a Season of Magenta

By

Brenda B Dawson

ISBN-13: 978-1463731670
ISBN-10: 1463731671

A 2fires Publication Co at CreateSpace
http://www.2firespublishing.com/dawson.html

Also by Brenda B. Dawson

THE SCOTT SERIES

Petals from the Judas Tree
A Touch of Jasmine
Sammy Blue

Regrets
Indian Blanket
Monster in the Goldfish Bowl

Published by
2firespubishing@gmail.net
P.O. Box 673
Barnsdall, OK 74002

ISBN-13: 978-1463731670

Printed in the United States of America July 2011

In memory of my mother, Willie Brouillette
A Southern Belle with a Yankee spirit.

My sincere thanks:
To my daughter, Bridgette Laramie,
For her belief in her old mom.
To my granddaughter, Racheal Tinsley, for her vision.
A special thanks to my good friend, Margie Knight,
For reading and reading and reading.
Thank you to my proof reader,
Anna Raye Lewis

Chapter 1

Beth Boudreau
Oleander, Kansas 1958

"You are such a stupid little fool, Beth. At least the other girls gave me some resistance, but not you, you little moron." The big man's voice was strained, struggling to conceal his excitement. "You willingly jump in my car, tell me all about yourself, your family, your address....how your sweet little dog would never bite anyone. Why would you do something like that, you dim-witted little puss? Are you really that dense?"

In horror and disbelief, the small girl stared in wonder at the massive man she'd considered her new friend. When she'd approached him a short time before, he seemed to be a nice man, neat, clean, well dressed. He looked like Pastor Johnson at church, but this man was not like Pastor Johnson, she discovered too late, and he was not a nice man. He was a very mean man, a horrible, evil man.

He wasn't tall, but he was big and appeared to be about the age of her Uncle Jack, her mother's youngest brother. Just like Pastor Johnson, he had thin red hair, thick horn- rimmed glasses, and a very large nose. To Beth, he looked like he was always smiling and would be friendly and nice, but actually, his teeth were too big for his mouth, causing him to wear a fixed smile, a lure he used on his favorite prey: the young girls at the skating rinks, movie theaters and other parental escapes.

With the mighty grip of a long-distance trucker, the powerful man steered the old Nash Rambler off the main road onto a remote side road leading into a secluded area of scraggly pine trees and dense brown overgrowth. Pulling up his emergency brake, he turned and glared at her as though reading her thoughts. "Because I dress well, you assume I'm someone who cares what happens to a little tramp like you. Well, I don't, Beth. I don't care about you one bit. You're no more to me than a piece of highway trash, a nuisance to decent folks, and a disgrace to your good parents. You're bad,

Beth. Bad."

Before he flipped the passenger seat down in the old car, he locked all the doors ensuring no escape and then turned to her. Carefully, he studied the angelic face of the dark haired girl huddled in the seat next to him, staring up at him with large questioning brown eyes. For an instant he hesitated, his large hands gripping the leather bound steering wheel in uncertainty. As quickly as he lost control, he regained it. His mouth tightened, his jaw grew hard. He squeezed the steering wheel until the threads in the leather broke. There was no escaping the smoldering rage inside him. Once again, it consumed him with a bestial intensity.

In his right hand, he flashed a square-cut athlete's ring: big, ominous, like himself, a reward for his brutality disguised as sport. As he smashed into her, she felt the corners of the ring tear into the soft areas under her eye and through her immature eyebrow, and she could hear the crunch of her nose under his angry fists. As she tried to defend herself, he kneed into her groin claiming his sick triumph over her youthful innocence. Exhausted, she gave in and experienced the savagery of the insanity that drove him, tearing her, wounding her virgin body. Mercifully, her mind went black.

Beth had come to her aging parents at a time in their lives when they'd given up all hope of having a child of their own and were so overjoyed with this impossible gift, this miracle from God, that they adored her, spoiled her, and nearly smothered her with parental concern.

She was a happy, loving child: eager to please, an astonishing beauty, surely kissed by the angels. Her complexion was as fair as vanilla cream, cheeks touched of strawberry, and huge chocolate eyes offset by a mass of dark ginger curls.

As her body matured into a young woman, she remained slender, with perky little breasts, slim hips, and a perfect height of sixty four inches. She was the President of the Honors club, one of the finalists on her seventh grade swim team, active in every social club in the school, and had been chosen the "Harvest Queen" by her peers. But with the maturing of her body and the changes within her, Beth became discontent with the safe, perfect life she knew and longed for adventure. Fascinated with the excitement of the outside world, she resented the restrictions of her doting parents and craved her independence.

She was thirteen years old, a "teenager" in an era when her parents knew nothing of the slang "teenager". But Beth knew, and she was the perfect teenager. She adored vanilla fountain cokes filled with peanuts, Rock n Roll, James Dean, and boys.

The first time Beth had seen *Rebel Without a Cause* in the local Bijou Theater, she sat through it three times until the owner finally asked her to leave. But every day after school, instead of going to the library as she told her Mother, she'd hide her school lunch money in her rolled-up-jeans cuff, and walk to the Bijou to watch love come alive with James Dean and her "twin", Natalie Wood. She knew she was Natalie's twin, because her friends said so. She had the same dark hair, clear white skin with the same delicate facial features and, astonishingly, she wore her hair in a pony tail just like Natalie.

But Beth didn't go to the movies to see Natalie, her twin, she went to see James Dean, and at night she would dream of a romantic rendezvous where he would hold her and love her and kiss her. She never got any further into her dream than that because she didn't want to venture into that dark world of sex of which she knew nothing.

After the movie left town, Beth missed the rebel, James Dean, and her daily theater visits, even though her nightly dreams of him continued. Eventually, someone told her that *Rebel Without a Cause* was an old movie and that James Dean had been killed in a terrible auto accident years before the movie came to their small town. Devastated, she screamed and cried and yelled that they were liars and she hated them. He could not be dead. He was her true love.

With that distress on her mind, she cultivated a friendship with an older, rebellious gang of kids at school, hoping to find second-hand love with a James Dean rebel. She didn't find that love, but soon she was doing everything her parents had warned her against. The lack of respect for authority she found exciting, seductive to her innocence, and that was how the trip to Hollywood, California began.

"It could be a wild new adventure," she suggested, hoping she didn't choke on the Pall Mall cigarette dangling from her lips, and in vivid detail, she described the brazen adventures conjured in her mind. They planned the trip with gusto, but they agreed to wait for the right time as Beth suggested, all unaware that the trip was her plan to find James Dean. The gang left the day of her freshmen high school class trip, her parents oblivious that she was on a trip of her own and not safely chaperoned by the teachers. To help pay expenses for the trip in his old green Volkswagen van, Beth took the allowance money she'd saved and gave it to the leader of the gang, Tony. They ran out of money a few days later and when they stopped to use the restrooms at a lonely rest stop, Tony told the girls they had to offer sex to the men for money. Horrified, Beth refused. Sometime later, at the filthy, dimly lit rest stop in the middle of nowhere, she stood terrified, staring at the exhaust from the back of the green Volkswagen van. She'd been left behind. After some time, a friendly, well-dressed gentleman came out of the restroom, and after Beth explained her plight to him, he offered Beth a ride to the next town. Gratefully, she jumped into his car.

"What happened to you is your own fault, Beth. I'll bet you consider yourself one of those "teenagers". You lie to your parents, read those nasty comic books, and dance that devil music." The sanctimonious brute paused, as if in deep thought, then he continued. "Yes, I know all about that music. It's a sacrilege, destroying good Christian music with all that humping and grinding. Elvis Presley running around shaking himself like a demon, causing young people to desecrate their bodies." He glared at her with contempt, as though she was responsible for all the wrongs of her generation.

"I know that's not how you were raised, Beth. I know you were running away from the good teachings of your parents. I know they taught you to never accept a ride from strangers, but that's what you did, Beth. You ignored their warnings, purposely strayed from good Christian teaching. Well, I hope you learned your lesson, Beth Boudreau, of 1927 Cherry Lane, Middleport, Illinois, because if you stay bad, I'll find you."

His warning voice roused her back from the darkness. She could feel blood running into her eye, but she remained still, crumbled into a tiny wounded orb. Clutching the dank seat, she knew her destiny had been planned as she felt the old car leave the rough country road and enter the lonely highway. When the car came to a stop he exited, the door groaning, and with the car lights illuminating his face, she saw him smile as though the icy rain was his accomplice. Pulling her door open, he grabbed her into his arms.

"Another lost soul," he bellowed as he lifted her high above his head, a sacrifice to some demented deity he worshipped. When it appeared that his offering had been accepted, he slammed her tiny body down to the watery drainage ditch far below. "Die," he whispered. "Doe, a long, painful death." Zipping up his leather jacket, he felt the spitting ice piercing his hands and he raised his arms in welcome, certain her cruel death was inevitable. Shoving his hands into his jacket pockets, he returned to his auto. Starting the ignition, his eyes filled with excitement as the ice turned into snow and covered the windshield. Soon her body would be covered with an icy-white blanket. She wouldn't be found until later. Shifting into drive, he pulled the old Nash Rambler back onto the highway. *It just didn't get any better than that.*

The icy water rushed over the back of Beth's head filling her mouth with the gritty slime, but Beth swallowed the muck, closed her mouth, and held her breath. Ignoring the screaming of her lungs, she concentrated on counting as though she were in an underwater contest with her seventh-grade swim team. But this time it was no contest. It was her survival.

Knowing the grief her aging parents would suffer at her death, Beth visualized herself wrapped in the soothing touch of their loving warmth, and miraculously, as though she was in a cocoon of safety, the frigid runoff soothed the burns on her arms, stilled the swelling of her nose and eye, and cleansed the blood soaked into her jeans. As soon as she heard the old car pull onto the highway, Beth lifted her head from the murky water and moved her arms and legs to regain circulation. Painfully, she pulled her small arms over her head and inched her body up to the world above. Several times in the darkness, she nearly slipped back into the watery pit below, but with the coming of dawn, she was able to see and grasp on to overgrown roots and clumps of grass, finding her way to the top of the ditch.

As Beth lay alongside the highway, exhausted, she could feel the warmth of the early morning sunshine. She knew that somehow she'd survived and would be returned safely back to her loving parents. But she also knew, she'd never let them know she'd been raped. She couldn't stand the thought of her aging parents suffering the visions of what really happened to her. No, she would never let them or anyone else know just how terrible it had been for her.

As she tried to pull herself upright, her strength gave way and she collapsed back onto the cold ground wondering how this had happened to her? Young girls weren't supposed to lose their virginity and that was the truth. That sort of thing was supposed to be for old married women, a duty they were forced to perform to have children. Oh my God! What if she had a child from this awful ordeal? What if she got some awful disease? It was just too shameful, and it was her own fault. He'd said it was her fault and all her friends would think it was her fault, too. Everyone would talk about her and laugh at her. She'd be forced to sit in the back of the school bus with the loose girls that liked to neck and pet with the naughty boys. Those same boys would expect her to put out for them because she was a dirtied girl. That's what everyone would think about her. Well, maybe she deserved the shame, but her parents didn't. No, she'd never let that happen to her parents. No one must ever know.

At exactly seven forty five, Officer Wayne Marquis of the Kansas State Police pulled his black and white onto Interstate Seventy for his early morning shift. As he prepared himself for the rush hour speeders, he spotted a small heap on the side of the road. It looked like a young girl.

Chapter 2

Randy James Scott
Poke, Texas 1958

"Papa, Papa. He's doing it! I saw him. Randy James is wandrin' to the neighbors again." Mary Ella raced into the kitchen clutching her dirty cotton-stuffed doll with the golden yarn hair and colorful embroidered face, her gift last Christmas. Her younger sister chased after her, dragging her dirty stuffed doll with dark yarn hair. Admiring the performance of her older sister, the small child collapsed on the old wooden floor of the small dark kitchen living room area.

"Papa?" Mary Ella continued, her smile curved into a smirk. "You told him not to go wandrin' on other folks' property. You told him, but he's doing it anyway. "

Her father ignored her as he rolled a paper around some dried tobacco, licked the edges, and lit the lean cigarette with a household match.

To be sure he heard her, the little girl raised her small voice into a childish screech, "Papa, did you hear me? Randy James is being naughty again. He's paying you no mind, Papa. Papa!"

Martha Scott turned from the kitchen sink and wiped her hands on her cobbler's apron scowling at her seven-year-old daughter. "Stop your tattling, Mary Ella, and leave your big brother alone. It's near bedtime, so get washed up and read your school book to your sister, till I come in to hear your prayers. Now scoot."

"It's not fair, Mama. Randy James gets to stay out past dark and we have to go to bed." Mary Ella stomped her feet in defiance, but her Papa's warning glance sent her off in a scurry.

"Wonder where he's going this time?" James Henry Scott asked as he pulled himself from the scarred wooden kitchen chair and crossed to the only window in the small room. Off in the distance he could see the dark head of his lanky son, Randy James. The boy was only thirteen years old, yet he was a head taller than he was, grew like a weed that summer.

"going to be a real big man someday," he said, scratching his stubble of a beard as he watched his only son disappear from view. "He's a good boy, real good boy. A boy any father would be proud to call his son. He never balked once when he handed over his weekly pay to help with the family needs, never asked for a penny, Martha." Sometimes, not very often, but sometimes in the summer when the boy worked a lot, James Henry was able to give his son a couple of dollars. Not enough. Not what he deserved. This life was not what any of them deserved.

With a big sigh, James Henry's shoulders collapsed in despair, allowing the top of his torn undershirt to slip from his bony shoulder down his thin arm. "Why can't he just accept the fact that he was born poor, raised poor, and most likely will die poor? Why can't he accept that, Martha? Why can't he stay off the neighbors' property like I told him, like I warned him about?" The frail man's shoulders collapsed further and he groaned in defeat. "Lord, I hate to use the strap on that boy, but I guess I'm gonna have to."

His tired wife smiled, pushing a strand of dark hair from her drained face. "The last time you used the strap on him, it hurt you more than it did him, James Henry," Martha replied, addressing her husband by his proper name, the only treasured inheritance left to him.

James Henry Scott, his ancestral namesake, had founded the once huge Scott Ranch in the early eighteen hundreds, and most of the land that now belonged to others around their small piece of land was still referred to as "Scott's End Ranch". It had been a proud ranch, a landmark in the community, a tribute to his early pioneer ancestors who'd fought their way from northern Illinois to Texas.

The Scotts' family had been farmers in Illinois, but the harsh Illinois winters would take the lives of their small calves, to be found dead the following spring, and as the bitter winters took their calves, the spring floods took their crops. After much research, James Henry Scott learned about this place called Texas. The land was cheap, the weather warm, and the land would provide good grazing for cattle. After much soul searching, he bundled his family into covered wagons, and began the long, arduous journey away from the snow covered lands of Illinois, through the storms of Missouri, past the rugged terrain of Oklahoma, and finally settled on the land north of what would eventually become Dallas, Texas. With its fertile ground and abundant creeks, the hard working Scotts managed to acquire thousands of acres of land and massive herds of cattle through their own toil, careful planning and dedication.

As time went on, the next few generations would buy more land. They would raise many head of cattle, and the calves wouldn't die in the winter, the crops wouldn't rot in the soil. They would prosper and gain wealth, but in time, this family got spoiled and used to the riches that their ancestors had worked so hard to achieve, and over the years, everything had been squandered by the lazy generations that followed. Instead of working the land to ensure a heritage for future generations, they chose to sell off sections of the once proud ranch to finance their own selfish desires. And sell they did. Gone were the land, the cattle, and the fine homes. For James Henry Scott and his family, there was nothing left except a few paltry acres, a couple of scrawny cows, and a three room shack that the ancestors would have found appalling, but James Henry Scott had his ancestor's name. A name he wore proudly.

"I don't think the neighbors mind him wandering about their land, James Henry. He doesn't hurt anything and all that exercise seems to help calm his temper a bit. You know he always seems more at ease when he comes home from those long walks."

"He's patrolling their land, like he thinks it's his. He just can't get it in his head that the land belongs to the neighbors. It's not our land, Martha, and it hasn't been our family's land for years. He just has those foolish notions and thinks he can claim what was lost to him, but he can't. I know. I had those notions too, when I was young, but my Pa beat that sort of nonsense out of me. I learned my lesson. Randy James has to learn, too, Martha, else he'll grow up no account, becoming a useless drunk like his uncle, or worse. It's for his own good. "

Martha Scott wiped her wet hands on her worn apron and sighed deeply. She longed to put her arms around the thin skeleton of a man that once was her strong healthy husband. She wanted to love him, touch him, console him, but instead, she turned from him and continued washing the dishes from supper.

Wiping the sweat from her forehead as she leaned over the deep sink, she thought about the love they once had. The love was still there, she knew that, but they no longer expressed their feelings anymore, nor had they touched one another since the birth of their youngest child five years before. Touching led to the bed. Bed led to babies. Babies, they couldn't feed. The two girls slept with her in the double bed. James Henry slept on a small cot in the second bedroom, and Randy James slept on a mat on the floor by the fire in the winter, and in the summer he slept outdoors somewhere. Randy James was thirteen, old enough to take care of himself and he did. That's the way he liked it.

Climbing over the barbed wire fence that separated his family's few acres from the large ranch adjacent to theirs, RJ, as he had started calling himself when his mama wasn't around, surveyed the land that wasn't his. What fools his ancestors had been to sell off this land just to enjoy their own selfish desires. They were just a bunch of lazy scoundrels and if they hadn't all been dead, he'd of killed them himself.

RJ was in a terrible mood. He was hot and sweaty, hair full of dust from the long walk into Poke, and for what? It was Saturday, and when he got off work at noon at the Angeles place, some of the boys told him they were heading to town to see some movie called *Rebel Without a Cause*. They said it was real good. So, he'd walked all the way into town, the hot wind blowing the dirt in his face, his toes killing him, and then he had to sneak into the movie. He figured that part wouldn't be hard. Anna Mae Smart, who was sixteen years old, was taking tickets and she'd let him pass, but he knew she'd expect him to come by to see her later and that wasn't to his liking. She'd want him to kiss her and hug her and he thought that was a bunch of crap, and he wouldn't do it. But he'd show up there anyway, so she wouldn't be mad. Nah, he wasn't ticked about Anna Mae. She was a good sort. Just a mushy girl he didn't understand.

No, what he was really ticked about was that movie was so stupid. All about some young folks rebelling against their parents, school, and every damn thing they could think of. He liked the looks of the dark haired gal in the movie, named Judy, but he sure couldn't see what those two boys had to rebel about. Looked to him, they had it pretty damn easy. He was fairly sure they never milked a cow at four o'clock in the morning and had the old cow kick the crap out of them. And he damn well knew that if they had a few cows to milk before they went to school, they'd be too damn tired at night to rebel against anything.

Taking long determined steps, the tall young boy could see the pond up ahead. It was a nice little place, real far away from everything. He could strip naked and get some of the dirt and heat off him. After he'd had a cool swim, it seemed he left a ton of worries behind him and he always felt better.

But today, even as he stepped out of the pond, he was still angry. He kept thinking about that dark haired gal in the movie, that gal, Judy. He envisioned her legs and the way that big skirt kicked up. He pictured her small breasts under that soft sweater. He wondered what she'd look like without that sweater, without the skirt, without nothing on. Damn it! He didn't like thinking about her one bit. She had a hold on him and he didn't like it. Always before, when he had a thought about some of the girls at school, he found a cold swim would take care of those feelings and thoughts. Not today. Damn it.

RJ climbed up the grassy slope from the pond and dressed himself. If he cut back South a bit, he could stop by Anna Mae's house. She'd be off work by now. After all, she'd let him in the motion picture show, so it was only right that he stopped by her house. Most of the time, he didn't want to get near her. Today though, something was making him feel different.

Even though it was getting pretty dark, RJ could see Anna Mae sitting on her front porch as he walked up the long driveway, but she didn't wait for him on the porch. Instead, she motioned to him to go around the side of the house and he did. RJ followed her past the main house and out toward the barn wondering just where the hell she was going. Usually, they just sat on the front porch in earshot of her folks.

As he came around the side of the barn, she jumped out at him and threw her arms around him. She started trying to kiss him and pulled his arms around her, begging him to kiss her and hold her like that guy in the movie. He wasn't about to do all that stuff and he told her so. All that necking and carrying on was just plain stupid, and so he started to walk away from the old barn and go on home. Then, she pulled her skirt up and her britches down and all of a sudden, he couldn't get his old jeans down fast enough. With her skirt pulled up around her middle, she kicked her britches off into the wind and plopped herself on a pile of hay, all the while grinning a big one at him. He knew he looked just like a damn fool when he fell down trying to run over to her with his jeans down around his ankles, but with her experience and his willingness, things happened real fast.

It was then RJ looked up and saw his Pa coming around the corner of the barn and he knew he was dead meat. Her pa chased him half way home and he didn't know what was gonna be worse, a beaten from her old man or a beaten from his. Either way, he knew he was gonna get one. He sure was right on that one.

After the beating from his pa, RJ was put on a pretty short leash by his parents. His ma started reading him long Bible passages every night and more on Sundays. His pa gave him so many chores, that getting that gal to pull her britches down again was the furthest thought from his mind, during the day, anyway.

By the end of that summer, RJ had grown big, tall, strong, and could carry his weight in work against any man, including his pa, and except for making sure he didn't get around the neighbor gals, RJ's parents left RJ to survive as best he could.

But as the crisp days of fall began, RJ noticed his Pa didn't seem to be able to keep up working with him anymore, and it worried RJ. He didn't mind carrying a part of his Pa's work load. He was young and strong, but his Pa just didn't look right to him. He looked so skinny. Course, none of them had enough to eat, not enough meat, anyway. They mainly survived on what his Ma grew and canned from her garden and the leftovers she brought home from the neighbors' houses that she cleaned.

The few head of cattle they had were as skinny as all of them, and RJ knew it was just a matter of time before they had to sell them, and there'd be no more milk to drink or to sell. He just didn't know what was gonna happen to his family, and that was an awful worry for such a young boy.

RJ's pa didn't know how close RJ had been watching him, but

RJ did watch him as the man who looked twice his age would sit out on the old porch staring out at nothing, rolling and smoking one cigarette after another from the small crop of tobacco he'd managed to harvest. He coughed a lot. RJ had seen him spit up blood more than once, and it seemed to RJ that he shouldn't be taking all that smoke into his body. He couldn't see where it would help him, but he knew better than to question his pa. Even though RJ knew he was a lot bigger and stronger than his pa, he also knew that if his pa decided to hit him, he'd never raise his hand in defense against the man. That wouldn't be right. So, he kept his mouth shut and watched as his pa got sicker and sicker.

The next spring, his pa died. "His body just wore out," the doc told them, but RJ knew that his pa had just given up on life. Life and its hopelessness was what wore him out. So, RJ had a decision to make. Either he could work part time and go to school full time, or he could work full time and go to school whenever he could. He chose the latter.

It didn't do any good, though. Two years later, his ma died. "Her heart just gave out," the doc told him, but RJ knew better. She died of overwork, frustration, and from trying, and trying, and trying. He knew she didn't give up and choose to die like his pa did, but he knew one poor little woman could just take so much. It was no heart attack that killed her. It was a broken heart.

RJ thought that if he worked hard enough, he could make a home for his two little sisters, but he also knew the lonely ranch was no place for two little girls to grow up. After some time, the State took the girls away, sending them to live with relatives some place in Iowa. He never saw them again.

Chapter 3

Elizabeth and Charles Carlton
Tulsa, Oklahoma 1995

He'd come for her. The square toes of his black boots protruded from under the hem of the heavy drapery, and abruptly, there was a storm of movement, as he plunged toward her amidst twisted draperies and flashing gold glints of his ring. The icy water was filling her eyes and nose and she gasped for air, and she was drowning, and she couldn't escape, and she couldn't move, and she was so cold. She waited, held her breath, listened for the engine of his car to start.

Gasping for air, Elizabeth lifted her face buried in her pillow and wiped the damp dark hair from her forehead. Had he actually come for her? Where was he? Terrified, her dark eyes scoured the eerily dark room, her lungs panting as though ready to collapse. After gaining her composure, she realized she wasn't trapped in the murky pit of death. As she rolled over and faced the ceiling of her dark bedroom, she pulled the pink comforter up under her nose, grabbed the lonely pillow next to her, and searched the room for the safety of her everyday life. Feeling her pounding breathe calm to a natural rhythm, she eased herself upright, knowing she was secure in her own bed. It was just that nightmare, again, so real, so unforgiving, her constant bedfellow since Charles' death.

Exhausted from sleep deprivation, Elizabeth had tried a night light, but the glow reminded her of the lights of his auto. She tried using the sound therapy machine that Anne had given her last Christmas, but the calming sounds of the gurgling brook became the sounds of the water rushing across her face. Trying to sleep on her stomach with pillows wrapped around her head, she would awake gasping for breath as she had that morning. In desperation, she bought a tape on self hypnosis and nightly, directed by the calm monotone voice, she practiced the rituals to the "T". Gratefully, she would be given a few hours of peaceful sleep, until as usual, the evil one came.

With the comforter up under her nose and clutching the pillow that had been Charles', she closed her eyes, but kept her ears vigilant. In and out of sleep she dozed for a few hours, careful to avoid the deep sleep where the evil one awaited her. Far off in the shadowy distance, she could see Charles, his golden hair blowing in the breeze, his tanned body healthy and strong, his beautiful smile meant only for her. It seemed impossible that this vibrant man had fallen so deeply in love with her so many years ago, but he had, even though she'd never done anything to attract a man's attention.

When Beth went back to school after the rape, she dropped out of all school social activities, quit her beloved swim team, and as she grew older, she refused to date. The only adventure she sought was found in books from the library.

When Elizabeth graduated from high school, she was awarded a coveted scholarship to Columbia University School of Journalism in New York. Although she was delighted and very proud of this honor, she declined it. She refused to leave the safety of her parents and insisted on attending the small college in her home town. There she met and fell deeply in love with Charles Carlton, a robust Adonis, with a gentleness that touched her heart, the first time she met him.

Charles Carlton was her prince, her knight in shining armor. He was handsome, tall, a beautiful man and he adored her, but after graduation, she'd refused to marry him unwilling to admit her past. She was perfectly content to go on forever, holding hands, and sharing innocent kisses. Charles respected her wishes and simply decided Elizabeth was unusually shy and just needed some time to adjust to him. He'd thought it odd that a beautiful young woman like Elizabeth had never dated, but he wouldn't push her. She just needed time. He would wait.

A short time after graduation, Charles was offered a position with a nationally respected law firm in Tulsa, Oklahoma. He realized that this type of opportunity only came along once in a lifetime and he'd be a fool to decline. Elizabeth would just have to marry him and go with him, but to his dismay, Elizabeth still refused to marry him. No arguing or begging or promises would change her mind. With deep regret, he accepted that she would never leave her parents, so he moved on with his life without her.

Elizabeth did not move on. She missed Charles, terribly. His smile, his humor. Desperate for his warm touch, and miserable without him, she realized that being away from him hurt much worse than sharing her past, which she knew she'd have to do. With him so far away, she realized she wouldn't have to face him, if he decided he didn't want a defiled woman as his wife. In November, she wrote him a long letter and explained her miserable past.

When he came home for Christmas, they were married.

Charles realized that Elizabeth was still that wounded child from many years ago, but he was certain that she could learn to accept his body and the magic they would share together. He was patient with her, and through his gentle love, he taught her that sex could be a magnificent experience when used as it should be. After some time, she accepted him and the loving intimacy that had been denied her so many years ago. Soon, she became an eager pupil, hungry for the fulfillment that Charles gave her and happy to share in their lovemaking. With his soft voice and warm touch, he tried to wash away the memory of the rape, which controlled her mind, and with heartfelt sincerity, he promised they would never speak of that awful night, again. And they didn't.

But regardless of Charles good intentions, the horror of that terrifying night was never completely washed away and forgotten as he'd hoped. It was merely hiding in a small corner of Elizabeth's mind, festering slowly; a puss-filled boil, waiting for the nudge that would cause its eruption. It was inevitable.

The room darkening blinds and the heavy lined drapes kept most of the darkness away, but now dawn had come. Elizabeth's eyes flashed open in enthusiasm. Today wouldn't be the same as her usual boring routine; play Bridge with the widows of the church, volunteer with the widows, attend church with the widows, sip the Vodka hidden under the sink.... alone.

Quickly, Elizabeth climbed out of bed and threw open the drapes and blinds welcoming the sunshine of a waking world. It was a beautiful day, a glorious day, now that the night was gone. Outside the window, Elizabeth could see the yellow daffodils lifting their happy little faces up through the dead leaves and the dirty snow of winter. Off in the distance she could see the flurry of magenta flowers as the Oklahoma Redbuds shook the last dredges of ice from their long, slender fingertips. It was that odd time of year. Winter refused to die and spring demanded life. It was an unnamed, unclaimed season. It was old and it was new. It was an ending and a beginning. It was a season of magenta.

It was this same season, twenty five years ago, when Elizabeth's body gave life. Against all odds, her children had survived nearly eight months in her damaged womb and even now, she remembered the long months in bed. Smiling, she glanced past the small bathroom toward the enclosed porch that she had called her "nest" for those eight months. Just as it had been so long ago, the porch was aglow with sunshine, tiny rays of life pouring into the many windows. Most of the time, heating wasn't needed on the small porch, but during winter and early spring, the heat from the adjoining bath and bedroom was necessary.

Over the years, as the children grew from toddlers into young adults, the porch became a sanctuary of sorts to all of them. For Anne, it was her place for slumber parties; all the secrets of young girls hidden inside the brick walls. For Adam, it was his place to study the works of his heroes: the deceptively simple style of Ernest Hemingway, the uniqueness of John Steinbeck, and the genius of F. Scott Fitzgerald. Even Charles had spent hours on the little porch, searching his law books for ways to help the innocent layman, who rarely could pay for the enormous amount of time he gave to them.

After many years with the large law firm that had brought him to Tulsa, Charles decided to open his own office. He loved the slower pace of the Sooner state, and he loved the gentle, kind people who lived there, but even though the state was rich with oil, so many of the people were terribly poor and often uneducated. Many times, Charles had seen these people lose what little they had due to subpar law defense, and every time he witnessed an injustice of this sort, it made him ashamed.

Eventually, with careful planning and the income Elizabeth received from the newspaper position she'd secured, he was able to open a small office in a respectable, but deprived neighborhood, and Charles knew he'd found his calling. He did have some wealthy clients, whose money he needed to support his family, but most of his clients were poor, but proud, so gratefully he accepted payment with the food they brought from their gardens, the fish they caught in the ponds, the fresh eggs from their own chickens, and the pecans they handpicked and shelled.

At Charles' funeral, rich and poor alike, lined up for blocks to pay their respects to the memory of this unusually honorable man. Elizabeth stood for hours shaking hands and accepting gratitude, as she listened to the hopes and dreams that Charles had managed to save for so many people. For some time after his death, the grateful people tried to take care of Elizabeth with food left on her doorsteps daily, but finally, she asked them to stop bringing food. There was no one to eat it and the food was going to waste.

At forty-five years old, Charles Carlton was too young, strong, and vital to be visited by the monster named "Cancer", but he was.

"It's just small polyps," Elizabeth told him for the umpteenth time placing her warm hand around his. He looked away from her, hoping she didn't see the fear in his eyes. She couldn't believe that any health problem could happen to Charles. He was so active and strong. He golfed, was a powerful swimmer, and had started running in the early morning. There was nothing wrong with Charles. Nothing could be wrong with him. It just couldn't be. She turned her head to his and kissed him softly on his tan cheek. "I know it's nothing, my love. We should just be thankful that the doctor is being so cautious."

As the short somber man in the white coat entered the room and sat down, he lowered his eyes to his paper work as though he were reading something he hadn't previously read over and over prior to this appointment. He cleared his throat and straightened the blue and white bow tie that enclosed his white collar. He fumbled with his horn rimmed glasses, removed them and began diligently cleaning them with a soft white handkerchief he pulled from his pocket. Warily, he refolded the cloth and placed it back into his coat pocket. Observing them without the shield of his glasses, they grasped the disturbing look in his eyes. Neither heard another word he said. They both knew.

"We'll fight this horrible monster, my love, and we'll win," Elizabeth whispered, pulling Charles' head to her heart as they collapsed on a cement bench outside the clinic, the brilliant sunshine mocking their sorrow. "We won't let this happen to us, Charles. You're too young, too strong." Her soft kisses settled into his thick blond hair and she felt renewed strength. "There are so many good treatments now, like Chemotherapy and Radiation. Lots of people who've taken those treatments have lived a long time, and you will, too.. Cancer is no longer a death sentence, and besides, my love, you can't die. I could never live without you, my beloved", she whispered, oblivious of the anxiety she'd caused this man who loved her.

"I'll always be with you," she whispered. And she was.

She was there through more tests and when they heard the dire results, and she held his hand close to her.

She was there during the radiation and the chemotherapy, and she read to him for hours while they waited.

She was there as he slowly shuffled across the room, and she gathered his silvery blonde hair that fell from his shoulders onto the floor, and she hid it, so he wouldn't see.

She was with him as he vomited violently, and she held the bowl and washed the bile from his gentle face.

She was with him when he soiled the sheets of the bed, and she washed the sheets, cleaned his body, and rubbed him with soothing lotion.

She was with him when he cried like a small child, and she cradled him and tried to force her own strength into him.

She was with him as his once tanned skin turned an ashen gray, and she watched.

She was with him as his skin shrunk around his head, as if held in place by saran wrap, and she prayed.

She was with him when they got the final results and she knew.

She was with him as she watched the monster ravage his body, suck away his beautiful mind, destroy his pride, and she was helpless.

Day after day, she watched and kept vigil beside him. Day after day, he clung to life only for her. Finally, she could bear his suffering no more. "I promise I'll be all right on my own, Charles, my love. I'm much stronger than you think," she whispered as she cradled his ravaged body in her arms. "Your battle is done now, my darling. Go now, be at peace."

At two ten, that morning, Charles Carlton accepted the peace of death. At last, he escaped his monster.

Elizabeth was alone.

Chapter 4

R.J. Scott
Poke, Texas 1995

RJ Scott pulled the blanket up around his aging chin, shivering as the cold wind pounded the torn shade against the open window of his dark, dreary bedroom. For an instant, he questioned his own sanity, sleeping with the window open when winter refused to give up to the warmth of spring, but quickly, he retaliated against those sissy thoughts and pushed the blanket off his hairy graying chest. Arrogantly, he defied the cold.

When he was a young cowboy, he thought nothing of sleeping on the ground in the snow. Just give him a decent bedroll and he'd be warm and happy as a tick on a brown dog. The problem was, he wasn't a young cowboy, anymore. He was an old man, fifty this past year. With that thought in mind, RJ pulled the blanket back up under his chin. He was over half a century old. How'd he get so old?

As RJ thought about his life, he wondered about his future. Maybe he should go a little easy on those big breakfasts of biscuits and gravy, and sausage and eggs that he ate every morning. Maybe he should cut out the burritos that Juanita loaded with all that cheese and greasy Chorizo sausage. Maybe he should give up hamburgers and those big thick slabs of prime steak that he loved so much. RJ's stomach roared in retaliation, so he didn't dignify those thoughts for even a second longer. He'd take his chances on life and if he croaked, at least he'd go with a contented belly.

Listening to the banging of the torn window shade, RJ tried to wiggle his toes. They refused. He knew a storm was coming. His toes were more accurate than any weather forecaster, he'd ever seen on TV. Hell, they'd been doing that since that summer he turned thirteen and did all that growing, shooting up over six feet tall. His legs, feet, and the rest of him grew so fast, all his pants were up to his ankles, his shirts barely buttoned, and his toes were scrunched up against the end of his old work boots. Times were so bad for his family back then, they were lucky to have a bit of food on the table, and he sure as hell knew he wouldn't get any new boots until things got better. And things never got better. So, he didn't say anything and his toes just got all twisted and curled and hurt like hell while he tried to work in the fields.

Staring into the darkness of his dreary bedroom, he remembered the day, that same summer, when he and his pa were helping Anna Mae Smart's pa at hay making time. When they stopped for lunch, he grabbed a sandwich from the old gray cooler on the back of the truck, and as usual, slipped off his boots to ease the pain a bit. Anna Mae's pa was watching him, like he always watched him, but the next thing RJ knew, her pa had gone back over to his house and came back with a pair of his old boots for RJ. Those boots were real big boots, because Anna Mae's pa was a real big man, but aside from being a bit loose, they fit fine. Besides, RJ knew he wasn't done growing yet, and he was right. That was a hell of a nice thing for Anna Mae's pa to do for him, considering what he caught him and Anna Mae doing, but he'd gotten his beaten for it and it was over. Her pa was a good man.

It seemed to RJ that he'd been waiting an awful long time for dawn, so he rolled over and checked the dark window, again. He didn't need an alarm clock. He got up when the sun came up and went to bed when the sun went down. Pretty damn routine, but he didn't mind it. Never was anything to watch on the TV except maybe an occasional episode of *Discovery* or *National Geographic*. So, he just went to bed and waited for the next day's sunrise when he'd have his coffee on his front porch and watch the coming of a new day. The torn shade had stopped banging and as RJ glanced toward the window, he saw the soft pink hint of dawn. Lowering his long, muscular legs down to the floor, he looked up and grinned at the nearly naked gal in the pin up calendar, her long blonde curls partially covering her full naked breast.

RJ grinned as he ran his big fingers through his dark gray hair, anticipating the night to come. It was finally Friday. He'd been counting the days till Friday, his turn in the back room at "Big Goldie's Roadhouse". Of course, he knew he had to wait his turn. There were only a few gals that worked at Goldie's, but it seemed to RJ, this had been one hell of a long week. Grinning an even bigger grin, he gazed at "Miss March" and knew she was his problem. Damn, she was something else. He'd almost be glad when the month was done and he wouldn't have to look at her every day, almost glad, anyway. But he knew he couldn't throw her picture away. No, that picture he'd save in the old case under his bed along with the other gals he'd favored over the years.

Leaving his tousled bed with the blankets hanging on the floor, RJ tucked his faded denim shirt into his worn jeans, pulled his brown bull-hide roper boots over his gray socks, grabbed his stained gray felt cowboy hat, and headed for the kitchen to get his coffee. In long Texas strides, he sauntered to his front porch and lowered his large body into his weather beaten wicker rocker with the faded red and white plaid cushion. Soon, the Hummingbirds would return and RJ was ready for them. He'd hung several little red feeders from his front porch roof, so he could watch the hungry little buggers enjoy the sugar water he'd put in the feeders for them. They were a welcome sight to see after the long, cold winter. Sort of like the first sign of spring.

Taking a sip from his coffee cup, RJ stared out in wonder over his land, as though this was the first time he'd laid eyes upon this picture. It amazed him that this beautiful scene that was always the same looked so different when the seasons changed. As the light of the sun peeked up from the shadows of the East, eager to begin her routine journey to the darkness of the West, RJ always felt a sense of peace at her being. It was as though she was trying to remind the world that life was merely a season of time: always the same, but always changing.

Slowly, he sipped his hot coffee, watching as the sun made her journey up into the sky, allowing the world to see her golden pink image: her glowing beauty, framed by the blue of the protective sky. As she rose further into the sky, she grew larger, pregnant with the energy inside her, causing RJ to shade his turquoise eyes from the glare. To RJ, it appeared that the "Lady Sun" simply chose to hide her glorious body: a grand dame' of purity and class, allowing no one to look upon her nakedness. Respecting her privacy, RJ rose from his chair to begin the chores of the day, his two dogs faithfully leading his way.

RJ poured another cup of coffee into his black faded travel cup and walked toward his 1983 Ford F-350 truck he called "Big Red."

The big red truck stretched just shy of 20 feet-bumper-to-bumper, with a ten-foot bed, a back gate that refused to close anymore, and one green fender he'd replaced when he hit the ditch some years back, through no fault of Big Red's.

Positioning his battered hat low over his eyes, RJ smiled as his two Red Heelers pranced excitedly in front of him knowing they'd get their ride in the back of Big Red. He remembered the day he'd found them. They were just newborn pups. Some mean spirited son of a bitch had put them in a gunny sack and thrown them in the creek to drown with no chance to survive, but the sack had caught up on a branch and washed up on RJ's land.

He'd been out looking for a lost calf when he came upon the wet gunny sack, and he watched it cautiously, noticing the movement inside the filthy sack. With his knife, carefully, he cut the sack open and found three dead puppies and the two that were still alive. They were nearly dead too, but he wouldn't leave them there to suffer starvation. He buried the three dead pups and brought the other two home and nursed them back to health. Now, his boys, Red Heelers, were almost always with him. Best damn cattle dogs he'd ever seen.

Traveling down the two-lane country highway, RJ looked in the rearview mirror and chuckled with amusement, as the wind blew through the red and white fur on his boys guarding either side of the truck bed, always on the lookout for something. They loved the ride, so he always took them with him when he went to town, his town, Poke, Texas. Poke, Texas, was an old town. Old people lived there. Old ways presided over the town. Old friendships lasted a lifetime. Old hatreds lasted forever.

People helped each other as much as they could there, but no one took responsibility for others successes or their failures, and they never criticized others; however, they tried to make a living. And it was hard to make a living in Poke, Texas. Strangers rarely came there to enhance the sales of the businesses, but if the truth were known, that's the way the people of Poke liked it. They didn't like outsiders coming in to Poke bringing their crude city ways to the innocent little town. There was no real reason for strangers to come to the Poke anyway, because it only consisted of a church, a retired doctor, and a few small businesses. But on the very edge of

Poke, partially inside the town's limits, was the town's best kept secret and its biggest moneymaker, "Big Goldie's Roadhouse."

"Goldie's" had been a part of Poke for so many years, most folks couldn't remember when she started the place, and though it might seem strange to outsiders, Goldie, the woman, was respected in the community of Poke.

She was a very charitable woman and when there was a need in the small community, Goldie was the first to offer help which had always been accepted. But, no one had ever invited Goldie into their homes for dinner, or to sit on their porch to enjoy a glass of ice tea on a hot summer day. She'd never been asked to sit on the town council, nor the school board, even though she was a brilliant business woman. And never had anyone suggested she be invited to join the church, although she gave more to charities than anyone else.

But in their own way, the citizens of Poke took care of Goldie. They protected her business because of the money she brought into the community, and if there was ever to be a raid, she was the first one the sheriff called. They wanted her money; they just didn't want her near their families. But that was the way it was there in Poke, Texas, and Goldie accepted it.

"Big Goldie's" was sort of a private place, though. You could sit and drink all you wanted; even strangers could drink in the front bar room. But to get into the back rooms, you had to have a key. You had to be someone special. RJ had a key. He was special.

Most of the gals that worked there were older and had been with Goldie for years. She took care of them and made sure they were clean. RJ knew they were clean, too, because old Doc Henry checked them all the time. He had a key, too.

The back room at "Goldie's" was only opened on Friday and Saturday nights, so that the gals could be home with their families on Sunday and during the week, but make enough money on the weekends to put food on their tables. And, of course, it made it easier for Larry, the Sheriff of Poke, because he didn't have to keep his eyes shut too long.

Some people thought that being a bawdy gal was wrong, but to RJ it was just a way for someone to survive. It wasn't honorable, and probably not decent to some folks' thinking, but those gals took care of their familys and didn't ask for help. Besides, the nearest big city to find work was Dallas, and those gals couldn't afford to drive that far. Most of them didn't have cars anyway, so they did what they had to, and he respected that. All of Goldie's customers felt that way too, otherwise, they weren't welcome in the back room. Goldie wouldn't allow it. She took care of her own.

As the years passed, the back room keys, mainly belonged to the older widowed men of the community, who'd come just to have someone talk to them: someone to listen to their stories about their past lives with their wives when they used to be happy. Sometimes, they'd just want someone to hold their hands, touch them gently, and pat them lovingly. And for this human touch they were willing to pay money, and Goldie, always a business woman, provided the service. And everybody was glad she did.

As RJ passed "Goldie's Roadhouse" on his way back home, he noticed that it was quiet and dark in the early morning hours. Grinning, he contemplated the evening ahead. It was quiet now, but tonight the beer signs would be flashing, music would be playing, folks would be laughing, and he'd be in the back room with one of the big saucy gals from Goldie's. As RJ remembered "Miss March" her voluptuous bosom, and the promise in those big blue eyes, he wondered if he'd make it till tonight. *Damn.*

As RJ headed home from Poke that morning on the two lane highway next to his property, he heard his boys barking and he knew there was a missing calf somewhere. Sure enough, he could see the little fellow standing right there in the middle of the road. Quickly, RJ stopped Big Red and his boys jumped out of the back and ran to the little calf, carefully staying on either side of it, so it wouldn't run further into the road.

Jumping out of the truck RJ picked up the small animal, but he didn't know what to do with it. He couldn't throw it into the back of the truck, because the tail gate wouldn't close, and the calf would probably jump out of the back and hurt himself, but, RJ sure didn't want to carry that calf all the way up the lane to his house. It was a damn long walk to begin with, but carrying that squirming little calf all that way would be rough, and he wasn't as young as he used to be. He was still strong, but he wasn't the young stud he used to think he was. When he did something out of the ordinary now, things hurt on him, and carrying that little calf all that way would sure give him some new places to hurt.

For once in his life, though, RJ was glad he had such long legs, because he realized that if he put the seat way back in the truck, he could drive and hold the calf in his arms till he could return it to its mother. Entering the gate to his property with the calf on his lap, he knew his idea was working. The only thing he didn't think about was that the calf was not "lap-broken". The smell was awful. RJ was covered in calf poop all the way to his boots.

"Son of a bitch!" RJ shouted, as the calf looked up at him with its big black eyes, wondering what he'd done to arouse such a noise. "Oh, it's not your fault. You were just out trying to have a little fun and you got into a bit of trouble," RJ smiled at the innocent creature sitting on his lap. Quickly, he rolled his window down as far as it would go.

Like the inquisitive little calf, RJ remembered when he was young and had gotten into a bit of trouble. Only, his trouble was not a simple fence. It was a woman. He'd learned his lesson the hard way about women, and he'd made up his mind that he'd never get caught like that again, and he'd kept that promise to himself for over twenty-five years. He'd learned quickly, that any needs he had for a woman could be easily met for a few dollars over at "Goldie's". That's the way he liked it. Pay his money up front with a woman and no surprises later on.

Returning the little calf safely back to its mother, RJ slipped out of his soiled clothes, threw them into the aging burning barrel and started them on fire. Quickly, he walked into his house in his underwear, threw his billfold and some change on his dresser, and grabbed a pair of dirty jeans and the same shirt he'd worn the day before. Didn't matter how he looked or smelled. Nobody'd see him, anyway, but later on, come early sundown, he'd take a shower and get all dressed up. He'd get to "Goldie's" early that night, because he sure as hell didn't want to miss his turn in the back room. "Miss March." *Ah damn.*

RJ Scott pulled the brim of his hat further down his forehead sheltering his blue eyes from the morning sun. Carrying his tools in one hand and a round of wire in the other, he moved his large aging body down the lane from his house, following his two wiry boys, who were racing back and forth in front of him. It never ceased to amaze RJ how those two dogs always stayed ahead of him, but seemed to know exactly where he was going.

In long, swift strides, RJ walked back down the lane to where he'd found the calf earlier and began to search for the hole in the fence. His boys seemed to immediately know what he was looking for, so they raced right to the small hole. That would be an easy fix. It was just a small hole, but a mischievous little calf could sneak through it. Quickly, he mended the small hole and picking up his tools, he stood up rubbing his aching back.

Off in the distance, he saw his son, Jason, driving his SUV through the range toward him. RJ could also see that he had Anne with him this time, and he was glad he'd gotten the fence fixed so easily, so he could spend a bit of time with them. Anne had never been out to see him before, and RJ was beginning to think Jason was ashamed of his place. Smiling a big grin, he waved to them.

Chapter 5

Hoping to dispel some of the horrible odor from her hands, Elizabeth climbed into the shower and worked the clean smell of the shampoo into her hands and then into her hair. Sniffing her finger tips, she could still smell garlic and fish, the main ingredients for the "Courtbouillion" she'd serve when the kids came home for the long Easter weekend.

In the "*Distinctive Dining*" cookbook she'd borrowed from one of her wealthy widow friends, she'd found the fancy sounding recipe for the dish and hoped it would impress the young man Anne was bringing home for the weekend. It wasn't really a fancy dish, but it had a fancy name, and it did have a lot of expensive fish in it. That should impress him.

After she purchased the shrimp, she discovered to her horror that the smelly shrimp was not "ready to cook", but had to be shelled, deveined and cleaned. Fresh crab was too expensive, so she'd bought canned crab which smelled so bad that she'd raced the empty cans to the garbage outside, hoping she didn't attract every cat in the neighborhood. Her garlic press fell apart from age and lack of use, but the recipe had said "gently press the fresh garlic", so she "gently pressed the fresh garlic" with the only thing she could think of. Her fingertips.

The gourmet meal turned out to be more expensive than she planned, because she never cooked anymore. Even the basic items in her neglected kitchen cabinets were suspicious and had to be replaced. The aged spices had no smell, the ancient olive oil smelled rancid, and the flour had taken on a life of its own. "What are those little crawly things in there, anyway?" she grumbled as she rushed the flour outside to the garbage.

Anne was bringing home a young man from the Dallas law firm where she worked and that was quite unusual. In the past, Anne had compared all men to her father and none of them stood the test, so Elizabeth knew he must be important to Anne. Elizabeth also knew that to get into that prestigious law firm where Anne worked, you had to be brilliant, influential, or just plain rich. Anne had gotten in on her brains and her father's reputation, certainly not on her father's money.

Living in financial stress as she'd been forced to do these last few years, Elizabeth hoped Anne would never bring home a golden knight in shining armor bent on saving the world, like Anne's father. Elizabeth simply wanted Anne to find a man who loved her, came from a respectable family, and was super wealthy. That's all.

Coming from such a fine, affluent family as she was sure he must have, Elizabeth knew it was vital that this young man see that Anne's family lineage was of class and respectability. Maybe then, he would ignore some of the eyesores of her failing home, especially the awful mildewed ceiling ready to collapse at any moment. Elizabeth had hired a roofer to patch the roof, but it took him such a short time to do the job, she wondered exactly what he'd done up there. Now, anytime it rained the ceiling got worse, and when she'd called him, she discovered his phone service was disconnected.

Money had meant little while Charles was alive. He kept up the lawn, maintained the house, and knew how to invest their money. He knew everything about everything and never bothered her with the upkeep of anything, including the home and the finances. He only wanted Elizabeth to have her role as a happy wife and mother; a role she cherished, but a role that left her totally unprepared for the outside world.

To take care of them in their old age, Charles made many wise investments and Elizabeth knew that with time and reasonable growth, they could retire in comfort. But, how were they to know Charles would die so young while the investments were still immature and unavailable for distribution. To save money, Elizabeth had considered selling her home and moving to a condo, but the condo cost more than her house, the monthly fees were ridiculous, and the taxes were exorbitant. So, she stayed in her modest home.

She tried to return to work at the newspaper, but most of the people she remembered were gone, replaced by new, young faces; none interested in her twenty-five year lapse from the busy newspaper scene. She had limited skills from her assistance to Charles in his law practice, but her limits became obvious when she applied at various law firms. Everything was computerized now and her computer knowledge was limited. She was unqualified. When she applied for lesser employment, she was told she was overqualified. Giving up hope of having any additional income, Elizabeth struggled by as best she could on the small monthly income from an annuity Charles had left her.

Stepping from the shower, Elizabeth towel dried her dark hair, checking for any new gray hair that needed to be retouched. Finishing her thick hair with the hair dryer, she shoved the dark mass into a severe French Twist. She knew this style made her look more matronly, but she'd die before she'd let the widows at the church on "Widow's Row" suggest she was looking for a man. "Trolling for a fellow," was what Alma Green would sneer about any widow who refused invitation into her select group of widows. Elizabeth knew it wasn't that those widows wanted to find a man. They just couldn't stand Alma Green.

Many times Elizabeth wished she hadn't become involved with Alma, she was such a gossip. Often, Elizabeth thought the "facts" stated by Alma were just a bunch of lies, but Alma had been there when Charles was so sick, and after he died, Alma quickly latched onto Elizabeth with the jaws of a python. Being alone for the first time in her life, Elizabeth hoped that, somehow, being a member of the chaste widows of the church, she could ease the soiled memories of her childhood and absolve her of her heavy burden of guilt. It didn't. Now, after all these years, she was afraid to leave the small bit of security she found there. Maybe the other widows felt as she did, but she'd never know. No one would dare go against Alma. Things would never change, anyway.

Examining her face in her magnifying glass, Elizabeth searched for any brittle hairs that had left the presence of her legs and settled under her chin. Satisfied, she stared at her appearance in the mirror and welcomed the small age wrinkles around her eyes, minimizing the old scars of her youth. With the skill of a makeup artist, she used her eyebrow pencil to fill in the white scar that cut through her dark eyebrow. As she scanned herself in the mirror, it seemed that her body was a lot like the items in her kitchen. Her soft parts had turned hard, and her hard parts were soft. Weird.

Remembering her "Courtbouillion", she hurried back to the kitchen and gave it a quick stir. It certainly smelled delicious.

Gasping on a hot taste, Elizabeth spilled a spoonful of the sauce onto her recipe card over the part that said "one something" of rice. One what? Teaspoon, tablespoon, maybe it was a cup? It was a pretty big pan full of the stuff, so it must have been a cup. One cup of rice was added to the pot. Checking to be sure the stove was still set to simmer, Elizabeth gave a quick stir and returned to her bedroom down the hall.

Leaning over her bed, Elizabeth smoothed the pink floral sheets and the matching pink comforter and stood the silken decorator pillows up at crisp angles across the brass headboard. She loved this bed set and not just because Anne had given it to her for Christmas last year, but because it was so feminine and elegant; something, she could never buy for herself. Anne said that the new bedding might help her sleep. It didn't, but she hadn't told Anne.

With a final pat of approval to the bed, she gazed out the window at what used to be Charles' pride and joy, his garden. Several times in the past month, she'd called "John's Complete Lawn Care" to come and clean some of the winter's aftermath of fallen limbs, decayed leaves, and scraggly overgrown bushes, but he hadn't come. He only came when he wanted to.

Charles hired "John's" to do the yard work, when he could no longer do it, and John had done a fine job until Charles died. Then, everything changed. John never finished the yard work he started, if he bothered to show up. When Elizabeth complained, John goaded her, suggesting she find someone else to do the yard. "They're all expensive, Mrs. Carlton. None of them worked for peanuts, like I do," he grunted, scowling at her as he spit tobacco juice into Charles' once prize Crepe Myrtle bush.

Elizabeth wondered if that tobacco juice was what killed the bush. Horrified, she realized what he suggested. What if he quit? She couldn't mow the lawn and she couldn't afford anyone else. Who else could she get? What would she do? After that, she didn't argue with him anymore, just sent him a monthly check and hoped he'd come.

Drawing little circles on the frosted window panes, Elizabeth thought about the lazy yardmen, the useless roofer, and the mechanics who always told her there was something wrong with her car. She knew they were lying, but she couldn't fight them. She did what they told her to do and greedily they snapped up her small income. Elizabeth sighed with disgust at the pitiful coward she'd always been. Remembering the horror of her youth, she wondered if she would always be some man's victim.

Shaking her head in disbelief, she walked to her closet and began searching for something appropriate to wear for the first time meeting with Anne's new friend. She needed something that said "simple, but classy. Casual but chic." Her gray wool slacks and matching gray cashmere sweater set would be perfect with gray hose and simple gray loafers. When she heard them pull into the driveway, she'd slip on her grandmother's pink diamond earrings that she never dared to wear. Jewelry that expensive and worn so casually would make the young man assume that the big spot in the ceiling was just simply an eccentric oversight and not what it really was. A lack of money. Standing back from the mirror, she checked her appearance and knew she portrayed the look of a self assured, proper lady.

As she gazed at her charade in the mirror, she had the first nauseating wave of aroma from the kitchen. Something smelled God awful, terrible. The "Courtbouillion".

Chapter 6

RJ stared out of the back seat window of Jason's car as they neared Poke, Texas, noting that "Goldie's" was still closed. He hoped whatever it was that Anne and Jason wanted him to see wouldn't take too much time. He thought about "Goldie's" back room and smiled.

Staring at the back of Jason's dark head as his son steered the car down the two-lane highway, RJ felt an overwhelming sense of pride for his son, a successful attorney with a big fancy law firm in Dallas. Smiling to himself, RJ thought how Jason always wore a fine suit, not a western one, but a dark business suit and always a tie. And Jason wore funny shoes, not boots like he wore, but low cut shiny shoes, and sometimes they had little tassels on them. RJ thought that was sort of weird for shoes, but what the hell. That's what fancy people wore.

Jason looked tired, awfully tired. Usually, Jason was so careful about his appearance, but today he looked like a bum. His hair was shaggy, ragged looking, and sticking straight up on top of his head like a bandy rooster. He needed a shave in the worst way, and RJ couldn't imagine Jason owning that awful gray sweat suit he was wearing. From what RJ could see it had red writing on it that said, "**Rednecks Do It on the Run**", whatever the hell that meant, and there was a little red stick person supposed to be running wearing big red tennis shoes. That was just plain stupid, but Jason could wear whatever the hell he wanted. His son was a big shot now.

RJ was grateful Jason never had to work or fight his way through life as he'd been forced to do. He'd made sure Jason never witnessed the miserable times he'd experienced or faced the injustices of life that were constant to his father, but RJ knew it had all been worth it. He'd made a decent life for them, and his son was a son to be proud of. Jason was smart. Why, Jason had read so many books, that it was hard to believe there was that much to learn, but Jason had learned it. Jason didn't love nature much, but RJ decided that was okay, too. He loved nature enough for both of them.

Glancing out the window, RJ sat straight up in his seat. They had passed Poke and were headed toward the interstate. Where in the hell were they going? It better not be too far. He had to get back home and get himself cleaned up, so he didn't miss his Friday night at "Big Goldie's. Hell, he'd learned a long time ago, that if a man didn't get his juices cleaned out at least once a week, stuff could back up on him and make him damn sick. RJ sure didn't want that.

Watching the local countryside pass by, it gave him cause for alarm to the point of near panic. What the hell was going on? As they neared the interstate, he decided that if they went on the interstate, he'd tell them to take him back home. He couldn't go with them. He had plans for the evening.

RJ's scowl deepened. Yeah, and just what plans would he tell them he had? Anne was a nosey little gal and wouldn't quit drilling him until she found out. Now, just how could he tell them he was going to the local whore house, and he sure as hell didn't want to miss his turn? *Oh crap.*

Just before they entered the interstate, RJ heard Jason whisper something to Anne and she nodded her head in agreement. He couldn't hear what they said, but he could tell it wasn't something good and he knew it concerned him.

Jason pulled the car to a stop and got out. Anne got out, too. RJ opened his door to get out, but they shut the door on him. Pretty soon, Anne was driving and Jason had extended his seat back and was in deep sleep. Where the hell were they taking him? RJ wondered. Maybe they were taking him to the old folks' home and dumping him there.

Watching the changes in the Texas landscape, RJ realized that wherever they were taking him, he was their prisoner whether he liked it or not, so he decided to just accept whatever they planned for him. It couldn't be that bad. Maybe he could get into "Goldie's" on Saturday night. Yeah, that's what he'd do. Missing Friday night would be all right. What was one more day?

Having made peace with his Saturday night decision, RJ felt himself relax. He smiled at his sleeping son and would have liked to run his fingers through Jason's hair like he did when Jason was little. But he didn't.

RJ thought about the major court case Jason had just won. He shouldn't have had that case in the first place, because he was just the new kid in that pricey law firm he worked. He'd never handled a law case on his own before, so the big shots at the law firm shoved a minor case off on him for practice. They figured it would be a shoo-in and nothing would ever come of it.

The sixteen year old son of one of their rich clients got picked up for a DUI, and money talking the way it always did, the DUI was shoved under the table and forgotten. The kid went on with his spoiled rotten life, never learning one damn lesson except that his daddy could buy him out of any crap he got himself into. Much to everyone's horror, three weeks later a reporter named Ronald Moore woke up from a coma at the hospital, and started talking about a little red Ferrari that had hit him when he pulled off the highway to fix a flat tire.

Ron Moore remembered seeing the car coming up behind him weaving back and forth over the center line as though the driver was drunk. With a reporter's quick thinking, he memorized the license plate before the car clipped the back bumper of his car and tossed him into the ditch leaving him there to die. After his recovery, the first person Ron Moore called was one of his buddies in the DA's office. It didn't take long to figure out who owned the car.

Naturally, all hell broke loose at the prestigious law firm. The big boys in the firm wanted to take the case away from Jason because of the new charges, but Jason refused to relinquish the case. He had nothing do with the DUI cover up, but he was the attorney of record and could lose his license if that bit of hanky panky got out. Jason was adamant, so the big boys assigned a team of their top lawyers to assist Jason in the trial.

RJ thought about those hotshots assisting Jason, chuckled to himself, and saw Anne glance at him in the mirror. She watched him for a moment and smiled. She probably figured he was senile.

Running his big dirty fingers through his grubby hair, RJ wondered how Jason and Anne could stand the smell of him in the closed car. He could barely stand himself. He just plain stunk from the smell of the calf that morning. RJ examined the grime underneath his close cut fingernails and wished they'd stop someplace so he could at least wash his hands. They didn't and soon his mind wandered back to Jason.

Jason looked like a little boy when he was sleeping and certainly not the grand stander he turned out to be in court. RJ almost felt sorry for the father of that young boy on trial, because he knew how he felt when Jason was a kid and got into trouble. It looked like that man's son was in some real deep trouble, but RJ decided that doing some time at a detention center for kids might do him some good. Maybe the kid would learn something about responsibility and honor, if he could get away from his father's easy money.

RJ knew things didn't look good for Jason's case, and it seemed all bets were for Ron Moore's lawyer winning a big settlement for him, putting him on easy street for a while. There was just one small thing that nobody thought about except Jason.

Jason must have spent hours with the mechanic looking at Moore's hazard lights, which Moore claimed he'd turned on that night. Then Jason saw it. At just such an angle as the car was sitting on the highway, a short had occurred in the electrical system causing the back lights to shut off intermittently. Therefore, it wasn't certain if the car's lights were on or not, and at the angle the car hit the ditch, it was possible that no front lights could be seen either. The jury determined that it was possible that the boy didn't see the car in the dark rain whipped night, and when he'd felt the thump, he really did think he'd hit a small object on the highway as Jason suggested. Because of his youth, the boy got off with a simple slap on the wrist.

Ron Moore didn't fare so well, because the judge ticketed him for neglecting to have his Texas Vehicle Inspection tags up to date. Moore was madder than a hot hornet and swore he'd be watching Jason and someday he'd get even with him. Hell, Jason didn't care about his threats. He was the firm's young hero and could probably name his own price from then on, but the whole thing bothered RJ. Seemed to him, the boy got off without learning any sort of lesson, except his pa's money could buy him out of trouble, but RJ knew that's how folks thought when they'd been born rich and never had to work for a damn thing. It was sort of sad, if you thought about it.

As RJ looked out the back seat window to the world passing by, he glared at the signs telling him they were heading towards Oklahoma City. *Damn it.*

Chapter 7

The "Courtbouillion" was a disaster, the smell was worse, leaving a burned up mess and a ruined pan to boot. It was so bad that Elizabeth had to throw the ruined pan in the garbage with the dinner. Dropping her tired body into one of the large brown leather recliners in the family room, Elizabeth thought about the time and expense she'd wasted, and now the horrible, nauseating smell seemed to permeate every single room. She'd sprayed a floral room freshener around the house, but she was certain it only made it smell worse. She couldn't tell. Her nose was numb. She just hoped Anne's young man had a cold or sinus trouble, so he couldn't smell it either. It was awful.

Gazing at the clock over the fireplace, Elizabeth realized that it was nearly 8:00 pm. It never took them this long to get to Tulsa, even stopping in Oklahoma City to pick up Adam and Kathy. Elizabeth wanted to call Anne's car phone, but she didn't dare. Her kids thought she was a neurotic, psychotic old woman. Always worried, always afraid. Afraid to drive places she didn't know; afraid of the dark, afraid to meet strange new men.... afraid, afraid, afraid. Always afraid. Why couldn't she stand on her own two feet and stop being so afraid? It just had to stop and she knew it, but she just didn't know what to do or how to stop it. All she knew was that she was sick to death of always being afraid.

Exhausted, she closed her eyes. Off in the distance, Elizabeth could see Charles healthy and strong, his thick blond hair blowing in the wind, his beloved smile meant only for her. She raced toward him, her thick dark hair bouncing on her shoulders, her small bare feet cool from the touch of the dewy green grass. As she neared him, she dropped the hem of her white and pink gauze night gown and held out her arms for his embrace, an embrace that never came. Always, his warm body was just out of her reach, always. As she slipped deeper into sleep, she found the realm of the evil one. W*as he there hiding? Where was he? Open your eyes! Open your eyes*! *The noise! The noise!*

Elizabeth opened her eyes and in a daze grabbed the telephone next to her chair. Shaking, she put the phone to her ear and heard Anne's soft voice. Quickly, she tried to bring herself back to the present, so Anne wouldn't know how terrified she'd been.

"Mom, are you all right?" Anne asked. She and Adam had been worried about their mother for some time. Since their father had passed away, their mother seemed to become more peculiar, and those damn nightmares never let her have any real rest. She wouldn't talk to them about those dreams. She wouldn't talk to anyone about those damn dreams. How long could she keep her fears to herself?

"I'm just fine, Anne. I was just taking the garbage outside and heard the phone ring. I'm just out of breath, that's all."

Anne listened as her mother rambled on about the garbage. Her mother would never walk outside in the dark, never. It was well past eight o'clock and a dark overcast night. Nope, she was hiding things, again, probably, those awful nightmares. Anne had thought a change in her living arrangements might help her mother, and begged her to come and live with her in Dallas, but she'd refused to leave her home and live with either of her children. Her mother wouldn't even leave Tulsa to visit her or Adam, anymore. Finally, they just gave up and came to visit her.

Anne decided she wouldn't waste time arguing with her mother. They'd be there soon and she and Adam could try and figure out what to do with her this time. "Mom, we just picked up Adam and Kathy, so we should be there within a couple of hours. We got a late start this morning, and stopped by Jason's dad's place, and we'll......."

The line went dead. Those car phones were wonderful, but Elizabeth knew they'd never amount to anything. They just weren't reliable, always seemed to go out when you needed to say something important. Well, what was there to say, anyway? She couldn't say how disappointed and upset she was, expecting them by early afternoon, and now they wouldn't be there until late.

Well, at least they came. They came on all the holidays, anymore. Thank God, they'd quit trying to get her to come to see them. It was so much better this way.

It was exactly ten forty-five when Elizabeth saw the flash of lights in her driveway. Quickly, she grabbed the pink diamond earrings from their hiding place in the secret drawer in the ancient buffet and slipped them on. Ten forty-five! Ten forty-five! Never had they gotten there that late. *Good Lord.*

Elizabeth hugged her children as they came up the steps to meet her. Adam and Kathy were first to greet her. Kathy made it clear before she married Adam that she wanted no children, which seemed to be fine with Adam, but Elizabeth always hoped their form of birth control would fail just once, so she could have a grandchild to love.

Anne came next dragging her new friend by his hand. "Mom, this is Jason Scott. He works at the firm where I do." Anne was glowing, obviously happy. Elizabeth hugged her daughter and pressed her hand into her fresh blond hair. Gone were the schoolgirl pigtails, replaced by a chic short cut that relayed the look of a successful young woman of the world.

Jason Scott reached out his hand to her and Elizabeth couldn't believe her eyes. Anne's choice of men was a fairly handsome young man, but one who was desperately in need of a shave and a haircut. His dark hair was standing straight up on top of his head like a chicken, and he wore the most ridiculous outfit Elizabeth had ever seen: a gray sweat suit, hiked up about four inches up his ankles, black socks surrounded by black dress shoes with little tassels on them, and written on the front of his sweat suit in big red letters was "Rednecks do it on the Run." Elizabeth wondered just what Anne had gotten herself into living in Dallas, and exactly what sort of people did this rumpled young man come from.

Barely able to contain her disappointment, she held out her hand to the young man and tried to smile. She'd make him welcome, he was a guest in her home, but she'd get Anne alone later and make sure she understood this young man was wrong for her future. Elizabeth glanced in the hallway mirror at her Grandmother's pink diamond earrings sparkling at her in jest and felt sick.

Elizabeth motioned for the group of young people standing on the steps of her home to come inside, but Jason didn't come into the house. Seeing him motion to someone in the SUV, she stepped back out on the steps where she could get a better look at the young man. Jason smiled at her and again motioned to someone in the SUV to come and join them. Anne hadn't said anything about bringing another person. *Now what?*

RJ looked at the little clock on the console of the SUV and cursed angrily. For God's sake, it was ten fifty at night. He should have been asleep hours, ago. After such a miserable long ride, sharing the backseat with Anne's brother and his wife, RJ tried to stretch his long legs and get comfortable. Shoving his feet across the seat, he noticed the red clay drop from his dirty work boots. That was mud, wasn't it? Didn't look like mud. Sure didn't smell like mud. Oh well, Hell. He didn't want to be there, anyway. The vision of "Miss March" and "Goldie's" crossed his thoughts, again. *Damn!*

RJ watched his son and Anne walk toward what he decided was Anne's mother's home. He knew he was in for one awful long weekend. He hated being in the city. He even hated going to Dallas on Sundays for dinner with Jason and Anne. Now, he was stuck in Tulsa, Oklahoma, for the whole damn weekend. Could this day possibly get any worse? *Crap!*

With enormous dreaded anticipation, he stared at the modest brick home with the small enclosed porch on the front. It was Anne's fault! Yes, indeed, it was all her fault. *Damn her.* RJ was furious with Anne and he was more furious with himself. Not only had his son fallen for Anne, but much to RJ's dismay, he'd gotten so he liked Anne, too. Well, as much as he'd allow himself to like her. But, **she** was the one who told him there was something they wanted him to see that morning, and being stupid and falling under her spell, he went along with what she wanted. He knew better. Damn women. He'd gotten screwed again. Now, here he was away from Texas, his ranch, "Miss March", and "Goldie's". *Damn it.*

From his car window, RJ observed with great caution, the small woman he decided must be Anne's mother. As he examined the woman, it appeared to him that the woman was giving his son dirty looks. He wondered why she would do that. Surely, it was his imagination. Jason was a perfect son, an outstanding young man, and a whole lot smarter than that stupid woman.

RJ's suspicious eyes continued to peruse the woman. He determined she probably was just about his age, but he really couldn't tell. That woman had her hair up in a do like old ladies wore, like his Gramma had worn over forty years ago. RJ observed too, that the woman was plain, very plain. She had no color about her at all. Every piece of her clothes was the same drab, dreary gray, and her clothes were so loose and baggy, that hell, she might as well have an old, gray gunny sack thrown over her body. This woman had no style at all. He didn't know anything about women's fashions, but damn, he knew when a woman's appearance wasn't appealing to a man, and that woman wasn't appealing one damn bit. In fact, she had to be the most displeasing looking woman he'd ever laid eyes on. She was just pitiful looking.

As RJ carefully observed the woman, again, he noticed her frown at Jason, flashing her dark eyes up and down his long lean frame. Why, that snooty woman really was judging his son, deciding if he was good enough for her perfect little family. "Jason is a fine young man!" RJ wanted to shout at that woman. He was smart, educated, very polite, and a catch for any woman. Anne had chased Jason till she caught him, and RJ knew that because his own son was not the type to chase after a woman. Jason was just like him. He'd never chase after any woman. *No, sir.*

RJ knew Anne wanted Jason to come to Tulsa for Easter. He'd heard her going on about it last Sunday, and he knew Jason didn't want to come either, but he came, just trying to make Anne happy. Jason was a good man. The more RJ thought about it, the madder he got. His good son had agreed to come all the way to Oklahoma to meet that snobbish woman, when he was so tired he couldn't stay awake, and now, that nasty woman was sticking her nose up at him. A typical, rotten woman! Who the hell did she think she was?

Glancing past Jason, Elizabeth noticed a man in the back seat of the car, but the man made no effort to leave the car. Jason motioned for him to join them again, but the man turned his head and ignored them. Elizabeth knew the man had seen Jason motioning to him, but still he refused to get out of the car. She couldn't help but wonder what in the world was wrong with that silly man.

Jason walked down the steps and shouted to the man, his hands hiding in his sweat pant pockets against the cold blistering wind of March. "Dad! Please Dad, come on in the house." Jason's voice sounded as though he were begging, almost pleading with the man.

RJ ignored his son's pleas. He was fit to be tied. He was over fifty years old; an old man, a man used to making his own decisions and doing exactly as he pleased. Now, he was supposed to cow tow to that critical old biddy, a captive in her home. No sir, he wouldn't do it. He'd take Jason's car and find a motel. Hell, he'd spend the weekend at the motel and Jason could kiss up to the old gal, but not him, by God.

From what Elizabeth could see of the man he looked just like Jason, so she decided he had to be Jason's father. Why in Heaven's name did he come? She certainly hadn't invited him, and it was obvious, he didn't want to be there. Jason practically had to beg him to get out of the car, Elizabeth noticed as she watched and wondered about these strange people. The father certainly was no gentleman, and appeared to be an obstinate, most uncooperative person. He'd probably ruin the whole weekend with his pigheaded attitude.

Jason smiled awkwardly at Elizabeth and then turned to glare at the car where his father remained. Elizabeth could hear the frustration in Jason's voice. "Dad! Damn it. Behave yourself. Come in the house, right now." For some time, Jason stood at the bottom of the steps glaring toward the car.

RJ glared back at his son while looking through his pockets to see if he had his extra key to Jason's car, so he could get the hell out of there. To his horror, RJ discovered he had no key, no money, no credit card, and no means to pay for a motel room. He'd left all of that on his bureau that morning when he changed his clothes after the event with the calf. Now, he'd be forced to spend the whole damn weekend at the mercy of that hateful witch. That or live in the car for the weekend. *Oh crap!*

"Dad!" Jason bellowed.

RJ thought about the situation for a moment. Soon, a wicked sneer settled on his rugged face. He could be just as nasty to that hateful witch as she was to his son. He'd teach the old bat a lesson on this long, miserable weekend from hell. Give him something to do till he could get the hell out of there. "This might even be fun," he snickered out loud, but something deep inside his mind warned him that this was not to be his finest hour. After what seemed like a duel of wills between father and son, Elizabeth watched the tall stranger emerge from the back seat of the car, taking his time, not giving a hoot about them shivering in the cold. Even with everyone waiting for his grand presence, the stranger managed to stop, stretch, kick each foot against two different tires, and to Elizabeth's disgust, he kicked the bricks lining her walkway. All of them.

After some time, his own time, the man sauntered toward them in a slow John Wayne swagger. Elizabeth gasped. This man, who obviously was to be a guest in her home for the weekend, was a dirty old cowboy. Good Lord, he even had on a John Wayne cowboy hat. Well, it was some sort of dirty old hat, she noted. He was a large, tall, aging man, with blizzard cold eyes; eyes so cold they reminded Elizabeth of turquoise ice. His body projected a bullish dominance, threatening to trample anything that might venture into his path, and Elizabeth was well aware, she was in his path. When he neared Elizabeth, he stopped and glared at her, a smirk on his face, his arrogant blue eyes piercing into her soul, searing her, challenging her.

This man had never met her, and yet he seemed to hate her. Elizabeth wondered why. She didn't even know him. Well, two could play this game, Elizabeth decided. She'd taken all the nastiness she could possibly stand from men, and now this big threatening bull was subjecting her to his domination in her own home. This power play, he was trying to gain over her would stop, and it would stop now.

Elizabeth held her head straight and rigid, her black eyes flashing warnings to him. He eyeballed her back. Finally, she brought her dark eyes from his face down to the rest of him. He stood facing her proud and tall, and didn't seem one bit ashamed of his appearance: his shirt wrinkled, his jeans torn, that horrible old gray cowboy hat covered in sweat stains, and spots of God only knew what.

When he removed his hat to give her a cold "Howdy, ma'am", she noticed his salt and pepper hair pasted to his head from the weight of wearing that dreadful cowboy hat far too long. His gripper tight, faded denim shirt bulged around his expanded waistline, and his torn jeans settled low on his hips held in place with the wide brown belt clasped with a worn steer's head buckle.

Elizabeth wondered how on earth he kept his pants from falling down around his filthy boots. As she looked at his boots, she smelled something strange. Was that awful smell coming from Jason's father? Surely, that wasn't the smell of cow manure. *Good Lord.*

"Mom, this is Jason's father, RJ Scott," Anne explained, looking expectantly at her prim mother, wondering how she'd accept Jason's rather unkempt father. "We kidnapped him and brought him with us."

Elizabeth felt for the tissue secured in her sweater sleeve and covered her nose. "Does Mr. Scott have a real name, or do we simply address him by his initials?"

"RJ will be fine," the smelly man growled, holding his head high and rolling his dirty hat around in his large calloused hands.

"My gramma named Dad after Randolph Scott, the old time western movie star", Jason interrupted. "His middle initial is for his father, James."

"Yes," Elizabeth said, as she attempted to ignore the large, smelly man. "Thank you for clarifying his name, Jason." She forced a smile, but she noticed that having the conversation directed toward him seemed to make the large man uneasy.

RJ stood on one foot and then the other. His personal business was his own and no one else's. That woman didn't need to know one damn thing about him, and he wished Jason would just shut the hell up. He continued to glare at Elizabeth.

"Come in the living room," Elizabeth said, holding the door for Jason and Mr. Randolph James Scott, who ignored her as he brushed past her. *My, God. That* a*wful smell.*

Elizabeth's original sleeping plan, before Mr. Randolph James Scott came and ruined everything, was to put Adam and Kathy in Adam's old room. Anne would be in her old room, Jason would sleep on the sleeper in the den, and of course, she'd sleep in her own bed. Now, everything would have to be changed, and Elizabeth wondered where in the world she would put this man that he wouldn't stink up her whole house? With the size of him, he'd be too tall for the daybed in the sunroom where she wanted to put him. There she could open the windows and air the place out quickly, but with the size of him, Elizabeth realized that wouldn't work. Now, she really had a big dilemma. Where would she put him to sleep? Why in the world was he here, anyway? Who invited him*? Horrible man.*

"Is anyone hungry or would anyone care for a drink? I have soft drinks, or wine. Maybe I have…." Elizabeth remembered the half empty gallon bottle of Vodka hidden under the kitchen sink.

Before she could go on, she was interrupted by Anne, her cheeks glowing with hidden excitement. "Mom, we want to celebrate. We brought champagne, so will you please get your champagne glasses?"

Elizabeth knew she was going to die right then and there. Silently, she prayed against the inevitable, knowing in her heart she would lose. Her prayer stopped, but her thoughts continued. Jason might be a nice boy, but Anne could do so much better. What sort of a family would Anne be marrying into? His father was straight off the back forty. People might not have the money for expensive clothes, but his father wasn't even clean. How could anyone come to meet their future in laws without at least taking a bath and putting on clean clothes?

As Elizabeth crossed the room to retrieve the glasses, she passed the massive graying man. His blue eyes looked tired as he rested his head on the back of her crushed velvet accent chair, his long legs stretched out in front of him. As she passed by him, he allowed his legs to stay in her pathway forcing her to step over him. That did it. That man was the most uncouth, most disgusting man she'd ever seen. He was a crude, rude, smelly man, and he didn't belong in her nice home with her lovely family. Obviously, he knew it. Or he should know it. She wondered if he resented being there as much as she resented having him. *No, that wasn't possible.*

Anne passed around the six crystal glasses Jason had filled with Champagne. "And now", Jason began, "Anne and I wanted all of you together to tell you our first big surprise! We're planning to get married soon, but we haven't made any plans, yet."

Waiting no longer, Adam jumped from his chair with his hand outstretched in congratulations. His sister would join the ranks of the old married folks.

"No! Not yet, Adam. Anne has another announcement." Jason said as he beamed with adoration at Anne.

Elizabeth's nerves were on edge, her dreams for Anne shattered. Refusing to give up hope, she decided that if she could get Anne alone, she could bring her to her senses. Surely, she could get her to see that a union of two people with such different backgrounds could never work.

Anne took the center stage next to Jason amongst the clapping and shouting of her brother and his wife. Laughing, she held up her hand to show the center cut diamond Jason had given her earlier.

"Mom, RJ," she smiled a gleaming smile first at Elizabeth and then at her future father-in-law, her eyes searching for their approval. "Jason and I want to be the first to congratulate both of you, also." Her face turned a slight pink as she grabbed Jason's hand. "You will become grandparents at the end of September."

Elizabeth choked on her Champagne, coughing and gasping for breath. Wiping her mouth with the sleeve of her cashmere sweater, she glanced at the large, graying man, sitting silently, cautiously observing the festivities. Elizabeth was certain she noticed a scowl from him when his son announced the engagement, but when Anne mentioned the baby, a wide smile crossed his face. Obviously, he was delighted. Quickly, he rose from the little accent chair, the crushed velvet, very crushed now. He was not a fat man, Elizabeth observed. Even though he had the past-middle-age pot belly, he was very muscular, and from the deep tanned color of his skin, it appeared that he was outside most of the time.

Cautiously, Elizabeth watched the large cowboy towering over everyone, as he walked to Anne and gently kissed her on the cheek and hugged her. Without the least bit of awkwardness, he walked to his son, put his arms around him and kissed him, also. "Now, I understand," he said, quietly. And with the thought of a grandchild in his future, RJ Scott could feel himself relax a bit. He understood why Anne wanted him and her mother to hear this news, together. It was very good news. And it was only fair that they hear it together, but he still didn't like that nasty mother of hers. As he glanced in Elizabeth's direction, his happy smile was replaced with a snarl.

Elizabeth wondered what she'd done to deserve his nasty snarl. She'd been nothing but gracious to him and his son since they arrived, even though his attitude, his appearance, and even those cold blue eyes made her angry. And she hadn't been angry in a very long time. Then Elizabeth remembered she hadn't felt anything in a very long time.

Anne knelt close to her Mother, her hands resting on her Mother's lap. "See my ring, Mom," Anne's voice was breathless with excitement.

"Yes, dear," Elizabeth replied. "It's very beautiful".

Anne stared curiously into her Mother's eyes. She knew her Mother, and she knew when her Mother wasn't pleased, regardless of what she said. Anne just hoped that Jason and RJ hadn't picked up on her mother's disapproval as she had. Normally, she was such a loving, kind person. She was just tired, Anne decided, and it didn't matter anyway, because as soon as she could get her alone, they'd work out this problem. Her mother would come to adore Jason, she knew she would. She just wasn't sure how she would feel about his father, RJ. She wondered about that as she watched her mother start toward the kitchen carrying the tray of glasses.

RJ almost gagged when that woman opened the kitchen door and that terrible smell escaped into the living room. He'd never smelled anything worse. Smelled like burnt garlic fish with a cup of perfume thrown in. He gasped silently. Was that what she'd cooked for them to eat? And here he was with no billfold, no money; couldn't even sneak out for a hamburger. How could he eat that slop? He couldn't and he wouldn't. He'd figure a way to avoid her cooking somehow or other.

Looking about the room, RJ was as uncomfortable as he'd ever been in his entire life. The little chair that he was sitting on was too small for his large body, and he felt a spring prodding him in the butt. The smell of her cooking coming from the kitchen was indescribable, it was so bad, and the mildewed ceiling was ready to fall any second. And there sat that stupid woman flashing those expensive, pink diamond earrings like she was a rich bitch. Why, she should sell those ridiculous earrings and get the damned roof fixed. Hell, she could put on a new roof with the price of those diamonds. RJ glared up at the nasty ceiling, because he was tired of glaring at that woman with those stupid, pink diamond earrings. He knew how expensive pink diamonds were. Carla had begged for a pink diamond ring when they got married. She never got one. RJ chuckled, taking great pleasure in some old memory. Then he remembered his misery, and the scowl returned to his weathered face.

Gathering the empty glasses onto the tray, Elizabeth carried the tray back into the kitchen. She put her hands on the sink and stared into the darkness of the backyard. Her thoughts were worried thoughts, thoughts of uncertainty. How she'd dreamed of the day she'd be told she would become a grandmother, but not like this. This was not the way it was supposed to be.

"Mom", it was Anne's gentle voice. "Mom, don't be upset with me. I am so happy, and I want you to be happy, too."

Elizabeth put her arms around her daughter and cradled her with her mother's love. "A child, Anne? When I saw you at Christmas, you didn't even mention Jason".

"He just started at the firm in January, Mom", she replied, burying her mouth in her mother's hair, hiding her face from her mother's questioning gaze.

Elizabeth did some quick math. "Good Lord, Anne. What did you do? Sleep with him the first minute you met him? Didn't I teach you any morals?"

"Mom," Anne whispered, putting her hand over her mother's mouth. "You know I've never brought anyone home to meet you. I've never loved anyone before Jason. But when we met, it was so perfect. Like you and Dad".

Elizabeth cringed. She could have lived without that remark. What about the wedding and all the arrangements that had to be made? Anne was living in Dallas and she was in Tulsa. How could they order invitations in time? Get a wedding dress? Where would they have the wedding? What church? Surely, they would be married in Tulsa by Pastor Jim, the minister Anne had known all of her young life. He'd baptized her. He led the funeral for Anne's father. Elizabeth composed herself and let the worries lie idle for the moment.

"Anne, I just want you to be happy. Jason seems to be a nice young man, and maybe he can provide a fair living for you, but he's such a hick, a nobody; the son of a beaten up old cowboy! Look at that awful sweat suit he's wearing with that ridiculous saying, Rednecks do it on the run. Now what decent person would wear something like that?"

Anne doubled over laughing. "Oh, Mom, you're a classic. That's my sweat suit! Jason came in late last night from a trial, and stayed at my place, because it was closer to the courthouse than his place. He didn't have anything to wear for the long drive, so I insisted he wear my old sweat suit. Trust me, Mom, Jason is fastidious about his appearance, but right now, he's just exhausted."

"All right, Anne, but just look at his Dad. He looks as though he came straight out of the barnyard. I swear he smells like cow dung."

Anne broke out in a whoop of laughter. "Yes, Mom, he does. And he isn't very happy about it." She clapped her hands in delight. "Jason and I found him working out on his land mending fences. We knew if we took him back to his house and said we were coming here to meet you, he wouldn't come." she giggled as if still a young child. "He would've made some excuse about not being able to leave his cows, or his dogs, or the snakes or the varmints or any excuse that he could come up. So, before he could object, we told him we had something to show him. We got him in the car and kidnapped him. He didn't know what was happening until we hit the interstate. Boy was he mad." Again, she giggled in delight.

Elizabeth realized that the horrible man was not someone her daughter was the least bit afraid. Of course, Anne wasn't afraid of anything. Not like her mother. "Well, who is going to feed the cows and take care of his dogs?" Elizabeth snapped, thinking what foolish children they were. Getting married, having a child, starting a life together with such an uncertain future.....and that big, smelly man. Lord. Just the thought of Elizabeth's grandbaby being held in the smelly arms of that backwoods cowboy was just too much. It just absolutely enraged her. But Anne was pregnant. There would be a new life, and she would have a little child to love and watch grow; and like it or not, the nasty man was Jason's father. They'd be forced to share the love of this child, together.

"Mom, there are people who will care for RJ's cows and dogs." Anne said, breaking into her thoughts. "We took care of that before we got to his place. Everything's fine."

Anne took Elizabeth's aging hands in hers and stroked them lovingly. She stared searchingly in to her Mother's dark beautiful eyes, remembering those soft eyes glowing with approval when she'd been a child and accomplished some small feat in her young life. And now, even though she was grown, she longed to have her mother's approval.

"Mom, we really wanted for you and RJ to learn of our wonderful news, together," she whispered. "You are both the best parents anyone could ever want, and we want you to be happy for us." Anne's blue eyes were begging her mother for approval.

Elizabeth searched her heart for all the happy memories that this child had given her, and she knew there would be more happy times and more happy memories. Gently, with only the love that a Mother could feel for a child, Elizabeth placed her arms around her only daughter.

"Now, my dear Mother," Anne whispered glowing with renewed happiness, "Give me a kiss, tell me that you love me more than any other little girl in the world, and wish Jason and me much happiness." And Elizabeth did.

Anne joined Jason, Adam, and Kathy in the den, where Adam lit the gas log in the large brick fireplace. Many happy times had been spent in that room when Charles was alive, Elizabeth remembered. Biting her lower lip to ward off the memory of his loss, Elizabeth walked through the living room toward the den. She heard a loud rumbling sound, snorts followed by deep growls. There, scrunched up in the little gold velvet chair, was Mr. Randolph James Scott, his head on his chest, sound asleep.

Elizabeth knew the man was exhausted, as she watched the rising and falling of his large body, with every snore. Being a proper hostess, she decided she had no choice but to let him have her bed, but then she realized she might never have to see him again after the wedding. She'd done her part. Throughout it all, she'd shown herself to be a very gracious hostess, a real lady, and she was sure that awful man had seen that. Of course, she didn't care what that big overgrown cowboy thought of her. He just didn't matter one tiny little bit.

Elizabeth walked into the den leaving the large man to his slumbers. The kids were laughing and joking, talking about baby names, but absolutely no discussion of wedding plans. Elizabeth wondered what on earth Anne was thinking. Had she no pride?

Upon entering the room Elizabeth cleared her throat, and the kids grew quiet. "Anne, Jason will sleep in here on the sleeper sofa and you will sleep in your room". She made her statement in such a tone that no one would dare object. "Mr. Scott will sleep in my bed." Doubting herself for a moment, she mumbled in a small voice, "I hope he doesn't mind that I slept on the sheets last night. Of course, I could change them now for him."

"I guess Mr. Scott can stand your smell for a couple of nights", the growling male voice came from behind her. "But for God's sake woman, let Anne and Jason sleep in her room and you can sleep in your own room. I'll sleep on the sofa bed."

Elizabeth felt the anger welling up inside her again, her head jerking angrily toward him. Who did this ignorant fool think he was to be telling her what should happen in her own house? She spun around quickly and glared at him with the vengeance of a mother whose superior knowledge had been questioned. She faced him squarely and fearlessly in defiance, hands secure on her small hips, "I don't care what sort of indecency you allow in your house, Mr. Scott, but in my house, people who are not married do not sleep together."

RJ stood his ground, glaring back at her. "Look lady, that's as stupid as bolting the chicken coop after the fox's run off with the chicken. The damage is already done. And for your information, they're both over twenty-one years old, and sure as hell don't need your outdated parental consent to sleep together. They're having a baby in a few months, for God's sake woman, so I'm pretty damn sure they've already slept together at least once, and probably have a hell of a lot more times than you'd like to believe."

RJ's blue eyes had turned a stormy raging blue as he scowled into her defensive, flashing brown eyes. Aware that she refused to back down over the ridiculous issue, he gave her a condescending smile, acknowledging her as the most stupid woman he'd ever met. He continued his angry tirade. "Lady, you do know, don't you, that a baby is made when a man beds a woman." RJ knew he should stop and for a moment he paused, but seeing the indignant smirk on her face, he just couldn't help himself. "Or has it been such a long time since anyone's bedded you that you've forgotten how it's done?"

There was a stunned silence in the room. No one dared breathe. Elizabeth's mouth fell open in shock. RJ seemed surprised what had come out of his own mouth, but he was even more surprised that he'd gotten so angry, that he'd aimed the nasty remark directly at that woman. He had better manners than that. Never in his life had he insulted a woman until that day. He looked off into the distance for a moment, shuffling from one foot to the other, trying to figure out what he should do.

After what seemed an eternity of uncertainty to everyone, he began, "I truly am sorry for that remark, ma'am. I'm just tired and would like to go to bed....somewhere, anywhere, I don't give a damn where. Hell, I'll go and sleep in the car."

Elizabeth composed herself into the true lady that she was, ignoring his comments. She'd love to tell him where he could go sleep, but she didn't. She was a proper lady. With her head held high, Elizabeth marched from the room, a tiny smile hiding at the corners of her mouth. She'd exposed the intruder's real behavior. She had him, and he knew it. "Under the circumstances, I will accept your apology, Mr. Scott. It's been a long day for both of us. Please come with me." Triumphantly, she marched on.

"Mom, where will you sleep?" Adam called watching the huge beaten man follow his small mother from the room.

"I'll be fine on the sun porch," she replied with such a tone of authority that it even made her blush.

"It gets cold out there, Mom", Anne called after her.

"I'll be fine", Elizabeth snipped. "There's plenty of heat from the bathroom."

RJ turned to face his son before he walked from the room. "Jason, you mind your manners. You sleep in here and no sneaking off to Anne's room. We will respect the rules of her house." RJ knew the horrible woman had gotten the best of him. He couldn't let her get away with it. He continued, "even though her stupid rules don't make a lick of sense."

Elizabeth was no longer smiling. He just had to get the last word in, that horrible tyrant. Onward she marched from the den, down the long hallway to her bedroom, the anger bristling up around her neck. She dared not turn to look behind her for the man, but she didn't have to. She could smell the odor of cow dung following behind her.

"Now, Mr. Scott, I will show you where you can sleep," she stated gaining control of her emotions as she flipped on the light in her bedroom. Both elders stood erect, arms akimbo, the silence deadly.

Elizabeth knew the nasty man was in awe of the pristine bed where she was allowing him to sleep, with the pink brocade comforter, the matching pillow shams, and the pink silk designer pillows. All perfect, all clean. Ignoring RJ, Elizabeth opened the bathroom door, hoping he'd take the suggestion. "You can shower here and there are plenty of clean towels in the cabinet. I know you will be comfortable. Good night, Mr. Scott." As she bristled past him, she grabbed her pink polka-dot nightgown and her pink robe and slippers from behind the door. Not bothering to acknowledge that he was standing there, she slammed shut the door to the sunroom.

"Good night, ma'am," she heard him quietly reply through the closed door. Then she heard him comment in a low tone, "Is every damn thing in this house pink?"

Elizabeth ignored his comments and tucked in the white frilly eyelet comforter around herself. "Not everything in this house is pink," she thought. "Not everything." Sick with disappointment, Elizabeth settled herself in for the night. It certainly hadn't been the day she'd hoped for, and the longer she had to tolerate that big smelly man, she knew it would only get worse.

For some time there was complete silence. Elizabeth wondered if the man would bother to bathe, or would he just crawl into her lovely bed, encrusting it in the odor of cow dung and the memories of the weekend from hell. Finally, she heard her bedroom door open into the bathroom. The shower started and she heard the unmistakable man sounds coming from the shower. Elizabeth wondered if it was some sort of male ritual that men had, that they felt they had to pass gas in the shower? *Absolutely disgusting.*

She heard the shower stop, the slamming of the linen closet doors, and the man grumbling loud enough so she could hear him. "Stupid, tiny little towels! Got to use two of the damn things just to dry my head." The light went out in the bathroom. And then it was quiet.

Chapter 8

Elizabeth was running naked through the night. The snow was falling on her dark hair and dancing down around her nude body, as tiny dancing fairies performed a ballet on the dais of her skin. The snow was growing deeper, whipping up above her ankles and wrapping her in a blanket of solid ice. Opening her eyes, Elizabeth tried to make some sense of where she was. Oh yes, she was on the sun porch. She was freezing.

"Only in Oklahoma, could you have daytime temps of seventy and nighttime temps of thirty," she shivered to herself. Squinting in the darkness, softened by the shadows of the streetlights outside, she was able to see the closed door to the bathroom. That stupid man had closed the door, leaving her no heat. She'd specifically told him to keep it open. She **had** told him not to close it, hadn't she? Or was it the kids she'd been talking to? She couldn't remember. Her brain was probably frozen.

Elizabeth crept along the cold floor, making her way to the bathroom door. Pulling the door open, she could see that the door to her bedroom was also shut. She had no other choice but to wake the awful man and remind him to leave the doors open after he used the bathroom.

Elizabeth pushed open the door to her bedroom and could feel the heat of the warm air circulating about the room. The man was snorting in and growling out in the perfect rhythm of two pigs performing some weird barnyard musical. How could he possibly sleep through all that noise?

As she made her way through the room in the light of the moonlight shining through the window, Elizabeth observed his massive body breathing up and down in unison with the snorting and growling. Longingly, she gazed at her side of the warm, cozy bed which appeared to be as untouched as she'd left it that morning. Obviously, he'd designated her side of the bed and wanted nothing to do with it. Watching him thoughtfully, she wondered if her smell on her pillow sickened him to the point that he chose to remain in one spot avoiding any trace of her. Elizabeth lifted her chin higher dismissing the man. She could care less how he chose to sleep in her warm snuggly bed. If not for her generosity and kindness, he could be the one sleeping on the porch freezing to death. But no, she'd given up her comforts for him. *Dumb, ungrateful, hick.*

"Mr. Scott," she whispered. "Mr. Scott, please wake up for just a minute. I need to tell you about the bathroom door." He continued his in and out snorting and grunting. "Mr. Scott", she spoke in a louder voice, "You must wake up, please." Cautiously, she touched his hairy, muscled arm, but he didn't respond.

The first blast of warm air, upon entering the room, gave way to goose bumps around her arms and shoulders. Her feet were so cold her toes were numb. Teeth chattering, she stood shivering in the moonlight, staring longingly at her untouched spot in the captivating bed. Grabbing his arm, she shook him with both of her hands. He growled a little and resumed the barnyard symphony. Nothing was going to wake that big mountain of a man.

Elizabeth hurried around the bed to her own side, the coldness of the floor seeping upward into her ankles. She spent a short moment in contemplation, listening as the loud barnyard symphony grew ever louder. He'd never wake till morning, she was certain of that. He'd never know. Quickly, she threw all the pillows onto the floor and slipped her small body in beside him. She'd stay just long enough to get warm and then she'd return to the cold porch which should be warm soon.

Elizabeth snuggled into her side of the bed and felt the silky softness of the down pillow caressing her head in loving familiarity. The weight of her brocade comforter swaddled her body, as she envisioned the comfort of white sanded beach, the sun gently toasting her skin. Very soon she felt the heat radiating from the intruder in her bed, and without the slightest effort, she found what she'd lost a long time ago, the blissful, oblivion of deep sleep.

RJ Scott sat straight up in the bed, his chest heaving, his blue eyes flashing about the room. "Where the hell am I?" He gasped to himself, half afraid to find out. There was some sort of terrible noise coming from the other side of the bed, and he wondered what in God's name that awful noise was. It sounded like some sort of a wild bird, maybe a Loon. No, Loons made laughing sounds. Good God, whatever it was, it was just damn scary.

Trying to adjust his eyes to the early dawn, he remembered where he was and could see what appeared to be a lump in the bed next to him. Hesitant to touch the thing, he reached down beside the bed and found his old boot. Very carefully, he took his dirty boot by the heel and touched the thing next to him with the toe of his boot. It didn't move. He gave it a whack and to his amazement, the thing rolled over and faced him.

"Good God, Almighty." He exclaimed under his breath. That nasty woman had crawled into bed with him. Pulling the comforter up around his naked chest, RJ was clearly puzzled. What the hell did she want? Remembering his angry remark to her earlier, his own voice raged in his ears. '*Has no one bedded you in such a long time, that you've forgotten how it's done?*' RJ cringed to himself. Yeah, she was mad when he said it, and so was he. So, what the hell was she doing crawling in bed with him? Did she think that he made an offer to bed her? God, he hoped not. No, sir, he had not offered to bed her. If that old gal wanted sex, she would have to look somewhere else. He was not putting out for her. He chose his women, not the other way around.

Cautiously, he stared at her in the darkness, wondering about the strange woman. What the hell sort of a horny old gal was she, crawling in bed with a stranger. He'd never been forced to put up with any in-laws before, so he wasn't sure what to do. Just how much was expected of him as an in-law? Surely, bedding the old widows in the family was not expected of the single men. Hell, society was nuts anymore, but that was ridiculous. RJ scratched his gray head in wonder. What the hell sort of a crazy family had Jason gotten tied up with, anyway?

RJ remained very still with the covers pulled up tightly around his body. He knew the strange woman had to be sleeping deeply with all that bird call snoring. After some thought, he decided that he'd just sneak out of the bed without waking her and avoid having to argue with her about her sexual desires. That'd just be too embarrassing for him.

Cursing softly, RJ remembered he'd wrapped himself in the comforter and put every stitch of his filthy clothes in her washing machine after everyone was asleep. He'd been waiting to put them in the dryer, but he'd fallen asleep. Now, here he was naked, with this crazy woman next to him, the comforter snuggled up around her. If he pulled the comforter off the bed, she'd wake up and he'd have to face her. He sure as hell couldn't go running down the hall to the laundry room naked, so what could he do? He was just stuck and it was dawn, damn it. Time to get up!

After studying over several means of escape, RJ accepted his fate and settled back into the comfort of the warm bed. Listening to the horrid bird calling, he stared at her for a moment, his blue eyes squinting for a closer look. She really was a pretty thing, he decided. Her hair was loose, all messed up and hanging in soft curls around her dainty pink, polka dotted nightgown, which sure was more pleasing to the eye than those ugly, drab, old lady clothes.

Feeling the first blast of cold air coming from the bathroom, RJ pulled the comforter up further on his chest. She must have frozen her ass off out there on the cold porch, he decided, not feeling one bit guilty. But she had given him her warm bedroom, and he thought that was decent of her. Maybe she wasn't so bad.

RJ continued to observe her in the safety of her deep sleep. Her hair was the color of Juanita's sweet Mexican coffee: dark auburn, rich and thick flowing down around her shoulders, soft dark strands covering her cheek. Her skin was the whitest skin he'd ever seen, smooth as a baby's butt. A few small wrinkles of age had started around her mouth, but still her mouth was almost perfect, lips like a small heart. Damn, she was a looker, or at least she could have been in the past. Oh hell, she still was.

Carefully scrutinizing her face, RJ noticed around her eye were a few small scars which seemed out of place in the rare beauty of the woman, but, he decided, those little flaws just made her human and not so damn fake. She reminded him of someone he'd had a crush on a long time ago when he was a kid, but damned if he could remember who it was.

Continuing to watch the aging beauty as she slept contentedly, RJ remembered her type from years ago when he was a young boy. The pretty ones were always the worst: stuck up, mean, cruel, real bitches, and this one was a prime bitch. She'd shown her true self when she glared at Jason, turning that perfect little nose up at his good son. He wanted nothing to do with her. Yes, he knew her type well.

Rolling over, staring up at the ceiling above him, his jaw clenching hard against his rugged skin, he remembered the shame he suffered over one of those pretty girls in his first year of high school. He'd saved every penny he didn't have to give to his folks, so he could meet Rebecca Ames at the school dance. It was Rebecca's idea for him to meet her there. She'd even made a big deal about it in front of all her friends and half the football team. He was such a stupid fool. He'd believed what she said. Hell, he'd no reason to think any different.

So, he'd been all excited about his first date, and it being with the prettiest girl in school. He'd even bought her a flower. He didn't have a car, so he'd walked all the way to town on the old dusty road, carrying a paper bag of his Sunday clothes, planning to put them on at the gas station before the dance.

Like an idiot, he sat at the damn dance for three hours holding the stupid flower waiting for Rebecca to show up. He could see some of the gals giggling, and the football team pointing and laughing at him, but he just kept on waiting for Rebecca. She never did show up as she'd promised, so he just threw the flower in the garbage and walked on home.

He learned a good lesson with that pretty gal, but not good enough. He'd married Jason's mother, another pretty one. That's when he really learned his lesson. She taught him real good. The pretty ones were bad, and this gal next to him in the bed was real pretty. She'd be nothing but trouble. Trouble was something he didn't need and was too damn old to put up with, but for some reason he couldn't understand, she fascinated him.

RJ rolled over and stared at the woman sleeping beside him watching her intently in the quiet peacefulness of the early morning. She looked so sweet and innocent as she slept. He wished she'd stay like that, but he knew she wouldn't. As soon as she woke up, she'd return to her mean, hateful self, and he'd have to be on guard against her, again. But for that moment, he decided he'd just lay there and enjoy her clean smell, her soft warm breath, and her incredible aging beauty.

As RJ watched her, to his complete bewilderment, the sleeping woman nudged herself close to him, and pressed the length of her soft body against him. Claiming him in a wifely manner, she slipped one leg over his. This warm intimacy was something new to RJ, something he'd never experienced with Carla. It amazed him that this woman seemed so completely satisfied with his closeness. Watching her as she contentedly recaptured a lost dream, she slipped her warm arms through his, and nuzzled her soft lips into his naked shoulder. RJ didn't pull away from her touch, nor did he move. Instead, he kept his arm very still and didn't care that she was using him in her dream of another man. He simply wanted to be there with her for just a little while. She was asleep. She'd never remember. What did it matter anyway? Tomorrow, she'd be the bitch again. But tonight, he'd take whatever she'd give him in her dreams. Still, he knew damn well he wasn't supposed to be there.

Submerged in the tranquility of the early dawn, RJ found absolute contentment in the closeness of the woman nestled against him, and for the first time he could remember, he knew peace. Soon, with the warmth their two bodies radiated to one another, RJ joined Elizabeth in the blissful, calm oblivion of deep sleep.

Elizabeth was running barefooted through the sandy beach as the waves of the ocean licked at her ankles, dried quickly by the warm breeze that caressed her. Dropping down onto the sand, she closed her eyes and basked in the warmth of the sunshine that kissed the tiny pebbles of the golden beach around her. She listened in contented awe to the lapping of the waves, swaying back and forth in perfect tempo. Charles was there and came and laid his long body down beside her. She moved her leg over his and in total contentment slipped her arms around his arm and pressed her lips into his familiar warmth. How wonderful to touch him again, to feel his body next to her. Everything was as it should be. Everything was perfect.

The flickering of the sunshine danced on Elizabeth's eyelids causing her dark eyes to blink open in utter shock. Good Lord! She'd overslept and was in bed, cuddled up no less, with this strange man, and he was no longer snoring. What if he was awake? What if he knew she'd crept into **his** bed after she'd made such a scene about Anne and Jason sleeping together?

Elizabeth heard him cough and then she winced as he passed some very smelly gas. She lay totally motionless. Even her eyelids refused to blink. When he began snoring again and she felt it was safe, she began to inch her way out of the bed. As she lifted the comforter to escape, his powerful arm landed across her chest. She was trapped. Her mind darted back and forth in question. Was he awake? Did he know she was there? Fearfully, she turned her head slightly so that she could see him, hoping she would not see his mean blue eyes peering back at her. He was soundly asleep, and for that, she thanked Heaven. Studying him, she realized that he really was a handsome man, if he wasn't such a pig.

He lay sleeping on his side and continued snoring, so Elizabeth took the opportunity to examine him more closely. She wasn't really spying on him as he slept. She just wanted to take a closer look at him without him knowing it.

The age creases at the sides of his eyes were white, obviously from squinting in the sun and deeply inset into the ruddy dark tan of his face. His hair, now that it was clean, was a mixture of black, brown, silver, and sun bleach. His teeth were clean, but somewhat stained, probably from years of coffee use.

He had a strong male nose like the noses of the Romans she'd read about in her novels, a gladiator's nose. Yes, that's what he seemed to be: a ferocious, fearless, powerful gladiator. Elizabeth pictured him strutting proudly around the arena in Rome, the crowds cheering for his victories and wondered if she would cheer for him. *Definitely, not.*

Elizabeth continued with her inspection of him. Around his ears were unruly curled wisps of the dark, salt and pepper hair, which formed a union with the stubble of his graying beard. Oh, how she'd love to get her fingers into those unruly little curls and force them into obedience, submission. Feeling daringly brave with the big man snoring, she pushed the comforter down from his chin where she observed the mixture of black and gray curly hair matted over his white muscular chest, such a contrast to his ruddy suntanned face.

He was an appealing man, she couldn't deny that, but she knew her interest in him was just some sort of silly curiosity, like her fleeting interests in the mavericks in her romance novels. No, this man was no one special. He was no hero's gladiator, just a worn out backwoods cowboy straight off the back forty. Even realizing that, Elizabeth couldn't take her eyes off him. He'd been such an ogre, earlier: ranting and raving about the sleeping arrangements, carrying on like a fool. But when he was asleep, he looked so peaceful, almost harmless.

Her conscience begged her to leave the poor man alone. Ignoring her better instincts, she pushed the comforter down past his chest to his…. "MY, GOD! Where was his underwear?" Elizabeth gasped. She was in this bed with this man and he was naked! Good Lord! What if he woke up and found her there? What if he thought she was there to have sex with him? What if he just couldn't control himself?

Oh yes, she'd read stories about those oversexed cowboys and their uncontrolled lust for women they desired. What if he threw his hard naked body across her, his hairy chest touching her breasts, his massive hands searching into places they had no permission to be? She wouldn't be able to scream, because she couldn't let the kids know about this. What if he became so overcome with passion for her that he seduced her into surrendering to him? She'd just have to let him have his way with her. Let him make ardent, passionate love to her. Elizabeth felt a slight shiver. *Oh, my goodness.*

For a minute, Elizabeth gave some vivid thought to this minute-movie she'd created in her mind, grateful that he was still asleep, unsuspecting his lead in the torrid scene racing across her mind. She felt her face flush and her body warm, and knew she was in trouble. What if he did wake and find her staring at him? What would he think of her? She knew she'd better get out of there fast.

Carefully, she lifted his large hairy arm from around her chest and laid it down on her pillow. She located her slippers under the bed, grabbed her robe, and tiptoed from the bedroom into the safety of the bathroom. Oh, so carefully, she closed the bathroom door, holding the doorknob so that it didn't click and wake him. She felt her heart racing inside her chest, but she'd made it. That awful man would never know she'd been so desperate that she, Elizabeth Carlton, had stooped to share a bed with him...a*nd him, so very, very naked.*

Chapter 9

Adjusting the tie on her pink chenille robe, Elizabeth walked down the long hallway, through the utility room and into the kitchen. With the aroma of fresh coffee tantalizing her, she was ever grateful to the person who invented programmable coffee pots. Pouring herself a cup of the hot brew, she sat down at the table in her bright, cheery kitchen with its many tall windows, alive with early morning sunshine.

Grabbing her Granny glasses to read last night's paper, she was reminded once again, she wasn't getting any younger. It was just a matter of time before she'd be forced to wear the glasses constantly and not just to read. Lifting her head quickly from the newspaper, she heard movement in the utility room. It was **him.**

"Mind if I use your laundry facilities, ma'am?" His husky voice called from the utility room.

Elizabeth wondered how he knew she was in the kitchen. The door to the utility room was shut. Alarms went off in her head. She ignored them and answered in her most agreeable voice. "Of course not, go right ahead. Do you need any help, Mr. Scott?"

"I know how to use a washer and a dryer," he growled.

"Oh, great," Elizabeth muttered to herself, "another day with Mr. Sunshine." Quickly, she decided she would not allow him to bother her that day. For the first time in ages, she felt really good: totally rested and wide awake, eager to meet the day, even a little happy for a change.

"Come and have a cup of coffee, Mr. Scott," she offered cheerfully.

"Can't ma'am," he replied in a droll voice. "I'm standing out here naked with a blanket wrapped around me."

She heard the dryer start and wondered when he'd washed his clothes. Had he known that she'd been in bed with him? A sick feeling overcame her happy thoughts.

In answer to her thoughts, he responded, "I washed my clothes last night. Now, I just need to dry them."

Elizabeth felt a sigh of relief. He knew nothing of her little escapade of the night before that involved him so intimately. Thank

God.

"I have a large green chenille robe with a tie belt in my closet, Mr. Scott. Just put that on and join me for some coffee while you wait for your clothes to dry." She heard the utility door open and close and then heard heavy footsteps exiting down the hallway.

Elizabeth was on her second cup of coffee when she heard the heavy footsteps returning. Slowly, he pushed the door open, hesitating upon entering the kitchen. Looking up from her paper, she caught a glimpse of the green robe through the partially opened door. She smiled at the large man. "Come in, Mr. Scott. I won't bite."

He entered cautiously and stood facing her, his blue eyes glaring, defying her to say one word about his attire. Elizabeth smiled in acknowledgement of his presence and peered down into her coffee cup, knowing she couldn't look at him and not laugh. She started to get him a cup of coffee, but he seemed determined to take care of his own needs.

With large steps he strode to the coffee pot, and poured himself a cup of the black steaming coffee. Elizabeth took a quick glance at him. He hadn't been able to get the robe to extend around him, so he'd put it on backwards. Fully aware that his rear end was exposed, he'd attached a pink towel to the belt of the robe as a flap to cover his exposed rear end.

Elizabeth pulled the paper up around her face and felt the laughter welling up inside her. Gasping for breath, she forced back the laughter, knowing he would be furious if he saw her laughing at him. She truly didn't want him to ruin the glorious day, so she decided to concentrate on sad thoughts. Sad thoughts would control her laughter.

Taking a sip of coffee, she heard him sit down at the table, and choked on her coffee. *Sad thoughts. Sad thoughts.* With the paper up around her hidden face, Elizabeth tried to make small talk. "Do you have cattle, Mr. Scott?"

"I have a few head," he growled, offering no further communication.

They sat in silence as they sipped their morning coffee. Time passed. The only sound was that of the clock quietly ticking away, not missing a beat, taking its job very seriously. Feeling that she now had her feelings under control, Elizabeth decided that she could take a quick peek at him without cracking up with laughter.

The large man had placed himself at the side of the table, but it seemed to Elizabeth he tried to stay as far away from her as possible. He was reading the other part of the newspaper and she observed he didn't need glasses to read. Everyone their ages had to wear glasses to read, but not him. Oh, no, not him. She peered down his long body barely covered with the green robe and spied the white hairy legs and the brown roper work boots.

Seeing his cold blue eyes leering back at her, she grasped the paper back around her face, hoping he didn't notice the paper shaking uncontrollably as she tried to stop her laugher. Holding her breath, she tried to think of sad things, but all she could visualize was him in that stupid green robe, his hairy white legs, and the brown boots.

Elizabeth snorted, stifling her laughter for a quick moment. "Would you like more coffee, Mr. Scott?" *Sad things! Sad things!*

"I can get my own damn coffee," he growled, angrily stomping across the kitchen to get his own coffee.

Elizabeth knew he wasn't just angry, he was infuriated with her. She had to stop thinking about how funny he looked in that ridiculous getup. She hid her face in the paper as he walked over to the coffee pot. In vain, she scanned her memory for sad things.

"Well, son of a bitch!" She heard him yell. "That is just the last stinking straw!" Quickly, she forgot about searching her mind for sad things and pulled the paper from around her eyes wet from tears of laughter.

In his hasty independence to get his own coffee, he'd stepped on the hem of the pink towel. As he bristled across the kitchen floor, stopping at the coffee pot, the towel had fallen down around his ankles, exposing his very white, shiny hinny.

He didn't move, but stood perfectly still. She didn't move either. She couldn't. She was holding in her laughter so tightly, she was afraid she'd wet her pants.

Slowly, he turned and looked at her as she sat motionless. Looking up at him, her eyes glistening from suppressed laughter, she noticed that the anger seemed to slip away from him. His cold blue eyes softened into a clear soft turquoise, the age creases at the corners of his eyes eased. His snarl changed into a wide grin.

"All right," he said towering over her, staring down at her as though she was a naughty little girl. "Now, you can laugh".

And laugh she did. At first she let out a small giggle. Then, with loss of all self control, Elizabeth doubled over in laughter, tears running down her cheeks, as she clapped her hands in sheer relief.

RJ started to walk from the kitchen, but instead he turned and faced her, grinning broadly. "Well, hell, woman. If I'd known that dropping my drawers was what it would take to get you to laugh, I'd have dropped them a long time ago." With his shiny hinny glistening in the sunlight, her green robe nipping at his pale white knees, and his brown boots completing the picture, Mr. Randolph James Scott proudly exited the kitchen.

Elizabeth plopped herself down in one of the big brown leather chairs in the informal family room, away from the mildewed ceiling, the crushed velvet chair, and the memory of the debacle of the night before. She'd dismissed all thoughts of impressing the man who would become a grandparent with her. She shuddered thinking about him. He was too crude to know the difference between class and crass, anyway. She just gave up.

It was the Saturday before Easter and every since the children were babies, her family had attended Saturday night Easter services, missing only one service in all those years. That was when both children had the chicken pox.

Pastor Jim had encouraged the young families to attend Saturday night services, so they, too, could enjoy the excitement of the Easter egg hunts planned for their children on Easter Sunday. He was a kind, good man, but he was also a smart minister. He knew there wasn't one child who could sit still through his Sunday service, squirming this way and that, anticipating the goodies that the Easter Bunny had hidden for them. Consequently, he knew that as the parents struggled to keep their active children in tow, no parent in the congregation would hear his sermon. So, Saturday night church, the day before Easter, became a ritual to almost all the parents with young children. Thinking back over the years, how her family had maintained the Saturday ritual, Elizabeth knew this

Saturday night Easter service would not be like the others which her family had faithfully attended. Anne, her precious little blonde haired girl, was pregnant with a child of her own. *Unmarried and apparently in no hurry to get married.*

Elizabeth wondered if she should mention this to Pastor Jim. How would he take it? What would he say? How could this have happened? Had she been such a lousy mother that her child had become a woman without morals? Elizabeth cringed. They must act quickly, hurry the wedding along. Often, girls got married hastily and discretely. When a child was born seven or eight months later, most people said nothing and welcomed the new child into the world, but Anne was three months pregnant with absolutely no plans to marry. Her belly would grow large soon and everyone would talk about her. Anne was a new age woman, yes, and Anne had always lived life on the edge, so to speak, but for God's sake, had she no old fashioned pride?

Like the crush of fine crystal, horrific memories of Elizabeth's childhood rape shattered her happy mood. Remembering all she'd given up to hide the stain of her youth, Elizabeth's small shoulders lowered in the old familiar shame. She remembered the cruel accusations made against her when she'd been returned to her parents. No one knew she'd been raped, but the gossip had run rampant about her, and she vividly recalled the shame she'd experienced. She couldn't let shame haunt Anne and possibly her new grandchild as well.

Alma Green and her widows would have a ball with this news. The things they'd say about Anne would be awful. Anne didn't care, she knew that, but Anne had never faced gossip before. She had no idea of the pain. Elizabeth thought about that for a minute as she swung her leg over her knee and clutched her hands together. Maybe Anne didn't worry about what they said about her, but she did. Elizabeth shrugged in acceptance. Maybe going to a Justice of The Peace was the answer. No one would know when they got married, if she could just get Anne to keep her big mouth shut.

Elizabeth continued to mentally argue with herself, nervously swinging her leg back and forth across her knee and clenching and unclenching her hands. It just wouldn't seem right not having Pastor Jim officiate at the wedding. The kind, gentle man was the core of their moral code, even though Anne had chosen to ignore it.

The morals, or rather the lack of morals of her child, gave way to an even more urgent problem for Elizabeth, Anne's future father-in-law. The man's clothes were awful. They were clean, yes, he'd washed them, but he couldn't go to church dressed like that. She couldn't ask him to stay home, but she couldn't have her handsome family walk into church with that ruffian strolling in with his torn jeans and the shirt that barely covered his stomach. He had to get some decent clothes. Even if she had to drag him shopping, he would get something respectable to wear to church. Alma Green and her gang of widows would most definitely be there gaping and gossiping about this ludicrous, backwoods cowboy. God knows, they didn't need more gossip than Anne would provide.

After much thought, Elizabeth came up with an idea. She'd take everyone for lunch at the "Flaming Dragon Buffet", which wouldn't be too costly for her. The restaurant was located right next to that nice new men's shop. What was the name? Oh yes, "Mr. Enrique's Distinctive Men's Clothing".

With the clothing store next to the restaurant, Mr. Scott would never suspect she was embarrassed by his appearance. She'd insist on buying him a nice shirt and a decent pair of dress slacks. "My treat!" she'd say, sweetly. He'd be pleased, and everyone in town would never know that Anne had chosen an indigent for her father-in-law.

The morning rolled on. A light rain gently kissed the grayed winter grass, as it glistened in delight with this gift from Heaven. Elizabeth peered out the window, progressing in her worries as her leg continued to swing back and forth over her knee. Sunday might not be a good day for an Easter egg hunt. The kids would get their little shoes wet. The dye would run on the Easter eggs. The traditional "Peeps" would be soggy. The chocolate candies would be ruined. The children would be so disappointed. All the goodies purchased by their parents would be wasted.

Elizabeth uncrossed her legs from their nervous movements, and forced herself to calm by deep breathing as she'd learned on her hypnosis tape. After many deep breaths, she felt more at ease. Maybe the parents could hide the Easter eggs in the house. Yes, that would be good. They could make deviled eggs later. The children could help. They would enjoy that.

Thinking about food, Elizabeth wondered just how she would bring up lunch? When should she announce that they were all going out for lunch? How could she be sure she could get him there? He was so obstinate; he'd probably fight her about going anywhere to eat. He probably wasn't used to eating in restaurants. He'd even refused the breakfast she'd offered to fix for him that morning. Maybe he was embarrassed by his country manners. She breathed deeply, again.

Elizabeth fine-tuned her plan, hoping someone would mention food. As if an answer to her dilemma, she heard Adam's voice calling her. "Hey, Mom. There are some people here who're getting pretty darn hungry. I won't mention any names, but it could be the only rounding lady in the group." She heard Anne slap him as though they were still kids, and the familiar laughter filled the room as the childhood retorts began.

Elizabeth knew her master plan was working perfectly. This was her opportunity. "Yes," Elizabeth answered. "I was just wondering if anyone was hungry. I have such a taste for Chinese food today. I hope everyone likes Chinese food."

RJ's blue eyes flashed open at the thought of eating someone else's cooking other than hers. He'd refused the breakfast she'd offered to cook that morning, even though he was half starved. The sickening memory of the smell of her cooking cured his appetite, then, but now, the thought of decent food quickly rekindled his starvation. "As long as you're buying, it sounds good to me," RJ answered quickly, arms closed, leaning against the doorway eyeing her cautiously.

Today would be *"brown day,"* he decided, as he scrutinized her high necked, long sleeve brown shirt, baggy brown slacks, brown jacket, and of course, her old lady brown shoes. RJ was sure she knew the weather was supposed to get up past seventy that day, but that silly woman had on that ugly hot outfit. RJ turned away from the group so they wouldn't see him laughing. *She was gonna burn up.*

RJ faced the group and tried not to laugh. She was wearing all those damn hot clothes, but she sure as hell wasn't wearing those pink diamond earrings, she'd worn to impress them the night before.

She learned damn fast she couldn't pull the wool over his eyes. No, sir. RJ chuckled devilishly to himself.

Elizabeth all but purred, hoping not to rile RJ. "Well, of course, I'm buying. I'd never have my guests pay for their own food." Smiling her sweetest smile, she thanked God that much was settled, and now all she had to do was get him to the restaurant, fill him with food, and when he was fat, happy and satisfied, she'd march him over to the men's store and buy him some decent clothes. Quickly, Elizabeth ushered everyone outside.

As Elizabeth hurried down the back stairs from her kitchen, she came up with another plan. With the six of them, they'd have to take her car, too. She'd suggest that Anne ride with her, and while they were alone, she'd insist Anne quickly begin making wedding plans. The thought of Anne waddling down the aisle, her big stomach covered in a white wedding gown, made Elizabeth wince, and at the pace Anne was planning this wedding, Anne might deliver the baby on the way down the aisle. *Oh lord.*

Elizabeth had to take charge. It was imperative. "Anne, come ride with me," she called as she motioned to her. Anne didn't seem to hear and crawled into the car next to Jason. The big man was coming toward her car. She almost swore as she released the electric lock on his side of the door, but she didn't. Instead, she forced a smile as he lowered himself into the seat beside her.

"Son of a bitch," RJ yelled as he hit his head entering the small car. "What the hell kind of car is this? It's too damn low for a person's head. Hell, you can't even stretch out your damn legs!"

"That's why it is my car and not your car, Mr. Scott", Elizabeth snapped as she backed out of her driveway. "If I wanted a big boat of a car, I would have purchased one. This car, I can handle like a dream." Then she heard the bump. She'd run over her mailbox. Elizabeth dared to look at RJ. He was glaring back at her. His expression said it all. She was as dumb as any woman he'd ever met.

"Yep, you can drive this little piece of crap just like a dream." He snarled in contempt.

Crawling back out of the car, he hit his head again. Slamming the door, he uttered some words Elizabeth had never heard used in decent company, but she knew that sort of reaction should be expected from an ignorant pig like him. Watching him in her rear view mirror, he picked up the dented mailbox and shoved the mangled post back into the ground.

When RJ returned back to the car, he ducked very low upon entry, a smug, satisfied expression on his weathered face. "That will hold it until we get back and I can fix it." RJ considered tormenting her mercilessly about her lousy driving, but instead, obeyed his growling stomach. "Well hell, what are you waiting for, woman? Let's go find food".

Everything had worked like a charm for Elizabeth. She'd watched as this large man devoured three plates of food, returning time and time again to the buffet bar. She could only imagine the sounds and smells that he would emit from her bed that night. Finally, he shoved back from the table, a contented look on his face, and Elizabeth knew he was ready for her next move.

As they exited the restaurant, she continued on with her big master plan. "Kids, why don't all of you go on ahead", she said sweetly. "I know Mr. Scott was hurried from his home without bringing a few nice clothes to attend church." She smiled more sweetly. "So, I would like to take him to "Mr. Enrique's" and let him pick out a nice shirt and some handsome trousers. My treat!" Elizabeth tried to smile even wider and look excited. "What say, Mr. Scott, will you let me treat you to some new clothes?"

RJ's cold, suspicious eyes studied her face, wondering what the hell she was up to. "Now, let me get this straight, lady. You're gonna take me over to that fancy men's store and buy me some new duds. Is that what you're saying?"

Elizabeth smiled in faked delight. "Yes," she answered, gulping softly. Again, she sweetly repeated, "My treat!"

RJ stared at her cautiously, a slight smile edging the corner of his mouth. He had plans of his own. "Well, all right then," he said, "let's go get me some fancy new duds." With Elizabeth struggling to keep up with him, RJ strode over to meet "Mr. Enrique".

As the two entered the store, Elizabeth was awed by the gold marble tiles on the floor, the deep mahogany chair railings enhancing the rich gold-flecked wallpaper, and displayed predominantly throughout the store were tall mahogany wood sculptures of men in various poses in work and at play. Then, to her horror, at the end of the store standing tall above all others, there appeared a sculpture of a nude male, his genitals standing out proudly for the entire world to observe. "Oh, my God. What sort of a store is this?" she gasped under her breath.

Out of nowhere, a young, pale, blonde man approached them wearing a colorful three-piece green suit, a perfectly contrasted yellow silk shirt, and a plaid yellow and green bowed ascot. Elizabeth decided he resembled a life size Easter Bunny.

"May I be of assistance?" he asked provocatively, pushing his hair back from his diamond studded ear lobes, while displaying an acre of shiny white teeth.

To her horror, Elizabeth realized the young man was flirting with Mr. Scott. "Oh, boy!" Elizabeth whispered to herself and wondered how the tough old cowboy would handle the young man.

As though he hadn't noticed the obvious flirtation, RJ smiled at the giddy young man. "Are you Enrique?"

"No, sir, I'm not, " he giggled. "Mr. Enrique services only his special clientele, but I've been with Mr. Enrique for many years, and I know I can be of assistance to you."

RJ leaned over and squinted at the name badge on the young man. In a booming voice, he replied, "Well, you see, Mr. Andrew, I think I am pretty dang special too, and I want Enrique, himself, to assist me in buying some new duds. No objection to you, son, but your sign out front says this is Enrique's shop, and he's the one I want dressing me".

Elizabeth felt her cheeks grow hot and thought she'd die of embarrassment. Should they leave or what? She bit her lower lip and rubbed her fingertips, nervously.

Quickly, an older gentleman approached them dressed in a black satin shirt, black slacks, black platform shoes, and a white satin tie secured with a black pearl. "I am Mr. Enrique. Is there a problem?" he asked, pursing his lips together in question. His long pointed nose was adorned with tiny round glasses, and his dyed cold black hair was secured in a pony tail, exposing his black pearled ear lobes.

RJ took charge, "Yes, there's a problem, Enrique. I'm just as special as any of your other clients and I want **you** to help me pick out some new duds. This lady here," he motioned with his thumb to Elizabeth, "has offered to buy me some new clothes, cause she doesn't want me to look like a damn hick when she shows me off to her lady friends tonight. I want to do right by her, so you show me some of the best stuff you got." And with that, RJ Scott's gripper tight shirt popped open. "Whoops", he said, squeezing the grippers back into place.

The elegant little man stared at the scruffy, large man for a moment, pressing his finger against his lips, contemplating the creation of a masterpiece. He couldn't resist. With an austere flip of his hand he motioned for Elizabeth to sit down in one of the gold brocade Queen Anne armchairs located near the grand entryway. "Come with me, please," Mr. Enrique stated as he sashayed across the room with the large man swaggering along behind him.

As Elizabeth sat swinging her leg back and forth in nervous contemplation, the two men stopped. Mr. Scott said something to Mr. Enrique, but he had his back to Elizabeth so she couldn't hear what he was saying to the small man. Without warning, Mr. Enrique clapped his hands together and began to squeal in delight. Elizabeth wondered what in the world that awful man had said to Mr. Enrique to cause such a reaction. With his little arms swinging in grand gestures, Mr. Enrique ushered Mr. Scott into a room separate from all others, and above the entry to the little room, inscrolled in elegant gold letters, were the words "Private Guest Only**"**. Elizabeth wondered in amazement how that big scruffy cowboy had managed to get in the private room. Then it began.

Elizabeth observed Mr. Enrique as he carried load after load of shirts and slacks back to the "Private Guest Only" room. She gazed helplessly as he held shirts up to slacks, colors against colors, fabric against fabric. Time after time, he returned with a load of clothes and selected new clothes. Every time, he would cast a quick wave to Elizabeth, and she worried just how long this was going to take. What had started out as just a quick stop to buy one pair of slacks and one shirt had turned into an ordeal. Why, Mr. Scott took more time trying on clothes than any woman dressing for a formal ball. It was ridiculous.

Because she'd put herself on such a strict timetable, Elizabeth remembered they'd come in the store at exactly one o'clock. It was imperative that she talk to Anne about this wedding, and if nothing else happened this weekend, she would make certain her daughter set a date for the wedding very soon. She looked at her watch. Good God. It was four o'clock. He'd been trying on clothes for three hours.

Elizabeth was desperate. Her nerves shot. Silently, she sat bouncing her leg on her knee, wringing her hands, and fretting over when she'd get a chance to speak to Anne. Anne must begin planning this wedding. Time was urgent. And there *he* was, trying on every single item in the store.

Knowing that her irritation was beginning to show, Elizabeth tried to calm herself by counting the marble squares in the floor of the large entryway. She counted the gold sparking ceiling tile. She counted all the recessed lights. She counted all the clothes racks in the store. She counted the statues, even the naked male with his prideful genitals. *Good God! Would that horrible man ever stop trying on clothes?*

Time passed. Mr. Enrique came out of the room again, and this time he held his thumb up to her. "I think we've narrowed it down to just a few selections that will look so grand on that beautiful man of yours." He smiled a wicked smile, and then added, "no one will ever suspect you've hired him for your male gigolo."

Elizabeth came out of her chair. "What? What did you say?"

Mr. Enrique raced over to her and grabbed her by her arm and giggled, "Please don't be ashamed of your needs, dear. As we age, we all need a boy toy or two, and that handsome devil that you picked, wearing *MY* gorgeous clothes...." Mr. Enrique paused kissing his fingertips. "My dear madam, your lady friends will be green with envy. They will all want a gigolo, too."

"But, I didn't hire him", Elizabeth began, but in a flash, Mr. Enrique had returned to the mysterious little room marked "Private Guest Only".

What had that horrible man been telling Mr. Enrique, Elizabeth fumed. Mr. Enrique actually believed that she was paying for Mr. RJ Scott to be her gigolo. Elizabeth Carlton forced to hire a boy toy? What insanity. And what was worse, he thought that pig was the best she could get.

Exasperated, Elizabeth glanced over the rows of clothing of

every style, color and fabric. Spotting the price tag on one of the shirts, she couldn't believe her eyes. She rose from her chair and walked quickly to the shirt, gasped, blinked in disbelief, and put on her glasses. Did that shirt say two hundred dollars? Surely, not. No shirt off the rack could cost that much. If the shirts were that expensive, just how much would the slacks cost? Did she even have enough money to cover the shirt in her bank account, let alone pay for a pair of slacks? Fingers twisting nervously, Elizabeth got out her checkbook to refigure her bank balance.

Philippe Enrique waved to Elizabeth as he noticed her fiddling with the price tags of his exclusive garments. Quickly, he entered the "Private Guest Only" room, closing the door behind him. Entering the luxurious green room with the masculine mahogany leather chairs, his eyes caressed the large, handsome man lounging in the massive chair. "She's getting really angry," he giggled.

RJ Scott looked up from the stack of National Geographic magazines he'd spent the afternoon flipping through, and stretched in comfort in the large chair he was reclining. He grinned in satisfaction. Why, he'd even gotten a quick nap while she sat there waiting for him. He chuckled to himself as he pushed the matching foot rest aside and took a sip of coffee from the cup labeled, "Special Guests**".** "What's going on out there? What's she doing?"

Philippe smiled, describing how she was walking around checking price tags, biting her lip. He related how she'd examined her checkbook and appeared to be refiguring her bank balance. Giggling in his high pitched laughter, he explained to RJ in great detail how he'd comforted her, being forced to purchase a gigolo for her "boy toy". Choking with laughter, he reveled in a grand gesture, how he'd held her hand, sympathized with her needs, and told her how he understood how difficult it was to grow old without a man. Both men exploded into laughter, the little man clapping his hands in delight; the large man slapping his thighs as though it was the funniest thing he'd ever heard.

RJ was beside himself, barely able to control his laughter. He was teaching that nasty woman a real lesson. She'd think twice the next time she decided to stick her nose up at his son and him. He stood up and set his "Special Guests" coffee cup down on the little table. "I've drunk so damn much coffee sitting here all day, my bladder's about to burst, Enrique. Where's the Gents' Room?"

Philippe Enrique rose from his chair, facing the large man, whose company he'd enjoyed so much during the afternoon of trickery on the silly woman. Motioning to him, quickly Mr. Enrique sashayed along a dim cobblestone hallway lit by quaint lamp post reminiscent of an old Spanish back street. At the end of the hall, he gestured toward a large red door. On the outside of the door, in very large black letters, it clearly stated "BULLS ONLY".

RJ opened the door to the "BULLS ONLY" room, hesitated for a moment, and gave a warning to the strange little man. "You stay out here, Enrique. Don't you dare come in to help me." As RJ started back into the "BULLS ONLY" room, he stopped and turned back to the little man. His blue eyes softened into a cool turquoise, and he smiled warmly at Philippe Enrique, someone RJ knew had suffered in his life from no fault of his own; someone, who was just born different. "You remember what I told you about that bill, don't you Enrique?" he asked in an unusually gentle voice for such a large man. "And don't forget that little snip, Mr. Andrew." With a quick wink of camaraderie, RJ left the little man standing alone in the hallway.

"Of course, Mr. Scott, I would not forget your instructions." Philippe Enrique mumbled to the closed door.

In a few moments, RJ exited the "BULLS ONLY" room and followed back down the little hallway. "Well," RJ said as he acknowledged Mr. Enrique waiting for him, "I guess I better go face her." Then, with little apparent interest, he asked, "What'd you pick out for me to wear, anyway?"

Philippe Enrique's tight Botox face broke into a smile, "I picked out the very first outfit that I brought you, even though you barely looked at it." He wagged his finger at RJ as if scolding a naughty child. "You will look so gorgeous, and the color of the blue shirt will so compliment your beautiful blue eyes."

"Yeah, yeah," RJ grumbled. "Thanks for the help with the clothes and for helping me put one over on that silly woman, Enrique, but enough with that pretty stuff."

Philippe Enrique beamed at the large, handsome man and considered what could have been. Then, quickly, he brought himself out of his dreams and back to the matter of making money.

"But, really, Mr. Scott," Mr. Enrique pleaded, "I wish you would at least try on this handsome outfit. What if it doesn't fit, properly?"

"Nah, there's no reason for me to have to strip down to my drawers and pull off my boots. As long as you got me the size I always wear, they'll fit. They'll be just fine." Stopping to think for a minute, RJ continued, "So, do you think she's had enough? Think we've taught that ornery, snooty, old gal a lesson?"

Mr. Enrique giggled in delight, carefully adjusting his glasses and flipping his pony tail. "We'll just have to see, Mr. Scott. I guess we'll find out by her reaction." Gently caressing the soft blue knit, long sleeve shirt and the navy slacks he sashayed out of the door of the "Private Guest Only" room, the large man stomping along behind.

"All done", Mr. Enrique announced, pursing his lips as though he were offering a kiss.

Elizabeth tried to smile at the two men as she silently thanked God the wait was over.

"Sorry, we took so long, my dear," Mr. Enrique said to Elizabeth as he pursed his lips, again.

"Oh, I didn't mind a bit," Elizabeth lied. "I'm just so happy you were able to help the poor slovenly man, Mr. Enrique. But, we can't judge him, too harshly. I imagine he rarely gets out of the barnyard and into decent society with normal people."

Mr. Philippe Enrique picked up his gold pen and touched it lightly to his lips as he glanced at RJ Scott. Without warning, he threw up his hands in dismay. "Mr. Scott," he gasped, holding his hands to either side of his face. "You must have a new belt for that lovely outfit. That old belt will never do. And maybe," he grinned "we need to look at some lovely bolos to match that shirt. I just got them in, today."

As the two men hurried off together, Elizabeth heard RJ reply to the little man in a too loud voice, "Maybe, I should look at some new boots, too. You do have a big assortment for me to choose from, don't you? I just **love** looking at the different brands."

Elizabeth glared in disbelief as this odd couple continued their shopping, well aware she'd been made a fool. That awful man had done her in. He'd infuriated her to the point she'd lost her self control. Meditating over this humiliation, she slipped back down into the little gold chair. For some time, she stared through the large window to the world outside and its promise of the coming spring. Spring brought freshness in its arrival, a beginning of life, an end to the misery of winter and so many senseless worries. But spring wasn't here, yet. It wasn't winter and it wasn't spring. It was that season of uncertainty. Still, it was a season of hope.

With that thought, Elizabeth felt renewed vigor, new strength. She'd regained her composure, as she began counting again. She'd show those two awful men, even if she had to count every floor tile, ceiling tile, rack, statue or whatever she could find to count in the whole God forsaken store. She was Elizabeth Carlton, a proper lady.

Ever so carefully, ensuring she didn't miss even one thing, Elizabeth began counting the many racks, the male statues, including the nude male with the prideful genitals, the ceiling tile, and the many marble tiles of the entry to "Mr. Enrique's Distinctive Men's Clothing".

Elizabeth was running down the street barefooted, racing to get to the church before Anne's wedding began. In her haste, she'd tripped in her high-heel shoes, so she took them off and carried them under her arm. Down the street she ran, up the church steps she raced. She could hear music and was certain she'd never make it to the front of the church where she was supposed to sit. Powerful reverberations from the ancient organ filled the small church as she hurried down the aisle.

As the wedding march began, everyone stood and Elizabeth grabbed a seat midway down the aisle. Securing the straps of her hi- heels around her ankles, she caught sight of the bride. Anne was enormously large. She wore an empire white wedding gown and even though the waist line was fitted securely under her gigantic breast, her big belly stuck out even further than those monstrous boobs. Elizabeth sank back into the pew and pretended to be praying, mortified, hoping no one saw her.

Then, as if things couldn't get any worse, she heard Pastor Jim ask, "Who gives this woman?" Before she could stand to say anything, she caught sight of her green bath robe. That horrible man had arrived. He was giving Anne away and he was wearing that awful green bathrobe, the pink towel flap over his hinny, and those stupid boots that accented his white hairy legs. Suddenly, Mr. Enrique ran up to the big man, pursed his lips into that stupid kiss thing and slapped a price tag on the flap over Mr. Scott's hinny.

"No! No!" Elizabeth yelled. "Please, stop this insanity!"

"Are you all right, Madame?"

Elizabeth heard a voice calling. Her dark eyes flashed open. Where was she? "Oh yes, Mr. Enrique," she answered. "I guess I dozed off." She did not smile.

Mr. Enrique and the large man stood staring at her, united in some secret code. "Do you think we're set for today, Mr. Scott?"

"Yes, Enrique, I think our shopping mission is definitely complete." Turning to Elizabeth, RJ Scott gloated in victory. "Ma'am, are you ready? Have you had enough **shopping** for one day?"

Elizabeth ignored him and glanced at her watch. It was five o'clock. They'd wasted four hours with his ridiculous shopping. He did it on purpose. She knew he did, just to make her angry and look the fool. "Figure the bill, Mr. Enrique", she snapped, knowing she'd have to transfer money from her savings for his little shopping spree.

Mr. Enrique smiled in delight. "Oh my dear, you don't pay now." he chirped, glancing quickly at RJ. "We bill you at a later date. That is how it's done in the better clothiers."

"Fine," Elizabeth snipped. "That's just fine and dandy." Without a glance at RJ, Elizabeth rushed out of the grand entryway of "Mr. Enrique's Gentlemen's Fine Clothing". Locating her small car, she flung the door open, jumped inside, and slammed the door shut. Racing the motor, she watched RJ shake hands with Mr. Enrique as he followed RJ out the door. Anger raging through every cell in her body, Elizabeth pulled out of the parking place, leaving RJ running after her, his arms laden with gold and green packages. Watching him running down the street behind her, she knew the kids would be furious if she left him as she wanted to do. Seething with anger, she stopped and waited for him to catch up with her.

Damn you! She swore silently, as she pressed the knob that released the electric locks.

"Sorry, it took so long", RJ said sweetly. Quickly he took his seat next to her before she changed her mind and left him in the street, again.

"Sorry, my foot! How stupid do you think I am, you arrogant, pompous jackass?" she hissed, as she rammed her little car into drive, not bothering to check for oncoming traffic.

"What? What did you say? I didn't hear you," RJ snickered grinning into his side window, smugly aware he'd won their latest battle. The day just had to be perfect now. He had her so damn mad she was swearing at him. Whistling a happy tune, RJ truly wished Philippe Enrique could've heard her response. When he got back to Texas, he'd give Enrique a call. Her reaction was just too good not to share.

Elizabeth stomped out of her car and slammed the door. Quickly, she raced up the stairs of her back porch and into the utility room, slamming that door shut, too. Entering the door to the kitchen, she slammed that door so hard that the door knob fell off inside the utility room.

"Damn it to hell! That arrogant pig!" she yelled.

Out of nowhere, her family appeared, alarmed to hear the softly reserved voice of Elizabeth Carlton yelling and even more shocked to hear her swearing. Anne hurried toward her mother and put her hand on her arm, "Mom, are you all right?"

"No, I'm not all right," Elizabeth shrieked, throwing her purse at the kitchen table, the contents scattering across the floor.

Jason hurried to pick up the scattered contents of Elizabeth's purse. Quickly, he knelt on his hands and knees to retrieve her lipstick that had rolled under the refrigerator. He stood and placed her lipstick and the rest of the contents next to her purse. He had an idea what had happened. "Ma'am, have you been with my dad all this time?"

"Jason, you are a nice young man, but, your father…." Elizabeth spotted the turning of the broken doorknob as the awful man tried to open the door.

"Oh, never mind!" she hissed, as she strutted to the utility room door, pulled the doorknob stem from the kitchen side of the door and threw it on the floor.

She turned and glared at the two young people gaping in wonder at her. "Do **NOT** put that door knob back into the door. I mean it," she warned, grabbing her purse. With a gloating smile, Elizabeth marched through the door to the dining room, leaving Mr. RJ. Scott and all his lovely packages locked in the utility room.

Chapter 10

For the Easter service, Elizabeth had chosen her plain navy blue pants suit, a long sleeved pink and white stripped silk blouse with a high lace collar, her blue two-inch wedge heels, and pulled her dark hair tighter than usual into the twist at the back of her head. Indeed, she looked **very** puritanical, even though puritan thoughts weren't on her mind. Knowing she'd be stuck walking into church with that awful man, she didn't want the widows' group gossiping about her and that arrogant slob. Grabbing a small navy clutch purse, she walked toward the den where Anne and Jason were talking quietly.

Jason looked up at her as she entered, wondering if she was still as mad as before. "Ma'am, I know how ornery my dad can get when he puts his mind to it, but he means no real harm. He's a good man and a good father, but sometimes, he just gets a bit cantankerous."

She knew Jason was just trying to soothe her, because he didn't want any trouble with her as a mother-in-law. Elizabeth didn't want to lose him either, as a son-in- law, not with Anne growing larger by the minute.

"Jason, you are not your father…."

Jason interrupted. "Ma'am, my Dad's had a hard life, and I guess he just doesn't trust women"

Anne poked him, "Well, he likes you, Anne, you know that. But, ma'am, something happened to my dad after my mother died and he's never been the same, never looked at another woman. I guess he just loved her so much that he never got over the pain."

"How old were you when your mother died, Jason? I don't mean to be nosey, but I just wondered, if you don't mind talking about it."

"I know her name was Carla, but I was just a baby, so I don't remember her. Juanita, my dad's friend, raised me. She's the only mother I ever knew."

"I thought you said that he hadn't looked at another woman since her death?"

"Are you talking about Juanita and my dad?" he roared laughing. He sounded so much like the awful man. "No", he said softly. "Juanita and Carlos are my dad's oldest and best friends. It was like having three parents when I grew up. I couldn't get away with anything."

"What are you trying to get away with, son?" the booming voice asked as he entered the room. "Personally, I think you got away with plenty. You're gonna be a daddy. You did some things without us catching you."

Elizabeth refused to look at him.

RJ ignored her.

The two aging delinquents sat on opposite ends of the room, avoiding each other and the explosion that silently roared between them.

The phone rang and Anne eagerly raced to get it; anything, to escape the hostility in the air. After a few minutes, Anne returned. "Mom, that was Jan. She said she heard that James Donnelly has a girlfriend. Remember, I dated him. Sure glad I didn't hook up with him. Wonder if his wife knows about the girlfriend."

"That's idle gossip, Anne. It's none of our business." Elizabeth answered briskly, keeping her eyes lowered as she swung her knee over her leg and clutched her little blue purse.

RJ studied Elizabeth. She was a bitch, but she wasn't a gossip. That was one good thing about the woman, probably, the only good thing. RJ remembered the gossip that never seemed to stop concerning him and Carla. He'd also heard the things that were said about his son. That hurt.

"Mom, Jan and Danny asked us to stop for a drink after church," Anne said. "Will you and RJ be alright, together?" Anne reached over and touched her mother's hand, her meticulously tweezed brows wrinkled in concern.

Elizabeth could feel the anger seething up to the very top of her skull. She could never remember being as furious with anyone as she was with this arrogant Texas hick.

"Mom?" Anne repeated, "Will you and RJ be all right tonight, together?"

"Well, I suppose we will," Elizabeth snipped, her voice gaining momentum as she spoke. "We spent the whole damn wasted day together.....trying on clothes, shopping. Yes, we just love being together." Elizabeth was so mad she was panting. Angrily, she pushed a loose strand of dark hair back from where it had fallen on her forehead. "Oh yes, indeed, I spent all this time with this horrible man while he was trying to make a fool of me."

RJ came unglued, snarling back at her. "Oh, I didn't have anything to do with making a fool of you, lady. You did that all by yourself."

"I tried to be nice to you, you ungrateful ass, but, oh no. You and your little friend, "Enrique", as you called him...both of you just had a ball with me!"

"Now, you just hold on a minute, Mrs. Perfect. You're such a damn fake. What in the hell did you expect? Why, I could see right through you. You acting so sweet, offering to buy me clothes like I was some poor bastard that had to take handouts from a woman!"

"And that is exactly what you did, didn't you, you despicable bastard!

"Mom! RJ!" Anne shouted, "Stop this. It's ridiculous. Both of you are behaving like little children, worse than children. You're adults who should know better. Just don't talk to each other if you can't say anything but nasty things. Shame on both of you. You're ruining this weekend, because you're **both** so damn pigheaded!"

RJ and Elizabeth turned and looked away from each other, both livid with anger.

RJ knew he'd pushed her a bit too hard. She'd blown her stack, and he was delighted, but he was a gentleman and a guest in her home, so he figured he'd be the first to make amends. "All right, we'll call a truce," RJ said, expecting her to reply in kind.

"I accept your apology, Mr. Scott." Elizabeth sneered, her nose held high in triumph.

"Wait a dang minute, here!" RJ began the familiar anger racing through him.

"Dad, please let it go," Jason begged, "Let's just get through the rest of the weekend. Please, Dad."

"Mom", Anne warned. "That means you, too. Now, stop it."

The drive to church for Elizabeth and RJ was silent, deadly silent. RJ didn't swear when he hit his head on the door, again.

Elizabeth didn't thank him for fixing the mailbox. They didn't speak when they got to the church, or when they entered the church and sat down. And RJ had no idea that they had passed the select ladies of "Widows' Row", and instead, sat one row ahead of Elizabeth's usual seat with the widows. Elizabeth had decided to just let the old gals wonder. They'd think she had a fellow and be secretly jealous. They didn't know what a pain he was.

Quickly, Elizabeth sat down in the pew followed by RJ, allowing ample room between the two of them. As the church became overly crowded for the yearly Easter service, the two elders were forced to scoot further and further across the once empty pew until they were huddled tightly at the very end of the pew. Being crowded closer and closer, Elizabeth found herself sitting uncomfortably close to RJ. It didn't seem to bother him, she noticed, as he rested his long leg against Elizabeth's leg. Quickly, she crossed her legs away from him. Seeing he had more room, RJ moved his long leg closer to her.

Elizabeth shifted in her seat, sending hateful thoughts to RJ and grumbling silently that she was happy he was so comfortable.

But RJ was not comfortable. He was miserable. His legs were too long to fit under the pew and he was forced to sit with his knees spread apart. His arms were compressed against his chest so tightly, he knew he'd get a crick in his shoulder. Then he realized how he could get a little more room. Carefully, he lifted his arm up and around the back of Elizabeth's shoulders. RJ had more room, but he wondered why he didn't feel more comfortable. It was that woman. He was just too damn close to her. There was something about her that bothered him, and he didn't like it.

Elizabeth was in shock. That awful man had put his big arm around her as though they were very familiar with each other. No. They were not familiar and certainly not friends. She felt the weight of his arm around her shoulders and the movement of his fingers as he unconsciously played with the shoulder of her jacket. Frustrated beyond words, she glared at his long leg still touching hers.

The congregation stood as Pastor Jim read the gospel of the day and Elizabeth was relieved of the burden of RJ's arm around her. Thank God. His arm around her was just too much. Who did he think he was that he could put his arm around her, play with the shoulder of her jacket, touch her.

They sat back down for the sermon. Back came the arm around her, only this time he seemed to be even closer to her. He was so close, she could smell the scent of her bath soap on him; she could feel the strength of his powerful body moving against her as he breathed, and the warmth of his hand as he played with the shoulder of her jacket. Oh, yes, she could certainly feel him playing with her jacket. *He needed to stop that.*

Elizabeth felt the unwanted heat of perspiration break on her forehead. It'd been forever since she'd been near any man, and here she was trapped against this big man. He too, was warm, she noticed, aware of his big powerful body next to her; moving against her, breathing on her, doing all those unnecessary things to annoy her. What was she to do? Did he have any idea what effect he was having on her? God, she hoped not.

Pastor Jim's sermon was a memorable one for everyone. The aging minister spoke of good and evil, hoping his small congregation would wonder on these thoughts. "Where did good end and evil begin?" was the topic of his mind. How could the two be so different and yet so connected? How did a person become an evil person? Surely, God would not allow a child to be born evil. What events in a person's life caused him to pass from a loving child to an evil person? Was it his fault that he became an evil person? Could an evil person accomplish one truly good act and become a good person? Was this person a good person or an evil person?" And he continued after a moment's hesitation, "Could a person who'd done good works all his life, commit one horrendous act and become an evil person?" Almost in a whisper, Pastor Jim concluded his sermon. "But, we are not here to judge our neighbors. Only God could determine that."

He stepped from the podium and the Choir began singing "Amazing Grace", a song that seemed to Elizabeth, a perfect closing to the sermon. Nearing the end of the service, Pastor Jim prepared to release his flock, and asked them to stand. "Now, if you're comfortable doing so, please take the hand of your neighbor as we offer the final blessing." Elizabeth had been dreading this part of the service. She did not want to hold hands with RJ Scott, but she didn't know what else to do.

The person sitting next to RJ offered her hand in friendship, which RJ took. Hesitantly, RJ put his large, calloused hand around Elizabeth's small, soft hand. He held her hand tightly, a strong, secure touch. Without realizing what she was doing, Elizabeth wrapped her fingers around his hand, as silently they accepted the final blessing. Somehow, the hand holding out lasted the final blessing, and with instant shock, the elders quickly released each other.

Before the procession out of church, Pastor Jim made one more announcement. "Be sure all of you join together for cookies, coffee, and fellowship in 'Group Together' in the reception area."

Elizabeth thought she'd surely die. There would be no 'Group Together' for them. She needed to get away from that man. He'd gotten too close and she wasn't comfortable. He'd brought up feelings in her, unwelcome feelings. Elizabeth followed the tall man as they tried to exit the pew, crowds of people filling the aisle, anxious to get on with their hurried lives. When they got to the end of the pew, RJ stepped out into the aisle, grabbed Elizabeth's arm and pulled her into the aisle in front of him sheltering her from the moving crowd.

RJ put both of his big hands on Elizabeth's small shoulders and steered her toward the end of the crowded church. As RJ pressed his long body next to Elizabeth in the crowded exit, he realized this intimacy with her seemed so natural. For a moment he reveled in her closeness, remembering waking in the early dawn with her sleeping beside him. With his fingers pressed into her soft shoulders, he knew she had to feel the heat from his hands. He sure as hell could feel it. Every step was worse, and RJ didn't like it. He had to get away from the woman fast, but he was certain that without his pushing on her shoulders, the silly woman would fiddle fart around, and he'd never get away from her, so he kept his hands on her. It was necessary.

As they exited the end of the aisle, Elizabeth felt a hand on her arm; the bony fingers of Alma Green, the undisputed ruler of the widows' group. "Elizabeth, dear, please introduce us to your new friend", she giggled, and then she whispered, "We know you aren't interested in him, dear. You would encourage no man's attention in that proper outfit you wear." She smiled, her teeth aged with many years of wear. Seeing the surprised look on Elizabeth's face, the old woman flashed her most concerned smile and whispered to her, "You aren't interested in him, or are you, dear?"

Elizabeth shook her head defiantly, "Of course, not."

"That's good, dear." The old woman whispered. "Above any hidden desires you might savor, you must honor the memory of your dear, late husband, Charles."

The widow's false concern for Elizabeth's welfare was a subtle threat and Elizabeth knew it. She'd seen it many times. Now, with Anne pregnant and unmarried, Elizabeth knew it was only a matter of time before the tongues would wag, and Alma Green's widows' group would begin their unmerciful attack on the morals of her daughter.

In an effort to discourage the coming attack, Elizabeth tried to radiate an air of happiness at the upcoming marriage of her wayward child. "Ladies, this is RJ Scott. His son and Anne are planning to be married very, very, soon. He's come all the way from Dallas, Texas, to share in the joy of the announcement of their uh, upcoming wedding. He's not really my friend", she added quickly, and regretted that statement as soon as it came out of her mouth.

Hearing that RJ was free game, all the old widows swarmed about him. One grabbed him by one arm and another by the other arm. He was strutting, eating it up like he was the cock of the walk, a debonair, handsome gentleman. Elizabeth watched him, captivating the old widows as his muscles flexed under his blue knit shirt, the navy blue slacks wrapped around those long legs. He was *no* debonair gentleman, Elizabeth thought. But Lord, he was handsome.

Off the widows took him, swarming around him like he was some sort of sacred cow, but Elizabeth knew that any older available male was a sacred cow to those old biddies. Ignoring their silliness, her mind recalled his nearness as they exited the church, the warmth of his hands on her shoulders. Elizabeth gasped to herself, as she realized her attraction to the man. Good Lord! What was she thinking? She was in church, for Heaven's sake, and yet she was experiencing this ridiculous tingly feeling when she looked at him. She was committing a sacrilege. *My, God.*

Elizabeth ignored RJ and all the widows. Being away from him, she reminded herself that he was a crude, nasty, man, and she was Elizabeth Carlton: a staunch member of the church, a respectable lady. Besides, she'd paid for those clothes that made him look so handsome. Wait until she told the old gals about that. Elizabeth turned away from RJ and ignored him, smothering the uncomfortable, unwelcome rush she'd known for him. The man was a nobody; a backwoods cowboy, a very nasty man.

Elizabeth made her way to the reception area alone, and watched as the man excused himself from the swarm of widows and walked toward Pastor Jim. Elizabeth wondered what in the world the man had to say to the kindly minister. Not knowing what secrets he'd reveal about Anne, quickly she hurried toward the two men.

"Howdy, Preacher," RJ began. Elizabeth gasped as she overheard RJ's remark. Pastor Jim had a doctorate in theology and this country cowboy was addressing him as "Preacher".

RJ continued, "My name is RJ Scott, out of Dallas. And I want to tell you what a fine sermon you gave. You really give a person something to think about; makes me question a lot of things. Now, I'm not a church going man, Preacher, but if I was, I'd come to your church."

Pastor Jim smiled at the tall man. "You know, RJ, that's probably the most sincere and truly kind thing anyone has said to me in years. Thank you, sir, for making my day." As Jim Walsh shook the hand of the tall visitor, he remembered the telephone call he'd received from this same man in early January concerning the Carlton family, especially Anne.

Smiling, he saw Elizabeth approaching. "Elizabeth," Pastor Jim said, taking both Elizabeth's hands in his. "It's so good to see you. I haven't had a chance to visit with you, lately. You always run off after church with the other ladies. Do you have any good news, Elizabeth, any bad news?"

Elizabeth was certain the nasty man had said something about Anne being pregnant before she could get there to shut him up. Him and his big mouth! She had to set this right.

"Well, I suppose you already know Anne is marrying Jason, Mr. Scott's son. That's the only reason we're here, together. And yes, she's pregnant!" Elizabeth glared at RJ.

"I didn't know that, Elizabeth," Pastor Jim said, scratching his chin in thought. "Do they love each other?"

Elizabeth stood gaping with her mouth wide open. She was the big mouth. Not him. Why hadn't that awful man nudged her? *Oh Lord!*

RJ butted in ignoring her fumbling for words, "They sure do seem to love each other, Preacher. And I want you to know, I'll be proud to have little Annie as my daughter-in-law, and I'm just happier than a pig in shi….uh, mud, about the baby. Best news I've heard in a year of Sundays."

Pastor Jim noticed the glare Elizabeth had given this large, weathered man, and wondered why she appeared so angry with him. A little too angry, it seemed to him. What she was hiding behind that widow's cloth? Did she have some hidden feelings for this man, some deep awakening that she refused accept?

Jim again remembered when RJ Scott called him about this family in January. He'd not asked about their finances, or their status in the community. He just wanted to know if they were "good folks" he'd said, and was concerned about Anne, who was dating his son. At that time, Pastor Jim would only tell the stranger on the phone that he wouldn't give out any personal information about any of his parishioners, good or bad. Now, meeting the man in person, he had a feeling about this RJ Scott; a feeling that he'd been merely trying to protect his own son from unhappiness. Possibly, it was from some unhappiness that RJ had suffered in his past. RJ Scott was a decent man. Pastor Jim was sure of it.

"Well," he said, "I've known this family for many, years, RJ. And all the members of this family are very strong, good people.... especially, Elizabeth. She's a real trooper. You and your son are fortunate to have found such a wonderful family. Anne will make a good wife, RJ, a reflection of her own sweet mother."

Pastor Jim reached over and shook hands again with RJ and patted Elizabeth's hand gently. As he noticed other parishioners waiting to speak to him, he put one arm around Elizabeth and the other around RJ, pulling both of them close into his outreached arms. "I do weddings and even baptisms," he whispered. Smiling to himself, he returned to his flock.

Anne's mother seemed to have disappeared, RJ noticed, so he went to get himself a cup of coffee. Feeling a hand on his arm, he turned. It was one of the older ladies who'd been introduced to him. Smiling a big smile for him, the older lady ushered him to a large round table where the other older ladies were sitting. A cup of coffee was waiting for him, and RJ smiled as he realized they'd planned for him to sit with them. As they chattered away, RJ put in the necessary polite yes's and no's and smiles expected from his presence.

After a few minutes, RJ watched with interest as Anne's mother sat down at a table by herself. Still answering the old gals with the appropriate yes's and no's, RJ continued to watch Elizabeth. She was a real looker. Even with that granny hairdo and those old lady clothes, she was still something else. If she'd just loosen up, the way she'd been that morning; dark hair spilling over that soft ivory skin: laughing, teasing, tempting him in her pink robe.

Without his consent, his mind recaptured her in the early morning sunlight, as she lay innocently snuggled against him in her bed. He could almost feel her leg over his, her mouth on his shoulder, the soft fullness of her breasts against his arm.

It was all right if he thought about her like that, he decided. They weren't innocent children and nothing would ever come of it, anyway. She wasn't the type of woman he usually fancied, but as long as she didn't know what he was thinking about her, it didn't really matter. It was just a silly fantasy. Giving himself permission to explore her further, he wondered what she'd look like in normal clothes....tight clothes....no clothes at all. Someone turned up the heat, RJ was sure of that. Beads of sweat formed on his forehead and ran down the sides of his face. *Oh damn.*

Seeing that the widows group had given her chair to that man, Elizabeth found a chair at another table and sat down, alone. She could see he had them going. All of them were chattering away, telling him their entire life's stories in a short matter of minutes. Cautiously, she observed him ensuring that horrible attraction for him, that tingly feeling, had disappeared. She watched as he laughed and smiled at the old biddies, seeming to agree with whatever they were saying. *God, he could be a charmer.*

With so many people gathered in the small room, it appeared he'd become very warm, sweat trickling down the side of his face. She watched as he took a paper napkin from the center of the round table and wiped his brow, his dark hair falling in small ringlets around his ears. Elizabeth remembered their morning in bed together and how she'd longed to get her fingers in those little curls. She smiled to herself. He knew nothing about their little early morning rendezvous. She even knew what he looked like naked. What a joke on him, she thought. Then to her horror, she realized the tingly sensation had returned.

RJ took a sip of the hot coffee and was jolted back to reality. He remembered the last woman he'd taken a fancy to, Jason's mother, Carla. That woman had made his life a living hell, and here he was now, casting an eye at Anne's mother. He knew better than to do that. Damn it. It would stop right now. That was final. He'd stay a far distance from that mean old gal, and if he had to be near her, he'd just recall how she'd scowled at Jason when they first got there. That should handle those feelings he was having for her.

From the safe distance, he watched her as she sat by herself. He was sure she usually sat with the old gals, but they'd given her seat to him. RJ thought that wasn't right, but he decided that she probably deserved it as hateful as she was. Still, she sure looked lonely sitting there all by herself. RJ watched her for a moment. He'd go sit with her just so she wouldn't be alone. He'd do the old gal a favor. Besides, he was tired of yes'n and no'n and grinning at the old gals around the table. He wasn't going to sit with that woman because he wanted to be near her. No, he was just going to sit with her, so she didn't have to sit alone. It was the decent thing to do.

Pastor Jim Walsh poured himself a cup of coffee and lovingly surveyed his flock as they joined in Group Together, noticing that the widows' group had grabbed the new man and ushered him to their table. He also noticed that there was no place left for Elizabeth. They'd filled Elizabeth's chair with a possible flirtation for one of them, and that was more important to those lonely, unhappy woman than the real friendship Elizabeth had offered them.

Pastor Jim had known Elizabeth and Charles for years, and even though they hadn't been able to spend their twilight years together, he knew their married life together had been blessed. How he wished Elizabeth would get away from the widows' group and find herself a new life. Over her years as a widow, she'd changed from the vibrant, happy, loving person she'd been with Charles, and all that was left of her now was a frightened, lonely, insecure woman, clinging to the widows' group for support. Pastor Jim shook his head in wonder. How could they support her when they had no idea of the powerful love Charles and Elizabeth had known together.

Yes, some of the widows had known similar love, but Alma Green, the leader of the group, had never been loved by her husband. She was just a matter of means to him and she knew it. Her parents' money was what he really married, not Alma. The substantial inheritance of her parents' money had been tightly controlled by her greedy husband, allowing Alma only life's barest necessities. After his death and the passing of time, no one even remembered the hateful man she'd been forced to abide in their loveless, childless marriage, and once her miserable marriage lay safely hidden in her memory, a new image was created in her mind. It was a false image, but one that suited Alma Green. Desperate to have some tiny bit of meaning to her pitiful life, she'd claimed the undisputed title of "Grieving Widow". Consequently, she demanded all the new widows follow her example, and those who refused suffered her vicious mouth.

Jim watched as Elizabeth sat silently at the table by herself. He picked up his coffee cup and started to join her, but as he stood, he noticed RJ Scott stand. Towering over the unhappy collection of widows, RJ flashed a big grin at all of them and excused himself. Completely secure within himself, the tall man walked over to where Elizabeth sat alone. As he moved his big body next to her, it seemed to Pastor Jim that RJ belonged next to Elizabeth. His place was with her. But it wasn't the same for Elizabeth. She hadn't acknowledged RJ when he sat next to her. She didn't look at him, and RJ didn't look at her. They were together, but they were purposely ignoring each other. It was so obvious. *Why?*

Pastor Jim scratched his head in wonder as Elizabeth and RJ Scott finished their coffee. Something was going on between the two of them and he was delighted to see it. It could be a new beginning for both of them, if they'd just allow it to happen. Pastor Jim smiled to himself. He'd discovered a wonderful secret. Quickly, he walked over to the widows' table and took a seat in the empty chair.

Elizabeth attempted to pull her little car out into the busy street where all the other cars were trying to exit the church at the same time. "Just let them go," RJ said, shoving his long legs forward as far as the little car would allow. "We can wait. We're in no hurry." Elizabeth put her car into park, and they sat silently until the road was free. Slowly, Elizabeth pulled the small car onto the empty street wondering what in the world she would do with this man for the rest of the evening.

RJ halted her worries. "Hey, that's an ice cream parlor over there," he announced, motioning to the small black and white cement block building ahead of them. Perched on the top of the small building was a large sun faded plastic ice cream cone. The place was completely deserted and appeared to be closed except for the flickering of the ancient neon sign announcing that "THE ROCKABILLY HOP" was "OPEN". Half of the dingy fluorescents surrounding the front of the small building were burned out and the rest were covered with bugs that had crashed and burned into them. Elizabeth cringed.

"Yes, I guess it is." She answered hesitantly, her eyes cautiously scouring the ancient building.

"Would you buy me an ice cream cone?" RJ asked, remembering how mad she'd gotten at him over the trip to Mr. Enrique's.

"Would you like for me to buy you an ice cream cone?" she responded, remembering how mad he'd gotten at her over the trip to Mr. Enrique's'.

"I would," he answered.

“Then, I will,” She stated, and pulled her little car into the ice cream parlor parking lot where worn speakers greeted them with the sultry voice of Wanda Jackson belting out "Let's Have a Party", followed by Carl Perkins and his "Blue Suede Shoes”. In complete difference to the outside of the building, the inside was immaculately clean; the floors gleaming with large, worn, black and white tiles. Booths of torn black vinyl lined the stucco white walls, which were adorned with black forty-five records, silently capturing famous artists' voices of years gone by.

The day’s light rain had quickly given way to a warm, inviting evening, much too beautiful to waste sitting inside the little parlor, the two elders agreed, so they chose a small table outside in the clean evening air. As they finished their ice cream cones, they listened as Elvis Presley wailed over the "Blue Moon of Kentucky", Johnny Cash lamented "The Folsom Prison Blues", and Fats Domino found his thrill “On Blueberry Hill. On and on the old songs played, serenading the empty "ROCKABILLY ROC" and its two silent guests, in no hurry to leave, both enjoying the music, lost in their separate worlds of memories.....good and bad.

Issuing an announcement for the two of them to leave, the little store flashed its’ lights, the music ceased, and one by one, the overhead lights shut down. Still, RJ and Elizabeth stayed, content with the night and each other's company, neither making the first effort to leave. But as the night settled on them, the air cooled, and RJ knew Elizabeth would soon be cold. Careful not to touch her, RJ reached past her, picked up her ice cream cone napkin and walked to the trash where he deposited it. When he returned, RJ stared down at Elizabeth, and to his surprise, he realized he hated for the night to end. But it had to. “Well, are you ready to call it a night?” he asked.

“I am,” she replied, allowing him a small smile.

With the ending of the day, the battle of wills ceased between them. They were at peace with one another. They could rest, renew their strength, but the truce would only last for a short time. Tomorrow was another day.

Chapter 11

Elizabeth poured herself a cup of coffee and noticed the clean cup sitting alone on the sink drain, obvious that Mr. Scott had his coffee earlier. Having washed his own coffee cup, she realized he was a very independent sort of man. No need for women in his life. She shook her head as she recalled that silliness she'd felt for him last night, and knew it was just some weird old lady hormone surge. She'd experienced these same hot flashes a few years back, a simple hormone thing. Today, she was fine. No tingly feelings, no sweating, no feelings for him at all. But, she reminded herself, he wasn't around either.

Stepping from her shower, Elizabeth dried herself quickly with a 'stupid, tiny towel' as he'd called them. She slipped on her robe and quickly brushed her damp hair. When she walked into the bedroom, she noticed that the bed was made exactly as she'd made it on Friday before he came. The pillow shams stood at attention against the brass headboard and the decorator pillows were exactly in place as they should be. He'd paid very careful attention to every detail.

Carefully peaking through the room darkening blinds of her bedroom window, she could see RJ tromping up and down her back yard. She could also see that he wore a new pair of jeans and a light denim shirt from his little shopping spree. More of her money spent on him, she thought, but decided it was worth it. Those awful clothes he'd worn yesterday would be getting ripe by today. She watched as he stood still a moment, staring at the ground, carefully observing something. Quickly, he knelt down on the ground.

Without warning, he stood up and strode over to the window where Elizabeth was watching him. She tried to pull back from the window, but knew he'd seen her watching him. He was yelling as though she could hear him. Silly man, didn't he realize the window was closed. She watched him rant and rave as he neared her and Elizabeth knew that the peaceful spell of last evening was broken. They'd returned to real life. The battle was back on.

Struggling with the aged, jammed window that hadn't been opened in years, finally she managed to lift it to hear what he was yelling about.

"Good Lord, woman, aren't you dressed yet?" Without waiting for her answer, RJ continued yelling. "Hurry up and get out here. I have something you need to see." Glaring at her still dressed in her pink robe, he bellowed, "And put on a sweater. It's nippy out here and I know you don't like to be cold".

Elizabeth stared at him in wonder. Just what had he meant by that remark? Did he know she'd snuck in his bed on Friday night? Was that how he knew about her sensitivity to the cold? Oh, Lordy. She remained still, waiting for him to make another snide remark.

"Hurry up," he shouted, turning his back to her and walking off into the large yard. "Time's a'wastin, for God's sake. I can't wait out here all the damn day long!"

Elizabeth heard him growl something derogatory about city folks and their laziness, but chose to ignore him and closed the window. Then it hit her. What had he found in that overgrown jungle of her backyard? It could have been anything. She didn't know. She didn't go out there anymore.

Chewing a broken fingernail from forcing the window open, Elizabeth gasped, bile surged into her throat, and the old familiar panic hit her square in the chest. Maybe it was a nest of rattlesnakes. How do you get rid of rattlesnakes? How did he know it was rattle snakes? Maybe it was copperheads. Were copperheads worse than rattlesnakes? Who do you call? What do you do about snakes? Do you put out traps for them? If that's the way to catch them, then how do you get them out of the traps? *Oh, dear Lord, please, no snakes.*

Quickly, she pulled on her denim jeans, grabbed her magenta crew neck sweater, pulled it over her head, and slipped her bare feet into her sneakers, terrified of what he'd found in her neglected, overgrown backyard.

Racing down the hall to the utility room, Elizabeth slammed the door closed, hurried across the back porch, and ran down the steps leading to the yard. He was watching her as she raced across the yard to where he stood. She could see he was really mad. As she came to a stop directly in front of him, gasping and panting from her unexpected early morning run, she tried to not look terrified of his findings.

"More pink?" He quizzed, observing her sweater, as though he'd completely forgotten what he wanted to show her in the first place.

"Magenta. Magenta is the color of my sweater."

RJ scrutinized her natural untouched beauty, near perfect against the deep pink of her soft sweater. Her dark ginger hair was damp, slightly messed as it hung down about her shoulders. Her porcelain skin had a cast of crimson over her high cheeks, and her dark eyes were big and full of wonder as she stared up at him. He cast his eyes down past her face to her rounded breast, her small waist, and her curved hips encased in tight faded jeans. Damn, she reminded him of someone, but he had no idea who. Nobody he'd ever met, he was sure of that. A gal like her, he'd never forget.

Out of nowhere, he felt that old feeling. A feeling he didn't like; that funny feeling he discovered the first time he noticed girls were more than creatures to tease and taunt. It was the same feeling he'd had while watching her at church. He didn't like that feeling, and he knew damn well it wasn't something he could control. It had to be stopped, but he didn't know how. He just wouldn't look at her, anymore, he decided. He'd ignore her. That was final.

Quickly, he pulled himself back into reality, and reminded himself that she was a snotty, hateful, old broad that had stuck her nose up at his son when they first got there. With that thought in mind, he could feel himself getting angry with her, again.... finally.

"Magenta," he repeated. "Well, magenta looks a whole hell of a lot like pink to me!"

She ignored him and nervously searched the ground with her eyes. "What is it that is so important? Did you find snakes?" She stood rigid, her fingers clutched tightly.

"Hell no, I didn't find snakes," he roared. "I found something worse than a poor old snake that won't bother you, if you don't bother it." Quickly, he knelt down on the ground and shoved his knife blade into the ground. "There you are, you little son of a bitch! I got ya."

He stood up and held out the knife for her to observe. His conquest was a nasty little grub worm shriveling around in a circle in an effort to escape the knife's blade. He flipped the nasty little worm into his large palm with the dirt still clinging to it. "Now, listen and learn," he began, avoiding looking at her.

He wasn't wearing his hat she observed, thankful there were no snakes, and that she could relax and enjoy the warm early spring day without any new worries. She really wasn't very interested in the life story of the grub worm either, but he turned and scowled at her, so she responded, "Yes, I'm listening".

"See all those tunnels in your yard?" He said, pointing to the uprooted rows of grass. She looked down at the many small tunnels burrowed under the surface of the grass. She had watched those tunnels increase over the years, but she didn't have a clue what to do about them.

"Those are caused by varmints tunneling under the ground. And you know what those varmints are searching for? Those varmints are looking for these little bastards, the Grubs. You get rid of the Grubs, you get rid of the varmints, and you get rid of the destruction in your yard." He threw the Grub to the ground and smashed it under his heavy boot, sneering in triumph; Caesar, reveling in his great victory. Then, they walked along in silence.

Elizabeth remembered years ago when she and Charles had moved into the old home, and how happy and excited they'd been; how eager they were to start their family, and how they'd planned to grow old together here. One of the things that Charles loved so much about the home was the huge back yard and the possibilities it offered. It was a large, narrow, weed-filled yard extending almost over into the next block. Bound with eagerness, Charles had explained his dreams about the yard, before they'd even signed the papers to purchase the place.

"First, the yard needed to be tilled" he'd explained, so excited that he could barely wait to get his hands on the rented tiller. The yard was somewhat shaded, so Fescue grass seed, fertilized lightly, and watered carefully would be perfect for their yard.

He would plant Photinia bushes that would grow tall and green in the summer and offer leaves of flaming red to offset the drab of the dreary winter, and they'd provide a barrier against the neighbors' ugly wooden fence at the end of the yard.

Pink, white, and red Azalea beds he'd enclose with the clay rocks that he'd dig from the crude, unkempt yard enabling the Fescue to thrive. Then, just about the time the Azaleas wilted into healthy green bushes, the white and purple Crepe Myrtles would come to life. Everywhere in his garden there would be color. Flowers, bushes, everything would flourish in the rich soil. It would be a grand garden.

And so, this yard became a Charles'garden. His personal creation to love, and in turn, it loved him back. He sowed the rich ground with fescue and faithfully watered it daily for fifteen minutes. And the grass responded, staying green and lush summer and winter; a deep green carpet, soft to the touch, yet strong and enduring. Just like Charles.

Charles built his Azalea garden as he'd planned, carefully following his instruction book on yard care, and his Azaleas were a show piece of vibrant spring color. He planted the Crepe Myrtles, giving them just the right amount of water and fertilizer, weeding around them, and carefully spreading mulch around their tender stalks to protect them from the scorching sun. His Photinia covered the ugly fence at the end of their property, and he trimmed it into a beautiful, soothing green hedge in the hot summer, and as he'd planned, in the winter it flowed as a mass of flaming red leaves to chase away the winter drab. Daily, he talked to his flowers like they were his little children, and they rewarded him with the glorious colors of life, standing tall and proud. Just like Charles.

But now, after all these years, the Photinia limbs were too big and they folded themselves over in shame. The Azaleas had given up years ago and were no more than spindly twigs, distant memories of times gone by. The Crepe Myrtles tender stalks were covered with weeds, unmercifully scorched from the summer sun, refusing to bloom anymore. His garden had died. Just like Charles.

Elizabeth returned to the present as she hurried to keep up with the tall man striding so angrily through the jungle of her yard. Onward he marched, trudging forward, inspecting everything, missing nothing. He stopped to examine every overgrown half dead bush like a dog that had to pee on everything in its path. He dominated this jungle, and he was not happy. He was very angry.

He shook his head in disgust at all the weeds and the decay of Charles' garden. She heard him swearing under his breath, and she knew he was right. She'd let it go. She'd let Charles' garden be destroyed. It was her fault.

After inspecting most of the yard, he turned around and stared at her, his piercing blue eyes filled with disgust. "What in the hell do you have a garden for, woman, if you don't take care of it? Just look at those Azaleas! They're all dead!" Stooping over what used to be Charles' prize Azalea patch, he knelt to the ground and began digging with his big hands into the dirt around the dead bushes, as though ministering the sacraments of death.

Elizabeth felt the lump forming in her throat. The tears welled in her eyes and ran down her cheeks. She wiped them away and said nothing. She remembered how lovingly Charles had chosen the perfect colors of the sweet spring flowers; how he'd worked the peat moss into the dirt, giving it just the right amount of the hard acidic addition to make the ideal Azalea garden. Oh, how she missed him….his warmth, his touch, the intimacy of their lovemaking. *Oh God, why did he have to die?*

RJ stood up, certain he'd overcome that teenage boy feeling he'd felt for her. He was back in control, again. He was angry, damn it. And he knew he had to stay angry. He couldn't let her see how she affected him. He'd get her back for how she treated his son when they arrived on Friday night. She'd acted like a hateful bitch, and he'd be damned if he'd miss this chance to let her have it. He'd make her pay for her actions. He'd make her so damn mad, that maybe she'd stay away from him for the rest of the weekend. God, he hoped so.

Quickly, he turned around and glared at her, ignoring the tortured look on her face, seeing only what he chose to see. "What's the matter with you, lady? You can dish it out, but you can't take it. Where's the snooty old broad I met Friday night; the superior old lady that eyeballed my son like he wasn't good enough to be a part of her snobby little family? Where's your superiority now, Mrs. Perfect?"

Seeing her tears begin to well in her eyes, RJ knew he was winning the latest battle. He was making her mad enough to start bawling, so he continued his tirade. “You don’t enjoy anyone criticizing you, do you, Mrs. Perfect? Well, you can criticize me all you want, but don’t you *ever* turn your nose up at *my son*!”

“It was Charles’garden.” Elizabeth whispered, her trembling hand covering her mouth, tears rolling down her strawberry cheeks, the lump in her throat strangling her voice.

“What? Speak up! I can’t hear you, when you’re blubbering.” RJ shouted, arrogant in his defeat: the conqueror, the master of all things. Things she'd obviously never learned. He was right. She was wrong.

“It was my husband’s garden!” she yelled back at him, defying him and her tears. “When he died, every bit of his garden died with him. It never bloomed again,” she sobbed, standing boldly in front of him, tears of yesterday's sorrow running down her face; a lost soul grieving over lost gardens, lost memories, lost love.

For a minute, RJ stared down at her trying to comprehend what was happening. He hadn’t meant to hurt her that bad. He just wanted to teach her a lesson. She just couldn’t go around being so self-righteous and judgmental of people. She was wrong, damn it. It was her fault. She brought the tongue lashing on herself. If she couldn’t take it, she shouldn’t try to dish it out. Now, here she stood in front of him, bawling her eyes out.

RJ watched her for a moment as the dark hair spilled onto her wet cheeks. She was crying so hard she didn't even bother to wipe the hair out of her eyes, just let it mix in with her tears. RJ handed her his fairly soiled handkerchief and expected her to refuse it, but instead she grabbed it, blew her nose heartily and continued with her tears. Never in his life had he ever seen a woman cry like she was crying. Never.

Studying her for a moment, RJ tried to figure out what to do. His big old grizzled heart was aching for the pain he saw in this woman, but he couldn't let her know it. She'd take it as weakness on his part, and before he knew it, she'd be pulling her feminine crap on him. He'd learned his lesson in the past and was too old to get burned, again. He'd suffered too much grief with the women in his life to ever let one get close to him again. It just wasn't worth it. That's the way it had to be.

He'd get control of himself. He would. Damn it. He wouldn't touch her. He wouldn't even pat her on the shoulder, nothing. Let her cry her eyes out for all he cared, she'd just have to take care of herself. He wasn't going near that woman. No, he would not.

Elizabeth couldn't stop crying, and hated herself for allowing this man to see her raw emotions. She'd never let anyone into her private world of pain and she certainly never wanted to let this man into it. She just couldn't help it. Somehow, this big, burly cowboy had hit a nerve in her, and all the grief and pain she'd held in for such a long time was pouring out on to him. And somehow, she knew it was meant to be.

As RJ watched her, he realized the woman wasn't crying over anything he'd said to her. She probably hadn't heard a word he said anyway. She was off some place in her own world, a world of deep, searing pain. She seemed to be facing hidden memories that came alive in her husband's garden; something she'd never faced before, or something she'd hidden inside her. Whatever it was, she was in a world of hurt. RJ hated himself for his foolish weakness, but he just couldn't stand to see her hurting like that. Damn. He was almost hurting as bad for her, as she was hurting over whatever was hurting her. It was awful.

RJ was damn sure he was going nuts. She'd made him nuts. From the minute he'd met her, she'd made him nuts. She'd made him so damn mad that he'd insulted her in her own home, and now all he wanted to do was comfort her, ease her heartache, and make everything right for her. *Damn it all!*

Unsure of himself, not knowing what to do, RJ walked slowly toward her until he was so close he could feel the heat of her gasping sobs on his own face. With the same hands that he'd held the dirty grub worm and caressed the dead Azaleas, he brushed away her tears and lifted her quivering chin up toward him. Staring into her tear filled, baby doll eyes, he wondered if she could ever have some tiny bit of feeling for him; some little shred of need for him other than a soiled handkerchief. He doubted it. She was too far out of his league and he knew that was a fact, but something sure as hell was happening between them. He knew it. He just couldn't figure out what.

As Elizabeth looked up through her own tears into gentle turquoise blue eyes, she knew an instant communion with this man; a locking into each other's souls in some powerful, emotional maze of discovery and wonder. She saw it, and welcomed it.

RJ Scott was almost knocked out of his boots. Never, in his born life had he ever experienced this unbelievable sensation with a woman. He'd known lust for the bawdy gals and compassion for a few women, he was not an unfeeling man, but what he felt for her....what he felt for her was all those things and more. Lust, compassion, concern, and he wanted....no, he *needed* to protect her and take care of her. All this was so new to him. It was confusing.

"All right, now," he whispered. "All right." Without thinking, RJ very gently slipped both of his large arms around her and pulled her close to him. Softly, he stroked her hair, a little girl whose father had saved her from the darkness. He'd make everything all right for her. He'd comfort her and protect her. He'd keep her safe.

It was at that point, RJ realized what he was doing, but he couldn't stop it. He wouldn't stop it. He didn't care anymore. Let her hurt him. So what? Didn't matter one damn bit anymore. Not right now. Not now, damn it. RJ pulled her closer to him. *Just for a little while. Just for now. To hell with tomorrow.*

Elizabeth didn't want him to let her go. She just wanted him to hold her, to stay secure in his strong arms and let her fears and worries drain away. This was the first time in years she hadn't been afraid. Just his touch made her feel safe. But finally, feeling a little ridiculous, Elizabeth forced herself out of this strange new place that she'd found in him and composed herself. "I'm sorry," she began, but he quickly interrupted her, as though her tears and this new awakening between them had never happened.

Quickly, he pulled himself away from her, "Hey, that's neat!" he said, rapidly walking away from her toward the little gazebo that Charles had designed and built for her. She hurried behind him, trying to keep up with him in his long strides, as he continued the inspection of this pitiful part of her property. In the distance stood the little gazebo, and she knew he'd be determined to inspect it just as he'd inspected every other thing she'd neglected over the years since Charles' death.

Elizabeth remembered years ago when Charles built the gazebo. He'd always worried about her skin that tended to burn so quickly without warning in the Oklahoma sun, but he also wanted her with him when he worked in the garden. So, he designed and built her the gazebo. He built it into a square with three walls of lattice work, a large open entryway, and a solid roof to keep out the rain and sun. Inside the gazebo, he'd built a settee with wooden arm rests and a cutout at the end of the armrest that was the perfect size for an ice tea glass. With the solid ceiling protecting her delicate skin and the lattice walls offering a gentle breeze, she could easily enjoy the garden, read her books, and be close to her husband.

As they neared the small building, he stopped and admired it. "Did your husband build this little house?"

"It's called a gazebo," she replied, "and yes, Charles built it for me".

RJ examined the house from top to bottom, running his hand along the now withered, and somewhat mildewed remains of what was left of it. "He did a fine job, fine job." He repeated, as he bent over to enter the little house. He set his sprawling body down on the settee and patted the seat beside him for her to sit down also. "Your husband was a good man," he said as if he knew him personally.

"That he was," she answered, feeling the familiar lump welling in her throat.

"Who do you have to take care of this yard?" He asked, gazing around the yard, a frown creasing his weathered brow.

"John's Complete Yard Service takes care of the yard." She answered, hoping the discussion was over.

"He's ripping you off. You know that, don't you?" RJ asked.

"Everybody rips me off." Elizabeth answered.

"Some people are assholes," he grumbled. "What does it mean *John's Complete Yard Service*? Doesn't that mean he trims the bushes, takes care of the critters, and keeps the yard looking good? That's what it means to me." RJ was silent for a moment, thinking about the awful yard and her obviously poor financial situation. "Does this John come on a regular basis or do you just call him when you need him?" He didn't give her a chance to answer and continued on. "Does John charge different rates for different services? Doesn't he have some sort of package plan that includes everything, so you don't have to worry about this damn big yard?"

Elizabeth knew he was purposely trying to drive her insane. “I don’t know. There were different plans, and I took out the best plan he offered. I thought that meant he'd keep up the place as Charles had wanted.”

“You’re getting screwed.” RJ answered.

“I know”, she sighed.

For some time, the aging couple sat silently enjoying the beauty of the day content in a way that neither understood. After some time, their solitude was broken by the sound of Anne‘s voice calling them.

“Anne, we’re over here”, Elizabeth and RJ exited the small gazebo waving to her.

Anne was breathless as she raced toward them. “Where have you two been all morning? We were ready to call the police. We thought maybe you’d been kidnapped again, RJ” she laughed. She didn't say they'd been worried the two elders might have killed each other. “I’m starving, Mom.” Anne smiled, seeing the relaxed manner between the two former enemies.

“I’ll fix us some breakfast. We’ll skip lunch, have an early supper,” Elizabeth said.

“Skip lunch?” Ann laughed. “We’ve already skipped breakfast and lunch, Mom. It’s past noon.”

“No, it’s not,” Elizabeth and RJ answered in unison.

“We just came out here and it was 9 o’clock,” Elizabeth answered.

“It was 9 o’clock for her” RJ said, “but a lot earlier for me.” RJ remembered earlier, how he’d watched her bedroom window for any sign of her; noisily tromping up and down her yard, throwing branches around, kicking clumps of dirt, swearing overly loud, waiting for her. And now, he admitted it to himself. He definitely had been waiting for her.

RJ ignored his foolish thoughts and squinted up at the sun staring straight down upon them. “Damn. It is past noon”.

"I'm dying for some Guido's Pizza, Mom. I swear, I've been dreaming about coming home and getting some of his special combo pizza with the spicy crust. That's all I can think about".

"Anne, I think you might be having your first taste of baby cravings?" Elizabeth said, patting her child's stomach.

"Annie," RJ interrupted. "You should be craving steak, not pizza. That baby's papa is a Texsan, not Italian,, he teased, considering Texas a nationality of its own. RJ would have preferred steak or even a hamburger, but he decided that if he ate this "Guido's" pizza, he wouldn't have to eat her cooking. Quickly, RJ made it known his suddenly acquired love of pizza. "I'm just kidding, Annie. I love pizza. I've been having the same hankering, for pizza I mean. Course, your mom will have to pay for it. We know I don't have any money." Anne smiled as RJ wrapped his arm around Anne's shoulders and they started toward the house, Elizabeth following behind.

After a few steps, RJ stopped, turned back toward Elizabeth and waited for her to catch up to them. He smiled as she approached. "Hurry up, slowpoke. Do I always have to wait for you?"

"I don't have six foot legs like you do." Elizabeth snipped back at RJ. Walking toward him, she could see his blue eyes twinkling in the sunshine. He was actually smiling, and he was smiling at her. Something good had happened to them in the garden. There was a new understanding between them, even a small admiration. She could see it in his eyes. In response, she was filled with a sudden awareness. A tiny glow had started inside her, and it felt good. She felt good.

As they walked toward the house, the big man slowed his step and shortened his stride, allowing Elizabeth to walk in ease beside him.

Chapter 12

Elizabeth was running through her backyard, bare feet tripping over the mole holes. From some distant land of light and goodness, she could see Charles waving to her, his thick blond hair blowing in the soft, warm breeze, his body clothed in an aura of the light from which he'd come. As he appeared to glide slowly toward her, she held out her hand for him to come to her. He remained out of her reach, as usual, but this time he seemed to be guiding her closer to the little gazebo he'd built for her. Effortlessly, he hovered above the little house beckoning her to come to this place of happiness. He smiled at her, and though he didn't speak, she knew there was something he wanted her to understand. As she raced toward the little gazebo, toward Charles, he began moving away from her, waving goodbye as he floated mysteriously away. Soon he was gone, but Elizabeth understood his message.

Mesmerized, she watched as the beam of light returned to the mysterious world far above her. Turning her gaze from the sky back to the garden, she could see the little gazebo. There was somconc standing inside the gazebo. Someone she knew: someone real, someone alive. He was a large man with graying sun burnt hair, experience aged in his worn face. He was smiling at her, and she could feel the warmth of happiness beginning to grow deep inside her chest. He walked toward her, his arms open wide as he saw her running toward him. Her heart pounded in her chest as she visualized his strong arms around her, the warmth of his body next to hers, the passion of his kiss, the….

The sound of the telephone startled Elizabeth awake. She'd been dreaming, and even though she couldn't really remember the dream, she knew a rush of tranquility. Charles had come one last time to tell her goodbye and ask her to go on with her life and stop her grieving. Suddenly, she remembered seeing herself running toward RJ as he stood in the gazebo. Did anyone know what she'd been dreaming? What if she'd called his name in her sleep? Quickly, she glanced over to RJ who was asleep in the large brown leather recliner next to hers. He awoke and gazed over at her, smiling. He was completely unaware of her dream. *Thank God.*

“That was Tom and Sandra on the phone,” Adam announced. “They wanted to invite all of us to dinner as their guest at the club. They said to invite you and RJ, Mom. How about it, guys? If they’re buying, I’m for eating and sipping a few cold ones”. He looked at his sister and remembered the child growing inside of her, “Well, Anne we don’t have to go. I just thought it might be good to see the old crowd, again.”

“I’m going,” Anne said as she pulled herself up from the floor. “I don’t have to drink. It will be great to see all of the old gang. They can meet my honey and all the women will be jealous because he is so cute.” She stopped and kissed Jason on the cheek, “I’ll be the designated driver.”

“What say, RJ, Mom? Are you in?” Adam asked as the others left to dress for the evening event.

RJ looked at Elizabeth. “Go on and go with them,” he said. “But, I have no desire to go clubbing with the kids.”

“I’ll stay home, too,” Elizabeth agreed to use RJ as an excuse. “It wouldn’t be polite to leave Mr. Scott at home by himself”. Elizabeth knew the last thing she wanted to do was go dancing and eat more food. She just wanted for the two of them to sit and relax. Maybe they could go out in the yard again, walk around a bit. Maybe they would sit in the gazebo for a while. Elizabeth's wavering emotions hit her again, and her thoughts wobbled like a see-saw. Maybe he didn’t want to go back to the back yard again. Maybe he was suspicious of her dream. Maybe he knew the feelings she was developing for him. Oh, Good Lord! Maybe they better stay out of the back yard.

“I can only sit for so long and then my butt gets sore,” RJ announced. “How about we go for a walk?” He pulled his large body up from the soft chair and rubbed his butt.

“That’s a good idea,” she agreed, ignoring his gesture. “I need to work off some of that pizza. Where would you like to go?”

“Doesn’t matter,” he answered. “Let’s just go.”

Elizabeth knew there was a park over on the next block, but she’d never walked there before. She'd driven past it often on her way to the store, so she decided it wouldn’t be too far for them to walk. It was a beautiful day, sunny and warm. For this perfect day,

Old Man Winter had taken a rest, and Princess Spring was tip toeing forth. There was no need for jackets today.

The two aging people walked along in silence along the shaded streets of Redbud Lane. "There's a park a little way from here," Elizabeth said. "There's a pond and some ducks and a walking trail, if we still feel we need more exercise."

"All right," RJ answered, as they walked to the end of the block and turned onto Silver Pond Road. There was a steep hill that they'd have to climb to get to the park, but Elizabeth didn't see that it would be a problem. They were both fairly strong; well, he was anyway.

As they climbed the steep hill, RJ turned and looked at Elizabeth as she struggled up the steep hill. "You okay?" he asked.

"Of course, I'm okay. Do you think I'm some old lady that can't even climb a little hill?"

"Just wondered," RJ answered. "It's not a little hill."

Elizabeth was nearly gasping for breath. Hiding it from RJ was even worse. She wondered if they would ever get to the top of that stupid hill. Stopping for a moment to catch her breath, RJ turned and looked at her. "Have you ever walked to the park, or have you just driven by it in your car?"

"Well, it just didn't seem to be so far," Elizabeth answered, "but, I guess I didn't realize how steep this hill is. I'll be okay. I'll make it. I just need to rest for a moment."

"Uh huh," RJ said. Quickly, he walked back to Elizabeth and placed her arm through his, so she could hang onto him as they made their way up the hill. Finally, they entered the park area.

"I'm about done in after that walk," he said, smiling at her. "Damn, lady, you know how to wear a person out. Hope you don't want to try one of those walking trails now" RJ laughed softly and motioned toward a bench facing the pond.

Elizabeth smiled as they walked toward the little bench refusing to comment on walking the additional walking trails. She wasn't sure she'd even make it to the bench.

"I thought you said there were just ducks here?"

"Well, what do you call those brown and white things? Those are ducks."

"Hell no, those aren't ducks. Those are Canadian Geese, and those damn geese can be meaner than a wild boar if you get in their way. When I was a kid, we had a few geese and those little bastards would sneak up on me when I was doing my chores. Hell, they'd bite the crap out of me. If you come back here by yourself someday, stay away from the damn geese. They look all cute, but don't trust any of them.

"Back in 1982, Wisconsin sent a bunch of those Canadian geese down here to Oklahoma so they could multiply further south, I guess, or maybe Wisconsin just wanted to get rid of a few of the nasty little critters. Anyway, those damn geese did a good job of multiplying. Now, nobody can get rid of the geese. They're all over the place."

Elizabeth was listening to what he was saying and wondered how he knew so much about nature. She listened as he talked, but she couldn't take her eyes off of the mother and her two little children, who'd been feeding the few white ducks at the edge of the pond.

She was a young woman with a little blond headed boy, just a toddler; and she had another child, evidently an infant, in a stroller. They finished throwing their supply of small pieces of grain to the ducks, and soon the mother, with her infant in the stroller and holding the hand of the little boy, walked away from the ducks and sat down at one of the many cement picnic tables in the small park.

"I've got to go to the can; got to go pee." RJ announced. "I'll be right back."

Elizabeth smiled at him and for some reason, didn't find his detailed bathroom explanation offensive anymore. That was just the way he was.

After watching him take his long steps away from her, she turned her vision back to the mother and the children. Watching the mother with her children, Elizabeth realized that now, for some reason, she could barely wait for Anne to have her baby. How she longed to feel a small child in her arms again. Smiling, she envied the busy little mother, she'd been watching.

The mother had evidently planned a picnic for them, because Elizabeth saw her push the stroller up to the table and watched as the mother gave the little boy instructions to stay close to the stroller and not to move until she returned. Leaving him alone for just a moment, she hurried to her car to get a small picnic basket. Seeing his mother had gone, the small boy completely ignored her warning and took off running toward the ducks and geese as fast as his little fat legs would take him.

RJ stood in the small, smelly, block bathroom, reading all the dirty words and invitations on the wall as he washed his hands. He determined that kids now days were sure getting creative, and he grinned as he read all the phone numbers you could call to have a 'good time'. Chuckling silently to himself, he wondered who'd answer all those phone numbers, or if they were just pranks. As he continued reading more of the smut on the walls, he could hear noise coming from a distance outside the little toilet area. Wiping his hands on his jeans, quickly he walked out of the bathroom and looked toward the bench where he'd left Anne's mother sitting. There was no sign of her.

Peering quickly around the small area, he didn't see her, and decided maybe she'd used the ladies room. From down by the pond area, he could hear the geese hissing and honking, flapping their wings in attack. As he scoured the pond area, right in the middle of all the commotion, he could see the magenta sweater and the dark hair of Anne's mother. She was standing very still with her back to him, and he wondered what in the hell had possessed that woman to walk into the middle of those mean ass geese, when he'd warned her about them. As he walked quickly toward her, he could see the geese pecking at her naked ankles, jumping up towards her knees, and flapping their massive wings as they honked their warnings to her. But, she didn't move one step. She just stood there.

Somewhere behind him, he could hear a young woman's voice screaming in terror, and he knew the woman was close behind him. He turned around and motioned to the woman to be very quiet. Calmly, he walked toward Anne's mother who remained still, frozen in fear.

"Move back very slowly and don't turn your back on those geese, ma'am."

Hearing RJ's voice, she turned to look at him, and RJ could see she was holding a little blond haired child. Remembering his own childhood, he recalled when his pa had warned him about the gaze of the geese. "Stare them down," his pa had said. "Make them scared of you."

Quickly, RJ put himself in front of Elizabeth and the child, diverting their attention to him. He stood large and silent, facing the geese, which by now, were near a frenzied state. "Get behind me and start backing out of here, ma'am. Don't turn around and run, just back away, slowly."

RJ stood with his arms stretched out, but remained perfectly still, showing the geese his dominance over them, and hoping he didn't attract the females who were protecting their eggs. He'd been through that event before when he was a kid and still had the scars to prove it.

Watching the geese begin to walk away from him, RJ felt confident to begin backing away from their nesting area himself. Quickly, he caught up with Elizabeth and took the little boy from her arms as they walked back to the frantic mother.

As RJ slipped the small child back into the safety of his grateful mother's arms, she thanked them repeatedly for their help. Elizabeth leaned down and looked at the sleeping infant in the stroller, completely unaware and uncaring of the events that her big brother had brought about. "What a little angel," she commented. "We'll be grandparents at the end of the summer. I can't wait."

Elizabeth heard her own voice speaking, but she couldn't believe she'd spoken so happily about her first grandchild who still needed his parents to get married. But it was more of a surprise to her that she'd spoken of RJ and herself as "we".

The young woman gripped her inquisitive little son's hand tightly as she calmed herself from the near disastrous day. "Oh, you and your husband will have a ball with your first grandchild. I know my parents did." Elizabeth didn't dare look at RJ and he didn't look at her. They let the young woman's comment slide by, both lost in their own dreams of their future grandchild.

As they walked back over to the little bench where they'd been seated, they waved as the young mother packed her children into their car seats and drove away.

RJ looked down at Elizabeth's ankles and saw the bloody streaks from the pecks of the angry geese. She was one hell of a woman. She didn't look it, but she was one tough gal. He was damn sure she wasn't the same woman he met Friday night. No, sir. That stuck up old biddy would never get down and dirty with the geese like this gal had. The woman just continued to amaze him. He scratched his graying head and wondered why in the hell she acted like such an old witch when he first met her? She really was a good woman. So, why would she pretend to be a nasty person when she wasn't?

"Let me look at your ankles," RJ said, knowing that Elizabeth wouldn't allow him to help her until she knew the young woman was gone.

"I'm fine," she laughed. "I get more scrapes than this from other people ramming their carts in my ankles at the grocery store."

She was lying and he knew it, but he'd check her over when they got back to her house.

"Why in the world would they allow those awful geese to be in the park where they can hurt innocent people?" Elizabeth asked, watching the geese hiss, honk and raise their wings at each other and the ducks.

"They're not so bad. They won't hurt you unless you get near their nest like that little fellow did. That old gander was just protecting his lady and what was theirs. We're lucky the old female goose didn't come around, 'cause damn, they can be even worse. But, that's just a good mother protecting her own. That's why I got my butt kicked by the goose when I was a kid. I was trying to get her eggs, and by God, she wasn't gonna let me have them." RJ laughed softly, remembering the old goose, a good mother.

The geese seemed to have left the area, so the two elders sat together quietly enjoying the peace of the small park. Elizabeth smiled, but in the back of her mind lurked the dread of that awful long walk home and this time the addition of her sore ankles. As if reading her thoughts, RJ said gently, "The walk back will be easier, but we'll have to be careful that you don't slip and fall on that steep hill. You'll hang on to me."

The sun had started its descent in the west, as the two elders started the long walk back to Elizabeth's house. At the top of the hill, RJ took her arm and placed it back under his and they began their journey. They made it down the steep hill without incident and turned back onto Redbud Lane. They could see her house in the distance as they walked under the cover of the swinging arms of the magenta Redbud trees that lined the street of her neighborhood. Entering her driveway Elizabeth realized that she still had her arm through RJ's, but she decided her driveway was pretty steep, too. She'd just hang on to him until they got to the doorway.

Elizabeth and RJ entered the house and headed immediately for the comfort of the big brown chairs in the den where they both collapsed. Hearing the sound of John's car backing down her steep cobblestone driveway, the elders found themselves alone, again. After some time, RJ stood up and stuck his large hand out to Elizabeth. "Come on into the bathroom. We need to check those bites on your ankles."

"Oh, for heaven's sake, I'm just fine." She answered. He wouldn't move, so finally she accepted his hand and followed him into her bathroom.

"Sit down, there." He pointed to the toilet and began rummaging through her medicine cabinet. RJ knew she'd raised two kids and he was sure she knew about first aid, but he wanted to touch her again, and he decided this was a good enough excuse. He didn't know why he wanted to touch her. He didn't care. It's what he wanted.

Finding a tube of antibiotic ointment, RJ laid it on the side of the sink and filled the bathroom sink with warm water. Checking the temperature of the water, he knelt down before her, untied her tennis shoes and pulled the shoes from her feet. With a sudsy, warm washcloth, he began washing the scrapes, explaining to her in great detail, how necessary it was to clean such wounds, no matter how small they appeared.

As Elizabeth listened to him, she knew he was aware she'd raised two healthy children and certainly knew all about first aid, but she just let him go on talking and working on her feet and ankles, while she peered into his dense, dark gray hair. The tingly feeling was there, as usual. She just accepted it as normal now. It never went away anymore, not when he was there.

Who was this man? She wondered. He was nothing like he appeared to be when he first arrived, acting like a hateful old bear, tormenting her. Why would he put on being such a mean man, when the man she'd come to know was a kind, thoughtful, caring man? And why hadn't some woman managed to marry him? She watched him, as he told her about all sorts of illnesses that she'd get if she didn't get her wounds cleaned properly. He was so handsome and just about the sexiest man she'd ever met. Why hadn't she noticed it before? She'd been afraid of him before, she decided. Now, she wasn't afraid anymore. Not afraid of him one little bit.

He'd been alone for such a long time. How could he possibly stand all those lonely nights? Maybe he wasn't alone. He didn't seem to be the type of a man who could remain celibate forever. Of course, he'd lost the great love of his life, Jason's mother, but still she'd been gone over 25 years. Surely, there must have been another woman somewhere.

Lightly he applied the ointment to the bites on her ankles. "There, you'll be good as new. I'll bet you learned a big lesson today, didn't you, missy....after your great battle of the Canadian Geese."

Elizabeth wondered where the "*ma'am"* had gone. Gone with the vicious geese, she hoped. "Thank you, Mr. Scott, you make a fine doctor." She smiled up at him, and he grinned back at her. "Would you like a drink, Mr. Scott?"

"I would if you don't mean soda pop and if you'll stop calling me 'Mr. Scott.'"

She smiled as she thought of how he constantly addressed her as "*ma'am*". Now, maybe "*ma'am*" had turned into "missy". Well, "missy" was better than "ma'am". At least it didn't sound so terribly old.

RJ followed Elizabeth into the kitchen and watched as she opened the door under the sink. "I'm sure I have something under here," she rambled. "Of course, it's been some time since I've offered anyone a drink, or had one myself," she lied. "Yes, here it is."

As she pulled the gallon jug of Vodka from under the sink, RJ noticed it was only half full. Someone sure as hell had been sucking on the juice.

Walking to the white cabinet, she pulled two tall glasses from the shelf. Smiling, she rinsed them both. "They're probably dusty from lack of use," she explained, as she walked over to her refrigerator door, put the glasses under the little ice spout, and partially filled the glasses with ice cubes. Very carefully, she lifted the bottle and poured enough vodka into the glass to cover the bottom of the glass.

"Hope you like Bloody Mary's". She smiled, as she filled the glasses with tomato juice. She put a small shot of Worchester Sauce in them, stirred the drinks with clean celery stalks which she left in the glasses for decoration, and handed one of the glasses to RJ to enjoy.

"Holy Crap, that's awful," he gasped. "How'd you get through a half gallon of booze drinking a nasty drink like this?"

Elizabeth breathed a long accepting sigh as she watched him take control of the drinks. They were pretty bad, but she didn't want him to think of her as one of those lonely old ladies who chugalugged the booze in the evening as she sat by herself, but then she remembered.... she was one of them.

He grabbed her drink and his and walked to the kitchen sink. Using the celery stalks as a spoon to guard the ice cubes, he poured part of the drink into the sink and filled the rest of the glass with the Vodka. Reaching into the cabinet, he found the hot sauce and began vigorously shaking the bottle over the glasses. Using the celery stalks as a stir, he returned her celery laden glass to her, and without hesitation, threw his celery in the garbage. He took a sip. "Now, that's a drink", he said, satisfied with his creation.

"A little strong," she commented.

"Too much booze?"

"Too much hot sauce."

Smiling at each other, they walked from the kitchen out to the backyard.

It was a beautiful time of day, but the sun was setting, and there was a chill in the air. Quickly, Elizabeth wrapped her jacket around her shoulders as they settled down on the top step of her porch.

"I think it is going to get down to 30' tonight," Elizabeth said, remembering the cold porch and Friday night when she'd snuck into bed with him.

"Yeah," he agreed. "When we left Texas, we had the same cold snap. Seems like the weather we get down in Texas heads right up here to Oklahoma. I had my jacket with me, but by the time we got here, it'd warmed up so much that I just left it in the car."

From this site on her back porch, they could observe the entire yard and all of the pitiful, neglected landscape. She cringed as she stared out over the disastrous mess, hoping he would just ignore it and let it be. She certainly didn't want to get him started on "*John's Complete Lawn Service*", again.

"RJ," she said, hoping to take his mind off her yard. "Please be sure that you leave the bedroom and bathroom doors open when you go to bed tonight."

"Got a little cold out there, did ya?" RJ turned his head away from her, so she wouldn't see him grinning over what he knew to be true.

"No, I was just fine," she lied, "but, I like to keep the heat evenly distributed throughout the house, so it doesn't take so long to warm." She knew she made no sense, whatsoever. "I mean..."

Noting her discomfort, he interrupted her. "I think it's getting nippy. You're probably cold. Let's go and check out that wonderful, warm, sun porch you love to sleep on." He stood up, grabbed her hand and pulled her up.

"Thanks," Elizabeth nodded. "Guess I'm getting old."

"Me, too," he agreed.

As they entered the kitchen, he took her glass and refilled both of them with his Bloody Mary concoction. It really was a pretty good drink Elizabeth decided as she watched him, or maybe her taste buds were just fried. Maybe, after this, she'd never be able to taste anything again ever.

As they entered the sun room, she walked to the large swing mounted onto the ceiling many years before. She sat down and waited for him to sit beside her.

"Are you sure this thing will hold both of us?" He asked, as he scrutinized the installation.

"Oh, just sit down", she said. "If we fall, we'll get up".

Cautiously, he eased himself onto the soft pink floral cushion of the white wicker. Together, the two aging people began to swing back and forth together, enjoying the events happening on the quiet street in front of her home.

Remembering past experiences of their own lives, they watched as the father helped his son stay upright on his first experience on a bicycle. They smiled as the father picked up his son when he fell to the ground, hugged him and encouraged the boy to keep trying. Trusting in the word of his father, time after time the young boy crawled back onto the baffling bicycle. After some time, the boy no longer needed his father's hand and rode freely about the silent street as RJ and Elizabeth applauded in approval of his great feat. Soon, the father and his son left and disappeared into a house down the street.

After some time, they watched the older lady walking her feisty Jack Russell. The little dog was in such a hurry to get to its destination, that it all but dragged the little lady with him. Just as the lady and the dog arrived in front of Elizabeth's house, the dog stopped, hunched his body into a squatting position, and relieved himself of his day's meal. They watched the lady slip a piece of plastic paper around the dog poop, examine it carefully as though she had just secured a prized possession, and slip it into another plastic bag. As the little lady and her feisty dog hurried on to their evening walk, the elders laughed out loud as they watched her.

RJ told her about his two boys back in Texas, and how he'd found them nearly dead in the creek, and brought them home with him. He explained how he'd fed them with an eyedropper, but not being with them all the time, he'd been afraid they'd starve, so he'd put them in with an old cat that had taken up residence in his barn. The kittens she'd delivered hadn't lived, so she accepted the newborn pups as her own and suckled them back to life. He smiled as he told her how the two dogs now slept on either side of the old cat to protect her, her faithful children.

The skies grew dark and the participants of the street had long since ceased their unknown performances. Still Elizabeth and RJ continued swinging together, only the squeak of the rusty spring breaking the silence of the night.

After some time, RJ began talking to Elizabeth softly, quietly, and almost in a whisper, so as not to break the spell that had captured the two of them. Elizabeth listened with interest, asking questions and making comments in return. For hours, the two talked quietly together, reminiscing of times gone by….good times, bad times.

RJ told her of how many generations past, his family had come to Texas from Northern Illinois in covered wagons searching for a better way of life; how they'd been able to buy unsettled land so cheaply, even before Dallas, Texas, had become a city. He explained how as time went on, the next few generations would buy more land, and would raise many head of cattle. They would prosper and gain wealth, but in time, his family got spoiled and used to the riches that their ancestors had worked so hard to achieve.

Bitterly, he spoke of how the "lazy scoundrels", he called them, the children of his ancestors, would sell the acreage to gain their own careless, foolish desires. RJ cleared his throat, hesitant to talk about his own miserable life, but finally he went on. He told her about how poor his family had been, and how both his mother and father had died so young, and how he'd never seen his sisters, again.

He explained that he'd married Jason's mother in his mid-twenties, but she was gone when Jason was just a baby. That's when he met Juanita and Carlos, he told her. "Juanita and Carlos had lost their baby to a heart defect, and since I needed someone to help with Jason, and she needed a baby to love, we sort of became a family.

"Juanita raised Jason alongside her own kids," he laughed. "When Jason did bad things, like all kids do to learn, she paddled his little butt. But when he fell down and hurt himself, Juanita was the one who picked him up and loved him. She was his mother, and you couldn't find a better mother or a better woman."

Elizabeth smiled, thinking of her son and his own childhood. "Where are Juanita and Carlos now?"

"Oh, they live over by me. Carlos has a small landscaping business. He can't do much anymore, because of his arthritis, but his youngest son, Marco, works the small business for his dad."

In a hushed voice, Elizabeth began to tell RJ about her life with Charles; how she'd gone to college in the town where she'd grown up, and then married Charles and moved to Oklahoma. And RJ visualized her as a beautiful young woman that he knew she'd been.

Elizabeth continued to tell him how she'd worked and supported them while Charles did his internship in Tulsa so that Charles could have his dreams. And RJ admired her grit in their marriage.

Smiling, she spoke of the happy day she knew she could finally stay home and become a full time wife and mother. And RJ was happy for Charles that he'd been able to watch this magnificent woman's body grow, carrying the seed of his children, and witness their amazing arrival into this world.

She told him about their lives together and how they never had wealth, but they had happiness. And RJ felt the cruelty of envy lurking inside his memories of his own life.

The smile on her face ceased as Elizabeth spoke of their terrible battle with the monster, Cancer, and how they'd lost. And RJ was sorry for Charles that he'd been taken so soon from their perfect life. After a few moments, Elizabeth became silent.

It seemed to RJ that her whole life revolved around her husband and children. It occurred to him that this vibrant creature felt her own life was finished. He wondered what her dreams were. She spoke of her husband's dreams, but what happened to hers? What happened to her passion for life? RJ knew her passions were still inside her, somewhere. He'd seen those flashing eyes glaring at him Friday night when he'd challenged her about the sleeping arrangements. He smiled as he remembered her being so angry that she swore at him.

Yep, there was still plenty of fire in her, RJ knew that, but it was clear to him that this little woman sitting next to him was stuck in a time warp. She couldn't go back and she was afraid to go forward, so she did what she could at this point of her life….nothing. Elizabeth Carlton was as lost as that ornery little calf he'd carried back to its mama before he left Texas. He hated to see that poor woman lost like she was, but he knew he couldn't help her. He had no right to get close to the woman, no matter how bad he wanted to. Truth be known, he'd allowed himself to get too close to her as it was, and now for her sake, he knew he had to stay away from her. Getting close to her just wouldn't be right. It wasn't fair to her.

All was quiet for a few minutes, and RJ and Elizabeth watched as two young people, barely in their teens, came from behind the house across the street. It was obvious to both the elders, that there'd been some hot and heavy happenings in the bushes behind that house. "My word, aren't they too young to be carrying on like that?" Elizabeth asked.

RJ chuckled, remembering his first '*carrying on'* with Anna Mae behind the old barn.

"What's so funny?" Elizabeth asked, smiling at the large man.

Without meaning to, RJ found himself telling Elizabeth all about the barn, Anna Mae, and the beating he got when he was thirteen years old, his first sexual encounter. Both of them found themselves laughing as they shared thoughts of the amorous RJ Scott with his pants down around his ankles, falling to the floor and crawling as fast as he could to get to the gal, hoping she didn't change her mind about being with a stupid oaf like him.

Then for some reason that she could never understand, and without even knowing what she was doing, Elizabeth began to tell RJ of her nightmare rape when she was thirteen years old, her first sexual encounter. She spoke of how she had denied the rape to her parents so they wouldn't worry about her, but how she'd secretly feared a pregnancy or worse. Elizabeth spoke of the awful lesson she'd learned from her first crush on James Dean, and her terrible first adventure out into the world….a horrible lesson she'd never shared with anyone except Charles, and now for some reason, RJ.

RJ sat quietly trying to absorb the horrors this little woman had lived through. She'd overcome the terrible nightmare alone in some secret place inside her young mind, and he knew she must have been terrified. But, she'd accepted it, lived with it, and had gone on to build a strong marriage and a good life in spite of her past. Hearing the quiver in her voice, RJ knew she still suffered the grueling pain of those awful childhood memories.

Elizabeth stared down at her clasped hands and the pink of the magenta sweater that covered her arms. Slowly, she pulled up the sleeve of her arm closest to RJ. RJ could see small round scars covering the entire length of her forearm. “He was a smoker,” she said. “I was his ashtray.”

Quickly, she pulled her arm back toward her and replaced her sweater sleeve tightly down around her small wrists. Immediately, she was sorry for allowing him to see the cruelties branded upon her youth.

RJ was aghast. He was in shock. Not because this rare beauty's arms were so disfigured, but because he couldn’t imagine how she’d lived through such a terrible ordeal and never told anyone. He wondered how much of the nightmare she’d actually shared with Charles. Charles sounded like he was such a moral and virtuous man that RJ doubted that she’d ever really told him the worst of it. He would have been too shocked. He could have been a saint for all RJ knew or cared, but it was obvious to RJ that Charles wasn’t callous enough to shoulder her pain. No, a gentle soul like Charles couldn't do it. He was too soft, too good. But, someone sure as hell needed to help that little woman, and RJ was damned sure what she needed at this point of her life was some hard-nosed old cowboy who wasn’t afraid of the Devil himself. RJ knew just the old cowboy.

Without looking at her, RJ pulled her right arm back under his arm and covered her nervous fingers with his left hand. With a gentleness that seemed rare in such a large harsh man, he pushed her sweater back up to her elbow and carefully scrutinized each and every pitiful reminding scar that she had been forced to endure for all these years. As though he were offering some magical salve of healing, RJ circled each round scar with his large finger as he journeyed the length of her arm. “Tell me,” he whispered. “Tell me every single thing you can remember about that night.”

“I’d rather not talk about it,” she answered. “Charles never wanted me to talk about it, and so, I’d just rather leave it buried in my past.”

“It’s not buried, missy. It’s living your life for you, and it’s smothering you. Now, it’s time to let it go. Face the nightmare and be done with it. Tell me everything you can remember. Everything. Don’t leave out one little miserable memory. Tell me over and over till you’re so sick of remembering it, it won’t dare haunt you any more, ever again.”

"RJ, please.... I just can't talk about it."

"Oh yes you can, and you will, little missy. It's time to slay the demon. Don't let him lay hidden in the far corners of your mind ready to grab you whenever he wants. Pull him out of those shadows and make him face you. You can begin talking, now."

"I don't know, RJ. I'm not sure....how do I begin?"

"How about starting with James Dean?" RJ smiled at her and continued drawing small encouraging circles around her arm. Finally, he remembered who she reminded him of. She was Judy, the girl of his dreams from that movie, *Rebel Without a Cause.* RJ shook his head sadly. Years ago, he'd given up his dreams of Judy or someone sweet and wonderful like her. Carla had seen to that.

"I was thirteen years old, the first time I saw the movie with James Dean." Elizabeth began hesitantly at first, but the more she remembered, the more she talked. And she talked, and she talked, and she talked, and as she talked, her soft voice became so enraged, it no longer sounded like the same woman. She ranted and raved on and on, and as RJ had suspected, once she started talking, she couldn't stop until she'd purged the demon. As she poured out the horrible memories, she talked faster and faster; and the faster she talked, the harder she grasped RJ's hand, until he was certain he'd never have any feeling in it again, but he didn't say anything. He just let her go on and fight her demons.

"That fiend took away my childhood," she gasped, as though this was the first time she'd realized it. "No, he didn't just take away my childhood, he took away my future. If it hadn't been for Charles, I'd probably still be living in my parents' home, an old maid afraid to face the world. Afraid! Afraid! Afraid of everything and everyone! Always trying to live a pristine life, so no one would suspect that I was a bad woman! He told me I was bad! He told me that, RJ. That maniac told me I was bad and in the back of my mind, I let him control me all of these years, because for some reason I accepted his word as gospel. Why did I do that, RJ? Why did I give him my life?" She asked, her rage turning into a tiny whimper.

"You were a baby who faced a demon disguised as a kind, caring adult, missy. He tricked you, yes, he did, but now just think about all you've accomplished in your life, even while you were carrying around his quilt."

"His guilt!" Elizabeth looked like she'd had a revelation. "His guilt, RJ! It *was* his guilt, wasn't it? It wasn't my guilt. I was just a poor innocent child."

RJ squirmed and felt a bit like a barnyard philosopher, but he didn't need a college degree to see the wrong that had been done to this poor woman. "No child can be held guilty for the actions of an adult, and no child should ever have to endure what you did, little miss. That's not just a crime against you It's a crime against all that's good and decent. Your preacher said that no one is born evil, but I'm not sure he's right on that one. Some children are mean and cruel, and they get worse the older they get, no matter how good folks are to them. There are real demons, missy, whether they appear as a kind, caring gentleman, like you found," RJ paused for a moment deep in thought, and then he continued. "Or maybe they appear as a beautiful young woman. We can't understand such evil and that's why they can get into our souls. They thrive on innocence and spoil the good they find. I think sometimes nature just makes a mistake and forgets to build good and kindness into some folks. Doesn't happen very often, but when it does, we find the real demons."

"He was a demon, wasn't he RJ?"

"Yes, he was a demon."

"But, I survived, and had a good marriage and I raised two fine children."

"Yes, you did."

"And I have survived without Charles. I have done it on my own."

RJ patted her hand gently. "Yes, you have, little one. Yes, you have."

Elizabeth sighed into the depths of her soul. She leaned back into the little swing and released her grip on RJ's hand. For all these years she'd let the demon terrorize her, and in just one weekend, with this big cowboy's patience, she'd faced the demon. At long last, she was free. It was over.

After some time passed, RJ pulled away from her, remembering his warning to himself and hoped he hadn't overstepped his boundaries within his own mind, but as he pulled away from her, she slid her arm through his and placed her hand on top of his hand resting on his leg. As she sat so close to him, he could feel the softness of her arm under his and the roundness of her breast, as he felt her breathe the very same air he was breathing. He didn't move, in fear she'd pull away from him, and he ignored the warnings that his brain was flashing to him. He pushed all caution from his mind and simply relished the few moments they had left together.

Soon, they heard the hall clock sound the beginning of a new day. As they spent these past hours together, they'd accepted the clock's announcements of the passing hours, knowing they still had time together, but both of them had been dreading the sound of this new day; the announcement that their time together was over. Just like "Cinderella's" story, they could put it off no longer. Their time together was finished. Tomorrow he'd leave, but both of them knew their lives would never be the same....good or bad, neither could tell.

They said their goodnights, and Elizabeth grabbed her pink nightgown from her top drawer and changed into it in the little bathroom. She snuggled up under the white eyelet comforter on the daybed in the little sunroom and heard the shower begin and end. Finally, she heard RJ open the doors to the bedroom. She'd be warm on the little porch that night.

Chapter 13

RJ couldn't sleep. He turned from his left side to his right, from his stomach to his back. He pushed the covers off and pulled them back on. She was less than twenty feet away from him, and hell, it might as well have been a mile, a thousand miles. He couldn't go to her. He couldn't. And it was real funny, too, he realized, because he wasn't thinking about sex, when he thought about her, and he was always thinking about sex. All he wanted to do was have her close to him. Hell, he wanted her close to him all the time, and he knew it that morning. He just hadn't accepted it. He'd even banged on her bedroom window that morning to get her to hurry up so he could be close to her. She didn't answer, so he figured she must have been in the shower....so he just watched the bedroom window until he saw a movement. Then he acted like he hadn't been waiting for her. He might as well admit it to himself. The woman had gotten a hold of him, and damn it, he liked it. Still, he had no right to her.

RJ got out of bed and stared out the window. In the distance he could see the small building Charles had built for his wife. Charles' wife. Elizabeth Carlton was Charles Carlton's wife. She was not RJ Scott's wife. RJ Scott had a wife. Carla was his wife. A wife who never cared about him, a woman who never cared about anyone but herself.

"That was a long time ago," RJ mumbled under his breath. It had been years since Carla had been gone, and damn it, Elizabeth Carlton was not a wife. She was a widow, and she was alive. She was beautiful and warm and sleeping less than twenty feet away. RJ started toward the bathroom door to the small porch where he could hear the little bird calls of her snoring, but then, he stopped in mid step. What was the matter with him? Was he totally nuts? He couldn't go to her. He couldn't. It wasn't right. Of course, if she came to him, he'd have to let her in his bed. It was her bed, for God's sake.

A wicked smile turned at the corners of RJ's mouth as he walked into the small bathroom. Oh, so quietly, but oh, so deliberately, he closed both the doors. Silently, he returned to the warm comfort of the bed. He shut his eyes and waited.

As Elizabeth lay snuggled asleep under the little comforter, she began to shiver. Her nose was cold. Her feet were freezing. She woke and could see in the moonlight that the door to the bathroom was closed. RJ must have gotten up in the night to use the restroom and forgot to open the door. Quickly, she hurried across the icy floor, her slippers in hand. Silently, she cut through the small bathroom and into the warmth of her bedroom where she knew he was soundly sleeping.

She didn't try to wake him. He was snoring and she knew that he was out like a light.

Quickly, she hurried across the room to her side of the bed, pulled off the decorator pillows, then the pillows covered with the shams. Carefully, she pulled back the blankets and crawled back into the warm comfort of her own bed.

RJ stopped snoring and rolled over on his side facing her. Elizabeth could feel him staring at her in the darkness of the room, but he said nothing and for a moment, he just lay there.

She lifted the comforter from her and began to quietly exit the bed, hoping he'd go back to sleep and forget she'd been there. It was then she felt his arm slip across her chest, his large hand securing her shoulder. Turning toward him, she could see his blue eyes staring at her in the moonlight.

"Stay," he whispered. "Don't leave me."

Not knowing what to do, she turned from him and faced the wall as if the wall could give her the answers. But, it couldn't. This situation, she had to figure out herself. She'd only known this man for three days, but my lord, they'd spent almost every waking minute together...and yes, one complete night. If she willingly stayed in bed with this man, what would it mean? Would it mean one thing to her and another to him? She was not an easy woman, surely he knew that. If she stayed willingly in a bed with a man, that would mean she was making a commitment to him. Would RJ be willing to make the same commitment to her? RJ had to know there could be no other way for her, but did he understand what it was she expected of him?

Elizabeth felt RJ pull his muscular arm from around her

shoulder, releasing her. She was free from him. But, still she lay quietly next to him, questioning if she wanted this freedom. RJ had asked her to stay with him. Stay in the shared warmth of their two bodies. Oh God, how she wanted to stay. Was it wrong to want to feel his strength wrapped around her near nakedness? Was she such a bad woman to want this? No, she was not a bad woman! She was a lonely woman! Hadn't she suffered the penance of loneliness for the last seven years? Wasn't that enough?

When she'd met Charles, they'd dated for two years before they made their commitments. They had time to get to know each other, time to fall in love. But she and RJ were not young, and they didn't have the luxury of youth. They didn't have time for a courtship in the usual sense. They couldn't count on tomorrow. And damn it, she wouldn't throw this away. She wouldn't lose RJ, regardless of a lack of commitment on his part. She'd take whatever he had to give....however small.

Quickly, she leaned over and grabbed his arm, placing it back around her shoulder. Without hesitation, she scooted snug against his warm, waiting body, and as she did, she realized she'd been nearly starved for this soothing intimate touch.

RJ slipped his other arm under her encircling her entire body, and pressed her to him, laughing softly against her ear. They lay quiet and still in near overwhelming contentment; a contentment that could only be known and understood by those who'd been abandoned by love's human touch.

"Now isn't this better to just sleep in here with me, rather than running back and forth to the porch like you did, Friday?" RJ whispered, pulling her even closer to him, content with her small body snuggled so close to his, and intoxicated with the sweat smell of her soft clean hair.

"What are you talking about? I didn't sleep in here with you on Friday night," she answered, running her fingers along his massive arm to his hands clasped tightly around her.

"Oh yes, you did," he said, moving his long legs close to hers. "Your wild snoring woke me up out of a dead sleep. God, I thought some weird bird was loose in here. And I don't mean any little canary. How can you sleep through that racket?"

"Well, what about you and all that barnyard snoring?" She

answered, moving her legs apart slightly, feeling his leg move between hers. "It sounded like it was a chorus of pigs."

"I don't snore."

"Neither do I."

"All right," he laughed. "All right."

"RJ?"

"Yes, Beth."

"Beth?" She asked, remembering the name of her youth.

"I can't call you Elizabeth", he whispered. "Elizabeth was that nasty old broad I met on Friday, but when she finally let loose, Beth was the real woman I found inside." They were silent for a few minutes basking in their new found contentment.

"RJ?"

"Yes, Beth"

"RJ, will you make our kids get married as soon as possible?"

"I will," he mumbled, "I will."

Happy and contented, finally without worry, Beth took his large hands and pulled them up under her neck, kissing them with gentle tenderness. They had found each other. The commitment was made. Life could be good, at long last.

RJ could hear her breathing softly, steadily, and knew she was asleep. He nuzzled his nose under the hair on her neck, euphoric in the soft smell that could only belong to this woman. He held her closely to him, securing her to him; a thief who'd stolen a treasured possession. He knew she wasn't his to keep. He'd have to give her up, but for now, he could hold her. She could be his for a little while. Knowing that he could ask no more from her than what they had this night, he would be content. In the morning, he'd let her go. In the morning, he'd push her away from him.

He couldn't let her become a part of his life, his living hell. No, he wouldn't ask that of her. But for this short time, he'd savor being with her, feeling her close to him. His Beth.

Gently he caressed her small hips, daring to move his large fingers across her soft breasts while capturing this memory in his mind. This one night, he could enjoy every inch of her as she slept so innocently next to him, but his heart was heavy. He dreaded the morning, knowing what he must do. RJ hated this night to end and he fought sleep like a bitter old enemy, but slowly, inevitably, his blue eyes closed and the night slipped away. Morning would come.

Chapter 14

Beth ran her arm across the warm bed feeling for the man she'd fallen in love with sometime the past weekend. He wasn't there. She opened her eyes in the early morning sunlight and saw him sitting quietly beside her, watching her, studying her. Slowly, she sat up in the bed and stretched her arms toward the ceiling, smiling at the big man. "How long have you been up, RJ? Why didn't you wake me?"

RJ didn't answer, and he didn't take his eyes off the small woman. He didn't know what to say or how to begin. All he knew was that he hated himself.

Sitting up in the bed, Beth extended her legs to the floor, her toes searching for her slippers.

RJ knelt down onto the floor and finding her slippers slipped them onto her feet as gently as a caress. He stood from his crouching position, and without speaking, resumed his seat next to her on the bed.

She slipped her arm through his and placed her hand on his leg. "RJ", she whispered. "We're both adults and we have a little time until the kids wake up." She looked into his blue eyes questioning his thoughts. "Why don't we just crawl back into the bed and if you want…"

As if someone had slapped him back into reality, RJ stood up, dwarfing the small woman as she stared up at him. He knew what she was offering him, but he also knew he could only have her in his dreams. The magic of the night was gone. Reality was back. He knew what he had to do.

"What I want now is a cup of coffee," he said. "Get your robe on, and I'll meet you in the kitchen. I need to talk to you about something." Then he was gone.

Elizabeth wondered what in the world had just happened. Why was he so cold to her? There had to be some simple explanation. All they had done since the evening was sleep. There'd been nothing more between them that should cause him to bolt on her as he'd just done. No, it had to be something else.

Elizabeth pulled herself up and grabbed her robe still meditating over his strange attitude. It must be their differences in finances and social standing. Yes, she knew he was just an old cowboy, dirt poor, but money and society didn't matter to her anymore. He was a fine, decent man: a good man, a rare man. After all those years alone, Elizabeth knew that being with someone you loved was the only thing that really mattered in life. And yes, she loved this big old cowboy, and she was certain he cared for her. Maybe he didn't love her yet, but he would learn to love her. She'd make him love her.

Beth walked into the kitchen and saw RJ staring down into his coffee cup. Seeing that he'd set a cup of coffee for her at the other end of the table, she picked up the coffee cup and moved closer to him. She sat down close beside him, determined that she could make everything right for them.

Ignoring the hurt look on her face, RJ began, "Beth, I can't offer you a damn thing."

Beth decided it really was the money business and breathed a sigh of relief.

Quickly, she interrupted, "RJ, if you're worried because I have money and you don't, please know that money isn't a problem with me. I don't care about that. I wouldn't be a burden to you. It's not as though you'd have to support me. I wouldn't ask anything from you, RJ. Please."

RJ turned and faced her, enormous strains of anguish appearing on his rugged face, his blue eyes squinting, searching his memory. "Years ago, I got myself into some trouble and that trouble has followed me forever. I've tried to make things right, but I can't. I can't make it go away. I just have to live with it."

RJ," she tried again, but he wouldn't let her. He had to go on and finish it.

"The life I've brought on myself is nothing but a living hell and only a lowlife, cowardly scoundrel would ever bring some innocent into that hell. I sure won't! Damn it! I'm more of a man than that!"

RJ could see the devastated look on her face and it was killing him inside. Knots surged inside his stomach, and he wondered if he could survive this without vomiting, but he knew he had to finish it.

If he didn't hurt her a bit now, it would be so much worse for her later on. He had to do it, but he hated himself for the mistakes he'd made in his past.

"What is it, RJ? What could be so bad that you're willing to throw away this little bit of happiness that we've found together? We aren't young, but we've been given another chance at life. Please, RJ, I know you feel as I do." She reached over and put her hand firmly around his arm.

He pulled his arm away from her, stood and turned his back to her. "I was a damn fool. I could see this thing starting between us, and I just stood there and let it go on. Damn my lousy soul."

She wouldn't let it happen. She wouldn't let him walk away from her. Not now. Quickly, she placed her body in front of him and put her arms around him. Tightly she clung to him. "Please, RJ, don't do this to us," she begged, desperate to hang on to the dream she had for them.

He took her arms from around him and carefully pushed her back down into her chair.

"We'll get through the wedding of our kids, Mrs. Carlton. We'll be polite to one another, so we don't ruin their wedding. But after that, I never want to see you, again. Now, I'm gonna fix some breakfast, so I can get the hell out of here."

Elizabeth couldn't stop the pounding in her chest, and yet she couldn't breathe, and that terrible uncontrollable lump was rising in her throat. Tears forming in her dark eyes, miserable in her grief, she hurried from the kitchen.

RJ fumbled through the refrigerator, searching for something to make for breakfast, but he didn't really give a damn about breakfast. The memories of the night before tore at his heart, and tiny dreams of a future with her slammed to the floor. He wasn't stupid. He knew damn good and well that memories were all he could have. Not one damn thing more. He scowled as he remembered all the cruel injustices that hounded him his entire life, and anger raged inside him like a wild beast pounding its head against the rigid bars of captivity.

After some time, RJ calmed himself and waited for his breathing to slow in accord to his heart beat. As his rage simmered down, he pulled a carton of eggs from the door of the refrigerator and placed them on the counter. Ignoring the chore of breakfast, he walked to the window and stared out at the overgrown backyard. Like that overgrown back yard, his own life had been nothing but a tangled mess, and no matter how hard he tried, he could never clean up the damage. He had to accept it and go on. He had no other choice.

Elizabeth turned on the shower and stepped inside, feeling the hot rain falling down her hair and face, her tears as one with the shower drops. She didn't care. Nothing mattered, now. She wondered what happened. Why was he doing this to her, to them? What could he have possibly done that could be so bad that he would throw away what little time they had left together?

Elizabeth knew she'd humiliated herself, throwing herself at him as she'd done. She'd begged him; he'd rejected her. She'd clung to him; he'd shoved her away. She was like a dog begging for a pat on the head and receiving a kick in the teeth instead. After all these lonely years, she'd ventured from the safety of her cloistered world and found this man she'd been certain cared for her. He didn't.

Stepping out of the shower, she dried herself and observed her image in the mirror. A complete disaster peered back at her. Elizabeth's eyes were red and swollen, and her dark hair was hanging in strands around her shoulders. Her face was white, lifeless, like she was dead and didn't realize it. She didn't care. She just didn't give a damn.

Elizabeth grabbed the edge of her bathroom vanity and cringed as she heard Anne's laughter down the hallway. How she wished they'd all just leave. She couldn't handle polite conversation, even with her own kids. She couldn't be Mom, sweet and understanding, or Elizabeth, the prim and proper. Not now, damn it. Not now. But she was Mom and she was Elizabeth, and she would go on as she'd always done. Grudgingly, she put on her clothes and shoved her dark hair back into her usual stern French twist. With a heavy heart, she returned to the kitchen.

Entering the kitchen amongst much laughter from Anne, Jason and Kathy, she sat down at the table. RJ put some of his egg concoction on a plate and handed it to her. She pushed it away and sat silently waiting for them to leave. She couldn't look at RJ.

"Mom, it was so cold last night, when we came home," Anne said. "So, I stopped by the sun porch to check on you, but you weren't there. Where were you, Mom?"

Elizabeth ignored her daughter and hoped for once, she'd just let it go. But as usual, Anne wouldn't quit until she got her answer. "Mom, did you hear me? I was worried about you. Where were you?" What seemed like an eternity passed and Anne started in again, "Mom?"

RJ's booming voice was unusually soft and quiet, "She was with me. Your mother slept with me."

Anne threw up her hands, clapping and laughing. "I don't believe it! Is that true, Mom?"

Elizabeth didn't acknowledge her daughter.

Adam smiled as he walked into the kitchen hearing the happy sound of his sister's laughter. "What's so funny, Anne? It's too early for jokes."

"Oh Adam, you've got to hear this! Guess where Mom slept last night? Guess who Mom slept with last night? Mom, prim and proper Mom, slept with RJ last night! Woo! Who! Can you believe it? Mom and RJ slept together?"

RJ turned from where he'd been staring out the window at the garden and glared at Anne knowing she wouldn't quit until she got an answer. "Your mother is a fine woman and a dedicated mother, Anne. She's always been faithful to your father, to you, and to this whole family. But, what she does in her private life is her business and none of yours. Stop questioning your mother, Anne."

She wouldn't quit "Oh, RJ, you know what a prude Mom is."

"Be quiet, Anne", Jason whispered noticing his father's stern jaw clenching in rage as he fisted and released his large hands down about his jean pockets.

"But, RJ," Anne continued.

"SHUT UP, Anne!" Jason demanded. Then, he whispered, "Just be quiet, Anne, please."

He looked at his little bride to be and could see the hurt in her big blue eyes. He leaned over to her and gently kissed her on the cheek. "If you don't be quiet, I'll tell everyone how you've been sneaking into bed with me every night breaking all the rules of the house!"

Adam poured himself a cup of coffee and turning to look at the family, he grinned. "Well, damn, I guess Kathy and I were the only ones who got a decent night's sleep since we got here. The rest of you were up all night playing musical beds!"

Elizabeth threw her napkin down and walked from the room.

After picking up her newspaper, Elizabeth dropped herself down into her brown leather chair in the den. She couldn't see a thing; didn't have on her glasses, didn't care, either. She could hear Anne calling her, but she didn't answer. Anne found her, anyway.

"What are you doing, Mom?" she asked.

"Reading the paper."

"Since when do you read the paper without your glasses?" Anne asked, pulling the paper from her mother and placing it on the table as she knelt down in front of her mother. "I'm sorry, Mom. I wouldn't hurt you or make fun of you for anything in the world. I was just so shocked when I heard about you and RJ."

"There is no RJ and me. Look, Anne, if you must know my personal business, then here it is. We had a few drinks last night. I got cold in my bed and crawled in bed with him. Nothing happened. Today, we both go our separate ways. After your wedding, we'll never see each other, ever again. That's the way we both want it."

Anne could see the sadness in her mother's dark eyes and knew this weekend with RJ had started feelings between them, but something had happened, and now it was over. She hoped her mother's prudish ways hadn't turned RJ off. Probably did. Her mother couldn't possibly change her ways in one short weekend.

As Anne thought about her lost, little mother, she heard her voice again. "Anne, it's beginning to sleet outside. Everyone needs to get on the road before the ice storm gets too bad. If you head south right now, you'll miss the worst of the storm."

"Mom", Anne wouldn't quit, "The RJ, I knew was an old man; a tired old man. When he came to Dallas on Sundays to have dinner with Jason and me, he was never one minute late, and he never stayed past two o'clock. He was a quiet, gentle soul, and unless someone asked him a question, no one even knew he was there. He just existed. He lived to work." Anne placed her hands around her mother's. "But, when he came here and met you, he changed, Mom. That man got feisty. He was alive. He had excitement in his life. I should've known what was happening. I should've realized it when I saw it."

"Anne, you have it all wrong..."

"Mom, do you know what he's doing right now? He's outside working again, just like he does probably eighteen hours a day. He's out there scrapping ice from the windows of the car. It seems to me, that as long as he keeps working, he won't have to face living."

"Please Anne. Just let it go, please. The roads are going to get bad and all of you need to head south and try and miss it. Go!"

Anne could see that it was a lost cause. "All right, Mom, come to the door and kiss us all goodbye. He's probably in the car waiting for us, anyway."

RJ took the ice scraper from the glove compartment and chipped a small hole into the ice by the driver's window. He'd started the car when he first went outside so the ice would melt more quickly. And as he'd figured, he could put his chisel under the ice and lift the entire sheet away from the window. But, he didn't. He needed something to do, so he just kept chipping away at the small spot, grateful to be working. The ice wasn't so bad on the other windows of the car either, but he kept chiseling at it, anyway. He'd do anything so that he didn't have to think about her anymore. He'd be all right when he got back to Texas. Life would be just like it'd been for him for these many years.... every day the same. She couldn't be with him. It had to be this way.

RJ finished his job of clearing the windows of the sleet, sorry to be done with his work. Miserable inside his own head, he settled himself into the back seat for the long ride back to Texas.... where he belonged.

He'd tried to avoid looking at her, but now RJ watched as Beth kissed her children goodbye. He watched as the cold wind blew about her dark hair. He could see her small fingers clutch the green shiny parka around her, trying to keep the white fur lined hood from blowing from her dark head.

As much as RJ hated himself, he couldn't take his eyes off

Beth. He remembered her laughter, her tears of the night before, her soft warm body next to his. Sadly, his happy memories hurled away like the cold wind as he watched Jason put his arms around Beth. As he hugged her, Jason accidently knocked the furry hood from her dark hair. RJ cringed. She'd be cold without her hood. Cold like she was when she crawled in bed with him, last night. With the bittersweet memory still so vivid in his mind, RJ could almost smell the scent of her hair. Painfully, he watched the mental image he'd drawn in his mind as he stroked her small body, while she lay so still next to him. That was all he could have, he knew that. But, at least he had that.

RJ wondered about the memories she had of him. He'd given her absolutely nothing. He had taken the innocence from her and left her in pain. Hell, he was no better than that creep that took her virginity. She'd trusted him, believed him to be an honorable man, and just like that son of a bitch, he'd used her to fill the lonely void in his life. And now, he'd thrown her away.

No. Oh, hell, no. He couldn't throw her away. Never could he do that to her. As bad as it was, he would tell her about his life. It was the least he could do. It was only right.

Feeling the cold wind pick up around her, Elizabeth pulled the shiny green parka around her body tighter and pulled the fur lined hood up under her chin as she watched the car slowly back out of the sleet covered driveway. Turning around as she eased her way up the steps, she felt warm tears battle their way from her eyes and down her cold cheeks. She turned and waved again, bidding farewell to a dream. As she glanced back, she saw the car come to a stop in front of the house where the little boy and his father lived, and Beth decided someone must have forgotten something. As she waited in the cold wind, she watched as RJ got out of the car and made his way up the slippery driveway. With his heavy tan work jacket buttoned to his neck, he'd pulled the heavy knit collar up around the back of his head, his large hands in the jacket pockets. He'd forgotten his hat, she decided, and turned to go into the house. He knew where he left his hat. He could find it himself. He certainly didn't need her.

Beth could hear RJ calling her name. She ignored him. There

was nothing left for him to say.

“Beth,” he called as he quickened his pace up the icy walkway. “I need to talk to you.”

“Oh, I think you've said enough to me, Mr. Scott. I’m not interested in one more damn thing you have to say.” Without turning to look at him, she hurried up the steps.

“Beth, please.”

As she turned around, he was standing at the bottom of the steps. His ears were red and little pellets of ice bounced on the tan, stained, work jacket. He stood rigid, determined, his fists clenching and unclenching with nervous energy.

He'd hurt her beyond belief, and now he wanted to apologize or explain his actions. How dare he think her feelings meant nothing, and she would forgive him just so he could feel better about himself! No! She wouldn't do it.

He reached up and took her hand in his and pulled her down the steps toward him.

Cautiously looking into his blue eyes, she faced him. “What do you want?” she snarled.

RJ cleared his throat. He’d been practicing every detail of what he had to say. “Beth, I’ve never been close with any woman before.... like we were last night, I mean. Hell, I wasn't even close like that to Jason's mother.

"When we first got here on Friday, I was pissed 'cause they tricked me to get me here, and I guess I sort of took it out on you. But, the more I was around you, I guess I sort of got used to being with you. I liked being with you. Then yesterday, when you came running toward me in the pink…. magenta sweater and those tight jeans, my God, I thought I was gonna fall on the ground. I couldn’t even look at you. God, I had to keep my back to you so you wouldn't see me drooling, just looking at you.”

RJ paused for a moment and put his hands around hers, warming her hands against the icy cold.

“Beth, I don’t know what this thing was that happened between us this weekend, but I want you to know that I’m not one bit sorry for the time we had together. In fact, you sort of got a hold of me. I wasn't leading you on, Beth. I wanted to be with you."

“Yes, and then you changed your mind this morning, didn't

you RJ? That's the fastest kiss off I've ever received." Aggravated at the nerve of the man, Beth pulled away from him and hurried up the steps, her parka hood falling from her hair.

RJ grabbed her hand and pulled her back down the step to face him, a genuine sadness filling his face. "Beth, I have to tell you something, else. Please, hear me out, and you make your own decision. Then, you can walk away from me, and you'll never see me again. But Beth, I owe you an explanation."

Elizabeth looked at the waiting car and vowed his story better be a good one. Her brown eyes flashing hurt and anger, she answered. "Go ahead, I'm listening."

RJ leaned over and pulled her parka hood up around her face and tied the ties into a bow under her chin, so she'd stay warm while he talked to her. "Beth, Jason doesn't know this, and no one else knows it either, except Juanita, Carlos and a few others that don't matter."

RJ stood on one foot and then the other staring at the ground below him. "Jason's mother, Carla, didn't die. She abandoned us. She didn't want him and she didn't want me. Truth be known, neither one of us gave a hoot about the other. With me it was simple lust, and hell, I don't know what she wanted, but it sure wasn't me. After a quick roll in the back of a local bar in Poke, Texas, Carla came to me and told me she was in a family way. She wanted me to give her money for an abortion, but I wouldn't allow that to happen to my child. I told her that if she was sure it was my child, I'd take care of both her and the baby. She agreed, and I married her. After Jason was about a year old, she dumped Jason and me."

RJ glanced up at her, hesitant to continue, but finally he did. "Later on, she came back and said if I didn't start paying her money, she'd take Jason from me, and she'd be able to do it, too, being she was his mother, but Beth, I knew she wouldn't take care of him. She never took care of him when she lived with us. I couldn't stand the thought of my little boy dirty, hungry, or worse. So, I just paid her to keep her away from us. It was safer for him that way."

Beth watched his blue eyes as he glanced toward the waiting car at the end of the driveway, then he went on. "After Jason was grown, I tried to get her to divorce me, but she wouldn't. She said she'd tell him how she never wanted him, and how she would have aborted him, but I'd paid her to carry him to term. Beth, no kid needs to live thinking his own mother didn't want him, and would've done harm to him unless his pa paid to keep him alive. So, I've kept on paying Carla for all these years. Course, it was all right, because I had no life anyway. I just lived in my hell-hole that I'd created for myself, and kept going in my day-to-day existence."

RJ smiled at her, his blue eyes twinkling in the misty cold day. "I was doing okay, too, 'til I came here and met you and started acting like a damn 15-year old kid." He cleared his throat again and stood on one foot and then the other, staring at her, waiting for some reaction. Beth said nothing.

Bringing himself back into reality, RJ frowned, his blue eyes scowling, and he began again. "So, you see Beth, I am the worst sort of a scoundrel! I am a greedy, selfish, unfit poor bastard, and I can't offer you one damn thing. Hell, I'm married, Beth! I'm legally married to Jason's mother and I will be 'til the day I die, 'cause she'll never let me go! That's the hell I live with."

MARRIED! The shock raged inside Beth's mind, but she stayed silent, as she searched RJ's blue eyes. This was certainly not what she'd expected him to say. He was married. He'd never be free. He didn't love that woman, but still, he was a married man! If she allowed herself to love him as she wanted to, she'd be breaking the sacred laws of matrimony.

"Well, Beth, if being with me was what you were wanting, I needed to let you know the truth about me, and I know it's pretty damn ugly." RJ stared at the ground and made small circular holes in the ice with the toe of his heavy boot waiting for some comment from her. Finally, his big shoulders drooped in defeat. "I'm sorry Beth. I know this isn't what you wanted. I'm sorry."

Beth watched as RJ turned and started back down the driveway, beaten, all arrogance gone from his body. It was obvious he'd fought a terrible battle with himself and lost. Beth touched the bow he'd securely tied under her chin. In all his misery, he was still worried about her comfort. RJ Scott was an honorable, decent, kind man, and he was in pain. It was killing her to watch him, and she knew then, no matter the outcome, she loved him. "RJ." she called, grabbing onto the grill of the stairway, so she wouldn't fall on the ice. “RJ, come back here.”

Beth watched as RJ made his way back up the slippery driveway and stood facing her. She pulled his cold hands to her chest and looked into his blue eyes. “RJ, you’ve told me about your past. You've been honest with me. I won't lie to you and say this isn't a big shock to me, because it is. I'm devastated, but my feelings for you haven't changed. I know what I want. I want you, RJ. Somehow, I'll find a way to live with your situation, but what about you, RJ? What do you want? Do you want me?”

“Yeah, I guess that’d be all right with me.” Beth looked shocked at his answer, and RJ felt like a complete dithering old fool, an idiot. Hell yes, he wanted her. Good God Almighty, yes. He just didn’t have a clue what she wanted him to say, or how he was supposed to say it. Hell, he'd never courted, or sweet talked a woman before. He'd always thought that stuff was foolishness, but now....

As RJ thought over the situation, he realized what this woman had offered him even knowing about his marital situation, and he felt sick knowing the destruction that could happen to her because of him. He had to warn her. “Beth, there’s nothing in this deal for you, but shame and misery.”

“Aren’t you part of the deal, RJ? Isn’t that what this is all about? You and me, together?”

“Beth, I told you. I’m married.”

“I don’t care.”

“What? Beth, do you know what you’d be getting yourself into with me, the gossip from your widow lady friends? Folks looking down on you because of me.”

“I don’t care about anyone but you, RJ. And if you feel the same way about me, that’s all that matters. I love you, RJ.” Beth pulled back from him and stared into blue eyes that could not lie. He loved her, even if he didn’t know it.

Beth ran her hands up from his chest and put both her hands on either side of his face. Gently, she pulled him to her and kissed him on his rather startled lips. Her kiss was soft, warm, wet; urgent with the pent up passion of years of frustrated loneliness. She longed to delve further into this magnificent kiss, but she felt him rapidly pull away from her. As she looked up at him, his eyes were a kaleidoscope of whirling blue confusion, and then she knew.

"RJ Scott. Hasn't any woman ever kissed you like that before?" she asked, taking his calloused hands in hers.

"No. No, I don't recall any woman kissing me like that," RJ answered stumbling over his feet and his words. "I...I...I never had time for kissing and courting and that sort of stuff." RJ stared at the ground, covering the small circles he'd made in the ice with dead leaves he'd kicked from under the step.

Beth stared in disbelief at this giant of a man. She knew he'd been married and probably had known lust and passion with any number of women, but she was certain he knew absolutely nothing about the intimacies of love with a woman. Because this was all new to him, RJ Scott was unsure of himself, shy. Of course, he was shy, Beth realized. He'd never been loved by a woman. Well, things were about to change for RJ Scott. He was going to be loved all the way down to his big old toes.

"Didn't you like the kiss, RJ?" she teased, knowing what his eyes told her.

"Oh hell yes," he answered, grabbing her and kissing her so hard she thought her teeth would come through the back of her head. It was obvious. RJ needed a lot of work. Frantically, she pulled away from him before he smashed her.

RJ looked embarrassed. "Guess I didn't do very good with the kissing."

Beth looked at the car parked on the street and remembered her family waiting for him. "When we have the time, RJ, I plan to teach you all about the fine art of kissing."

"Well, Teacher. I sure as hell can't wait for the next lesson." RJ laughed softly and glanced at the waiting car. "I'll see you soon, Beth."

Beth watched as he turned and waved to her as he entered the waiting car. As they drove away, she noticed the sleet had stopped, and the sun was melting the icy glaze with its gentle warmth. All the people on earth that she loved were in that car, and now, she knew they'd be safe on their journey. Beth smiled in thanksgiving, certain that she and RJ would have a wonderful future together; a time to forget the past and go on with new beginnings. Surely, that's what the future would hold for them.

If only she'd had a crystal ball.

Chapter 15

RJ had been awfully sick since he'd returned home from Oklahoma. His stomach was upset, he couldn't sleep, he couldn't think straight, and he knew his problems were all due to Beth Carlton's hold on him. Every place he looked he'd see her. That pink....no, that magenta sweater, dark hair bouncing on her shoulders, big innocent brown eyes smiling at him. Every corner of his mind was filled with that woman.

While he waited for dawn to peak through the open window of his bedroom, RJ thought about their differences and knew their lives could never work together. Just too many things they'd never be able to agree on. He'd never leave his home ever, and she'd never understand what his land meant to him. After they'd been together for a while, she'd want him to move to Tulsa, Oklahoma, move to the city. Live so close to other folks that you couldn't belch, that folks would complain. He could barely stand Sunday dinner in Dallas with Jason and Anne. That was a damn nightmare, being cooped up in that little apartment for two hours. Just think how awful it'd be cooped up in that little house of hers in Tulsa. Forever.

"Oh, God, no," he uttered to himself. He'd never leave his land, and if she didn't like it, she'd have to stay away from him. Yeah, he'd gotten smitten with her in Tulsa, but now that he was back home in Poke, Texas, he'd had time to think about that thing that was going on between them. Hell, he knew it was just a silly old fart crush. He'd missed his Friday night at "Big Goldie's", and he hadn't done that in over twenty years. Beth Carlton was a good looking woman and she just got his juices flowing….real bad. Not having sex for a long time could do that to a man. That's all it was. No sex.

He might as well put a stop to his thoughts about her right now, he decided. No reason to worry about getting attached to her when they'd never be able to agree on a place to live and probably nothing else either. Yep, he'd forget her faster than he met her. RJ snapped his fingers as proof to himself that with the simple snap of his fingers, she'd be gone, and his life would go on as usual….like it had every day, week after week, year after year. That's the way he liked it.

RJ wiggled his toes and looked out the window, hoping for the first glint of dawn. It still wasn't there, but the vision of Beth Carlton was. "Damn it." he growled, as he watched her running across the yard toward him: magenta sweater, sweet smile, big eyes. He refused to see her in his mind anymore. Ignoring her vision, he rolled over and faced the wall.

He'd think about the storm coming in. His toes were aching something awful, sure sign of a bad storm. At least now he could afford good substantial boots that fit him, and he wasn't forced to wear outgrown boots with holes in the toes like when he was a kid. His choice of boots weren't exactly fashionable, like some folks wore, but they were damn comfortable. Of course, Beth would probably expect him to wear city folks' shoes, something like those stupid little tassel shoes that Jason wore. *Damn, she's back.*

RJ flipped over on his back and stared at the wooden crucifix that Juanita had insisted on hanging over his door. He hadn't said anything when she'd put it there. It was just easier than arguing with a silly woman about organized religion. Juanita went to church all the time. Beth did too. Pretty soon, Beth would make him join the church….force him to sing in the choir. *Oh, Lord.*

He just had to get himself straightened out, and he knew he could. He was an old man and no woman was gonna tear him up like she was doing. He'd think about other things. "Miss March"! She was always a good way to change his thinking when he was worrying. *Miss March.*

The first glint of dawn filled the room with its soft promises of the day. Eagerly, RJ lowered his long legs to the floor, ran his fingers through his graying hair and gazed up at "Miss March", just as he did every morning. Somehow, her blonde hair wasn't as shiny anymore, not like Beth's silky mahogany hair. Her lips were too red, too full, too pouty, not like Beth's soft, warm lips that captured his and nearly knocked the breath out of him. RJ felt a shiver run down his spine. *This just had to stop! It had to! Oh, God.*

RJ finished dressing, got his coffee, and headed for his front porch to do some serious thinking on overcoming the hold Beth Carlton had on him. As he leaned back in his old white wicker rocker, his boys ran up to him licking his hand, just as they did when he drank his coffee on the porch every morning. The lady sun was beginning her journey, like she always did, and he felt somewhat better, seeing his routine still the same. He placed his coffee on the floor, and gave each one of his boys a good scratching, just like he did every single day.

Things were getting back to normal. He was back in Texas and he'd forget all about Beth just as soon as he started his daily chores. He'd stay busy and pretty soon she'd mean no more to him than just a silly memory, but there was one thing he'd do before he forgot her completely. He'd call that damn John's Complete Lawn Service in Tulsa, and make sure that boy fixed up that awful lawn as he should have been doing all along.

RJ thought about her yard for a minute. It needed something else in that yard, something that he put there, sort of his final goodbye to her. Maybe some big Azalea plants next to the little gazebo door, some pink ones. No, some magenta Azaleas. Yeah, he'd do this for her, and then she'd be gone from his mind. Give up her hold on him.

After RJ contacted John's Complete Lawn Service, he gave John a good going over for cheating that woman all those years, and in a voice of fire and damnation, he explained to John in no uncertain terms what was to happen to her yard, how it was to be maintained, and how John was to send RJ pictures for his inspection as soon as it was completed, and that better be damn quick.

Gulping the last of his coffee, RJ walked around the back of his house and grabbed a sack of dog food from the barn and filled his boys' two bowls. Finishing that, he filled another big bowl with fresh water from the faucet inside the barn, and smiled down at his two boys, both wagging their tails and waiting, wondering what their master had planned for them, now that he was back home with them, where he belonged. Things were back to normal again.

RJ started toward Big Red, his two boys leading the way. He was a happy man. He'd defeated the hold Beth Carlton had on him. Why, he wasn't thinking about anything except the chores of the day, and one of the things he needed to do today was to go over to the neighbors and see if he had any hay left over from last summer.

Next year, he'd be sure to allow for more hay, being as his own cows were calving so good. Yep, life was just the same again.

As RJ climbed up into Big Red, he felt his stomach rumble and decided that was a good sign that he was getting over whatever ailment he'd picked up. He decided it was probably a touch of the flu, probably got it from Beth. RJ winced at her memory, but before he could stop himself, he was recapturing her long, endless kiss, the softness of her lips, her offering of simple pleasures he never knew existed....pleasures, he hungered to feel again. *Oh God, would it never stop?*

Beth wrapped the towel turban style around her dark wet hair, stared out her bedroom window, and envisioned RJ tromping up and down the ugly mess of her yard. Smiling, she wondered if he'd thought about her, even for a moment, after he'd left. She'd thought of nothing else but him, but as the day passed, she wondered if the weekend with RJ had actually happened, or if maybe it was just because she wanted it so badly.

He was probably home now, not giving her a single thought; chasing the chickens off the porch, cleaning the cow dung from his boots. To him, this weekend, probably had no more meaning than a summer camp romance like she'd found before she'd even become a teenager. '*Oh yes, we'll miss each other. Yes, we'll write daily.*' Then, as time passed, summer camp would be part of the past and along with it the summer romance. Beth wondered if this was what had happened this weekend. Was this simply a childish summer camp romance between two aging adults that surely knew better?

Walking back to the bed, she patted the spot where he'd slept and realized she'd kicked something under the bed. Leaning under the bed, she discovered his old gray cowboy hat. Picking it up, she stared at it for a moment. Running her fingers around the outer brim of the hat, she gazed inside the hat at the rings of long gone sweat around the hat band, every spot reminisce of honest hard work. The hat was worn and crusty around the brim, but inside it was soft and pliable, and overall it remained strong, enduring and honorable. The hat *was* RJ Scott.

She pressed the old hat to her chest, smelling the sweat that had been him. Closing her eyes, she clung to the old hat. This was no summer camp romance. With great tenderness, she placed the old hat back where she'd found it under the bed, where it would stay until he came for it.

Beth finished dressing, and stood in her kitchen drinking her third cup of coffee, waiting until she was certain, she could talk to John of "John's Complete Lawn Care", and not the answering machine that she'd become so intimate with over the years. She knew he'd been cheating her for years, and she'd had it. "No more, little Johnny," she declared. "No more."

Standing erect, with her shoulders back, she cleared her throat as she listened to him answer the telephone. "John?" she inquired. "This is Elizabeth Carlton, and I want to talk to you about my yard."

"Oh yes, ma'am," he answered, "I was just going to call you. We're coming today to do some work on your yard, and I wanted to be sure we could get in your back gate."

Well, this was a surprise! No arguing, no harassment, no threats. What happened? For a moment Beth almost fell back into her old gullible ways, but she caught herself. She'd made up her speech, and by golly, she'd let him know that she knew about that yard! That little troll would surely feel her authority.

"You see, John, the reason I have those ruts in my back yard is because of the varmints, I mean those nasty moles. They come after the grubs, and they tear up my yard! Now, if you get rid of the grubs, you get rid of the moles, and you get rid of the ruts in my back yard!"

"Yes, ma'am," he agreed. "We'll take care of that, too. My trucks will be getting to your house shortly. We'll fix everything for you."

A few minutes after she hung up from her very satisfying conversation with John, of John's Complete Lawn Service, Beth heard the sound of trucks entering her driveway. Quickly, she ran out the back porch and unlocked the gates. She knew she must have really scared him, because there were three trucks pulling into her back yard with three men in each truck.

Quickly exiting the trucks, they were all over her yard working. Working, not sipping a cup of coffee from the Stop Quick, or relating some story about the hot babe they had the night before.

They were actually working.

Beth watched in amazement as they put something into the mole holes and then continued with huge rollers all over the yard. They fertilized the yard, seeded the fescue, trimmed the bushes, cleared the weeds, replaced the dead Azaleas with healthy ones, and then mulched around the new plants. On and on, it went for the rest of the day and into the evening, and they were still working. She'd never seen them stay at her house past four o'clock, when they came, if they came.

Then, Beth began to worry. What if he'd misunderstood her? What if John were going to charge her some large fee? What if she was going to be cheated again? She got out her checkbook and checked her pitiful balance. It would be some days before the interest from her dividends would be transferred to her checking account. How would she pay for all of this? She hated to ask him to wait to cash her check.

As she looked up from her checkbook, she spotted two men placing two gigantic clay pots of beautiful deep magenta Azaleas next to either side of the Gazebo door. "Oh, no," she yelled. "I can't afford that!" Quickly, she raced down the back steps.

"John", she called. He turned and looked at her, smiling as she neared him.

Yes, you're smiling, you sneak! I know you'll stick it to me, now. Well, I'll be darned if I'll put up with this any longer. You work for me, Mister! I'm the boss here!

"John, I didn't ask for those pots," she said with authority, standing on her toes to appear larger as she'd seen RJ do with the annoying geese. "You'll have to take them back. I just want the yard to be maintained, properly."

The young man turned and smiled at her again. "Yes, ma'am," he replied. "But, you see, Mrs. Carlton, somehow we've managed to neglect your place, unintentionally of course, but we want to see it back like it should be, as Mr. Carlton would have wanted. There's no charge to you, ma'am".

Elizabeth was beside herself. She'd used her authority and it worked. She hadn't been afraid to stand up for herself and she was overwhelmed with her new aggressive attitude.

John continued as he turned to push a bee from buzzing too

close to his head. "Sometime this week, there'll be a fellow coming over to fix up the Gazebo for you, too. It's pretty old, but he'll try and stabilize it and repaint it inside and out. It'll be what you want, Mrs. Carlson. When we get done, your husband would be proud of this garden." He smiled at her and as he walked away from her, he yelled at one of the men who'd stopped for a cigarette break. As she watched John inspect the finished yard, she noticed he was taking Polaroid pictures of her beautiful transformed garden, and then was putting them in a file he carried. That was odd.

Knowing how proud Charles would have been of the garden, Beth smiled. He would have been proud of her, too. Through mist-filled eyes, Beth watched as the trucks backed out of her driveway and were soon gone.

Chapter 16

It was Friday. RJ had suffered a miserable week. He was frustrated and totally disgusted with himself. He couldn't get Beth Carlton out of his head. No matter how he tried, how he denied it, she was always there, waiting for him.... dark hair, magenta sweater, big brown eyes, and soft lips. Always there!

It was Friday night, his night at Big Goldie's and RJ couldn't wait to get there. Impatiently, he instructed his boys not to follow him as he gunned Big Red down the long driveway to the main road to Polk and to Goldie's. Shoving Big Red into gear, he pressed down on the gas trying to force the old gal to go faster, but Big Red sputtered and balked in defiance. RJ cursed and let her have her usual slow and steady pace.

Knowing he couldn't win with Big Red, RJ gave some deep thought to his problem. What he needed was a woman's body. He didn't need any silly little kisses. He needed a big buxom gal with an eager rump. One that could help him dump his frustrations and get over the damn hold that tiny little woman had over him. He needed sex, and he needed it in the worst way! Any way he could get it, and by the first gal that he could find. He didn't care. Just get it over and done with.

RJ pulled Big Red up behind Goldie's and parked in his usual spot with the rest of the Friday night regulars. Half loping around the side of the cinder block building to the front door, he threw open the steel door with the bars covering the peephole window and walked inside. The beer signs were flashing, the jukebox was playing, a couple of the gals were dancing with the men, and one gal was sitting with a little old man holding his hands, listening as though she cared while he poured out his love for his long deceased wife. The place was lively, and there was a lot of loud talking and more high pitched laughter. Goldie's bar was just like any other bar on a Friday night, almost.

RJ stood alone at the well-worn mahogany bar watching and wondering. Nodding his thanks, he took a long drink from the bottle of Lonestar Beer Goldie routinely set in front of him, her broken face frozen in the familiar grotesque smile. He slapped a handful of wrinkled dollar bills onto the damp bar and nodded as Goldie took two of them and punched the numbers down on the ancient, silver and bronze cash register. RJ heard the familiar ring as she pulled down the old side crank to total the purchase. The register totaled four zeros. RJ wondered if anyone would believe there was no money in that cash register on a Friday night as busy as the place was, but RJ breathed a sigh of relief seeing the cash register total zeros just like it always did. Things were the same as they always were. Nothing had changed at Goldie's.

RJ clamped the heel of his boot on the steel rung of the barstool and glanced around the busy room. A couple of the gals smiled at him in invitation to the back room. He smiled back at them, but quickly turned away, hoping they didn't come over to him. He'd driven like a madman to get to Goldie's, and now that he was here, his usual eagerness for the back room had just up and left him. He'd been tired and worried that past week, so his bit of reluctance was just a passing thing, he was sure of that. He just needed a few more beers, and maybe a couple shots of Johnny Red. Quickly, he gulped down the dregs of the bottle.

Moving his rear onto a torn black vinyl barstool, he turned from the crowded room and faced the colorful bottles of booze that reflected in the mirrors behind the large, glitzy woman with the canary yellow hair. "You working tonight, Goldie?" RJ scowled, setting his empty bottle in front of him.

Grabbing another beer from the cooler, Goldie popped the cap and placed it in front of RJ. "No, Sugar, I'm just handing out booze to a bunch of drunks, 'cause I enjoy it so damn much."

RJ smiled at the tough old gal. She smiled back, her twisted smile, closing only half of her mouth, spreading her thick red lipstick across her face, reminiscent of a circus clown. Some folks said they'd heard her step-mother had beaten her with a hot poker when she was a kid, and that's why she was so disfigured, but no one asked about it. It was nobody's business.

"Regular bartender, Joe, has the flu or so he said. So, I'm stuck working the damned bar. Damn, it's hard to get good help anymore."

"Goldie, he's been with you for more than twenty years. Give the poor bastard a break will ya? Maybe his wife is sick again."

"Well, aren't you Mr. Nice Guy tonight RJ, caring about the health of his wife?" Goldie studied him from the corner of her eye as she wiped the bar in front of him.

"Bullshit!" he answered, gulping down a slug of the cold beer and angrily slamming down the empty bottle for another round.

Goldie picked up the empty bottle, wiped the wet ring with a faded bar rag and replaced the empty with a full bottle. Cautiously, she watched RJ, knowing he was steaming mad about something. "You keep knocking them down like that, RJ, and you ain't gonna be worth a crap in the back room."

"And just what the hell business is it to you, Goldie? Keep your damn opinions to yourself and leave me the hell alone! I came here to drink, damn it, and I'll drink. When I'm ready to screw, I'll let you know! How's that, Goldie? Anymore advice you think you need to give? If not, shut the hell up."

Goldie moved her massive body down the bar and away from him. She'd heard about RJ's quick temper, but in all the many years she'd known him, she'd never seen even a glimpse of it until tonight. RJ was fuming mad, like he was fighting the world and himself right along with it. Something was definitely wrong with him, but she sure wouldn't ask any more questions.

RJ looked at his image in the mirror through the tall colored liquor bottles and felt sick. He saw a sorry, miserable old cowboy, who'd just offended one of the few women friends he'd ever had. He knew he was a real asshole. "Goldie," he motioned her over to him and when she stood directly in front of him, he handed her the full bottle of Lonestar she'd placed in front of him a few minutes before. "Take your best shot at me, Goldie. Hit me hard. I deserve it."

Goldie smiled her crooked smile, took the bottle from his hands and set it back down in front of him. "Never in all the years that you've come here, RJ, have you ever raised your voice to anybody. Everybody gets one chance. You just had yours, Sweetie." Goldie knew she'd give RJ chance after chance, if he ever asked it, but she also knew she had to pull him out of the mood he'd sunk himself into. "Okay, big boy, what's the problem?"

"I'm gonna be a grandpa, Goldie." RJ swirled the beer around in the bottle and watched the foam mount to the top.

"So, that's what's bothering you, RJ? What the hell? You love kids, or is it you're afraid of getting old? Hell, RJ, you either get old or you die. I like the first choice myself."

Goldie waddled away from RJ to get a drink for a couple of strangers down the bar who'd just walked in. They were an older couple and the woman had her arm through her man's and he was looking at her like she was his whole world.

"Where you folks from?" Goldie asked, playing the good bartender.

"We're coming from Tulsa, Oklahoma, heading for Houston. Just got married today and we'll be honeymooning on a cruise out of Houston on Monday. We've got reservations for a hotel in Dallas, but we decided to stop here for a drink before we get back on the interstate."

Goldie smiled her crooked grin. "Congrats, folks. Your drink's are on the house."

RJ watched as Goldie made small talk to the newlyweds and he felt sick. He was thinking about Beth again. God, couldn't he even go to the whorehouse without her following him? Ah hell, who was he fooling? He knew he couldn't find what he needed in the back room of "Goldie's Roadhouse" anymore than "Miss March" could squelch those awful feelings he was having. It was her, he needed. Beth. His Beth. He missed her so damn bad he just about couldn't stand it, and had no idea when he'd ever see her again. He was going absolutely nuts wanting to be with her, and there was nothing he could do about it.

"So, RJ, when's Jason getting married?" Goldie asked using the bar rag to wipe up sweat from his bottle, again.

"Damned if I know," he answered, staring down into his beer bottle avoiding Goldie's questioning eyes.

"Is she a decent girl?"

"Oh yeah, she works at the law firm with him. They seem to be crazy for each other."

"Well, what the hell are they waiting for? Maybe you ought to put a bug in his britches and get them married soon, RJ. I imagine the bride's folks will want to plan a big weddin' and all that crap, if she's a high falutin' lawyer like Jason."

"She's a widow." RJ answered, thoughtfully peeling the paper label from his beer bottle.

"The bride's a widow! Well, ain't that something, RJ. How old is this bride?"

"Not the bride, Goldie," RJ stammered. "The bride's mother's a widow."

Goldie raised her eyebrows at RJ. Why the hell was he talking about the bride's mother? They'd been discussing the bride, not the bride's mother!

Goldie checked her bar for empty bottles signaling another round, but she kept a close eye on RJ. Never had she seen anyone so intent on peeling every little bit of label off of the beer bottle as RJ was doing. He sure seemed to be doing some deep thinking.

Goldie watched her old friend, but stayed out of talking range. He seemed to be working something out in his mind, and she figured he didn't need her bothering him with idle chatter. She knew people and their needs. Hell, she made a small fortune from it. Still, she stayed close enough in case he did need her.

After some time, RJ slammed the half-empty bottle down on the bar, as though he'd come to a dramatic conclusion to his dilemma. He had. The wedding! Beth wanted him to hurry up this wedding. If he and Juanita got their asses in gear, Beth would be with him by next weekend, maybe sooner, he hoped.

Goldie took the bar rag and cleaned up the small pile of label that RJ had finished tearing off the bottle. Leaning close to him, she saw a satisfied look appear on his face, just like he'd made some miraculous discovery. "RJ, what's going on?"

RJ leaned over and patted her chubby hand, took a last swig of his beer, and started across the floor to the door. "Nothing's going on, Goldie. I just got to get this weddin' going real quick." Whistling off key, he was gone.

"Well, damn," Goldie wondered out loud. "RJ's missed two Friday nights in a row. What in the hell's got a hold of that man?"

Chapter 17

If RJ's head had been the knee Beth was drumming her fingers on, she'd have killed him. She was that furious. She'd been expecting his call since Tuesday and now it was Saturday. Still, he hadn't called. A gentleman would have called. Any normal man would have called. RJ should have called. He should have called!

Beth drummed her fingers harder, but it didn't help relieve her irritation with him. Being the obstinate character he was, he'd neglected this tiny, little nicety in their new-found relationship. He could have called, even if it was just to say "Hello", or in his case, "Howdy". Why hadn't he called? He should have wanted to call her. Beth pounded her fingers faster.

Yes, she knew she could call him, but she didn't have his phone number, and besides, it was the man's place to call a lady he was courting. Of course, RJ didn't know anything about courting a lady, and yes, he did don the hardnosed old cowboy act, but common sense would allow that he would miss her a little bit. Then the realization hit Beth that being as *country* as he was, maybe he didn't have a phone. "That's it," she decided, relaxing the drumming of her fingertips. "He couldn't call because he didn't have a telephone."

The telephone rang. "Howdy, this is RJ Scott from Texas," a gruff voice said.

"Hello, RJ Scott from Texas." There was a moment of silence. Then, she heard him laugh softly, and just hearing his voice, all her hostility melted and was gone.

"Juanita's here with me, Beth."

"Yes, RJ. Hello, Juanita." Beth heard him say something and then heard a small voice in the background.

"Juanita said, 'Howdy' to you, Beth. Now, you remember that you wanted our kids to get married real quick?"

"Of course, I remember, RJ. I've thought of nothing else," she lied.

"Well, Juanita's come up with a plan."

"What sort of plan?" Beth asked, and heard RJ turn to Juanita and repeat what Beth had said to him, and then she heard Juanita say something to him, and he was back on the phone.

"Juanita thinks it would be nice to have the wedding here at my place."

Then Beth heard the woman speak in the background and the two of them began to talk, but she couldn't hear what they were saying.

"Yeah," he said to Juanita, and then he was back on the phone with her. "Juanita wants to know what you think of that."

"Do you have enough room to seat everyone, Juanita?"

Beth could hear RJ speak to Juanita again, but she couldn't hear Juanita's answer. Soon, RJ was back on the phone, "Juanita said, 'It's okay', Beth."

Exasperated with the continual repetition of conversations, Beth said, "RJ, don't you have a speaker phone?"

"Yeah," he answered, "Jason gave me this phone last year and it's got all kinds of buttons on it."

"Well RJ, just put the two of you on the speaker phone, so we don't have to keep repeating."

She could hear him fumbling around with the phone, grumbling while Juanita fussed at him in Spanish. "Okay, Miss Smarty Pants, how the hell do I do that?"

"Just hit the little button that says speaker. Just press it down and let it go. Then we can all talk."

She heard more fumbling. "I can't find my glasses. I can't see these damn little names on this fancy little phone."

"When you were at my house, you didn't need glasses to read the paper," Beth answered.

"Oh, yeah, and I couldn't read a damn thing in that newspaper either, but I sure wasn't gonna let you know it." She could hear him laugh teasingly, and she smiled as she heard him thank Juanita for finding his glasses.

Hearing the distinct sound of the echo of the speaker phone, she knew they were on speaker. "Okay, RJ, we're on speaker."

"OKAY," he bellowed into the phone, **"CAN YOU HEAR ME?"**

"Good Lord, RJ, people in the next state can hear you! Stand away from the speaker phone and stop shouting for God's sake." She heard more fumbling and the two of them talking to each other.

"How's that?" He asked.

"Yes, that's much better. Now, we can all have a say in this wedding."

"Juanita," she asked, "Juanita?" She heard more talking between them. Now, they were whispering.

RJ spoke, '"Juanita said 'what', Beth?'"

Oh God, this was a disaster! Juanita refused to talk on the phone. Giving up trying to communicate with the elusive Juanita, Beth tried again. "RJ, is there enough room to have the wedding inside or do you have any place nice for the guests to stand during the wedding?"

He began to laugh, "Oh, I'll just throw out a few bales of hay, wring a couple of chickens' necks, fire up the old barbeque pit and we'll have a regular old hoedown."

She could hear Juanita fussing at him in the background. Then, she heard Juanita say, "We can have it in the garden. It will be very nice and the ladies can wear lovely dresses".

RJ began to repeat what Juanita had said. "Juanita said…"

"RJ, I can hear her" Beth began, "tell Juanita that I think that will be very nice." *Good Lord, she was getting just like those two idiots.*

"We can plan all we want," Beth heard Juanita say to RJ, "but tell the lady that Miss Anne will have to make the final decisions of what she wants for her wedding. Tell her that, RJ".

RJ began to repeat what Juanita said. "I heard her, RJ, and Juanita's right. We need to talk to Anne first, and we all need to talk to her, together. "

"Well, Miss Hi tech," he began, "you know so much about the telephones, don't you have one of those fancy phones that folks can visit three ways?"

"You mean a conference call. Yes, I do."

"Well, then, hook us up. Time's a-wastin."

Beth fumbled around for a minute. "I don't know how to use it," she answered.

"Well, what the hell are you paying for a service like that for, if you don't even know how to use it?"

"Do you have it, RJ?" He didn't answer. She knew he had it, too. "Do you know how to use it, Mr. Smarty Pants?"

"Hell no! I don't know how to use the damn thing, but I know who does. Anne does. I'll call her and she can hook all of us up."

After about 30 minutes, Beth's phone rang again. "Mom," Anne began, exasperation gripping her voice. "Now, Mom. I think I have RJ and Juanita on the phone! Maybe. I'm not sure! Damn it! I hope they're still there! RJ, are you there? RJ?"

They could hear him, but only in a whisper and Beth could hear the groan in Anne's voice. "RJ, what are you doing with the phone now?"

They could hear RJ's whispered response. "I can't hear anybody. Can anybody hear me?" Then, it occurred to Beth that he thought he was still on the speaker phone and was trying to talk from across the room.

"PUT THE PHONE UP TO YOUR EAR, RJ!" Beth yelled. "WE'RE NOT ON SPEAKER PHONE ANYMORE."

"Okay! Can you hear me now? Juanita's on the extension" he said, then they heard him say, "Juanita, say something." Silence.

RJ was back on the phone again, "Juanita says 'what'?"

"Well, so much for high tech, right Anne?" Beth asked, mockingly.

"You aren't any better than they are, Mom. When are you people going to join the 20th century and learn to use computers where we can see each other." Anne shuddered at the thought of what this group could do to the world of computers.

RJ interrupted "Well, hell, Annie, we just learned how to use the speaker phone! Give us some time."

"Yeah, in the next century," she laughed. "Okay, I have Jason here on my computer from his office. Don't ask, RJ. Just trust me, he can hear us."

About that time they heard Jason's voice, "Hi Dad, Elizabeth, Juanita!"

"Don't get the group started, Jason," Anne warned. "Just getting them this far has been a real trip. Just be quiet and talk to me. Don't try and talk to them. Trust me, Jason. You will lose."

Anne began in a very professional voice; a woman in charge was speaking. "Now, we were discussing our wedding, I believe. Jason, listen to this carefully. As I understand it, "the group" thinks we should get married as soon as possible. I know we'd talked about going to the Justice of the Peace next Friday and just doing a simple ceremony in front of the Judge, but, "the group" here, wants to throw some sort of a formal ceremony. It seems "the group" has decided that it would be nice to have the ceremony at RJ's, and Juanita has agreed that they could work something out for that same Friday night that we'd planned. I'm agreeable if you are, sugar pie," she added in her old soft voice.

"Whatever you want, Anne", he said. "But remember, we have a flight out of Dallas at midnight for Las Vegas for the weekend."

"Yes, that will be our honeymoon." She agreed. "Hey "group", this is beginning to sound like a real wedding!" Anne's voice was back to the old Anne Beth knew and loved. "Sounds like it will be wonderful. But we just want a few guests, just the closest of friends. Okay, group?"

Everyone agreed that a small wedding in his garden would be perfect. Anne would have Kathy as her matron of honor, and Jason would have Adam as his best man.

"Well, group, this has been fun, but Jason and I have to get back to work. Just let us know what we're supposed to do and we'll be there."

The executive voice had returned, but Beth knew that was the way it should be for Anne, for now, anyway.

Chapter 18

RJ rolled over in the twisted covers of his bed and looked for the sunshine of a new day. He was a happy man. This time next week, Beth would be with him. He'd have her in his bed. He felt the familiar shiver, as he envisioned their first time together, all the things he wanted them to experience, together. *Together?*

"Oh God," RJ gasped, remembering he hadn't the faintest idea how to please a woman. Hell, he didn't even know how to kiss one. He'd been with many women, but he'd never been a lover to any of them. It'd always been lust he'd felt for women, and in all cases he'd paid dearly, one way or another. Beth had been a widow for seven years, probably never even thought about being with a man anymore. Yeah, she'd offered more that morning in Tulsa, but she was probably just being polite. She was a church going widow, and probably not used to having her juices flowing like his did. That part, that sex part of her was probably dried up and forgotten by now. *Oh God!*

RJ sat straight up in his bed. What was he supposed to do if all she wanted to do was sit on the porch and hold hands? Damn! Would he be willing to give up sex for her? For a while he thought about Beth, then sex, then more sex, then Beth. He wasn't about to give up either one and he knew it, so he'd just have to find a way to make her want him as much as he wanted her. Then he came up with a plan.

He'd learn all he could about a woman's body, all the mysterious secrets that would make a woman want a man, and he knew he'd have to become an irresistible lover, a machine of sexual pleasure. RJ smiled in delight at his plan, knowing he'd have the best of both worlds, Beth and sex. He'd make her want him so bad, she'd beg. O*h damn.*

Old Doc Henry would have some books on the female body, he was sure of that. Maybe Doc could show him some pictures and point out the places on a woman's body that he could study to learn how to please a woman. Doc would get a good chuckle out of that, him being over fifty years old and so stupid about women. Well, it wasn't like he had a female person to practice his love-making style on. For a moment he considered the gals over at Goldie's but he didn't want to touch any woman but Beth. Not anymore. He just wanted to touch her all over her soft body. *Oh damn.*

While he was over at Doc's he'd get himself a good checkup too, just to be sure he was in perfect condition. Nothing in this world was going to spoil their first time together. After she discovered what an amazing stud he was, he was certain that he'd be busy pleasing her night and day. Hell, they might never get out of the bed again ever. *Oh damn.*

RJ gunned "Big Red" down the little two-lane highway toward Poke, his boys guarding his backside. He couldn't help but smile. Beth would be with him soon. His Beth, his woman. His Beth was the only treasure he'd ever received in his life that he hadn't had to work, fight or pay for. She was the grand prize with no strings attached. He wouldn't question it, or doubt it. He'd treasure her, protect her, and honor her above all that he'd ever had or would ever have in his life to come. That was his promise to heaven; his thanks for this unbelievable rare jewel that had been entrusted to him. His Beth.

RJ gazed at the clear blue sky hovering over the small town of Poke, Texas. His mind was at peace. If there really was a God, then for the first time in his life, God had taken notice of him. God had smiled down on him, RJ Scott. God liked him. Damn, he felt good.

Later on that day, Beth heard her phone ring again. "Howdy," RJ said, "This is RJ Scott."

His voice sounded tired, like the first time she'd met him. "Yes, RJ," Beth answered.

Beth heard RJ clear his voice and in her mind, she could see him scowling. "Hey, I… Juanita and me, we need to know when you're coming to Dallas, and if you're planning on staying in Dallas at Anne's, or out at my place."

Beth thought that was such a strange thing to ask and felt terribly offended in his gruff attitude toward her. She cringed, feeling those old summer camp memories crawl up her back. Naturally, she'd assumed she'd stay with him. She'd visualized early sunsets on his old front porch: the dogs, the chickens. *Chicken poop! Yuk!* But they'd be together and in her mind that was all that mattered. Then she remembered Juanita was a big part of his life. Maybe Juanita had changed his mind. Maybe Juanita didn't want anyone to be with *RJ.* Maybe they'd go back to "ma'am and Mr. Scott". "I'll stay wherever it's convenient for everyone", she answered softly, wondering how things could have changed so quickly.

"Well, I imagine it'll be best for you to stay here at my place." he said. "Folks won't have so much running back and forth to Dallas, and if you need to go somewhere, somebody can take you. So, you gonna be flying in?" RJ hesitated and then quickly continued before she could answer, "Maybe you should think about coming in a bit early. I mean you want to be sure you get here for this weddin', and don't miss it. Of course, whenever you want to come is up to you. Somebody, most likely will be here for you."

"Well, I certainly don't want to put *somebody* out," Beth answered curtly, feeling her own hostility growing. Remembering the flights were cheaper midweek, she continued, "I'll see about getting a flight there for next Wednesday morning, if that's convenient to *somebody's* busy schedule."

"Yep," he answered, "Sounds like a plan to me. I'll pick you up at the airport in Big Red, my truck. Just call me, and if I'm not here, leave a message." And he was gone.

Beth wondered how she could have been so incredibly stupid. RJ Scott didn't give a hoot about her, a frumpy, middle-aged widow. Sure, he acted like he cared about her when he was in Tulsa, but that was last week. A hundred years ago. Now, they were back to reality. His reality. A place where she didn't belong....just another summer camp romance after all.

Chapter 19

It had been a busy week for Beth. She'd finally been able to talk to Anne and learned from her very modern child, that the day they'd decided the wedding, she'd found the perfect wedding attire at a little shop next to where she'd stopped for lunch. It featured a champagne lace-fitted top, with champagne satin palazzo pants covered in chiffon. Perfect with four-inch stilettos and flowers in her hair. Very chic, very modern, and a quick change so they could be off on their honeymoon.

Beth wondered who this strange woman was that claimed her daughter's voice. Whoever heard of a "*palazzo*" pants wedding outfit? Lord only knew what that looked like. Beth breathed a sigh of relief knowing there'd only be a few people at the wedding to witness such an outfit. Besides, she couldn't imagine what sort of a fiasco the wedding and reception would be with RJ and Juanita in charge. *God help us all.*

Beth couldn't decide what sort of a dress she should get. RJ probably didn't have air conditioning. If it was hot, she'd wilt in a more formal dress, but she knew that Anne was close to a lot of the partners at the law firm, and if they came, Anne would want to introduce them to her. Consequently, Beth didn't want to look underdressed, regardless that RJ would probably wear dirty boots covered with the usual smell of cow dung.

After giving the situation much thought and knowing her latest interest check was deposited in her bank account, she decided to go with a dressy look and hope for the best. She wanted something in a deep pink, but couldn't find anything that didn't make her look like a matronly grandmother, and the good Lord knew she wasn't that yet. Desperate, she had settled on a mid-length long-sleeve sage shantung gown, with a bolero jacket accented with tiny green sequins around the front and hem. It was an okay dress. Not great, just okay. She was probably overdressed for the occasion anyway.

After much investigation into flights to Dallas, she found a very good deal. Instead of leaving on Wednesday, she'd save a substantial amount of money on her ticket if she left on Thursday morning. Realizing that RJ was in no hurry to see her anyway, she booked the ticket for Thursday morning to arrive in Dallas at 11a.m. She called his house, left a message, and hoped someone would bother to listen to it.

All of her clothes had been ready since Tuesday, including the great bargain she'd found on a pair of silver three-inch sandals, accented with Rhine stones on the ankle and toe straps. Those she'd pack in her small carry-on bag with her makeup and undies. After the purchase of the plane ticket, the dress, and the shoes, Beth still had enough of her monthly interest allotment to treat herself to having her hair done professionally, but hearing her dilemma over finding a good hair salon, one of her wealthy widow friends insisted on giving her a "mother-of-the-bride" gift. An appointment at the exclusive "George's".

George was certainly not what she'd expected. Dressed all in white, he appeared to be more of a surgeon than a hairdresser. As she watched him with his scissors in hand, she decided he probably thought he was. George pulled her hair up, he pulled it down. He pushed it toward her face, he pulled it back. It was rare that he got to work on a matron with such a full-length head of hair such as hers he'd told her. Most mature ladies wore their hair short, the fashion for the older ladies.

Beth didn't know if she should thank him or be insulted. She didn't have time for either. Without questioning how she wanted her hair styled, George made his decision. Her hair would be piled on top of her head, with curls pouring down the sides of her face. Without further discussion, his creation began. Beth had been warned by her friend that she was not to speak to George while he was creating her personal hair style, so Beth remained very quiet for the entire three-hour session. When George was finally done, he knew he'd created a masterpiece, and everyone under his command raved over his creation. Beth thought she looked like some silly twit out of a historical romance novel, and almost expected some white teethed hunk of masculinity to come riding in the door on a mighty stallion, but she didn't say anything to George. She praised him along with the others and smiled as he strutted like a proud peacock. Silently, she wondered if George knew Mr. Enrique. The thought of those two together brought on a severe case of the giggles, which George ended with a sharp glare.

Tomorrow would be a quick hour flight to Dallas and she'd be there. Beth sighed as she crawled into her bed, trying to keep her head straight so those strange banana curls wouldn't flop around her face. A million thoughts raced through her mind as she listened to the wind roar outside her window. The TV had forecast a bad storm, but that was south of Tulsa. "Everything would be fine," she told herself. "No need to worry."

Her dark eyes closed and immediately she found peaceful, deep sleep. The nightmares that controlled her sleep for so many years were gone now, never brave enough to venture into her dreams again. She had fought the demons and had won. RJ Scott had seen to that.

Beth found an unassigned seat on the small turboprop plane heading to Oklahoma City for passenger pickup and then on to Dallas. She settled into the small seat to relax and was glad she'd found this flight so reasonable. After the OKC pickup, it was a straight shot to Dallas.

The departure on the 70-passenger plane was a bit rough, and the captain kept warning them to keep their seat belts on, while the stewardess kept doing her little dance, swinging around the oxygen masks, issuing instructions on what to do in case of an emergency. The plane dipped. It rolled. They flew higher, then lower. Finally, the captain announced they'd be landing in OKC shortly.

After what seemed like a very long wait for takeoff, the Captain was on the speaker again. "Ladies and gentlemen: The storm and winds in Dallas will not allow a safe landing into Dallas at this time. We will allow everyone off of the plane until we can determine the safety of the flight. Thank you, for flying with Tentwosix Easy-Fly Airlines".

"What?" she asked the small dark lady seated next to her, "What does this mean?"

"Don' know", the Mexican lady answered. "My kids book me this ticket. Don' want to go to Dallas, no how." And then she was gone, happily exiting the aircraft.

Inside terminal D65 she approached the desk clerk for information just as he was leaving his post. "Where are you going?

What about our flight?"

"I don't know, lady. I was told there's a big storm in Dallas, and there's no way our small plane can handle that storm. Just get some lunch and come back and wait. That's all I can say. You can't control the weather. Next flight out will be at two o'clock p.m. and thank you, for flying Tentwosix Easy-Fly Airlines."

Beth called RJ's house and talked to his answering machine, again. She'd probably be on the three o'clock flight instead; hoped that'd be all right.

She grabbed a sandwich and a glass of tea at the snack bar, and after finishing the dry chicken salad sandwich, she walked the airport until one o'clock. At one thirty, she approached the young man at the terminal and inquired about boarding. "No," she was told, "no one could board." He was there to tell the folks that there was a real bad storm over Dallas coming up from the Gulf Coast and that it had done a lot of damage in the Houston area. She'd just have to wait until the six p.m. flight. "And thank you for flying Tentwosix Easy-Fly Airlines."

Beth called RJ and visited with the answering machine again, stating that she'd be there around seven p.m. At five p.m., she returned to the small waiting area. At five thirty, the young man returned. "When do we leave?" she asked.

"No flights out tonight to Dallas 'cause it's flooding there," he said. You do realize that six p.m. is the final flight of the day, don't you. And thank you for flying Tentwosix Easy-Fly Airlines".

"Final flight for the day?" she asked. "I wasn't told there were no flights after six o'clock."

"Can't you read the sign, lady? We only fly at ten am, two pm, and a final flight at six p.m. That's why you got your ticket so cheap. And thank you, for flying Tentwosix Easy-Fly Airlines."

"Well, what am I supposed to do now?" She asked, aware of the pronounced irritation in her voice.

"Don't know, lady. Maybe get a hotel room here at the airport if there's one available. So many flights have been cancelled to Dallas. You'd better hurry and check on a room".

As Beth hurried away from his final "thank you", nonsense, it occurred to Beth to call Adam and Kathy. They probably hadn't left for Dallas yet, and she'd ride with them. Why hadn't she called them before? Oh yes, she'd wanted to get there a day early.

Quickly, she dialed Adam's car phone and learned that they were almost in Dallas as they spoke. They'd left early due to the storm that was coming in from Dallas. Hadn't she heard about the storm?

Placing the wall phone back on its hook, she hurried toward the main gate. Maybe she could still get a hotel room for the night.

Watching the Friday morning weather channel on the TV in her hotel room, it appeared the storm had cleared in Dallas. It had moved up to Oklahoma City. Beth knew she couldn't let herself panic. That wouldn't help anything. Calling TentwoSix Easy Fly Airlines, she got the recording, "All flights out of Oklahoma City for Friday had been cancelled." And of course, "Thank you for flying Tentwosix Easy-Fly Airlines.

"Now, what?" She wondered out loud, trying to overcome the increasing panic. Giving it some serious thought, she wondered if the major airlines could still make it to Dallas. Beth started dialing numbers and pushing buttons for English over Spanish and for all the other crazy numbers to answer her questions, only to get a recording saying there was a delay. She repeatedly hit "redial", and eventually, a young man answered for the major airline.

"Yes, certainly we can get you to Dallas." He said, and Beth felt a wave of relief come over her. "You'll leave at three o'clock this afternoon, fly into St. Louis, Missouri, where you'll have a five hour layover. You'll arrive in Dallas at nine-thirty p.m."

"Nine thirty!" she groaned. She was going to miss her own daughter's wedding. *Good God!*

The young man sympathized with her, and when she said she could've driven there faster, he asked why she hadn't. "Just rent a car at the airport and go," he said. "You'll be there in six hours, tops."

"Six hours in Hell", she gasped to herself, knowing she'd be in a strange car, driving alone on unknown roads for hundreds of miles. The old familiar panic tried to paralyze her thinking as usual, but she knew how disappointed Anne would be if she didn't make it to her wedding. And regardless of his attitude toward her, she still wanted to see RJ. Quickly she regained her new found confidence.

Again she called Tentwosix Easy-Fly Airlines, and someone actually answered the phone. She needed her clothes, she told them. She was driving to Dallas. Where were her clothes? In the belly of the plane? Of course, they were. And of course, she knew they had no way to get her clothes without unloading all the other passengers' clothes in the pouring rain. Didn't she realize this?

"No way, lady," she was told. Your clothes are going to Dallas with or without you. And thank you for flying Tentwosix Easy Fly Airlines."

She hung up the phone in defeat, wondering how in God's name did this happen to her.

On her walk to the car rental, she found a telephone stall, and called RJ's phone number again to report her latest schedule change. Naturally, no one bothered to pick up the phone, so she visited with the answering machine knowing Juanita was standing right next to it. She wanted to kill the woman, but instead in her sweetest voice, she asked if someone would contact Anne to bring her a dress to wear to the wedding. Anything. It didn't matter.

Luckily, she was able to get a car at the car rental, but she didn't have a choice of style, they informed her. She should have rented the car sooner, but lucky for her, they still had one available. It was a 1989 red, two-door Geo Metro Hatchback, four cylinders for good gas mileage, not a big luxury vehicle, but it would get her there.

Luxury was an understatement. As she pulled the little two-seater out of the car lot, it stalled. She started the car again and managed to keep it going until she got on the interstate headed toward Dallas. As she hit a pothole on the interstate, the gas gauge on the panel flashed the empty warning. She glared at the panel and it flashed an angry red signal back at her. She'd checked the gas gauge when she left the auto rental, and it said it was full. The gas gauge didn't work. Of course, it didn't work.

Seeing a "Food and Gas" exit a few miles down the road, Beth followed the exit signs off the interstate to the small gas station and pulled up to the pump. As she exited the car, the rain pummeled down on her like she was standing under a waterfall. As she fought to pump the gas, the wind grabbed her scarf and shot it off into the distance. Pounded by the wind and rain, George's masterpiece was gone. The strange banana curls flattened into long tendrils around her face, and the hair piled on top of her head sagged like a deflated bladder. Muddy water filled her tennis shoes, and as she turned to put the hose back into the pump, a backlash of gasoline spewed onto her shirt and into her hair. Bracing against the bitter storm, she managed to secure the hose back into the pump. As she quickly turned, she caught her shoulder on a rough spot on the side rearview mirror of the car and tore her plaid shirt at the shoulder.

Beth jumped back inside the little car and holding the door open slightly, poured the water from her shoes, and laid them under the fairly warm heater vent to dry. Shifting her little car into drive, she laid her bare foot onto the gas pedal and pulled back onto the interstate. As she hurried to pick up speed in the merging traffic, she felt her little car swerve as it splashed through the rising water on the interstate. It would be slow-going in this storm, and she prayed the little car would make it through the beating it would be taking. Silently, she added a small prayer for herself.

Chapter 20

RJ had been fuming all week. Somehow Juanita figured out that he and Beth were more than friends, and Juanita hadn't pulled any punches, telling him how wrong he was getting involved with a respectable woman, him being a married man. He'd insisted they were just friends, but somehow Juanita knew better. She said he acted like a dog in heat when talking to Beth Saturday morning, so when he talked to Beth later that day, he tried to sound indifferent to her to keep Juanita's nose out of his business. Being unfamiliar with the female emotions, he had no idea how his indifference affected Beth, or how badly he'd hurt her. All he knew was that Juanita was listening to every word he said to Beth, and he sure as hell didn't want to hear her preaching any longer. Besides, he knew Juanita was probably right about him. She usually was. Since she and her family had moved in with him years ago, she'd treated him like a big sister. Now she was a big sister who couldn't keep her nose out of his personal business.

Sitting in his wicker rocker on his porch, he was livid with anger and sick with worry. He ignored the lady sun forcing her way through the cloudy morning and paid no attention to the hummingbirds delight in the red-sugar-water feeders hanging from the porch. All he could think about was Beth, and how it could never be right between them. Was it really going to be so bad for them like Juanita said? Would Beth eventually hate him because she'd given up her respectability for him? Him, a married man. Could he live with himself knowing the shame he'd brought on that innocent woman? He could become the greatest lover in all time, and she'd enjoy him for a while, but eventually, she'd regret what he'd taken from her. Eventually, she'd hate him. That's what Juanita said.

Why was it that every damn time he'd been given something decent, it was ripped away from him? RJ half-heartedly scratched the ears of his two boys as he wondered about his sorry situation. Was his life just a damned big joke? Did the big man above just need someone on earth to play with, laughing while he struggled?

RJ was not a man to feel sorry for his lot in life, and his

personal inner whining was getting on his own nerves. He'd always been a man of action, one who could make decisions quickly and accurately, and his decision now was that he had to get off his butt and correct this miserable situation.

RJ walked around the back of his house and jumped in Big Red. He had to be done with Carla. It wasn't fair to Beth. He knew Beth would accept him for who he was and that's what bothered him. Beth was such an innocent. She had no idea how bad it had been in his life or how bad it could get. Some folks around Poke still remembered Carla and blamed RJ for the breakup, claiming his temper was the reason. Although most people just minded their own business and didn't give a damn one way or another, there were still a couple of his old enemies who wouldn't let it die. They said he was hot-headed, worked too much, and was always gone. She just got lonely. Yeah, he'd heard the gossip, lived with it every day, but that's all it was. Gossip.

RJ never offered any reason for the split with Carla, because it was nobody's business but his own. Besides, he'd never tell anyone how shamefully she'd neglected Jason. Let them say what they wanted about him. As long as Jason never knew about his mother's neglect, he didn't give a damn what they said.

When Jason was little, he'd asked about his real mother, but he was told that she was gone. Nothing, more. After Jason got older, somehow he got the idea that his mother had died, so RJ never told him otherwise. Neither did anyone else. No one dared interfere in RJ's business. Most everyone in Poke knew RJ Scott as a fair, decent man who'd help anyone in need. Still, there were a few unfortunate folks in Poke who'd crossed his path in a deceitful manner and learned the fury of his temper, eventually suffering his legendary revenge.

Starting the engine in Big Red, RJ left his two boys staring at him as he drove down the driveway away from his house. He'd go to Dallas and confront Jason's mother for the last time. This time he'd demand a divorce. He'd always given in to Carla because of Jason, but now Jason was a grown man with a child of his own on the way. If Carla contacted Jason, then so be it. It was time for Jason to grow up, time for Beth to heal, and time for him to live.

RJ gunned Big Red down the two lane highway toward Dallas

and wished the old girl could go a bit faster, but he knew he didn't dare push Big Red. Cursing softly, he maintained his slow, steady speed, just like he'd have to do on the interstate to Dallas, but RJ couldn't complain. She was an old gal, just needed some new parts. It wasn't her fault.

As they neared Poke, RJ saw the "Big Goldie's Roadhouse" sign beckoning to all the lonely. Gearing down, he pulled off into the familiar site. Today he was making a break with his past and his past included Big Goldie's Roadhouse.

It had been a sunny, beautiful Friday morning, perfect for a wedding that evening. The storms that caused such havoc the past week had vanished, leaving the fresh clean promise of peace. As RJ pushed past the "closed" sign and opened the door of Goldie's Roadhouse, the sunshine flooded the dark cinder-block building, appearing to uplift the haven for lost souls into a similar realm of peace. As the door closed, the sunshine vanished along with the illusion.

Adjusting his eyes to the dark shadows, RJ spotted the heavy woman playing solitaire in her personal booth far away from the bar, her miniature black poodle staring adoringly at his massive owner. In the light of the small booth lamp, Goldie moved the cards to and fro, the twisting of the many cheap, gold bracelets tarnishing her portly wrists, further decoration of her gaudy style. Even in the early morning, she wore a bright red lipstick that simply accented the broken smile that lived upon her ghostly face, a fact she didn't seem to realize. Maybe she just didn't care. It was her business.

Seeing RJ, the little dog raced toward him and danced around his feet, eager for the ear scratching he knew he'd get from the gentle, big hands. RJ reached down and picked up the little dog, scratched his ears and placed him next to Goldie.

"How you doing, Goldie"? RJ asked as he sat down in the booth across from her.

"Can't complain, RJ," she answered, wondering what he was doing there so early.

"I've come to turn in my key, Goldie. Don't need it anymore", he told the massive woman with the yellow hair and the twisted smile. He reached over and placed the key on the table between them.

"Well, damn, RJ", she laughed ignoring the key. "What'd you do? Go find yourself a live-in hooker? "

"Nope," he said, flashing his big grin. "Found my woman, the only woman in the world for me."

"Don't want to bust your bubble, RJ, but unless there's something I don't know, you still got that damn Carla dragging around your neck. It's not Carla is it?"

"Oh, hell, no, Goldie. But right now, I'm on my way to Dallas to see Carla and this time she's gonna give me a divorce. This time damn it, whatever it takes, I'll do it."

"Well, RJ, I sure wish you the best of luck, but I doubt luck will do you any good. That damn Carla is just a nasty leach and she won't let you go till she's sucked you dry. Hell, that woman would die before she'd let you go RJ, and you know it too." Goldie knew she'd said too much about Carla, but couldn't stop herself.

RJ leaned over and petted the small dog that was now standing on top of the table. "I've got to do something, Goldie. My woman is a respectable widow woman, and I won't allow her name to be tarnished in this mess with Carla. Jason's a grown man now, so she can't hurt him like when he was a little boy, and that's what I always worried about. Her hold's broken on me Goldie, and by God, this time she's giving me a divorce. I'm done with that woman."

Goldie remembered RJ mentioning that Jason's fiancé's mother was a widow woman. Was this the widow he was willing to give up his key for? Goldie knew she had to be the one. No other widow women around Poke or Dallas, for that matter, had ever caught RJ's eye. It seemed pretty strange to Goldie that the mama and the daughter had both caught the elusive Scott men. In fact, it seemed damned strange. Maybe the mama and daughter had planned it, like she'd seen on TV some time back. Maybe this was all a scam. For RJ's sake, Goldie knew she'd have to get to the bottom of this situation.

"You say this gal of yours is a respectable widow woman, RJ. Then why is she cozying up with a married man?" Goldie lifted her painted eyebrows and stared cautiously through her thick mascara. "RJ, you did tell her you were married didn't you?"

"Well, of course I did, Goldie. But, she said she didn't care about that. She just wants to be with me." RJ could feel himself getting aggravated, again. He'd been forced to listen to Juanita rant about Beth and him.... about Beth's morals, and in his case, Juanita had emphasized his "*lack of morals*". Now Goldie decided she had to put in her two cents.

Goldie folded her cards and stacked them neatly in front of her, her lower red lip drooping to expose a gold tooth. "Now, RJ, stop and think about the situation for a minute. You've just met this woman. Hell, I'll bet you don't even know her maiden name."

"Boudreau! Damn it. She was a Boudreau from Illinois."

"Okay, RJ, so you know bits and pieces about her, but RJ, what do you really know about this woman? What decent woman is going to throw away her respectability by being with a married man?" Goldie poured RJ a cup of coffee and set it in front of him. "I've been shunned by everybody from here to Dallas for being what I am, but I admit it, RJ. I'm a whore. I gave up my respectability a long time ago, and I've accepted my fate. Now you tell me you have a respectable widow woman willing to give up her reputation just to shack up with a married man. Hell RJ, folks will shun her, call her a loose woman. Some will call her a whore, just like me."

"Damn it! It's not the same thing, Goldie."

"What's the difference, RJ? Just because you don't leave money to bed her, is that the difference RJ?" Goldie watched RJ for a few moments, but he didn't return her look. She knew she'd hurt him and insulted his woman, but Goldie was determined to figure out what it was the woman wanted out of RJ. It was better for him to be hurt a little now than for him to be hurt like he was when he first came to her place after the miserable Carla fiasco.

"Well, how's she in bed, RJ?" Goldie asked, propping her large doubled chin on her chubby hands and staring at him in wonder. He ignored her look, but she could see from his frown, she was getting some response from him.

Goldie pushed on. "Is she just horny? If that's the case, then sleep with her on the side and don't let folks ever know. Maybe she'll get her jollies cooled off pretty soon, and she can go on back to her little respectable world of suffering widow. In the meantime, you can crank off a bunch of freebies with her." Goldie smiled, knowing she was getting to him. “Uh, you did say she was good in bed, didn’t you, RJ?”

“Goldie! You’re getting awful damn nosey. I’m not telling you about my personal life with Beth.”

“Oh, I don’t care what you do with her, RJ! My point is that if she is such a good, respectable woman, there must be something wrong with her, if she’s willing to be with a married man who hasn’t a chance in hell of marrying her. Now back to my question. How’s she in bed?" Goldie watched as RJ scowled at her question. "You have bedded her, haven’t you, RJ”.

RJ took a sip of the hot coffee and set the thick, white mug back on the table. He hesitated for a moment, his blue eyes concentrating on the black coffee. “Well, not exactly.”

Goldie threw back her head in laughter, her broken mouth forming a red sideways triangle upon her layered face. “What in the hell does that mean, RJ, ‘not exactly’? Either you have or you haven’t”.

Goldie watched as RJ stared into the bottom of the coffee cup, his blue eyes lost somewhere in thought. She knew his woman had to be up to something and RJ just couldn’t see it, just like when he’d been taken in by Carla. Goldie hated to see it happen to him again. He was a real good man and didn’t deserve more crap. Then it occurred to Goldie that the woman might just be playing hard to get with RJ. She’d pretend to be a sweat innocent widow, and then when she’d hooked him, she’d dump him and take him for everything he’d worked so hard to accomplish. Maybe that was the widow’s plan.

Reaching over to him, Goldie slipped her fat stubby hand with the flaming fingernails over his, and spoke to him softly. “Sugar, I know you’re lonely, but you just met this woman. You don’t even know her, RJ. She just might think you got some money and then you’d be stuck again, like with Carla.”

“Hell, Goldie, she thinks I’m some sort of a backwoods cowboy and she still wants me, chicken shit on the porch and pigs running through the house. She thinks she’s gonna support *me*, for God’s sake.” Goldie watched RJ’s face come alive just thinking about that woman. Goldie sighed deeply, knowing she was losing this battle. Still, she pushed on.

"Well, I'm glad to hear that, RJ, 'cause you don't need another Carla. But, if you haven't bedded her yet, isn't that sort of like buying a pair of shoes without trying them on? She just might turn out to be one of them cold, frigid gals, and you know you couldn't handle that life, so there you'd be alone again. So, just keep the key, RJ. You can make up your mind later if you want to return it or not." Opening the large fingers of his hand, she laid the key back into RJ's hand and then closed his fingers back around it.

"Whatever happens, I'll take my chances with her, Goldie. For the first time in my life, I've found something with a woman that means more to me than sex."

Poor dumb bastard, Goldie thought. RJ had gone and gotten himself in love and didn't even know it.

RJ leaned over to the large woman and as gently as she'd given him the key, returned it back to her hand and closed her portly fingers around it. With his fingers wrapped tightly around hers, RJ and Goldie stared at each other for a minute in the wordless communication of long-time friends.

"Thanks for the coffee, Goldie," RJ said as he stood and patted her little dog sleeping contentedly sprawled across the table. As he started toward the door, he stopped, reached into his billfold and placed a wad of money on the bar. "Give this to the gals, Goldie."

"I will, RJ," Goldie answered, moving her large body from the booth and crossing toward the bar to collect the money. "Sure hope things go like you want them." Goldie took RJ's key and moved it onto a peg with a few other keys. "I think I'll just retire your key, RJ, along with a few of my favorite old boys that have passed on." Goldie's crooked mouth melted into the smile of the sideways triangle and her broken face flushed as RJ grinned at her.

As RJ closed the door behind him, Goldie knew that wasn't the last time she'd see him. Carla wouldn't let him go and that widow woman of his wouldn't wait forever. She'd give up on RJ and go on back to her own respectable life. RJ would be alone, again. That's just the way it was for RJ Scott. That's the way it had always been. She'd keep his key ready for him....for when he returned.

Staring out the tinted window, past the silent "BEER" sign in the front window of Big Goldie's Roadhouse, Nora Jean Desmond watched RJ as he climbed into his big red truck. She knew he didn't remember the first time he'd met her so many years ago. It was at his wedding, when he married her sister, Carla. He didn't remember her, and she'd never told him. That's the way she wanted it. Nobody from Poke needed to know who she was or anything about her real life. She was Goldie, the local "Madame". That's all they needed to know. It was nobody's business.

Of course, when RJ met her twenty-five years ago, she was a young pretty girl. Some even said she was a real beauty. But that was before her stepmother broke her face with that hot poker, and before her Pa sent her to live with his sister in Dallas. It was before she ran away from her aunt's abusive husband and learned survival on the streets of Dallas.

Way back then, her young, fresh body was desirable to some of the men, but after she'd been used enough, they lost interest in her because of her face. Even at that young age, she was a clever business woman. Nora Jean organized the other young girls on the street and eventually purchased a house for them to work from. As time passed, she prospered, and through careful management of the girls and thc moncy, shc had a thriving businccss that included some of Dallas's biggest names. But Nora Jean missed the community of Poke, and as soon as she had a chance, she sold her place in Dallas and moved back to Poke. In the beginning, when she first took over the roadhouse, she had no intention of starting a "stable", but as time went on she could see the need for the lonely ones. There were a lot of lonely men back then, and RJ Scott was one of them. After giving the idea some thought, her business sense took over and she and "Big Goldie's Roadhouse" were born.

She remembered the second time she'd seen RJ so many years ago. It was the first time he'd visited her place sometime after the Carla-split. She remembered thinking then that not only was RJ a magnificent stallion of a man, he was a real gentleman, quite a combination. That's when she offered him a key to her back room and he'd eagerly accepted it.

Goldie knew he'd thrown Carla out sometime after the boy was born because Carla had come begging money from her. Carla claimed Nora Jean owed her money for taking care of her after their mother died, but Goldie told Carla to go to hell, and reminded her sister that she'd never taken care of anybody except her own lazy ass. The best she could offer Carla was a job working on her back as she'd been forced to do. Take it or leave it, she'd told Carla. Carla left it and went on to contrive a comfortable life for herself leaching off the innocent.

Goldie never saw her sister again until a few months ago, when Carla called and asked her to come to her apartment in Dallas. Carla said she was terribly sick and thought she was dying. She said she wanted to give Nora Jean a key and the code to the private entrance in the back of the apartment building. If anything happened to her, Goldie could get into her apartment without anyone seeing her. Goldie thought that was odd, but her sister was dying, so she went to see her.

After Goldie arrived at her apartment, it took Carla so long to open the door, Goldie thought she'd already died. When she did open the door, Goldie could see that Carla was stoned, drunk, or both. Goldie waited while Carla washed her wrinkled face with cold water and hoped Carla wouldn't forget what she wanted to tell her. Slurring her words and jumbling her speech, Carla pulled herself together long enough to give Goldie the written combination to her personal safe. She told Goldie that if anything should happen to her, she was to burn the manila envelope that was in the safe without looking inside at the contents. Carla made her promise that she wouldn't open it on the word of a "sister". Goldie promised Carla, but not on the word of a "sister". She promised as the Madame, who'd been taught by the world that promises didn't mean a damn thing unless it was to someone you loved. She didn't love her "sister".

It seemed to Goldie that Carla appeared much older than she really was. Her stunning blond hair, once worn loose and shimmering down her backside, was now gray, ragged, and frazzled thin. Her skin was wrinkled and yellowed, like hard wax dripped from a lighted candle. Her body, once voluptuous, hung like deflated crust attached to her bones. Her skeletal finger no longer carried the weight of the gaudy ring that Carla, shameless in her lies, insisted Nora Jean had stolen from their stepmother many years ago. Back then Carla was older and bigger than Norma Jean, but not once did Carla try to help her ward off the blows, as her stepmother slammed her again and again with the flaming hot poker, destroying her face and leaving her with an ugliness that repulsed and appalled others.

As Goldie watched her sister sleep, finding relief in the dangerous concoction of drugs and alcohol, Goldie opened the small safe. Without any qualms of guilt, she unfastened the ties of the manila envelope. Inside, she found a bank book, three legal papers, and a copy of Carla's will leaving everything she owned to Jason Scott. The bank book showed a balance of one hundred thousand dollars. The interest hadn't been updated in years, so Goldie knew the account on file at the bank was worth much more.

Carefully placing the bankbook and the will back into the safe, she read the three legal papers. The first one was a record of Carla's marriage to RJ Scott in 1973. The second one was a death certificate for a stillborn infant girl, Misty Barham, born to Carla and Ronald Barham in 1971. The third certificate was a certificate of marriage of Carla Desmond and Ronald Barham in 1971, obtained a few months before the baby girl was born.

Goldie put the envelope back into the safe and locked it up securely. With a heavy drop, she set her large body down across from this person who called herself her "sister". Somberly, Goldie studied Carla as she found retreat from her pain and her tormented mind with the deadly cocktail. Goldie knew first hand, what a cruel, selfish person this woman had been all her life, and it didn't surprise Goldie that Carla had wound up like she was. She'd trudged through life, smashing others in the miserable storms of her own creation. Now she was forced to live in her own wretched desolation.

As Carla coughed and struggled for breath, Goldie could see how weak and vulnerable her sister had become. She almost sympathized with her. When Goldie first entered Carla's apartment, Carla begged her sister to help her put an end to her life. Carla said she was afraid she'd botch her own death and make everything worse. Goldie was appalled that Carla would ask such a thing of her. Yeah, her sister's suffering would be ended, but what if somehow the blame for Carla's death got put on her? She'd spend the rest of her life in jail, but Goldie knew her sister didn't care about what might happen to her. Carla just wanted to end her own pain. Heatedly, Goldie refused, but in truth, Goldie knew Carla didn't deserve the peace of death. She was reaping exactly what she deserved. Her own place in hell. And Goldie was content to leave her there.

Shaking her canary hair in dismay at the memories of her selfish sister, Goldie watched RJ's old, red truck travel down the two-lane highway and disappear. For months, Goldie hadn't given Carla another minute's thought until RJ mentioned her a few minutes before. Even though she knew she'd be the first to be contacted on Carla's death, she was surprised that Carla was still alive. She'd been so bad off the last time Goldie had seen her, she couldn't imagine how Carla had hung on through that night, let alone three months more.

Goldie wondered about her sister and the man she'd blackmailed over the years. She wondered if Carla had given any thought to her own son; what he looked like, how he did in school, did he have a happy life? Goldie shook her head in disgust. How could any mother abandon her own child without giving a moment's thought to the welfare of the child?

RJ loved that boy, though, and he was so proud of him. Since the boy started first grade, RJ brought her school pictures of Jason. He nearly burst with pride while she raved over the latest pictures, showing them around the bar to anyone who would bother to look. RJ had no idea how much she cherished those pictures of her nephew, and he'd never know how she'd sit alone nights, comparing Jason's changing looks from year to year. Under each year's new picture, she'd kept a running diary of everything RJ told her about the boy over the year. Eventually, she had to add more pages to the book. Jason and RJ were her own people. They just didn't know it. It was best that way.

Goldie's gnarled smile turned to a frown, thinking about her useless sister. Instantly, the memory of the manila envelope in Carla's safe filled her mind. Why did Carla want the envelope destroyed without anyone reading the contents? What information was so important in that envelope that it had to be burned on her death? Deep wrinkles filled the scars of her face as she wondered what her horrible sister was hiding.

Holding her little dog close to her, Goldie stroked the hair under his rhinestone collar, and wondered what happened to the Barham man. Where was the divorce paper from him? Did they have the marriage annulled, or did the Barham man die? If so, where were the papers? Carla had papers on everything, even an ancient bank passbook that was obsolete. Surely, she'd hang on to important papers that released her from her marriage to Barham. That's the only way she could marry RJ....or could Carla be so low, that she'd marry one man while still married to another?

Goldie clutched her large chest as she gasped in understanding. Carla could never divorce RJ. She'd never been legally married to him. RJ's son, his pride, was a bastard child. If RJ ever found out about Jason's illegitimacy, he'd consider that an unforgiveable betrayal to his son's honor. Discovering Carla's greed was the cause of his son's lack of birthright, Goldie knew RJ's temper would be uncontrollable. She'd seen that temper recently at her bar and could only imagine his rage when he found out about Jason and what Carla had done.

Damned if it wouldn't be just like Carla to use RJ's rage to end her suffering. She didn't have the guts to take her own life to ease her pain, but she'd have no qualms about using RJ as an instrument of her death. She'd goad RJ, torment him, and scream lies at him. She'd claim that Jason wasn't even his son. That would be the lie that would send RJ over the edge. A hearty push, even a harsh slap could crumble the frail Carla. RJ would unwillingly kill Carla, and there wasn't a damn thing that Goldie could do to stop it. Even now, he was puttering down the road in his old, red truck on his way to the end of his freedom....just like an innocent lamb to the slaughter. Goldie knew she could never let that happen to RJ. After all, he was one of her own people, and Goldie always took care of her own.

Chapter 21

RJ was driving her insane and had been since he returned from Oklahoma. Juanita had a pretty good idea what had him all crazy, but she knew she'd best leave it alone for now, anyway. Hurrying across the garage from the kitchen exit, Juanita opened the door of the blue Ford Bronco, grabbed the silver sidebar over the driver's door, and pulled her petite body into the small truck. For a woman well over sixty-years old, she was still spry and more active than many younger women, a fact Juanita wore proudly. Placing her brown hand on the gear shift, she shifted her small SUV into drive and raced down the winding driveway of the ranch.

The wet Texas ground was still soft from the week's past storms, and the small truck bogged slightly in the jagged fresh white and gray gravel laid during the past week. Putting the little truck into four-wheel drive, Juanita made a mental note to have someone smooth that gravel before the wedding ceremony. She didn't want any of those snooty city folks stuck out there with them. Satisfied in her memory, she hit the button on her car visor, opening the closed steel gate and pulled onto the county road that would take her to Poke. Checking the gate in her rear-view mirror, she saw the words "Scott's End Ranch" lock together, and knew it was closed securely.

Knowing there was a straight road ahead for a few miles, she rammed the gas pedal down and felt her small truck surge ahead. As she traveled the two-lane highway passing the sprawling subdivision across from RJ's ranch, it occurred to her that she barely noticed that place anymore, even though it had once been hers and Luis's land. But, that was all in the past. A hundred years ago, so it seemed....when Jason was small. Jason, her precious little white baby, the only baby she hadn't had to birth. Oh, how she'd come to love that little boy. Tonight he was getting married and soon he'd have his own child, he and Anne. Anne seemed like a fine girl and Jason adored her. They'd be good together, but Anne's mother was another story, Juanita was sure of that. From what she'd gathered on the phone and the way RJ was so smitten with her, she knew Anne's mother was up to no good.

Juanita wiped the beads of perspiration from her forehead with a tissue over the visor and placed the tissue in the side pocket of her blue chambray shirtwaist. Shaking her head in the early morning heat, she pushed the electric window controls to wide open and welcomed the feel of the breeze blowing through her short, dark gray hair, cooling her head and soothing her thoughts.

Again, her mind drifted back to Anne's mother. RJ said that Anne's mother didn't have clothes for the wedding. What a joke. Her only daughter getting married, and she didn't have any clothes for the wedding? What sort of a mother was that? He said her luggage was stuck in the belly of the plane in Oklahoma City. How could that possibly happen? Anne's mother was no fool. She just told RJ that story so he'd buy her a new outfit. As besotted as he was with that woman, RJ would buy her anything she wanted, just like he did for that last hussy he brought home.... Carla.

As she sped the few miles toward Poke, she remembered the first time she'd met "Miss Carla" as the horrible woman insisted Juanita address her, like she was someone special.

Everyone in town, except RJ, knew he was just the flavor of the month for Carla, and everyone in town knew she was just after a free ride on someone else's hard work. So, when she came up pregnant by him, as she claimed, he married her. RJ expected them to be a normal family and raise a bunch of kids, something he'd always wanted, so he built a big house and moved Carla into it. RJ knew nothing about women and never dreamed a woman could be so deceitful.

Carla lay in bed all day long, claiming to be sick carrying his child. RJ couldn't or wouldn't see through her, so RJ hired Juanita to keep the house clean and fix the meals. She did it too, even though she had five kids and Luis to care for.... and her own poor, little, sickly baby.

Juanita shook her head in disgust remembering the past, but she knew it wasn't RJ's fault. He worked so hard and was gone so much. He didn't have time to take care of that big house, so she took care of RJ's home, dragging her sick baby with her. After a while, her baby got so ill she had to give up her job with RJ. Remembering back to that time, so many years ago, Juanita could feel the tearing at her heart as she thought of her youngest son....

such big heart problems, such a sweet, little boy, such a tiny casket.

She and Luis had spent every cent they could beg or borrow trying to save the child, but he died anyway. Sometime after that, the man from the mortgage company told them they would take their place if they didn't pay what they owed and all that interest. He said Luis had signed some sort of a balloon note and now it was due. "Pay or get out," he'd said. They had two months.

Luis worked two jobs, barely had time to sleep. He couldn't do more. So, she'd walked back over to RJ's again, to see if she could get a job cleaning, cooking, and helping with their little baby, Jason; anything, so she could help save their home.

Juanita recalled that awful day when she walked into RJ's house, after banging on the door for such a long time. It was past noon, and at first, she thought nobody was home, but the kitchen door was ajar. Fearing something was wrong with Carla, she pushed the door open.

In the middle of the kitchen floor sat Jason, not even a year old. Green snot was running down his face and he was buck naked, except for a diaper caked with dark baby poop and soaked with yellow urine. He was smiling a nearly toothless grin as he shoved bits of cracker crumbs into his slobbering mouth with his chubby gritted fingers. His dark hair, his chest, and his dirty legs and toes were covered in cracker crumbs, obvious attempts to feed himself.

As Juanita stared at the dirty little face with the big innocent blue eyes, the sight of the small child overtook her senses. She wiped his nose with a tissue, and without hesitation lifted him from the gritty, kitchen floor, using a large dirty towel to confine his stench. Pulling the small child to her body, tears flooded her vision, a heavy lump swelled in her throat. Lost in the nostalgia of the rubbery softness of her own baby's arms, she smothered Jason with love, a starving animal feasting on the sweet milky odor of his pure baby breath. Ravenous, she buried her nose into his soft, dark hair and sucked in the musky scent of little boy sweat. As the baby squirmed from her tight grip, she regained her senses, offering soothing words of love, and tenderly wiping away the dirty sweat beads around his neck.

Carrying Jason in her arms, she searched for his mother. At first she thought "Miss Carla" had fallen ill and couldn't care for

Jason. Then she found her. The lazy pig was passed out on the sofa with the soap operas playing, a bottle of pills next to her. Juanita remembered how furious she'd been with that awful woman, leaving that dope where the baby could get it.

In total disgust, Juanita shook the glazed woman until she was half awake and told her she was taking Jason home with her. Carla snarled that Juanita better have him back to her house before six that evening, before RJ came home. "And give him a bath. He stinks," she murmured through half-closed lips, rolling her body away from Juanita and continuing her sleep.

So, that had become the routine. As soon as she saw RJ's truck pull out of his gate in the morning, Juanita would race over to his house, get Jason and keep him at her house all day. Before six in the evening, she'd carry him back to RJ's house, race back to her own house across the highway, and watch for RJ's truck to enter his driveway, knowing the boy would be safe when RJ got home.

That extra mouth to feed didn't help Juanita and Carlos' financial problem, but they knew it was only a matter of time before they'd lose their home anyway, so they just did what they could. Exactly two months later, a man came to their house and told them they had to get out within the week. So with heavy hearts, they packed their few things and prepared to leave, knowing they had no place to go.

Juanita agonized over what would happen to Jason without her. With the care she'd given him over the last two months, the boy had grown big, little doubt he was RJ Scott's boy. So, daily, as Juanita fretted over leaving the little boy with his uncaring mother, she'd hold Jason to her breast, frantically trying to force enough mothers' love into him to keep him safe. Nightly, on her hands and knees, she prayed her rosary, begging God in his mercy to take care of the little boy. But even though her faith in God was unwavering, she spent endless nights tossing and turning in anguish. Never, could she imagine the wonder of God's infinitely perfect plan.

A few weeks after they'd been given their eviction notice, on a cold gray afternoon about four o'clock, she saw RJ's pickup pull into his lane. She knew Carla wasn't awake, because Carla only woke when Juanita yelled at her that RJ was on his way home. Propping Jason on her hip, Juanita watched in dread as his truck neared his house. She didn't know RJ Scott very well, but she knew one thing, he would be furious.

Juanita sat down at her kitchen table waiting for the inevitable, and soon there was a heavy knock at her door. Without waiting for her to answer, the door was thrown open so hard the knob hit the side wood panel, shattering it into thousands of little splinters. RJ Scott stood so tall in her doorway that he had to bend down to enter her small kitchen. As he stood scoping out her home, his blue eyes flashing, his breath raging, his face was almost distorted in anger. She held her head down staring at the patterns in her worn linoleum, and prayed he'd go away, but he just walked in.

"You been taking care of my boy all this time?" He growled, his angry blue eyes searing her face. Juanita held her head down and nodded, afraid to speak to the intruding giant towering over her. Uncertain what she should do, she clung to his son sleeping contentedly on her lap, his face buried in her bosom.

It seemed RJ Scott was even angrier than she thought he would be when he found out about the boy, and maybe it was because he was such a big, overpowering man, but she almost feared for her own safety. But her fear quickly subsided, as she watched him gently cradle his son up into his burly protective arms and walk from her house.

Sometime later, she heard his truck pull out of his lane. When she looked over at his house, everything was dark. Early the next morning, RJ was back with Jason. He explained that Carla was gone and he wanted to hire her to babysit for him while he worked.

"What's all that?" he asked, waving his arm at the packed boxes as he held Jason in his other arm.

She explained to him that they were moving because the mortgage company was taking their land.

"Why in the hell didn't you ask me for help?" he yelled. Then, as suddenly as he became angry, he calmed down. "What's the name of the loan outfit?" he asked and as soon as she mentioned the name, he was gone leaving Jason with her.

Later that afternoon, she saw RJ's truck pull into her yard. "Those dirty bastards put the screws to you, lady. They want your place to build a housing development. We'll never get it away from them, now, those sons of bitching thieves." Wincing at his vulgarities, Juanita watched his blue eyes narrow into deep thought. "Give me a day or so, and maybe I can come up with something."

So, that's how it all started. RJ told Juanita what parts of his house he wanted to use for himself and Jason, and she was free to do with the rest what she wanted. The many children RJ had planned for his own life would never be, but the big house he built for them could easily accommodate RJ and his son, Juanita, Luis and their five children. None of her children were small anymore, so everyone had responsibilities.

RJ was the protector, the general overseer, the financial manager, and the person who'd funded her children's college educations. He'd see that they had received good educations, RJ told Juanita, but it would be their responsibility to learn, and to use the knowledge to secure good lives for themselves and their families. And they did.

Luis, without the burden of their place, developed a small landscaping business of his own. In his spare time, he created many gardens around the sprawling house and coaxed them to bloom into picture-perfect masses of color. In the shaded areas of the large courtyard, he created gardens of exotic ferns, topiaries of Boxwoods, Arborvitaes, and Junipers in spiral, square, and round shapes. Purple Hearts, Silver Dust and Lambs Ears settled in giant white clay urns. Baskets of huge variegated Hostas, Caladium, and Snow in Summer captured the essence of nature that Luis created as his offering to the grand home.

Without the stress of providing shelter and food for her five children, Juanita became the undisputed matriarch of the large house that she made into a home. She was a caring sister to RJ, a devoted wife to Luis, and a loving mother to all of them. They became a commune of souls, she thought. No, she remembered, in heartfelt gratitude. They became a family. *God's infinite plan truly was wondrous.*

Although RJ said he'd never contracted to have any water feature installed in the center courtyard, one was installed there anyway. With so many workmen hurrying to finish the home, so Luis, Juanita and their family could move in, no one seemed to remember who or why the fountain came to be installed, or who was to be paid for it. RJ said he knew he'd be paying someone dearly for the statue of the Lady in the Fountain, but after seeing her with her open arms, the cool water flowing around her, and the peace she seemed to offer, RJ agreed that the water feature would stay. "She's just like the rest of us," RJ said, "just another misfit trying to find a home." From that time on, she remained ever vigilant, never faltering in her offering of peace to one and all. The mysterious Lady in the Fountain had found her home. Just like the rest of them.

That's the way it had been for years. Now, all the children were gone and on their own except for her youngest son, Marco, who helped his dad with his small business. Marco cared little for the affluent city life that his brothers, sisters and Jason had accomplished after they graduated. Like his father, Marco seemed content to work with his hands in the fertile soil of Scott's End Ranch.

Juanita halfway hoped RJ could find a woman to share his life. Then again, she halfway hoped he wouldn't. She didn't want him hurt again. He was such a big goof with women. She knew he was lonely, and she knew about that Goldie's place he went for women. She knew about the old suitcase filled with nasty calendar girls exposing indecent parts of their bodies. She knew just about everything there was to know about RJ. So, when he came home from Oklahoma, she knew immediately there was something different about him. For a while, he was in such a foul humor, she thought that Jason and Anne's tricking him into the trip made him angry. After a week or so, though, he seemed to have worked something out within himself, and he became content. Excited, but content.

RJ never mentioned Anne's mother to her, but listening to the two of them on the telephone, she could have sworn there was sparks zooming between them, and it had nothing to do with the phone lines. For the first time that Juanita could remember, RJ sounded giddy, acted playful on the phone with Anne's mother. Then, she'd found that bill on RJ's desk from John's Lawn Service in Tulsa, Oklahoma, for two horribly expensive pots of deep pink Azaleas 'to be placed on either side of the gazebo', whatever a gazebo was. That's when she figured it out. It was Anne's mother.

Before RJ met Anne's mother, he'd locked up Carla's bedroom and never went into it, again. She'd told RJ that it was a waste of space, leaving it vacant the way it was, but he'd answered that he needed it left that way. He'd said it was a reminder to him of his foolishness. He never said anymore and she didn't mention it again.

And then Anne's mother came along. RJ said he and Anne's mother were just friends, but as soon as he discovered she was staying with them, he called the decorators and had every single thing in Carla's old bedroom ripped out and replaced with new. Everything! Wallpaper, furniture, drapes, bedspread! And everything had to be pink. No, "MAGENTA**!**" he'd told the decorators. Now, where in the world did he learn a fancy word like that? Anne's mother, of course.

Juanita pulled her little truck into a lonely parking place and stared at the large painted red bow ribbon over the door of "Elaine's Boutique". She was honestly worried about RJ. Placing the truck in park, she sat quietly for a few minutes gazing down the lonely two-lane street in the small Texas town. She wanted him to be happy, but he'd only known Anne's mother for a short time. He couldn't be in love with her. It was just his overpowering lust again. It was that same lustfulness that had gotten him in all the trouble with Carla. He'd evidently forgotten how bad it could be when he started thinking with his man parts. After she heard the two of them on the phone teasing like a couple of kids, she warned him again.

She thought RJ understood what she was telling him, but evidently he didn't because that very morning, during her heated argument with the Wedding Planner, RJ called her into his office. She couldn't believe it when he asked her to drive into Poke and get Anne's mother a dress for the wedding. "It had to be a dress with long sleeves," he'd said....and a nightgown. He wanted her to pick out a nightgown for a strange woman? Was he insane? She knew she had to set him straight on this woman, and she did.

"No, I don't know her," she'd told him. "But, I do know that either she's a bad woman who's going to hurt you, or she's a good woman who's going to be hurt bad in this whole mess. Because of your wanton lust, are you willing to destroy this woman's life, RJ?" He hadn't answered, just turned from her and stared out into the gardens. As his shoulders drooped, she watched his hands clutch into angry fists. Finally, she heard him breathe a deep sigh in acceptance. He knew she was right.

"I'll take care of it," he mumbled. "Just get her a dress for tonight." And then he added almost in an afterthought. "And don't forget the damned nightgown."

He'd stood there for some time staring at the garden. It was killing her to see him hurt, like his dreams had died right in front of his eyes. She walked to him and put her hand on his arm. "RJ," she whispered, not knowing what else to say. Ignoring her touch, he pushed past her, stomped from the room and left the house. The next thing she saw was his red truck racing down the driveway through the new gravel, tossing it about as though it had no more weight than a flurry of snowflakes. *"God, help him," she prayed. "God, take care of him."*

Juanita rested her head on the leather steering wheel and stared down at the clay-stained mud-mats on the floor. She wished she was smarter. She wished that someone could tell her what to do. Knowing that RJ's story had no solutions, Juanita opened the door of her truck and stretched her legs to meet the street below. Feeling the gripping tensions gnawing at the back of her neck, she pulled her shoulders straight and took a deep breath. As though she were in a trance, sleepwalking, she forced one foot in front of the other until she stood amid the finery of Elaine's Boutique.

RJ had done so many good things for so many people, and yet he'd never asked for anything in return. She'd do anything to make him happy, whatever RJ wanted. RJ wanted this woman.

Juanita searched deep into her heart. She'd get the woman a dress. She'd get her a damn nightgown, too.

It had been a rough drive for Elizabeth. Due to the storms over Oklahoma, she'd been forced to travel unknown detours that took her miles out of her way. At one point of the trip, she'd driven through water that appeared so deep she was certain her little car wouldn't make it, but it did. It amazed her that just a month ago, before she'd met RJ Scott, she would never have undertaken such an incredible unknown journey. But, here she was, Elizabeth, Beth Carlton, traveling down unknown roads in a car that, to say the least, was "questionable".

She'd stopped every hour or so to have any available full serve gas station fill her gas tank and look over the aged engine in the little car, but she'd forgotten about the tires. About 50 miles north of Poke, Texas, she found herself stranded with a blowout. Checking the small donut spare, it appeared to be as flat as the blown one. However, she realized it didn't matter. The jack was broken and she doubted she'd be able to get the worn tire from the rim anyway. Remembering a small town, a mile or so back, she had no other choice but to hoof it back to where she'd seen a small gas station.

The mechanic wasn't busy, so he hauled the little car back to his shop, happily announcing that all her tires were shot. "It wouldn't be good for the car to put on just one new tire," he'd said, shaking his head as though he gave a damn. "Lady, you need all new tires."

Beth took a penny from her purse and placed it into the tread of each tire, not knowing what she was checking for, but remembering she'd read someplace that's what you were supposed to do.

"No, I don't!" she argued. "I need one tire." She could hear him grumbling, so she walked away from him, smiling in her newly acclaimed independence.

As he put on the new tire, Beth put one dollar in a cold drink machine and got nothing. Walking into the small shop, she saw the gum-popping, bleached-blonde woman standing behind the counter watching a small black and white TV.

"I lost money in your machine," she said to the woman.

"Yeah." Was the reply.

"I'd like to get a cold drink," Beth continued.

"There's some cold drinks back in the cooler there".

Beth walked back to the cooler and pulled out a cold bottle of ice tea.

"That'll be one dollar," the woman said.

"But, I just lost a dollar in your machine!"

"That's a vendors' problem, lady", she snipped. "You can write them and get your money back, but I can't give you the money".

Small town friendliness, Beth thought with disgust, as she paid for the drink and walked outside to wait for the car to be finished.

When she'd paid for her drink, she'd seen the telephone sitting idly on the counter, but she dared not ask to use it. She knew what the answer would be.

Outside, while she waited for the tire to be changed, she spotted a telephone booth, and quickly climbed into the ancient booth, glassed walls held together by duck tape. Again she tried to call RJ's house. Again she heard a voice tell her that the number she'd dialed was "no service". Since she had not talked to a live person at RJ's house as of last Saturday, she had no idea how to get to his place. The never-ending trip just couldn't get worse.

Spring had come on with a vengeance of warmth, and the full Texas sun beat mysterious waves of pure heat onto the little car, as though its red color was an unwanted magnet to the energy of the sun. After realizing the air conditioning was useless, Beth opened all her windows and felt the hot air flow through her drenched hair. She was a filthy, smelly mess and she knew it didn't care either....way past the caring point....too tired to care.

Beth shook her head in disgust as she remembered the hours wasted in "George's" expensive salon. She wondered what "George" would say if he could see his creation now. Visualizing his frosty face, she managed to smile.

With a heavy sigh, she thought about the money she'd spent on the green dress that she wouldn't be able to wear and didn't like anyway. Maybe she could take it back and get her money. She still had the tags, somewhere. Where was that receipt? Where did she put it?

Beth thought about Tentwosix Airlines and vowed she'd never fly with them again as long as she lived. She'd write them a nasty letter when she got home, but she knew it wouldn't do any good.

She thought about RJ Scott and her heart skipped a beat until she reminded herself of his cool attitude toward her the last time she talked to him. Some men were just like that. A woman's feelings meant nothing to them, just something to be toyed with. He'd simply played games with her. He was a handsome, desirable man, who probably had beautiful, **young** women throwing themselves at him. Yes, young women would go for his type. There was something about a cowboy, even an old one....even a poor, old one.

She had actually thought, hoped anyway, that they could find a life together. They seemed to fit so well after she'd gotten to know him. Know him! She didn't know him at all. Why couldn't she get it through her silly head that there never was a "they"? Turning her sore neck from side to side, she tried to relieve the aches and stiffness from hours on the road. Finding no relief, she knew for certain that she'd feel this tension until she got back to Oklahoma, and away from RJ. When she got back to Oklahoma, she'd get over her lost dream for them. She'd get over RJ Scott. This time she'd do it.

Chapter 22

Sometime later, Beth found her exit to Poke, Texas. Keeping her tired eyes glued on the solid yellow line of the two lane highway, she crept along doing twenty miles an hour for five miles following an oversized tractor into the town of Poke. After what seemed an eternity, she pulled into a phone booth on the end of the small town. The broken glass in this phone booth was held together by electrical tape.

Putting her last quarter into the slot, she dialed RJ's number. The recorded voice informed her that the number she dialed was listed "no service". The phone kept her quarter. *More small town friendliness.*

Having no idea how to get to RJ's place, she searched for signs of life in the "two stoplight town", right out of early 1900's. Several two-story brick buildings lined the streets, and it was evident that at some time there had been life in this place. It appeared the townspeople had attempted to spruce it up somewhat, painting some of the brick, and putting colorful modern-day awnings up over the few store entryways. As she drove down the vacant street, she noticed the merchants had turned their little white signs on their doors to read "Closed". It was six o'clock. Business was over in the town of Poke, Texas.

Driving through the small town, Beth looked up and down the quiet, vacant street with its early-century stores and sleepy past. A town like this one had to hold a million stories, she thought, all of them circa eighteen hundreds, "old wild west".

Carefully, she searched for signs of life so that she could ask someone, anyone, how to get to RJ's place. At the last stop sign out of Poke, she spotted a small gas station. The thin gray man, wearing soiled gray overalls, had his "closed" sign in his hand as she sped toward him.

"Excuse me, please," she shouted.

"Closed for the day, Lady", he answered. "It's time for me to go home to supper." He turned and eyed her little dirty red car and shook his head in amazement as he turned his back and walked away from her.

Knowing he was her last hope, she put her little car in park and raced after him.

“I don’t want anything,” she yelled, closing in on the man. “But, do you know RJ Scott? I’m trying to get to his house and his phone is out. My daughter is marrying his son tonight, and I don’t know how to get there.”

The man turned and looked at her in amazement. “RJ Scott. Everybody knows RJ Scott. His son’s getting married tonight”.

“Yes, I know”, she continued. “Please, could you just tell me how I can find his place?”

“You’re not from around here, are you?” He lifted a coke can and spit some tobacco juice into it. “You won’t find his house very easy”, he declared. “He lives way out in the country.”

“Can you draw me a map or give me some directions?” she pleaded. “The wedding is supposed to be at seven o’clock and it's almost seven now.

“RJ Scott, you said....his place,” he mumbled, eyeing her disheveled appearance. She saw him wince as she got close to him.

“Please,” she begged.

Flipping the sign around on his door to show his business was “closed”, the old gray man took out a key from his pocket and locked the door. Beth felt her heart sink as he walked away from her. “Well, get in that little car of yours and follow me.” He said. “I’ll take you out to RJ’s place.”

It seemed they’d been traveling for hours on the little two-lane highway, but “Mr. Gray Man” was only traveling about twenty-five mph. Patiently, she followed him in his little dusty gray pickup, until he pulled slightly past an open gate and motioned for her to enter the drive. Pulling through the gate, she noticed the lettering on the large wrought-iron gate. She couldn’t make out what it said, but she wanted to remember the gate. It might be her only exit back to civilization.

As she continued down the road, she noticed in her rear-view mirror, a subdivision had been built on the other side of the two lane highway. In her rear-view mirror, the subdivision grew smaller and smaller as she traveled on the winding gravel road to somewhere

Chapter 23

Softly caressing the delicate embroidered flowers of her teal blue skirt, and carefully checking the buttons on her fitted teal suit top, Juanita took her seat in the spacious courtyard. "The garden," she called this place. Of the many areas of the large home, this was her favorite location. She relaxed her aching body to the soothing sounds of the water surrounding The Lady in the Fountain, who offered comfort and peace to all tired and weary souls. Today, Juanita was certainly a tired and weary soul.

Seated on the bench surrounding the fountain, Juanita leaned back and put her hand into the cool blue babbling water. She wondered if the Lady in the Fountain ever got tired. Smiling, she peered up to the pitched red tile roof overhead, spreading its protective wings over this spot she loved. God had surely blessed this garden.

Peering out of the black wrought-iron double gates of the courtyard, she could see for many miles the land known as Scott's End Ranch. Juanita had been sitting in that exact spot an hour ago, as the first of many luxurious autos made their way up the winding drive. She'd watched each auto as it approached, the valets appearing out of nowhere, eager to assist the guests from their fine autos and to ensure the expensive autos were parked securely. Men in white dinner jackets, black ties, and crisp black trousers graciously took the arms of their ladies dressed in glorious gowns of colors so vivid it nearly took Juanita's breath away. All that finery was a sight to see, and each new auto seemed to bring more elegantly attired guests than the one before.

Now the view from the garden was still, and the only sound to be heard was the rippling water and the sound of the band playing softly at the back of the house. The valets had gone on to other jobs behind the house by the pool where numerous wedding guests sipped the booze from the open bar. Under the porticos surrounding the lengthy yellow, blue and white Spanish-tiled pool, crisp white table linens clothed the large round tables adorned with small gray terracotta urns of yellow and white begonias. The unusual urns would have been Anne's idea, but Juanita was certain RJ had something to do with having flowers that could be replanted in the garden later and not just become garbage. She knew for certain that the silly Wedding Planner wouldn't care what happened to the flowers after he'd had his big show.

It would be a grand wedding, Juanita knew that, but why did Anne insist on hiring the Wedding Planner, anyway? Anne said it was too much work for Juanita to do in just one week, but Juanita knew she could do it with a little help. She had planned to have the wedding in the garden with its stately white pillars, red Spanish stone floor, and all the lovely plants. It would have been perfect to have the minister stand in front of the Lady in the Fountain with Anne and Jason facing the beautiful statue as she offered peace and comfort in the sound of the bubbling water. The garden was a sacred place. Juanita corrected herself. "It **is** a sacred place." That Wedding Planner had no respect, and Juanita was certain he was a blackheart. Maybe even a heathen.

She'd told the wedding planner, she wanted to have the wedding in the garden from the very beginning. "No", he'd told her. "The large Mediterranean furniture, the huge pots of plants and all the trees of the courtyard took up too much room. It wouldn't be practical." He'd said, strutting away from her as though she was just a pitiful nuisance.

"No!" The wedding planner answered to every suggestion she made during the week's events. Finally that morning, she'd gotten angry with the snippy little man. She'd argued profoundly with him when he even refused to use the beautiful garden as a receiving area.

"No!" he answered gruffly. Throwing a measuring tape onto the floor, he shouted at her, "I don't have time for this. Trying to get a wedding together in one week is pure insanity, and I certainly don't have the time or patience to argue with you, the *housekeeper.*"

Juanita was crushed as she watched him rush off to RJ's office. "I am not just the *housekeeper*", she wanted to shout back at him. But she didn't. *I am Juanita. I live here,* she thought instead, clenching her hands to her waist. Juanita remembered how she'd taken care of Jason all those years since he was a baby. She'd become his mother. The only mother he'd ever known. She was a good, loving mother to Jason. And how many times had she tried to steer RJ onto a moral path away from his lustful nature? It hadn't done any good, but she'd tried with RJ. Lord, how she'd tried.

"I am not just the *housekeeper*." She whispered again, remembering the wedding planner's ugly words. "This is my home, too."

Still, the wedding planner's words hounded her as she'd watched from the garden as the first guests arrived. She didn't mean to hide from them. She just wasn't ready to mingle with all those people. When she finally got up enough nerve to walk out to the reception area where they'd all gathered, the glamorous guests ignored her as though she *was* the *housekeeper.*

She'd tried. She really did. But Juanita knew she could never fit in with the fancy guests. Her own children certainly did, though, and now they were laughing and talking like old friends with the guests out by the pool. She was glad they fit in so well. Her children had worked hard to be successful, but she never let them forget that it was through RJ's generosity they were so well educated. Through him they could become professional people and act and dress like the elegant ones in the glorious clothes. Now her children were just like them.

Juanita thought about forcing herself to join the fancy people again, but knew she couldn't do it. She dropped her head and shrugged her shoulders in disgust at her lack of social graces. Her children belonged with those people. She did not. She *was* just RJ Scott's *housekeeper***.**

Accepting this fact, Juanita made up her mind that she wouldn't go near the reception area again until she absolutely had to. She'd stay away from those people as long as she could. She knew RJ didn't care anything about them either. He just kept running back and forth checking the answering machine for word from Anne's mother.

Juanita knew Anne's mother *would fit* in with all those uppity guests. Oh yes, she'd be the mother of the bride, the grand lady of the whole affair. Even now, everyone was waiting for her arrival. Juanita wondered if, just maybe, Anne's mother had planned to be late, so she could make a grand entrance. Probably, she decided.

Juanita pushed out her chin firmly, determined to remember her lowly place in life. She could hear the laughter growing louder as the guests sucked up the champagne and booze from the bar. Even the music seemed louder. If the grand lady didn't get there soon, everyone would be drunk, passed out, and falling into the pool. But that was their problem. The *housekeeper* didn't worry about those things.

Staring out at the road, she could see something coming. It was just a small dot far off on the long winding driveway, but it was moving closer. It seemed to be some sort of a little red car, but it was the ugliest little car she'd ever laid eyes on. Ah yes. This would be RJ's woman, the grand lady, Anne's mother. Juanita watched the little ugly car as it neared the front of the house. One thing for sure, Anne's mother might be a grand lady, but she certainly had a lousy taste in cars. Stepping back into the shadows, so no one could see her through the wrought-iron gates, Juanita stood back to watch her arrival.

Thinking that she'd made a wrong turn coming toward the huge Spanish-styled home, Beth stopped her car and rechecked behind her. Maybe she'd missed a turn, but she hadn't seen a turn. Continuing her drive up the circle drive of the sprawling tan adobe home with the red tile roof, Beth noticed the many porticos surrounding the front of the house, and the many coved windows partially enclosed with black wrought-iron grills. The window grills were similar to the massive double gate that appeared to be the entry to the home.

This couldn't be RJ's home, not this big spectacular place, Beth decided as she looked around for a small building somewhere in the distance. He'd mentioned he had a little shack. This was no little shack. Of course, she didn't expect him to actually live in a little shack, but this place was more than she could have ever imagined even in her wildest dreams. Placing her car in park, she stepped out onto the driveway and heard the sounds of a band playing somewhere behind the house. People were laughing, but she couldn't see anyone.

Out of nowhere, a young Mexican boy approached her, smiling

the innocent grin of a happy child. He wore a small blue print tie, with his long sleeve white shirt, which someone had tried to tuck into his small blue trousers. She smiled as she noticed he was shoeless and only wearing his blue socks. He'd get into trouble for that. Smiling at the little boy, Beth wondered where he'd left his shoes.

"Hi, there", she said to the child. "Is this the home of RJ Scott?"

The little boy shook his head up and down, over and over, grinning happily, as though this was his job. "You want me to go and get him for you?"

"Yes, please," she answered, smiling as she watched him race down another part of the driveway to the back of the home, his white shirt falling from its once neat tuck inside his blue trousers. A typical little boy.

As he ran off, Beth looked at the house in disbelief. It had to be something out of a magazine, a high-class magazine. Where was the old wooden porch? Where were the chickens? Thank God there were none. And no chicken poop either. There had to be some mistakc. Surcly, that dirty, stinky man, she'd first met in Tulsa wasn't the owner of this place. And if he was, why would he let her go on thinking he was some poor backwoods cowboy? He let her make a fool of herself. *Of course, RJ thought it was funny.*

Beth remembered their shopping spree. How he must have enjoyed that day. How he must have gloated over her worry. Leaning against her dirty car, Beth thought how she would love to kill RJ Scott. Yes, she'd definitely kill him....after she saw him. Maybe.

As quickly as he left, the little brown boy reappeared. He was running so fast in his blue socks that the front part of his white shirt had fallen from the tuck in his blue dust-covered trousers, his mother's efforts completely wasted. As he turned the corner of the house RJ appeared, towering far above the small child. As Beth watched RJ stride towards her, she felt her excitement build even though she tried to appear indifferent to him. My God, he was so handsome. His dark gray hair was almost the same gray as the western suit he wore, and as he neared her, she glimpsed the black onyx bolo gleaming over his crisp white shirt. Gray trousers swept neatly over his long, muscular legs, a perfect cut above his gray cowboy boots, the silver toe-tips gleaming in the remains of the lingering sun. He was stupendous.

Watching him come closer, Beth fought to keep from racing toward him, reminding her of the hurt she'd suffered at his indifference to her on the phone. Cautiously, she began to limp toward him, the dried stiffened tennis shoe rubbing against her sore foot. As she and RJ neared each other, Beth stopped and leaned down to untie her malformed tennis shoes, which were forming blisters on her toes.

Seeing that Beth had stopped, RJ stopped. His brow furrowed deep into his rugged face, weighty thoughts conflicting in his mind. Cautiously, he rubbed his sweaty palms against the sides of his crisp gray trousers.

Beth untied her shoes and stood upright, staring at RJ. She held her back straight, her head high, and despite her rank body odor and shattered appearance, she portrayed the perfect lady.

RJ remained motionless, cautious and brooding against the backdrop of the evening sunset, a massive stallion readying himself for battle in an unknown territory.

Worn out and exhausted, Beth was sick to death of this silly game of deception, insistent on truthful answers. She kicked one tennis shoe in one direction and the other in the other direction. She pawed the hot blacktop with her dirty toes, a chaste filly, demanding the attention of the mighty stallion. Hands clasped on her hips, defiantly she glared at RJ daring him to pretend indifference to her again.

RJ and Beth stood staring at each other, an overpowering need erupting inside them, clutching, twisting, fighting to come alive. Without warning, the caution they'd tried so diligently to maintain escaped like a puff ball in the wind. All reason of sanity was lost. The truth was in their hearts. Nothing else mattered.

Quickly, RJ abandoned his own worried thoughts and moved toward her, walking faster and faster until he raced past the little boy. His decision had been made. There was no doubt in his mind and no staying his path. His arms stretched toward her, the only balm that would soothe the pain within him. Abandoning all caution in his desire for this woman, he raced toward her.

Overcome with her own need for RJ, Beth gave in to the decision that was clear in her mind. She'd waited long enough for RJ Scott to accept his feelings for her, and now that she knew he had, hell and high water couldn't keep her from him any longer. Racing toward him, her naked feet barely touched the ground as she jumped into his open arms.

Juanita had remained silent, watching as the lady spoke to her little grandson, Eduardo, and knew she had asked him to find RJ. Quickly, Juanita moved to the opposite side of the doorway, still hiding herself in the shadows. She needed to see how RJ would handle seeing this lady for the first time again after she'd warned him about getting involved with her. Silently, secretly, she watched.

The lady looked up and saw RJ in the distance. The woman started toward him and then stopped. She seemed to have something wrong with her shoe.

Juanita could see RJ walking towards the lady, and watched as RJ stopped. He was remembering her warnings. Juanita was sure he remembered. Then he started moving toward the lady and she wondered what RJ was doing.

RJ raced past little Eduardo toward the lady, and completely barefooted, the lady raced toward him. As he held out his arms for her, she jumped into his arms, throwing her arms around his neck. RJ held her high up in his arms, kissing her, and her legs and bare feet were wrapped around his butt. It was crazy. The two fools were just tangled up so tight with one another, you couldn't tell where one body started and the other stopped.

Juanita knew this couldn't happen to RJ. Stepping outside the gate, she called to him repeatedly, but he wouldn't look at her. He kept his arms firmly around the lady, kissing her over and over again as though he were devouring every inch of her, and what he wasn't kissing on her, she was kissing on him. It was disgusting.

She thought about calling him again, but knew it would do no good. She'd just have to talk to him later when he wasn't thinking with his man parts. As though she were a ghostly shadow, Juanita slipped back into the garden quietly pulling the wrought-iron gates closed behind her.

Walking side by side with arms around one another, Beth stopped to pick up her shoes. Retrieving her soiled tennis shoes in one hand, she slipped her arm back around RJ as they neared the front of the grand house where her little car was parked.

"RJ," Beth demanded. "You told me you were poor. Why did you lie to me?"

"Me, poor? Oh, hell no!" he laughed, "I told you my family was poor. *I* had no intention of staying poor. I had enough of that crap when I was young!"

"You purposely led me to believe that you were some poor backwoods cowboy, RJ. You let me buy you clothes." Beth turned and looked at him squarely. "You had a great time at my expense, didn't you?"

"That I did, Beth," he answered, not apologizing, but grinning a smile of obvious delight. "I had more fun with you at old Enrique's than I've ever had in my life. You sure were mad." RJ pulled her close to him as they walked toward her car.

Beth remembered the chicken poop and the old porch, she'd envisioned. "Oh, never mind, RJ. Trying to get you to behave the way I think you should is a lost cause, and I'd rather have you like you are. Now, I need to get my makeup bag from my car."

RJ stared in disbelief at the little two-seated, dirty red car, and thought of the prim and proper, snooty woman he'd first met. He knew Beth had suffered a terrible long trip in that sorry, rickety car, but she'd made it. She looked exhausted, but she'd kept on driving for hours and hours all the way from Oklahoma all by herself. Grinning with pride, he watched as she got a small case from the hatchback doorway. She was something else.... this woman. His woman. His Beth.

RJ watched in adoration as Beth struggled to close the hatchback door. Reaching over her head, he grabbed the door and pushed it closed. "Beth, why in God's name did you get this car at the rental?" he laughed, staring into the hatchback. "I swear this is the ugliest car I have ever witnessed in my entire life and I've seen some uglies."

Hands on her hips, Beth pretended to glare at RJ. He ignored her as he walked around the car and kicked the tires. "You got one good tire, though, Beth." RJ doubled over with laughter. "Jesus, how did you make it here in this little piece of crap? I'll bet this thing hasn't got one more damn mile in it. Gazing inside the little car, shaking his head, RJ continued his inspection.

"All right Mr. Smart Aleck," Beth retorted, "I made it here, didn't I? Am I not standing right here in front of your old silly self? I like this car. We bonded."

RJ was choking with laughter watching her. He walked over to her and stuck his finger in the tear in her shirt, running his calloused finger over the soft skin of her naked shoulder, and stealing his long finger into the softness of her breast.

Beth felt his little sneaky feel. She smelled awful, was hot and tired, and in no mood for his teasing. Not then, anyway. Later, yes. Beth glared at RJ.

RJ grinned and removed his hand. He could wait….for awhile, anyway. Later….when they were alone. RJ looked down at her muddy jeans and her bare feet. "You're a mess." he whispered, nestling his nose into her hair. He gagged. "God Beth, I'd say you even stink!" RJ threw back his head and roared with laughter.

"Well, I have news for you, Mr. Smart Aleck", she sneered, "I don't have any clothes to change into either, so I will attend the wedding just as I am, and you're my escort! So there!"

"Not so, my lady," he grinned. "Not to worry, Juanita's got you covered."

"Juanita's got you covered," Juanita heard RJ say to the lady. Quickly she stepped from the shadows of the gate and pushed the gate open, forced to welcome the lady to the home.

"Juanita, this is Beth." The lady smiled brightly at her as though she'd done something wonderful showing up there.

"Welcome to Scott's End Ranch," Juanita said, trying to sound sincere.

"Beth's sort of a mess, Juanita," RJ said as he stared down at the lady. "She cleans up pretty good, though. Will you see what you can do with her?"

Juanita knew she was just feeling sorry for herself, but she couldn't help it. Now it seemed she'd become RJ's lady's *maid.*

RJ leaned down, kissed the top of the lady's dark head. "Yuck!" he said, and quickly walked away.

Juanita winced in the awful smell of RJ's lady. As she motioned for her to follow her toward the gate, Juanita saw RJ stop and turn back toward them. He stared at the lady as though he couldn't believe she was really there. Quickly, RJ returned to the lady.

RJ pulled Beth close to him, engulfing her in his big arms, wanting to say something to her, but the words weren't there. Moving back from her a few inches, he stared down into her dark eyes, his own blue eyes speaking the words his lips could not.

Beth pulled his big rough hands to her lips. She kissed them softly, stroking his big fingers with her mouth, rubbing the calloused hands against her soft cheeks. RJ cupped Beth's face with his hands, caressing her with his large fingers, adoring her with his gentle kiss. As she slipped her arms around his neck, he pulled her to him, locking her into him with his arms, his lips, his body; joining a passion that transcended time and place. Oblivious to the world around them, RJ and Beth felt their souls escape their bodies, floating far above them….touching, joining, dancing the waltz of surrender.

Juanita stood silently watching them, knowing she was an intrusion in their world. Allowing them their privacy, she turned away. They'd forgotten she was there.

Beth was the first to come back to earth. She opened her eyes and saw Juanita waiting. "RJ," she whispered, pushing him from her.

Opening his eyes, RJ spotted Juanita patiently waiting for them, her gaze off into the distance. Seeing her, he pressed his lips to Beth's ear. "Beth, you need a nice soapy hot bath…. and don't forget to use lots of clean smelling shampoo." Bellowing a roaring laugh, RJ strode to the back of the house. And as Juanita watched RJ walk away, it occurred to her that in all the years she'd known him, she'd never heard RJ Scott laugh like that.

Turning to the lady, Juanita motioned the lady to enter into the courtyard. She could see the lady's eyes grow large in awe of the beauty of the garden inside the courtyard.

"What an absolutely amazing garden," Beth exclaimed, staring up at the tiled ceilings, the pillars, and the many baskets of yellow and white begonias, the chosen colors for Anne's wedding. As though she couldn't resist, Beth sat down on the curved bench surrounding the Lady in the Fountain. Lowering her hand back inside the cool water, Beth closed her eyes for a brief moment. Softly she whispered, "I wish I could stay forever in this glorious place."

"I wanted to have the wedding here", Juanita said in a small voice. "But, I am only the *housekeeper,* so everyone ignored my suggestions. Please follow me, Mrs."

"This would be a perfect place for the wedding," Beth agreed following behind Juanita, nearly overcome with the beauty of the natural environment. "Absolutely perfect!"

Juanita smiled slightly, and continued, "As you can see, all the rooms face into the garden.... I mean the courtyard. The first room on the right is RJ's office. Next is the library, then the formal dining area. The formal dining area was never used, so when our daughters were young, we converted it into bedrooms for them. After the girls left and Jason no longer needed me in the night, Luis and I moved our bedroom there, because it was such a large area and it gave all of us more privacy.

Juanita moved her arm in a motion that clearly showed her pride in the grand home. "Next to our bedroom is a large bathroom which adjoins the family room. The family room leads into the kitchen that spans the back of the house. The kitchen and family room outer walls are glass so that your view of the pool and back gardens are unobstructed." Juanita paused hoping she sounded somewhat cultured. Then she continued, "There are walkways on either side of the courtyard leading to the pool area, the kitchen and the family room." Juanita purposely ignored the laundry room, assuming the lady would have no interest in how things got clean, or *who* cleaned them. That was the *housekeeper*'s worry.

Juanita motioned for Beth to follow her as she walked toward the left side of the courtyard. "There are five bedrooms on the left side, all leading out to the courtyard. This first room on the right is where you will have your bedroom. A large bathroom connects your room to RJ's room." Juanita stopped and cleared her throat, determined the lady not get any ideas about sneaking into RJ's bed. "Both those bedrooms are meant to be private from one another." she stated. "If you need to use the bathroom in the night, just pull

RJ's door closed if it is open. He is a very honorable, decent man, and would never dream of invading your privacy. I expect you will do the same."

Beth smiled to herself, remembering Tulsa and the feel of RJ's hairy legs wrapped around her legs. He'd thought she was sleeping, but she wasn't. Clearly she remembered him, stroking her body with his touch, possessing her in his tight embrace, nestling his nose in her hair. His touch had just felt so good and so safe, that she didn't want it to stop. That's why she hadn't turned to him. Tonight, she would. Feeling a shiver run down her entire body, Beth knew Juanita's firm words were all in vain. Beth followed the graying, brown skinned lady in the teal suit toward the room that would be her bedroom. "This will be where you will stay," she said as she pushed open the heavy sculptured mahogany door.

Stepping into the bedroom, Beth felt she'd stepped into another world. Gone were the massive bold Spanish features she'd seen in the courtyard. This room, her bedroom was beautifully feminine, done in soft magentas, cool greens, and golden creams reminiscent of a magnificent subtle garden.

The room was fashioned with furniture of French Provisional antique cream, and the tops of the dressers were covered in a muted green marble. The contrasting creams of the walls enabled the floral fabrics of the room to blend together softly. The two coved windows were adorned in antique cream plantation blinds with over drapes of magenta floral damask. The huge cream four-poster bed held a matching floral magenta damask coverlet, overseeing a solid magenta damask dust ruffle. Solid magenta pillow shams adorned the sculptured cream head board, and various shapes of floral decorator pillows lay in perfect contrast. If she ever had to describe the bedroom of her dreams, this would be it.

Beth looked down at her dirty feet and could smell her own body odor. She felt sick as she searched for a chair to collapse in, that she wouldn't get dirty. Exhausted, Beth dropped herself onto a small footstool. Looking up from her dirty feet to the tiny woman standing in front of her, she smiled awkwardly. "I'm so dirty and tired, I'll be lucky to make it through my own daughter's wedding."

Turning her back to Beth, Juanita opened the large closet door and pulled a dress bag from inside the cedar-lined closet. Closing the door to the closet, she laid the dress across the bed and removed the protective cellophane of Elaine's Boutique. "RJ called Anne and got your dress size," she said. "I hope it's all right with you, what I chose." Knowing the lady didn't have a choice, Juanita truly hoped the lady would like the deep mauve dress as much as she did. Gently, Juanita fluffed the chiffon of the full sleeves and pressed the sequined mauve top over the drop-yoke flowing pleats of the matching shantung skirt. "Will this be all right, Mrs.?" She asked as she looked down at the dirty tired woman.

Beth was overcome with gratitude. This woman had gone to so much trouble for her, and she knew it couldn't be easy for her to buy clothes for an outsider that she didn't know or want in her house. With renewed energy, Beth jumped up and threw her arms around the small brown woman. "I can see why RJ and Jason love you so much, Juanita. Thank you so much for helping me."

Juanita let the smelly lady hug her for a moment. She did not want to like this lady. She did not. "Mrs., you need to take a bath and get ready." She walked across the room and motioned toward the large bathroom. "They've waited to start the ceremony until you arrive, so you must hurry. I'll wait for you in the garden."

"Juanita, you're very sweet, but I don't want you to miss the party. Go, join the others, but maybe if you wouldn't mind, could you come back for me in a little while?"

"Mrs., I am only the **housekeeper**. I don't belong with the fancy people. I'll wait for you in the garden."

Beth thought about that for a minute. Something wasn't right, but she didn't have time to worry on it. She'd caused the whole wedding to be delayed. She had to get bathed and dressed. "Juanita, I do want a bath, but could you do one thing for me?"

"Yes, Mrs." Juanita replied, wondering if this was the beginning of RJ's lady's demands.

"Juanita, my name is Beth. Will you please stop calling me 'Mrs.' and use my given name?

"Yes, Beth", she answered. She did not want to like this woman. She did not.

Beth placed her small makeup kit on the vanity located closest to her bedroom. There were two vanities in the large bathroom separated by a large coved window dressed in antique cream plantation shutters. In front of the window was a bench with a long green cushion. Under the seat was a cabinet with louvered doors that matched the plantation shutters. Juanita said the cabinet under the seat contained extra large towels that RJ liked, but they weren't so soft. "They weren't lady towels", she'd said.

Juanita said she'd stocked the cabinet under the vanity next to Beth's room with items Beth might need, and Beth had no idea how anyone could get so much stuff packed so neatly into that vanity. There were delicate, fluffy bath towels, hand towels, and matching wash cloths: soft net puffs, floral soaps, a variety of shampoos and conditioners. There were curl boosters and curl shapers, curl relaxers, and wet-shine gels, extra-hold hair sprays and soft-hold hair sprays, scented and unscented. There were foot powders, body powders and deodorant powders all in a variety of scents….and one solid unscented. There were toothbrushes in soft, medium, and hard, a variety of toothpastes, mouthwashes in mint or cinnamon, hair brushes, combs, curling irons, blow dryers, any feminine item that a woman could possibly use was stocked neatly in the vanity. Juanita had gone to a lot of trouble to please her, and please her she did.

Curiosity overcoming her, Beth peeked inside RJ's vanity. It contained a bar of soap, deodorant, a shaving cup with a brush and razor, a toothbrush with toothpaste and a hair brush. Nothing, more. No frills. That was RJ Scott. Beth smiled. Yes, that was RJ.

As she pulled off her filthy clothes, Beth was awestruck as she gazed through the plantation blinds. In the distance, herds of horses galloped in the cool of the early evening breeze, baby colts playfully prancing behind. Massive black cattle milled around a giant feeder by the large red barn, feeding and meticulously chewing till their hearts were content and bellies full. Two red and white dogs, which she decided must be his 'boys', slept contented by the barn. One raised his head and looked around, but it took too much effort to bark, so he went back to sleep. Every place she looked there was peace and contentment. This was a good place. His place. RJ Scott's home.

Turning away from the beauty outside the window, she surveyed the bathroom equipped with a lavish marble whirlpool bath and a monstrous tiled shower. Inside the shower there were two seats, and so many shower heads she could only imagine how soothing that would be on her tired aching body. The only question Beth had was how did you turn on the water? As Beth leaned inside the shower trying to discover the secret to the water, instantly she was covered in warm sprays of soft water. She'd found Heaven.

Adjusting the hair dryer in the holster inside the vanity door, Beth decided to let her damp hair hang loose and revert to the curls of her youth. There was nothing she could think to do with it, anyway. George had cut it too short for her usual French twist, but she knew she'd never wear the tight strict twist again. It didn't suit her anymore. Tipping her shoulders in loose curls seemed right. It looked right. It *was* right.

Quickly, Beth slipped on her dressy heeled sandals, thanking the heavens that she had slipped them in her carrying case at the last minute. They were perfect with the beautiful mauve dress. Beth took one last glance at her appearance in the tall cream mirror; even if she did say so herself, she almost looked pretty. It was the gorgeous dress that caused her good looks, she knew that, but the shy Juanita was the person responsible for the dress, and she'd never forget her kindness.

Knowing Juanita was still patiently waiting for her outside the door in the garden, Beth wondered why Juanita refused to join the party. Beth remembered the horribly shy Juanita from the telephone and knew that all the grand, sophisticated people must have been a nightmare for Juanita. Juanita had referred to herself as "the housekeeper", but Beth knew that both RJ and Jason respected and loved Juanita. For some reason, though, Juanita had not claimed her own right as a member of RJ's family. The housekeeper**? S**omeone must have said something to hurt the shy Juanita. Beth was certain it had to be something like that. What could Juanita do about it? Nothing.

Grabbing the pull on the large door, Beth exited into the peaceful splendor of the magnificent garden. Juanita sat waiting next to the flowing fountain. She turned and looked at Beth, a sweet smile crossing her lips. "Don't you look lovely, Beth. Next to Anne, you'll be the prettiest lady at the wedding." Juanita stood and walked toward Beth. Juanita motioned for her to turn around so she could check that no tags or stray strings would mar Beth's appearance.

Juanita smiled in approval. "You must hurry, Beth. All those people are waiting for you.... the mother of the bride."

Beth slipped her arm through Juanita's and petted her softly. "They're waiting for you, too Juanita.... the mother of the groom."

Juanita didn't know what to say, how to answer. Somehow, Beth knew. RJ's lady understood her feelings. And what's more, she cared.

"All right, Juanita," Beth said, grabbing Juanita's arm and placing it under her own. "Maybe if we stick together, we'll get through this ordeal after all." As the two mothers walked toward the reception area, Juanita felt Beth squeeze her arm with her small fingers, and in Beth's secure touch, Juanita found the confidence she needed. Holding her head high, as though she were royalty, Juanita smiled in genuine happiness.

She didn't want to like RJ's lady. No, she didn't. But.... oh Lord, she really did.

Chapter 24

Pastor Jim Walsh was very pleased with the wedding and the commitment of the two young people he'd just married. When RJ called him last week and asked him to perform the wedding of Anne and Jason, he'd been delighted to do so, knowing it would make Elizabeth happy. Before the wedding, he'd thought a lot about Elizabeth and RJ and wondered how their relationship was going. There was a relationship between them, he was certain of that. But had they accepted it? He certainly hoped so.

Having put him up in a nice hotel in Dallas, RJ paid for a rental car for him to go wherever he wanted in the city. Everything he did while in Dallas was paid for by RJ Scott. On a pastor's puny salary, that was quite a treat for the little Irish preacher. He appreciated everything RJ had done for him, but the one thing Jim Walsh really wanted was to get to know RJ Scott, the man.

People he'd visited with in the Dallas area all knew RJ Scott, or said they did. The story went that RJ's ancestors were some of the original pioneers that settled north of Dallas. They worked hard and accumulated thousands of acres, but eventually the future generations lost almost everything, a fact RJ Scott resented bitterly.

After RJ's parents died and his sisters were forced to live with relatives, RJ turned the rage inside him toward regaining the land that was lost to his family. He set out on a path and never wavered, working night and day. With the help of a strong back, a good mind, and an uncanny business sense, RJ managed to reclaim all his lost land and a whole lot more. He was always on the lookout for a land deal, knowing that lazy ancestors were still around, anxious to throw away their inheritances for a few lousy dollars. There had been a time when RJ Scott owed almost everyone in the state of Texas and neighboring states too, but he kept on buying and remortgaging.... buying and remortgaging.

With the unrest of integration in Dallas during the late 60's and 70's, many of the people of Dallas chose to move North of Dallas, but they needed land to build homes. RJ Scott had land in abundance, above and beyond his beloved ranch. Land he could sell, at a substantial profit to himself. With this profit, RJ was able to reclaim title to his ancestors' vast ranch and still maintain a large fortune which he'd invested wisely. Word had it in Dallas, RJ Scott was a millionaire many times over, although no one would ever know it to look at him.

Those stories were all interesting to Jim Walsh, but what about the man, RJ Scott? He had a son. Did his wife die? What happened to her? No one seemed to have the answers to those questions. It was as though she was there one day and gone the next.

RJ didn't talk about her and nobody would ask. They just all figured she'd died, but no one could remember hearing of a funeral being held for her. The people said it was none of their business. They just left it alone. That's the way it was done, back then. People minded their own business.

As Pastor Jim walked toward the reception area, he thought about Elizabeth and RJ, again. When Elizabeth entered the garden to take her place for the wedding, he'd hardly recognized the beautiful woman with the soft dark curls floating carelessly about her dazzling pink dress. Her face was radiant with happiness, something Jim hadn't seen since Charles was alive. He watched as RJ Scott escorted Elizabeth to her seat and took a seat beside her, ignoring his own assigned seat across the aisle. Pastor Jim noticed the Wedding Planner throw up his hands in frustration when RJ did exactly what he wanted to do and not what he'd been told to do.

From his vantage point during the wedding, Pastor Jim caught the stolen glances and the hidden touches between Elizabeth and RJ. It was obvious to him, they belonged together. With RJ Scott beside her, Elizabeth had come alive. He was delighted to see it.

Returning to the festivities, Pastor Jim stopped by the open bar, hoping a Ginger Ale would settle his stomach after the huge meal he'd eaten. He'd been assigned a dinner seat with some interesting people from Dallas and he'd enjoyed their company, but he was anxious to spend time with Elizabeth and RJ, who rarely left her side. In the meantime, he'd wait until he saw an empty chair at their table.

The band played the smooth love song from the fifty's, "Crazy". Beth watched as a number of older couples took their places on the small dance floor in front of the band, holding each other…touching. Watching the couples glide across the floor, she decided RJ should dance with her, feeling that if she didn't have his arms around her soon, she'd definitely be "*crazy*". "RJ?" she whispered.

"No, Beth. I don't dance." He answered crisply, anticipating her question. Taking a sip from his drink, he ignored her, but kept his arm around her chair.

"I could teach you." Beth whispered, turning her head toward his neck and nudging him with her nose.

"No." RJ growled, determined to end her efforts toward the dance floor. He'd read all those damn books on sex, but never thought about dancing. He'd let her teach him one day, he knew that, but he didn't want to make a fool of himself at Jason's wedding. He hoped to silence her, by giving her his growling "NO" that scared the hell out of most people.

Beth didn't fall for it. His growl was just bluff. When he turned away from her, Beth slipped her hand under the table cloth and engaged his knee in her small hand. Quickly, he turned back toward her feeling the small hand touching him so intimately. Avoiding his warning glare, she pinched him.

"Good God, Beth. Stop that." RJ whispered in exasperation. "I mean it, Beth. Now, stop it." RJ reached under the table cloth and grabbed her hand.

Beth leaned toward him. He leaned closer so she could whisper her apologies. There were no apologies. "That's payback, RJ. Payback for that naughty *feel* you copped on my bosom earlier." She smiled innocently at him. "Simple payback, RJ. Oh, and by the way, Mister, I *will* teach you to dance one day, and you will not complain nor will you give me any of your silly growls. I'm not afraid of you, not one little bit." Beth held up her thumb and forefinger, making a circle and shoved it in RJ's face.

RJ turned his head away from her so she didn't see him laughing, or see the pleasure her independence gave him. Gaining his composure, he turned back to her. "I have a few things planned to teach you too, Beth, you little vixen. You better be afraid." He warned, thinking about all the books he'd read about sex. Damn, some of those positions he couldn't imagine how they were supposed to work, but he was sure eager to try them with her. His woman. His Beth.

RJ leaned closer to Beth placing one hand around her shoulder while the other hand found her knee under the table. In retaliation to her pretended defiance, he raced his hand high up her inner thigh.

Beth's eyes opened wide with the intimate surprise. "Stop it, RJ," she whispered. "My Lord, we're at our children's wedding, for Heaven's sake. Quickly, Beth moved her hands to the top of the table in retreat, for the time being.

RJ leaned close and brushed her ear with his lips. "It's called payback, my little seductress, and I'm real good at payback, Beth. Never, ever mess with the master."

RJ pulled his hand from under the table, discovering the feel of her soft, warm leg had created his own undoing. "Damn," he swore silently. The sweat ran down the sides of his face like he'd run a five mile race. He wasn't some young kid, pawing all over his first gal. Hell, he was an old man. Why the hell didn't he feel like one? He knew what he felt, and it had nothing to do with being an old man. Hell! Resting his arm around her shoulders, he breathed deeply.

Undaunted by RJ's growling or his silly warnings, Beth dreamed up further retaliation, the perfect scheme. She leaned toward him to issue her latest threats, but RJ was glaring past her toward the door. His face went pale, as though he'd spotted the Devil himself. His body went rigid, his jaw cracked, his blue eyes spit fire. Beth turned to see who or what had so enraged RJ, and then she noticed two newcomers had arrived.

The object of RJ's fierce glare was a heavy-set balding man with thick round glasses. He wore a wrinkled brown suit, an outdated knit tie, and a stained shirt that appeared to be too small for his massive neck. It appeared the little unkempt man had arrived with a tall, distinguished older woman. She was dressed in a conservative, but expensive, dark blue suit. Obviously, she'd come straight from work. Beth realized the two newcomers weren't together, separating as soon as they entered the reception area.

RJ whispered to Beth that he needed to speak to Jason and hurried across the reception area where Jason and Anne sat laughing with a group of younger people. Jason stood quickly, seeing his father approach him. RJ and Jason moved some distance from the jovial group, conversing in guarded whispers meant only for father and son. RJ nodded in the direction of the crude little man. Jason developed the same look of concern in his eyes as his father.

With a great flair of independence, the professional lady in the blue suit approached Jason, throwing her arms around him and hugging him. She grabbed RJ's hand, held it familiarly for some time, apparently old friends. She spoke to them for a few minutes, then glancing toward the little fat man, she tossed her hands as though she had no idea who the man could be. He wasn't with her.

Not taking his gaze from the man, RJ returned to his seat next to Beth placing his arm protectively around her shoulders. His other hand he placed over her hands settled in her lap. If possible, RJ would have pulled her inside him to protect her. Cautiously, he watched the nasty little man.

"Got room for one more?" Pastor Jim asked as he settled himself in the chair next to Elizabeth.

"Absolutely, Jim", Elizabeth smiled innocently at the pastor. It was obvious to Jim that Elizabeth hadn't caught the heated energy between the Scotts and the latest newcomer to the reception. It was just as well. Whatever was going on between them was very bad. No need for Elizabeth to be involved. Trying to get RJ's attention off the man was useless, Jim realized. Thoughtfully, he studied RJ as RJ's icy glare followed the man every step he took.

"Mom, Pastor Jim," Anne said as she stood behind them, arm in arm with the tall professional woman in the blue suit. RJ and Pastor Jim stood politely. "This is Clarisse Martel, the person smart enough to see what a wonderful asset Jason would be to the law firm."

Clarisse patted Beth's shoulder and grabbed Pastor Jim's hand, shaking it with the grip of a woman self-assured in her own power. "Sorry I was so late and missed the wedding. I got tied up in court and couldn't get away. I've been at it today since the crack of dawn, so I can't stay long," she said. "I'm exhausted but nothing could keep me away from these precious children's reception. I'm so glad they didn't run off to Vegas like they'd planned. I might be late, but not too late to offer my best wishes to these two on their wedding day. Oh to be young again, and in love," she laughed. And then she was gone, and so was the nasty little man.

RJ rose from the table. His blue eyes scoured the reception area for sight of the intruder he'd watched so carefully and now lost. RJ excused himself and in long determined steps walked into the house.

"I don't believe we've met," the voice came from behind Elizabeth. Quickly, the little man pushed his way into the chair that had been RJ's.

Not knowing what to do, Elizabeth smiled and Jim Walsh stood and offered his hand. The little man ignored his offer.

"So, you are Elizabeth Carlton," he snarled exposing gnarled, stained teeth. Sitting on the other side of Elizabeth, Jim Walsh could smell the odor of musty cigar smoke, mixed in the distinct rank of aged body odor.

"I'm Silas Stone. RJ and I go back a long, long way." he pulled a grimy handkerchief from his pocket and wiped his forehead, and shoved it back inside his wrinkled pocket. "RJ always did have a good eye for women. I always liked his taste," his bottle-cap glasses magnified his dark brown eyes, reminding Pastor Jim of a hoot owl waiting for its prey. "You're older than I like, but what the hell. If you're good enough for RJ, you're good enough for me." He cackled like an old hag, but gazed cautiously about the room.

"Move on Silas," RJ's voice boomed from behind them, "Get out of my chair and get out of my house. You know you're not welcome here!"

Silas Stone jumped up from the chair and circled around the table, ensuring that the table stayed between him and RJ. His owl eyes turned black, hard lumps of coal. "Don't get all pissed off, RJ." He sneered. "I was just admiring your little lady.... remembering old times. Is she as good in the sack as Carla, RJ."

Moving back and forth around the table, just out of RJ's reach, the fat little man continued taunting RJ. "Hell, RJ, let's share Elizabeth like we did Carla! You bed her one night, and I'll bed her next, RJ. You, me, and Carla. You haven't forgotten Carla, have you, RJ? Carla, your wife."

A white-jacketed chair fell to the floor as RJ lumbered around the table after the insulting little man. "Get out of here, you filthy little bastard", he threatened, grabbing the man by the back of his coat and twisting his arm behind him. “I swear to God, I’ll kill you if you ever come near Beth, again!”

Beth rushed to RJ‘s side, knowing how easily RJ could snap the small man’s arm. “RJ, don’t.” she said. “Let him go. He’s not worth it."

RJ motioned to two of his men hurrying over to him. “Get this trash out of my house,” he told them. “Take him all the way to the gate, and one of you stay there and be sure he doesn’t try to get back in. Tomorrow, I’ll have a security device installed, but until that's done, I want one of you on that gate.”

Jim Walsh quickly glanced around the room to see who’d witnessed this explosion between these two long-time enemies. Thankfully, he could see that most of the tables were empty, the guests having left before the incident. Then he saw Jason coming toward their table. “I’m sorry, Dad,” he said. “I guess Silas pretended to be with Clarisse and that’s how he got in.”

“It’s all right, son. He’s gone now, and you and Anne need to go, too”, RJ answered, eyeing the door. “You don’t want to miss your flight. It looks like the party here is just about over.”

“What was he saying about my mother, Dad? Did Silas know her?” Jason’s eyes scrunched in a way that reminded RJ of Carla. He turned away.

“Silas Stone is a piece of crap and everything from his mouth is lies, Jason. You know that.” RJ walked to his son and put his arm around him. “Better get going, Jason. That airplane won’t wait for you.”

Pastor Jim pulled a chair up next to RJ as he watched Jason and Anne leave the reception area. “Are you all right, RJ,” he asked? He’d stopped trying to understand RJ. Now he just wanted to help him.

“Oh hell, yes,” RJ returned from his deep thoughts, and smiled his big grin at the pastor. “I don’t have a worry in the world.”

Beth removed the many decorator pillows from what she’d determined would be her side of the bed. RJ could remove the others when he joined her, if he joined her. She pulled back the comforter and sheets in the luxurious bed and snuggled herself into the soft comfort of the silky sheets.

After the encounter with the man he'd called Silas, RJ had became distant, somber. Nothing she could say or do could bring him out of it. He'd told her to go on to bed; he had some thinking to do. Once and for all, he had to work things out in his mind.

RJ made his way past the many busy workers clearing out the tables from the wedding reception. Tables were being folded, chairs stacked onto carts, table linens put into big dumpsters to be washed and readied for the next grand event. Everyone was busy. The bartender was closing his station as RJ leaned over the small portable bar, his mind off in the distance.

"Evan Williams Bourbon, Mr. Scott?" the young bartender asked.

RJ nodded as the bartender poured him a drink and set it down in front of him. "You have such excellent taste in bourbon, Mr. Scott. Most people are unaware of the intrinsic qualities of such fine bourbon, but not you, Mr. Scott. Of course, I know you're a connoisseur on bourbons, but did you know that Evan Williams Bourbon is the first and only vintage-dated single-barrel bourbon? Each bottle contains the vintage date of exactly when it was put in an oak barrel to age." The young man turned the bottle around in his hand in pure admiration of the distinctive drink and inhaled the gentle fruit-like sweetness of the prized bottle he held.

"Even though it isn't the most expensive bourbon made, I think it is the finest sipping bourbon found anywhere, Mr. Scott. It has won many awards over the years. This particular vintage from 1991 that you are drinking now was awarded "Domestic Whiskey of the Year" by *The Malt Advocate* and "Spirit of the Year" by *Wine and Spirit.* But, I'm sure you know all that, don't you, Mr. Scott?"

RJ didn't answer as he picked up his tumbler of bourbon and headed for the front porch to do some serious thinking. As he walked to the front of the house, he found his old wicker rocker hidden behind a large imitation bush, and he knew it was the work of the damn Wedding Planner. Kicking the bush out of his way, RJ carried the aged white wicker rocker in one hand and his bourbon in the other, and after setting his chair down in his usual spot, he settled himself down to do some serious thinking.

Watching the many white vans of the Wedding Planner's crew

exit his drive, RJ was so damn glad to see them all go. Maybe things could get back to normal, he thought, but he didn't know what normal was anymore. He didn't want his old life back. Not the way it had been. No, what he wanted was asleep in the grand bedroom, he'd created only for her.

RJ had dreamed about this night with Beth. He wanted it to be so perfect. Silas Stone had ruined it by reminding him of all the horrible people that were his life's history. Hell, he didn't care about those people for his sake, they couldn't hurt him, but they could hurt Beth. That he could never tolerate.

When Jason first got smitten with Anne, he investigated her family in Tulsa. RJ didn't want Jason to know the hell he'd found with a woman with no morals and less concern for the lives of others. What he'd found upon his investigation was that Anne's family was above respectability. Hell, Charles Carlton was so revered in his community, he could probably walk on water right along with JC himself. Charles Carlton would never have allowed Beth to endure what she'd been subjected to a few short hours after entering the home of RJ Scott. Hell no, old Charlie would never be involved in any sort of scandal, and he sure as hell wouldn't associate with the taint that followed RJ Scott.

RJ took a sip of the superior aged Evan Williams Bourbon and wondered who he was trying to fool. Scowling, he remembered the bartender suggesting he was some connoisseur of fine bourbon. Hell, he had no idea if the bourbon was any good or not. After the guests had been sucking up the booze for some time, he'd noticed the bottle of Evan Williams Bourbon was still full and decided it must be some rot gut bourbon the Wedding Planner had tried to sneak in as high-dollar booze. The Wedding Planner had told RJ he wouldn't charge him for any unopened bottles of booze. He'd leave the opened booze with RJ and the rest he'd take back to his business and settle up with RJ later. RJ knew better. He'd be charged for all the bottles of booze, opened or unopened. RJ decided he'd be sure all bottles were opened. That little twit couldn't put one over on RJ Scott. *No, sir.*

All those silly city folks had just about driven him nuts trying to impress him with their fake uppity ways, asking him all those fool questions about how to make money. He wanted to tell them to work their asses off and quit asking such stupid questions, but he didn't. He just smiled.

Then, all those investment people were asking him about his views on hedge funds, short selling, and derivative contracts. He'd just laughed and didn't answer. All he did was find a stock that made sense to him, bought it, and when he felt it had topped its price, he sold it. He had no idea what all those investment fellows were asking him about, and when they asked him for stock tips, again he just smiled. They thought he had some big secret in the stock market, but his secret was that he didn't know what the hell they were talking about and didn't give a crap. He was no financial genius. Hell no. He was just plain old RJ Scott, a man with crooked toes that ached all the time, because being raised a poor kid, he didn't have shoes that fit him.

RJ looked down at the silver tips on his shiny new boots. Those fancy boots were killing him, the tight crease in his suit trousers was itching him something awful, and that damned bolo with the string tie was driving him nuts. Shaking his head, he wondered why he'd gone through all this discomfort just to impress Jason's friends. He knew different. He didn't give a damn about Jason's friends or his employer.

Hell, no. It was for Beth. He wanted to impress Beth. Everything he'd done was for her, even the expensive clothes he'd bought last week in Dallas were for her. He'd wanted Beth to think he was some sort of a fine gentleman rancher and not the sorry old cowboy with the crooked toes that he really was. Just so she'd think he was someone special, he'd been willing to forego the custom boots normally made for him, and had been willing to stand the pain in those store bought, narrow, silver-tipped boots that the salesman told him were worn by fine gentlemen. That's how bad he wanted her.

A fine gentleman? Oh, hell no! He knew what he was. Silas Stone had reminded him. He was just plain old cow chips and horse crap, and no fancy house and no amount of money in the bank could make him different. He was so far out of Beth's league, he shouldn't be allowed to walk on the same ground as she did. Beth was a class act, a thorough-bred: a rare Sabina White filly, with soft pink skin, and big dark eyes. He was just some dumb jackass following her around and no amount of special grooming or otherwise could make him any different.

RJ had to make this right and he knew it. Beth had to see who he really was and she had to understand that it could never work between them. The class difference between them was bad enough, but what was worse was that he knew he couldn't protect her from the people that were his history.

RJ pulled off the painful boots and aimed them into the front yard. With one mighty tug, he ripped the onyx bolo from his neck and tossed it after the boots. With a mighty thrust, he hurled the contents of Evan Williams Bourbon toward the boots, smiling as the prized bourbon sloshed on top of the silver tips of the boots. In his stocking feet, he turned and walked to the back of the house where he'd put his boys to wait out the big shindig in the barn.

Opening the gate to the barn, RJ smiled as his boys ran free into the yard, sniffing and peeing on the spots once held by all the fine cars. Returning to his side, they jumped on his immaculate crisp trousers, delighted he'd returned to them after their long wait. RJ petted them and scratched their ears ignoring the dirt from their paws. He knew he'd never put his boys or himself through an ordeal like that again. He'd learned his lesson.

Chapter 25

Beth didn't know when she'd fallen asleep; she'd been so exhausted, but she knew she'd been sleeping for some time. She opened her eyes and felt the empty spot next to her. RJ had been looking forward to tonight as much as she had, she was certain of that. Where was he?

Stepping out of the comfort of the warm bed, she crossed the room to the bathroom. The door was closed, but unable to hear any sounds coming from inside, she pushed open the closed door and walked in. In the moonlight, she could see RJ's outline against the window in the bathroom. He'd changed from his smart gray western suit into a torn denim shirt, faded jeans, and scruffy dirty work boots.

"RJ?" she said softly. "Why are you sitting in the dark?" She crossed over to him and sat next to him on the little green bench. She slipped her arm into his and softly kissed his shoulder.

"Beth," he said. "This thing with you and me....Beth, it's not gonna work." He stopped talking for a moment, dreading what he had to say. "I'm not the man you think I am, Beth. I'm just a no class, backwoods cowboy with a lot of really bad people in my past...people like Silas, Carla and more. These people just don't go away, Beth, and they don't care who they hurt. They're not like the people you have to deal with Beth, a few gossipy women, cheating yard men."

RJ paused for a moment and pulled himself away from Beth's touch, and stood in front of her. It was hard enough to do what he had to do, but her soft touch was killing him. He had to do it. "Beth, these people I got involved with in my past could really hurt you, and I can't let that happen. I won't allow it. You're a sweet innocent woman with a good heart and a lot of comfort to give some good man. But, I'm not that man, Beth. I would protect you with my life, if I thought it would keep you safe, Beth, but I can't protect you from my past. I learned that tonight. I can't have you suffer for my past mistakes." RJ clinched his hands together so tightly, they were almost knotted; his mouth so dry he could barely speak. He continued, "After breakfast, I'm taking you to the airport and I'm getting you a ticket on the first plane back to Tulsa. I want you away from me and my damn miserable past, Beth. I want you where it's safe."

Beth's eyes adjusted to the half moonlit bathroom. RJ's head hung low, a whipped dog. She wondered how he could possibly suggest they go back to their routine lives without each other. Surely, he couldn't turn off his feelings for her so quickly. Could he do that? No, she didn't think so. And she wasn't going to let him try. No, not this time. RJ said she didn't know him. He said he wanted to keep her safe. He wanted them to give up this promise of happiness, just so she could be safe. The more she thought about his words, the angrier Beth got. She was furious, the anger welling up inside her, crushing her.

Standing up, she glared at him. "Have you had your say, RJ Scott? If so, then sit down!" RJ sat down on the little green bench and Beth continued. "Are you through telling me how I should live my life? Do you have any idea who I am? Do you know me at all?"

He started to speak, but she continued angrily, "I'm no little child, RJ! I'm over 50 years old. After I was raped when I was a young girl, I hid in the safety of my parent's protection. I threw away my friends, because I was afraid of their questions. I threw away my beloved swimming, so I could hide my scars. I threw away a sought after college scholarship to a prestigious university, because I was afraid to leave my safe life. Yes, I was safe. Safe and miserable. I almost threw away Charles too, because I was afraid of the intimacy with him. But, I wanted him and the life we could build together. So, I gathered up all my hidden courage, tip toed from my safe place and told Charles about my past. Thank God, he wouldn't let me go and taught me what real love was. When I became pregnant, the doctor and Charles insisted I terminate the pregnancy. It wasn't safe for me, they said. But I wanted those children, RJ, and I did whatever I had to do to have them. I spent long months in bed, and against all odds, I bore two healthy, strong children."

Beth hesitated, her anger subsided and she sighed deeply, her voice became softer. "Seven years ago, my world came crashing down upon me when Charles' cancer was diagnosed as terminal. He was my rock, my safe place. To my horror, I watched the man I loved die, RJ. Every day, he died a little more right before my eyes. Every day, I watched that poor suffering man struggle to live, because he didn't think I could take care of myself. He tried to keep me safe, but Charles couldn't. He was barely alive. Still, he hung on and on for me in pain that had to be unbearable. Finally, I had to let him go. I knew the nightmares I'd face alone, but I couldn't stand to watch him suffer any longer. It was me that urged him to give into death, RJ. I gave him permission to die, to escape that horrible pain. I promised him that I could make it alone and I have. No, I've not been happy these last seven years, RJ. I did as I'd done as a child and escaped into my own safe little world.

Beth smiled down at RJ. "Then, out of nowhere came RJ Scott." She reached down and caressed his rugged face. "He forced me to face my fears and I did. I won."

RJ started to stand.

"Sit down, RJ," she said, and he sat back down. "Today, I drove for eight hours through wind, rain, and mud and I had no idea where I was going. I certainly wasn't safe. You weren't there to protect me. I took care of myself and I made it, too. You want me to be safe, RJ. How can you say that? Life doesn't give you a safety net. Life doesn't promise you one thing." Beth stopped for a moment, watching RJ in the moonlight. Seeing his head hung so low, her tone softened. "Life is what you make it, RJ. You taught me that."

Beth ran her hand through his dark gray hair, stroking him, pouring her love into him. "Yes, I was scared, RJ, I was terrified. But, I knew that I could only have what I wanted, if I went after it myself. I couldn't count on anyone else to do what I had to do. I wanted to be at my daughter's wedding and I wanted you, RJ. I made it to Anne's and Jason's wedding. Now I'm here with you, RJ, and you want me to leave so I can be safe?"

"Beth, I'm not who you think…." he started, but she stopped him, her fingers covering his mouth.

"You think I don't know who you are RJ? Well, I do know you. " Beth reached down and pulled his hand up to her face feeling his calloused strength as she kissed his fingers. "You're a proud, arrogant man, but you're humble and unpretentious. You're an angry man, but a seeker of peace. You're a mighty lion, but gentle as a lamb. You're a student of nature, a teacher to all." Beth moved and sat down next to him. She sighed and pulled his hand down to her lap. He didn't move away. "RJ, you think you can stand alone in this world, but you're wrong. You think you can turn away from me, but you can't, RJ. Not anymore."

RJ didn't speak. He knew she was right. He didn't question it.

"RJ," she said softly, "don't tell me I don't know who you are, because I do. I know you. I love you. I want you. I want you tonight, right now. I've waited long enough. Either you love me now, or you'll never have another chance to love me. Do you understand me, RJ?" Beth stood and held her hand out to him.

RJ stood beside her and took her hands in his. He felt the relief forming across his brow as he looked down on the defiant little woman with the flames of passion dancing in her brown eyes. She could take care of herself. Yes, she could. Now, all she wanted was him. He sighed deeply, in grateful acceptance.

With his large finger, he touched the tiny spaghetti strap of her nightgown that lay across her shoulder and slowly he pushed it down her soft arm. Tenderly, he nestled his mouth upon her soft silky shoulder, finding thc swcct smcll of this woman hc hungered for. He pulled her to him, pressing her into him, smothering her with lips that craved her touch, her body, her soul.

"All right, Beth," he whispered. "All right."

Somewhere out in the distance, Beth could hear nature's serenade sung by the creatures of darkness. Such peace. Such absolute serenity. Beth smiled up at the man she loved and saw the return in his eyes. Taking his big hand in hers, she led him into her bedroom. RJ closed the door. Everything was right and as it should be.

Chapter 26

Juanita finished mending the tear in Beth's shirt and hung it on a hanger with the rest of Beth's clothes that she'd washed earlier. She didn't mind washing and ironing them, because she got up early and was always looking for things to do. She hadn't seen RJ that morning. He was always up early too, but she decided that maybe he'd left to do some chores. Juanita picked up Beth's clothes and walked from the kitchen, through the garden and stood before Beth's door, knocking softly.

"Beth, are you up?"

"Yes, Juanita," she heard a sleepy voice answer.

Opening the door to the grand bedroom, Juanita stepped inside. "I have your clothes, Beth." Beth sat up in the bed and sheepishly glanced toward a large lump in the bed next to her. Horrified, Juanita realized Beth wasn't alone in the bed. "RJ!" she gasped embarrassed for her imposition on them.

"What!" he said, as he sat straight up in the bed coming out of a deep sleep.

"I'm so sorry, RJ," Juanita said, red color glowing in her dark skin. Quickly, she started from the room.

"Juanita," Beth said. "You don't have to leave. If RJ's being here bothers you, I'll fix it." She shoved one of the pillows over RJ's head and pushed him back down on the bed, keeping the sheet tightly about her shoulders. "There," Beth said, patting the pillow. "I'm alone!" RJ lay still in the bed with the pillow over his head.

Juanita ignored the immoral scene in front of her and looked down at the clothes in her hands. "I mended your shirt and washed it and your jeans, too, Beth, but, I think your tennis shoes might be ruined." Casting a glance around the chaotic, shambles of the once grand bedroom, it appeared a tornado had passed through the night before. RJ's clothes, from his shirt to his socks, were scattered from the bathroom to the bed, and his old work boots looked like they'd been kicked across the room. The delicate decorator pillows hadn't escaped the storm either, one landing on top of a lamp; others thrown all over the place.

Trying not to look at the two people in the bed, both obviously sated and happy as newlyweds, Juanita lowered her eyes to the side of the bed. There it was, discarded and abandoned. Lying beneath RJ's underwear was the creamy nightgown with the little pink flowers and the tiny spaghetti straps that he'd insisted she buy for Beth. Juanita knew the expensive gown was useless. Beth was naked as a jay bird under those covers.

Juanita remembered her own wedding night so many years ago. Beth was a good woman and RJ was a good man. Turning away from them, Juanita frowned in despair. RJ and Beth weren't married. RJ was still married to Carla. Juanita was sure RJ had told Beth about Carla. He was an honorable man. Regardless, he and Beth ignored the fact of his marriage. They'd made their choice. They'd chosen each other over the sanctity of marriage, morality, and all else that was respectable. She just hoped they didn't have to pay too dearly for their choices.

"I will put everything here next to the door," the little woman said, mentally crossing herself, hoping God would forgive them.

"You're just too kind to me, Juanita. Thank you," Beth said. "Today, I need to call the airport and see if someone can locate my other clothes."

"Yes, you do that later, but I'll fix some breakfast first. What would you like, Beth? " Juanita asked, turning her back to the two of them, as she placed her hand on the handle of the door.

"Just some coffee would be fine, Juanita. Thank you, but I don't care for any breakfast," Beth replied.

"I want some breakfast," a muffled voice came from under the pillow.

"Beth leaned over and patted him on the stomach. "You don't get any breakfast," she whispered. "You're not here."

"I'll fix breakfast, now," Juanita said. Pulling open the ornate door, she hurried from the room.

Beth pulled the pillow off RJ's smiling face and moved it down to his side. Moving her body so that she was lying directly on top of RJ, she propped herself up on one elbow on his chest and smiled into his sparkling blue eyes. Gently, she kissed his lips, wondering how he had become such an accomplished lover. He sought to further the kiss, but she pulled away and began to trace around the features of his rugged face with her finger, beginning with the top of his weathered brow. As her fingers followed the road map of his face, she continued across the lines in his forehead and down to his dark eyebrows. She caressed the white lines at his eyes hidden in the folds of his worn, sun weathered-face, and with great interest, she moved her fingers across his face to his ears. In vain, she tried to flatten the little wisps of curls that encircled his ears determined to control the rebellious wisps of curls. Licking her finger, Beth pressed the little curls into place, securing them tightly with her finger, but as stubborn as RJ himself, as soon as she removed her finger, the little ringlets flipped themselves back into bouncing curls.

RJ was fascinated with Beth as he watched her finger travel the crevices of his face. Lying very still, he remembered tracing her sleeping body with his hands in Tulsa. He knew it was necessary for her to explore his body. The books said that. The books had told him a lot of things, but they hadn't told him the feelings he would discover waking up next to Beth. The books just stated facts of the human body: the senses, the points of stimulation, the instance of sex. Nothing was said about what he now felt. No, RJ knew he'd found something that wasn't in those books, something much more. He didn't know what it was exactly, but it was something he'd never found with any other woman. It was something rare; something he'd been searching for all life, something he'd never let go.

Running her fingers over his lips caused RJ to wiggle slightly and he noticed her smile seductively. She was driving him insane with her tantalizing touch, but he lay very still and continued to allow her to seek out whatever she needed to find and touch on his face and body. Slowly, she moved her finger from his lips down his neck and through the silver and black curls that covered his muscular chest, twirling the little hairs around and around on her fingers. Apparently bored with that part of him, she returned her finger back up to his lips. Smiling, she watched as he moved his mouth away from the teasing torture of her fingers.

"You can't get away," she whispered kicking the sheet from both of them. Placing her elbow on the side of his head, she continued tracing his lips as he wiggled under her.

"You're just tormenting me, now," RJ laughed, "You're a

wanton tease, a vixen. You're driving me crazy and you know it."

"Yes, I do know it," she answered, nibbling on the top of his ear. "RJ," she whispered. "How long does it take Juanita to fix breakfast?"

"Long enough." he answered. Grabbing the pillow that lay next to him, he wrapped it around her head and pulled her down to him. Damn, he was glad he read all those books.

Beth walked into the large kitchen with the wide ceiling-to-floor windows. Every place in this house was conducive to nature. The house was RJ. She stopped and stared at the beauty that was before her. All of the large tables were gone along with the many people, and she could see past the crystal-blue pool out into the colorful, vibrant gardens that Luis faithfully tended. Outside at a large glass patio table, RJ was eating his breakfast under the portico adjacent to the kitchen. Juanita was talking rapidly to RJ about Silas Stone, and Luis was standing beside Juanita, interrupting her constantly in broken English. RJ just kept eating.

"What's everyone talking about?" Beth asked. All conversation stopped, as though she'd walked in on the family secret. Luis and Juanita both nudged RJ.

RJ ignored Luis and Juanita and finished his breakfast. "That was good, Juanita," he said. "Got to keep up my strength." RJ laughed softly, as he walked over to Beth and kissed the top of her head. "You sure smell better than you did yesterday when you first got here."

Pouring a cup of coffee for herself, Beth sat down at the table. "RJ, who was that awful little man, Silas Stone?" she asked.

"Long story, Beth" he answered. "We'll talk about it sometime later."

Beth didn't appreciate being put off, and her tone showed it. "RJ, he was horrible to me, too, and I don't even know the man. I have a right to know why."

Luis and Juanita looked in question at RJ. He was the one who should tell the story. RJ settled himself in the chair next to Beth and stretched his long arms onto the table. "Remember that subdivision you passed when you came here, Beth?"

Beth nodded and RJ continued. "That used to be Luis and

Juanita's place. They had a little boy that was really sick, so they signed a balloon note to a mortgage company putting their land up as collateral to pay for his expenses. But, what no one told them was that if they couldn't pay the whole thing off at the end of the term, they'd lose their place. And, of course, that's exactly what happened. We found out later that Silas Stone was behind the whole damned thing. He wanted their land, so he took advantage of their situation and he got it. His big plan was to turn their land into an exclusive subdivision catering to the rich, and he'd planned to buy another twenty acres right next to the subdivision and put in a golf course, a country club, a strip mall and all the crap that rich folks want. Being as the subdivision was located so far from the luxuries of Dallas, he figured he needed to have them right at the rich folks' doorstep. He knew he could never touch my land, so to finish off his big *get-rich-quick* scheme, he had to have the twenty acres next to Luis and Juanita's old place.

RJ stopped long enough for Juanita to pour him more coffee. "So, I got to thinking, and I knew how I could really piss off old Silas. I went to the old boy who owned the twenty acres and offered him double what Silas offered, but I told him he had to accept the offer right then. Hell, he was no fool. That property was a piece of crap and he knew it. So, we went off to the bank and signed the papers that same morning. That was the worst business deal I ever made, but it was so damn worth it. God, Silas was mad." RJ threw back his head and laughed, enjoying the memory.

Remembering the justice that'd been lathered on Silas Stone seemed to give each one of them a great deal of personal satisfaction. Beth wondered how Carla was involved in all this, but something told her that story was better left discussed between the two of them in private.

Taking a long sip of his coffee, RJ continued. "So, anyway, Silas wasn't able to put his plans into place and all those rich folks that'd been interested in backing his plan originally, up and quit on him. No realtors would deal with him, the bank wouldn't loan him any more money, and finally he was forced to sell the land off in lots. I suppose he made a little money, but it couldn't be much. And I don't care, he got what he deserved!"

RJ stood up, the conversation was over. Beth knew

someday she'd learn what happened between RJ, Carla and Silas Stone, but it wouldn't be today.

"I've got to call that security outfit," RJ said, and picked up the kitchen phone. "Well, that's funny. I can't get a dial tone. It was working yesterday, because I fixed the ringer. I wanted to be sure we could hear it ring if you called, Beth."

"Oh Lord," Beth said, "How did you fix the phone, RJ?" She moved close to him and looked at the phone.

"I just pushed one of those little buttons with the arrows on them that points to up. See, those arrows right there, Beth. I turned the ringer up." RJ pointed to two little arrows on the side of the phone.

Beth grabbed his glasses that were sitting on the table and put them on him. "Did you wear your glasses when you *fixed* the phones, RJ?" she asked, leaning down and moving the lever from off to on.

"Well, I didn't see any sense in stopping to find my glasses."

"RJ, you didn't turn the phone up louder. You turned it off completely." Beth scolded, glaring at him, remembering the many times she'd tried to call him the day before.

"Well, I'll be damned," he grinned sheepishly. "Guess I really do need to wear those glasses."

"Yes, RJ", she agreed. "I guess you do," but, she knew he wouldn't.

In a matter of minutes, the phone rang. RJ picked up the phone, "Yeah, RJ Scott. Oh, our phone was out. One of the kids around here was probably playing with it and turned it off. I just caught it and turned it back on," he lied. "You say you've been trying to call me since yesterday, Sheriff."

There was a pause while RJ listened to the voice on the phone. "That's too bad." RJ said and sat down next to the phone. "What about the funeral? Any plans been made?" RJ listened intently to the caller. "Well, good, she can have what she wanted then. Let me know if there's anything you need from me, Sheriff. Thanks for calling."

RJ hung up the phone. "Carla's dead," he reported, as though he were discussing a fact of the weather. "She fell from her third floor balcony, broke her neck. Sheriff Dunns from Dallas said she'd had her funeral planned for some time."

Beth watched as RJ walked to the front of the large sink and stared toward the garden. She didn't know what to say. And what was there to say, anyway? She just kept silent.

Juanita broke the silence. "How long's it been since you've seen Carla, RJ? Hasn't it been something like fifteen years?"

RJ pulled nervously at the collar of his blue chambray shirt, keeping his back toward the three of them. Ignoring Juanita, he reached around to his backside and tucked his shirt further into his jeans. Securing his shirt, he wiped his palms repeatedly against the sides of his jeans.

Juanita continued. "Did the sheriff say she fell from her balcony, RJ? I wonder how that happened. All those apartments have some sort of a guard rail around them, don't they, RJ?" Juanita walked to the sink and nudged him out of her way as she filled the sink with hot sudsy water, ignoring the convenience of the dishwasher. After rinsing the dishes in the side sink, she placed the dishes into the sink. RJ moved to sit next to Beth at the kitchen table.

No one said anything for a few minutes until Juanita turned and faced them, her hands soapy from the morning dishes. She wiped the soap onto her faded red cobbler apron. "RJ, I know it's wrong to speak ill of the dead, but I'm glad she's gone. Think about it, RJ. Now you're free. Now you can have some peace."

RJ looked down at his hands and rubbed them together in deep thought. "I don't know, Juanita, it would seem that way", he answered. "But, somehow, I don't think I'll ever be free of Carla, 'cause you never knew what was gonna happen with the woman. Sort of like when you're enjoying the fresh spring air and you notice a little cloud in the sky. You think a gentle rain is coming till you notice the cloud drop a tail and destroy everything in its path…..just like Carla.

Beth decided to change the subject. Carla was such a painful memory to everyone. "RJ, I need to get my clothes from the airport in Dallas today."

RJ seemed delighted to have the Carla subject changed. "Sure enough, Beth. Whenever you're ready, we'll go."

"I had planned to return to Tulsa on Monday, but I still need to get my clothes for the return flight."

RJ openly scowled at Beth sitting upright from his slouched position next to her. "Beth, you can't be serious about flying back to Tulsa on that crappy little airline you tried to get here on, are you? I don't think that damn thing's any better than a balsa wood toy with a rubber band motor. No, Beth. That won't work. Besides that, Monday I have to go over to this old boy's place west of here to look at some calves he's trying to sell me. You can come with me."

"Well, RJ, I suppose I could stay until Tuesday. Yes, leaving on Tuesday will be fine." She glanced at RJ and noticed he was deep in thought.

"Wait just a minute, Beth. I need to check my calendar in my office. Hang tight. I'll be right back." RJ patted her hand and hurried from the kitchen.

Far too quickly, RJ was back. "Damn, Beth. Tuesday just won't do for me," RJ said, oozing with sincerity. "I have to drive up north to Dennison to pick up some parts that I have to replace on my truck. The fellow called Friday and said they were in, so I better get my butt up there and pick them up before he sends them back. It's not a real far distance, but it's sort of a slow ride. It's real pretty though. You'll enjoy the scenery."

Beth wondered how the auto parts store could have called RJ on Friday, when she'd not been able to call him, but she decided, maybe RJ hadn't "fixed" the phone before they called. Beth placed her head on her hands, wondering what to do now. "Juanita, could you get me a phone book? Maybe if I call now, I can get a flight on a major airline on Wednesday. Maybe…."

RJ quickly interrupted. He had no intention of letting her leave so soon. Why, there were things she needed to see. Things he needed to show her. Wednesday was no good. "Wednesday, I need to go into Polk and take old Paul out for lunch for bringing you out to my place last night, Beth. You need to thank him again, too. That's the way it's done around here. Folks here are right friendly and he'll want to see you again. No, Beth. Wednesday's no good."

Exasperated with his excuses, Beth flipped the phone book closed and turned to glare at RJ. When she'd talked to him last week, it didn't seem it would be a problem for "someone" to take her to the airport in Dallas. After some thought, Beth's glare turned into a knowing smile. He didn't want her to leave. "I suppose you're busy on Thursday, too, RJ."

"Yeah," he answered, grinning. "Thursday's no good for me, either Beth. I need to run my boys over to Chandler to the vet. They've been looking poorly lately. On the way back we'll stop by this little greasy spoon that's got the best hamburgers in all of Texas. Well, except for Juanita's hamburgers." RJ's face melted into a big Texas grin. "You're gonna love those hamburgers, Beth."

Juanita watched RJ's two boys racing across the back fields. They sure didn't look sick to her. "I'll bet Marco isn't busy, RJ. He can take Beth to Dallas on Thursday." She turned toward RJ smiling innocently.

RJ's big grin dropped flat. "Hell. Well, now that I think about it, maybe I can take you to Dallas on Thursday.... if you're of such a mind to leave so soon."

Beth's heart gave a flutter. RJ had tried everything to get her to stay and the truth was, she really didn't want to leave, but she couldn't help it. She'd agreed to model for the Children's Hospital fundraiser, and she couldn't let them down. Still, knowing he wanted her to stay with him made her feel warm and gooey all over.

Hoping Juanita and Luis didn't notice, Beth slipped her arm under RJ's and put her hand on his leg. As soon as possible, she would return to RJ. She had to. She couldn't stay away from him. Coming back to reality, she wondered what sort of excuse she'd give her old widow friends, so they wouldn't find out about her and RJ. She'd use Anne. Yes, she'd tell them Anne needed her help doing something, but of course, she'd be staying with RJ. My Lord, what would she tell Anne? She could never let Anne know her mother was sleeping with her father-in-law. Beth thought about sleeping with Anne's father-in-law and felt her body tense with excitement. She was in love with RJ. It was a good thing.

"I have to go back to Tulsa, RJ, because I hadn't planned to stay here more than a day or so, but I'll come back soon when I can stay longer." Beth felt RJ stiffen beside her. "Honestly, RJ, I have to get back to Tulsa."

RJ glared at the kitchen table, pouting. "Why? What's in Tulsa that you don't have here?"

Forgetting about Juanita and Luis, Beth pulled herself closer to RJ and kissed him softly on his shoulder. “Everything I want is here, RJ, but I have commitments that I need to handle in Tulsa.”

RJ pulled her hand from his leg and examined it carefully, avoiding the interested stares of Luis and Juanita. He’d dreamed of her coming, but never thought of her leaving. Hell, since she’d been here, he’d been more content than he’d ever been in his life. She couldn’t leave. He wouldn’t allow it. He couldn’t stand it. Good God, he was in love with the woman. How in the hell did that happen, he wondered. Didn’t matter how it happened, it did happen and that was a fact. Now that he knew his dilemma, he’d be damned if he’d let her just go trotting away from him. Hell no. There had to be a way to keep her from leaving.

RJ turned and looked down at Beth snuggled so close to him. He wished they were alone, back in bed again, but they weren’t. It had to be done now, quickly, without warning. He’d catch her off guard while she didn’t have a chance to think about it. RJ cleared his throat and then spoke his thoughts. “Beth, I’m a free man now. If you marry me, you could stay here with me forever.”

Beth looked up in shock. Luis and Juanita hung over the table in excited expectation. RJ grinned.

“My Lord, RJ. Was that a proposal?” Beth asked, overcome with disbelief, shock, happiness. Could her dreams, possibly be coming true? This was just too easy. She loved him. Obviously, he loved her. Now he was free. Yes. Oh Lord, yes.

“We can’t have a proposal without a ring, Beth.” RJ grinned sheepishly. “I was thinking maybe one of those pretty pink diamond rings to match those earrings of yours. Course, you can have anything you want.”

Juanita couldn’t believe she was witnessing this beautiful proposal. Luis couldn’t believe RJ was so slick. Beth couldn’t believe any part of it. RJ couldn’t believe he’d live long enough to hear her answer.

Beth placed herself in position for a convenient kiss. “I do love pink diamonds, RJ,” she whispered.

Grinning, his big grin, RJ slipped both his arms around Beth and pulled her close to him. He smelled her hair and rubbed his face against her brow. He sought her lips with his. Soon, he was enjoying the wonders of a most convenient kiss.

Juanita and Luis stared at each other contentedly and remembered a long time ago.

Chapter 27

RJ shifted Big Red into gear and steered her down the two-lane highway toward Poke, Texas. Passing "Big Goldie's" he glanced over at Beth and smiled, remembering the warning Goldie had given him about Beth being a cold, frigid woman. Beth was no cold, frigid woman. She was a woman with a passion equal to his. She'd taken him to her bed and now she was taking his name; a name he was proud to offer her.

RJ was a happy man. He couldn't ever remember being really happy. Yeah, he was happy when Jason was born, but Carla ruined that. He'd been delighted to have a son, and he'd hoped to have many more children. Carla ruined that, too. She'd blackmailed him for twenty-five years, so he'd never been able to have a life of his own. Now she was dead and he was done with her. At long last, she couldn't touch him anymore.

RJ knew his happiness was because of Beth, and he wanted her to know how happy she had made him. He decided he'd let her know the only way he knew; he'd spend lots of his money on her. He'd buy her a gigantic pink diamond set in platinum with a whole bunch of white diamonds around it and pink and white diamonds around the platinum wedding band, too. He'd give her so many diamonds she'd hardly be able to life her hand. It would be a grand ring. RJ stopped his thoughts about the grand ring, and realized that such a grand ring would have to be custom-made. That could take a long time. Hell, she could change her mind about marrying him if the jeweler took too long. RJ thought about that for a minute. No, he decided, he'd settle on the biggest pink diamond set the jeweler had in the store. He'd buy it today. No reason to give Beth any chance to come up with some silly excuse and change her mind about marrying him. She loved him. He knew she loved him, but still, life had a way of screwing him personally. No, he wouldn't take any chances. They'd get the ring today. It would be done.

Beth admired the Texas landscape as they passed through the town of Poke, Texas. One day soon, Texas would be her home with RJ. Once he'd asked her to marry him, she could barely wait to become his wife. First, they needed a ring, RJ had said, and he was adamant about getting one that day. RJ was old-fashioned about such things.

Beth thought about the ring she would have. It would be just a simple ring. She didn't need a big flashy diamond engagement ring. A single white gold wedding band with a few tiny pink diamond chips would be perfect, nothing too expensive. She didn't care about RJ's money. She'd lived this long without luxuries, and knew she didn't need such things to make her happy. He made her happy. That's all that mattered. And the fact that he loved her, and he did love her.

RJ moved his arm around the back of the bench seat of the truck and grinned at Beth in invitation. Quickly, she scooted next to him and pulled his arm down around her shoulder. They were teenagers again: happy, aging teenagers.....passionate, aging teenagers.

Beth looked down at her hands and stroked the rings that Charles had given her in wedlock. RJ knew Beth was deep in memories and he had a sick feeling inside him. Had she changed her mind? Would they get to the jewelers and she'd tell him to forget it, she preferred her past life to a future with him. RJ could feel shivers starting up his back.

They'd come to a deserted four-way stop before entering the traffic-filled highway that would take them to Dallas. RJ stopped and watched Beth for a minute. She looked up at him and smiled. Slowly, she worked Charles's rings from her left hand, leaving a deep indentation on her empty ring finger. Quickly, she moved Charles' rings to her right hand.

RJ leaned down and took a convenient kiss. She was his.

"Looks like it's gonna storm, again", RJ said as he leaned over the steering wheel of Big Red. "Good thing we headed for Dallas early this morning and got our business done." RJ grinned and Beth smiled, both content and happy.

Beth looked down at the massive pink diamond marquis solitaire waiting patiently on her ring finger. One day soon, it would be joined by its partner, an eternity platinum band engraved in the simple words, "NOW AND FOREVER." A matching band was in her purse for RJ.

Picking out rings had turned into quite an event. She wanted simple and RJ wanted grandiose. It had taken quite a while for them to agree on the rings, and she'd felt sorry for Mr. Stein, the jewelry store owner. He'd shown them every matched set he had in the store, but none seemed right for Beth and RJ. In desperation, Mr. Stein left them alone so he could bring out catalogues for more selections. While he was gone, RJ found the perfect engagement ring. Beth found the perfect wedding bands. The combination was a little odd, but they'd found the perfect set for them, and Beth and RJ were delighted.

Beth couldn't be happier than she was with RJ and wondered if their lives together would always be so tumultuous, so exciting, so incredibly satisfying at the outcome. Lord, she hoped so.

Pulling through the gate to his ranch, RJ stopped to inspect the security system that was being installed on the gate. "Keep it simple," he instructed. "I've got a lot of folks around here that aren't too good with technology."

Beth smiled. He was the worst one of all of them. He couldn't even turn on the phone.

RJ jumped back into the old red truck and Beth heard the ancient seat cover split. "Damn, I've got to be more gentle with the old gal," he laughed. But, she knew he wouldn't.

That morning, when they'd started off to Dallas, Beth couldn't help but laugh when she realized that "Big Red" would be their transportation. "You laughed about that little car I came in, RJ, what about this old truck. I doubt it will make it to Dallas."

Softly, he'd patted the one green fender of the old red truck. "Don't pay her any attention, Red. She's city folk, has no appreciation for an old work horse like you. But, don't you worry, Red, she's gonna be your new mama, and she'll soon love you as much as I do." RJ turned away from the old truck and as he helped Beth up into the passenger side, he whispered, "Beth, never say anything bad about Big Red. She gets really mad."

Beth smiled as she remembered the events of the early morning. They'd picked up her bag at the airport in Dallas, and she was happy that tomorrow she could wear different clothes. It had been an interesting day, but she was glad to be home at Scott's End Ranch.

RJ guided Big Red into the garage behind the sprawling house and hit the electric garage door to close. He sat for awhile, leaning over the steering wheel with his hands gripping the cover.

"We had a nice day today, didn't we, Beth?" he said, not expecting an answer, "Just the two of us." He placed his large hand on her leg and rubbed it gently. "Beth, I love you more than anything in this world," he whispered. "I swear I love you now, and I'll love you forever....now and forever, Beth."

Beth smiled and placed her hand over his hand. RJ told her of his love for her over and over that day. Once he'd discovered it was love he felt for her, he couldn't stop telling her, and she never tired of hearing it. Just as she needed those perfect words, Beth knew RJ needed them too, and each time she spoke them to him, his blue eyes sparkled with happiness. "I love you, too, RJ Scott....now and forever."

Having accomplished everything they wanted to do that day, Beth and RJ settled by the pool, shaded under the portico roofs. Enjoying the comfort of the white wrought iron chaise loungers, with their plush cushions of white, yellow, and blue stripes, RJ had fallen asleep and Beth was reading a book. Listening to the steady drone of RJ's barnyard musical, Beth found herself getting sleepy. Putting her book marker in place, she stood and started toward the house

"Where you going, Beth?" RJ yawned, his eyes still closed.

"I think I'll take a nap myself," she replied, leaning down and kissing him on his cheek.

"Okay," he said and pulled himself up from the chaise lounge.

"Did I invite you to my nap?" she asked, as he followed her into her bedroom.

"Yeah, you did." he said. "You kissed me, and I knew what that meant. It was an invitation for *Afternoon Delight* he mocked, pointing to the novel she'd been reading.

"Lord", she said, smiling as she entered her bedroom. "You are something else, RJ." RJ slipped his clothes off and crawled naked into her bed. Beth kept her clothes on and got into the bed next to him.

"Well, damn, Beth! You really are gonna take a nap!" RJ

laughed, but knowing himself to be the world's greatest lover, he wondered just how fast he could get her naked. It wouldn't take long, he decided, as he pulled her into his arms and kissed her.

Beth slipped her arms around RJ's neck and felt the passion of the man she loved. She smiled as he kissed her in areas she'd never dreamed could cause such pleasure, and wondered how long it would take him to get her clothes off. Not long, she was certain of that.

"RJ?" they heard Juanita's voice calling from the courtyard. "RJ, are you in there?"

"Yeah, Juanita, I decided to take a nap. That trip to Dallas wore me out."

Juanita's voice was high-pitched and worried. "RJ, you got to come out here. Larry Willis is here. Larry, the sheriff. The sheriff, at Poke, RJ."

"Yeah, Juanita, I'm coming," he grumbled grabbing his jeans. Quickly RJ pulled up his jeans, zipped them, ignoring his loose belt buckle. He'd be right back. No sense in bothering with closing the buckle. "Now, what the hell does he want?" RJ asked, throwing his shirt on around his shoulders.

RJ turned and grinned at Beth. "You stay right there, Beth, and don't you dare leave. As soon as I get rid of Larry, I'll be right back to give you some of my own special, "***Afternoon Delight***." RJ opened the bedroom door and walked out into the courtyard pulling the door closed behind him.

Hey RJ," the sheriff said. "Caught you taking a nap in the middle of the day, huh?" he stared past RJ into the bedroom. "Who's the lady in your bed?"

RJ leaned back to the door and pulled it shut behind him, making sure the latch closed this time. "Nobody you need to be interested in, Larry. Now, what can I do for you?"

The tall aging sheriff, his blue police shirt stretched tightly around his mounded belly, stared at RJ for a minute. "RJ, I just hate to do this. I really do. It's just nuts."

"What? Do what, Larry?" RJ asked, squeezing the grippers closed on his blue chambray shirt.

The tall sheriff openly scowled. He put one finger over one nostril of his nose and sniffed, then repeated the gesture with the other side of his nostril. “Damn allergies” he growled and then continued. “RJ, just let me ask you up front and we’ll be done with this whole thing. When was the last time you talked to Carla, your wife?”

RJ wondered if that damn Carla would ever stop torturing him. “Look Larry, she’s not my wife anymore. Carla’s dead.”

Sheriff Larry Willis was certain RJ didn't have anything to do with Carla's death. Hell, he'd been friends with RJ forever, but he sure didn’t like RJ’s quick answer. Questioning RJ wasn’t going to be easy. “RJ, you need to tell me right now if you know anything about your ex-wife’s death.”

“Hell, I don’t know how she died. She fell. Maybe she jumped. She’s gone. I don’t give a damn?”

“Good God, RJ. You don’t have to act so pleased about her death. That don’t look too good in your favor.” Larry Willis pulled out a wrinkled handkerchief and blew his nose. He folded it into a square and carefully wiped his nose as he watched RJ.

“What the hell do you mean, Larry, ‘It don’t look too good in my favor?’”

Sheriff Willis, the only police officer for the town of Poke and its surrounding community, wondered if RJ might be trying to avoid his question. Larry didn't want to put any false statements in RJ's mouth, so he knew he needed to be careful. He asked again. “Ok, RJ. Let’s start over. When was the last time you saw Carla, your deceased wife?”

RJ looked at Juanita and squirmed noticeably. “I guess, the last time I saw Carla was fifteen years ago. Yeah, wasn’t that what you said this morning, Juanita? You said….”

“Ain’t no need in dragging Juanita into this mess, RJ. When was the last time you saw Carla Scott, Jason’s mother?” Larry figured if he put it like that, RJ wouldn’t become so defensive. He’d shot craps with RJ when they were kids, and he knew RJ had a bad temper when someone tried to push him. “Please, just answer the question, RJ, so we can be done with it.”

RJ’s blue eyes turned into thin slits of cold blue ice, his voice deep and irritated. “Damn it, Larry. I told you, I saw Carla fifteen years ago and that’s when I last saw her.”

“Ah crap, RJ. You got to do better than that. It seems the

Dallas police got a tip suggesting you might have helped Carla over that patio railing." Larry Willis hated this kind of crap. Nothing like this had ever happened in Poke, Texas, and he wasn't used to it.

"Me? Are you bullin' me, Larry? Why'd I do something like that? I've put up with that woman's crap for twenty six years. If I was gonna kill her, I'd have done it a long time ago."

"The Dallas Police said they have some real incriminating proof that you went to see her on Friday about the time she was killed, RJ. They want me to bring you in for questioning. Damn it, you know I don't want to do this, but I ain't got no choice. It's either me or them coming to get ya."

Beth heard the conversation from the bedroom and could feel her world falling apart. Quickly, she opened the large door and walked into the courtyard. "RJ, what's he talking about? Is he suggesting you had something to do with Carla's death?" Beth glared at Sheriff Willis in defiance. "RJ had nothing to do with her death. He's a loving, kind man, and he'd never harm anyone."

Sheriff Willis looked Beth over for a minute, scowling and sniffing. "Lady, if I was you, I'd get the hell out of here as fast as you can. The Dallas Policc got a tip that RJ wanted to get rid of Carla, so he could marry some gal he took an interest in. And ma'am," he continued, waving toward the bedroom, "it's pretty obvious to me, you're that gal."

"Ah hell, Larry," RJ said, trying to tuck his shirt into his jeans and buckling them at the same time. "She hasn't got anything to do with this and neither do I. But, I'll come with you, anyway, just so we can clear this up fast. Just don't say anything about her, Larry. She doesn't need to be another victim of the Carla misery. Hell, I'm a prime example."

"I know, RJ," Larry answered, his demeanor softening, his voice sympathetic. "It seems like Carla's hold on you just goes on forever. She's dead and it's still going on." The sheriff hesitated for a minute. "RJ, I sure hope you got a good alibi for Friday. Those boys in Dallas are tough. They can make a case out of bullshit! Sorry, ladies."

Remembering his trip to Dallas on Friday, RJ turned and gave a worried glance toward Beth. Things were going to get bad for him, he was certain of that. He couldn't have Beth dragged into his mistakes, not now….especially, not now. Regardless of what she'd said about being able to take care of herself, he knew she couldn't handle the mess that was coming his way. He had to get her as far away from him as possible.

"I've got to get Beth out of here right now, Larry. The shit's gonna hit the fan real fast, and the Dallas Police will try and drag her into this mess. RJ remembered Larry talking about his no-good nephew that worked for one of the airlines. "Don't you have a nephew that works for the airlines, Larry?"

"Well, yeah, I do, but I don't trust the little bastard. Excuse me ladies. I'm sure he can sneak her through. He does it all the time, but it'll cost you plenty. He's pretty much of a lowlife."

"Money's not the problem, Larry. I'll pay whatever he wants. I want Beth out of Texas today." RJ chewed on his bottom lip anxiously waiting for Larry to answer.

Larry thought about it for a minute. His sun burned face turned gray. "Damn it, RJ, if they catch me trying to help you get that lady out of Texas, I could lose my job."

"Oh hell, Larry. I'll pay you too, if that's what you want."

Larry Willis felt sick. He didn't want RJ's money. Hell no. He just didn't want to lose the only job he'd known for the last twenty-four years. Hell, in a year he could retire with benefits.

RJ watched his old friend as he stood on one foot and then the other, scratching his soaked armpits and wiping his nose without his handkerchief. It wasn't the money he wanted and RJ knew it. Larry had a cushy job in poke where there was never any crime. Being the sheriff of Poke was a joke. The only one who didn't know it was Larry. "Larry, nobody wants that job of yours. Hell, they'll have to force your kid to take it when you retire. Anyway, nobody's gonna ever find out you helped me. Go on and call that no-good nephew of yours."

"Okay, I'll help you. Folks trust me in Poke, so I can't see where they'd suspect me of helping you hide your lady." Larry pulled out his cell phone and hurried toward his almost new 1994 Chevy Impala 9C1 police cruiser.

The cruiser had been in an accident on a high-speed chase in Dallas and that's why he was able to get it. He'd managed to get the cruiser repaired for nothing by pulling in a debt owed him by an old boy who owned a chop shop over in West Texas. Of course, he'd had the repair shop owner give him a bill for a small amount which he presented to the town of Poke, so they wouldn't get suspicious. Larry knew he was pretty clever milking the town for the small repair, and of course, they thought he was a hero for getting it done so cheaply. Larry laughed to himself and caressed the fender of the cruiser. Hell. He was a hero.

He'd been waiting forever for this new baby and barely had time to test it out when he got the call to pick up RJ for questioning. He didn't mind, though. He'd get a chance to see what she was made of on the open highway into Dallas.

Beth walked back into her bedroom to get her purse, RJ following closely behind her. "Beth," RJ whispered. "I was wondering if maybe you'd give me back your engagement ring for a little while." Beth was certain she'd seen the mist of unshed tears in RJ's eyes, so she didn't ask questions. She just removed her beautiful pink diamond ring and handed it and their boxed wedding bands to RJ.

RJ felt he might bawl like a baby as he watched Beth pull his ring from her finger, and move Charles' rings back to her left hand. It was killing him and he knew Beth was just as upset. "When this mess is cleared up, Beth, you can show off your pretty pink diamond ring to all your lady friends, and we'll get married just as fast as the law will allow us."

Grabbing her sweater and her purse, Beth followed RJ back into the garden. "I'll put the rings in the safe in my office until this mess is cleared up." Beth watched as he crossed the courtyard to his office.

In a few minutes he returned, a little boy in very deep pain. Beth took RJ's hand and pulled him along with her until they stood in front of the lady in the fountain. "Here, RJ," Beth whispered. "This is where we'll be married, right here." Pulling his calloused hands to her mouth, she adored them with her kiss.

RJ knew she was just dreaming their sweet dream that they'd created together and willingly he joined her. As he pulled her into his arms, the sacred silence was broken. Sheriff Willis had figured out how to use the speaker of his new police car. In a loud authoritative voice he shouted, "*Time's up, RJ. Get a move on!*"

Then they heard Larry giggle in delight with his new toy.

"RJ, it's a good thing the airport don't look so crowded today," Sheriff Willis said, glancing into the rear-view mirror at RJ and Beth. Gleaming with joy, Larry had almost forgotten about the passengers in the back seat of the police cruiser as he admired the bells and whistles of his second-hand toy. Driving it all the way to Dallas had given him his chance to open her up on the super highway and with lights flashing and sirens blazing, he'd enjoyed every minute of the ride. Effortlessly, he pulled the car into the departure area of the airport and waited for his nephew. After a few minutes, he spotted the skinny, long body and pimply face of his nephew, who, he noted, was still a slime ball.

RJ exited the back of the car and opened Beth's door for her. Sheriff Willis stayed in the car, seeing no reason to get out with RJ. Hell, he was just bringing RJ in for a few questions. Besides, he wanted to play with the radio.

As Beth exited the back of the police car, she noticed a tall, thin, young man nervously pacing up and down in front of the "Departures" door. She knew he'd be the person to get her on the plane for Tulsa. As he spotted her and RJ, Beth thought she saw him motioning to someone across from the loading area, but decided it was her imagination.

Larry had told her to leave her luggage at RJ's, to ensure she carried nothing to trigger the electronic sensor at the security gate. No need to call any attention to her. Heeding his warning, all she had with her was a nearly-empty purse and a sweater.

Beth thought the whole situation was absolutely ridiculous. She couldn't understand why they were taking RJ in for questioning. He'd made it clear to everyone that he hadn't seen Carla for fifteen years, so why would they suspect him of any wrongdoing. Why had RJ gone even this far to appease the police? It wasn't like RJ.

The skinny young nephew of Sheriff Willis motioned to his uncle in a half-wave of acknowledgement. He had no use for his uncle. His uncle was a damn pathetic idiot. Immediately, he recognized RJ and he knew his big show was just beginning. It wasn't very often he'd gotten an opportunity like this one. He gave "a big thumbs up" to the shadowy figure hiding behind the pier across the street. Mentally, he fondled all the toys and whores he'd have because of RJ Scott and his money. That slut Angie better never think about pushing him away again. He had money now.

RJ slipped his arm around Beth's waist as he saw the scrawny boy approaching them. He hated to let her go, but he knew this was for the best. Beth turned and looked up at him, her big brown eyes filled with questions and uncertainty. He patted her hand softly. "Don't worry Beth. Everything will be all right." Giving her a quick wink, he started toward the waiting police car. Larry had turned on the flashing lights and discovered a new "Zip Zip" sound to the siren which he sounded on and off while he waited for RJ. RJ pulled the door open to the waiting police car and growled at Larry. The lights and siren stopped.

RJ sensed he was a condemned man. Justice had rarely been in the cards for his life and he knew it. This would be more of the same. RJ turned and looked back at Beth, dreading the long separation he knew would be inevitable. Leaving the police cruiser door open, RJ hurried back to his Beth, his electric blue eyes storing photos of her in his mind. With the fervor of a madman, he pulled her as close to him as their clothed bodies would allow: his nose gasped her soft clean smell, his mouth consumed her lips, his mind wedded her soul into his. Hearing a new form of siren coming from the police car, RJ released this woman he loved....his Beth. "Now and forever, Beth," he whispered and quickly returned to the waiting police car. In an instant they were gone.

As the police car's tail lights flashed to a halt and pulled back onto the distant highway, a cold wind flashed about Beth's neck and shoulders settling upon her with a dampness that seemed unusual for the warm day. "Now and forever, RJ," she whispered, the wind tossing her words about as though they'd never been spoken.

Larry's nephew cast his eyes across the street and smiled, smugly satisfied. "Come on Lady. The show's over." And before she knew it, Beth was on a plane back to Tulsa.

Chapter 28

As Beth paid the cab driver and walked up the drive to her home, she noticed a silver car parked across the street from her house, but paid it no attention. As she slipped her key into her front door, she turned and observed the silver car. There was a man in the car, and he had a camera that was focused on her. As she continued on into her house, she wondered why he wanted pictures of her. She was of no interest to anyone.

Checking her phone for messages, Beth could see there were none. She decided no news was good news, but still, her house seemed strangely different. Same smells, same ticking clocks, same Vodka under the sink. She poured herself a drink and walked out to the back steps and sat down. Setting her drink down on the step beside her, she could see far past the well-manicured yard and the perfect Azalea bushes. None of this mattered anymore. It was no longer her home.

In the distance of her mind, she could see horses and baby colts playing. Two red and white dogs slept peacefully in the afternoon sun. A statue of a peaceful lady in a fountain beckoned to her. A shy, brown-skinned woman touched her heart. A big, rugged cowboy loved her. That was her home.

For the first few hours after Beth returned from Dallas, she'd waited patiently for RJ's call to tell her everything was fine and they could continue their wedding plans. The call didn't come and neither did sleep. She wandered her house until she saw the sun begin to glow in the East, and flipping on the TV in the family room, she settled into her large brown leather chair and gazed at the emptiness of the big chair adjacent to her. She smiled, recalling happy memories with RJ, and vowed if RJ Scott was eating a big breakfast out on his patio while she sat there worrying herself sick, she was going to kill the man. Yes. She'd kill him, after she'd loved him into oblivion.

With the telephone ringing in her ear, Beth realized she'd fallen asleep. Quickly, she grabbed the phone hoping to hear RJ's deep voice. It was Anne. "Anne, you're back from Vegas so soon. I thought you and Jason would be staying until next Wednesday. "

"We'd planned to stay till Wednesday, Mom, but Clarisse Martel called Jason while we were there and said RJ had gotten himself in some real trouble."

Beth could feel the bile rise up inside her and felt like someone had kicked her in her stomach. She could barely speak. "Anne," she whispered. "Is RJ all right? Where is he now?"

"Mom, this really doesn't concern you. I just wanted to let you know about RJ in case you saw something on the news about his arrest."

"His *arrest*!" Beth grabbed the leather chair to steady herself.

"Don't worry about it, Mom. RJ has a good attorney. Clarisse Martel is the top dog at work and she'll see to it that RJ gets a fair deal."

"Anne," Beth pleaded, "I really do want to hear about RJ." Beth realized Anne had no idea about her and RJ. My God, they were lovers. They were planning to marry, and her daughter was talking to her as though they were casual acquaintances, but Beth knew she couldn't say anything. On the way to the airport, RJ said that for Jason's sake, they shouldn't mention their marriage plans until the Carla turmoil was over. He knew Jason would be angry because his mother had stayed away from him all those years, and Jason needed time to accept it. RJ said Jason would probably never have noticed her small obituary in the newspaper, but now that the sheriff thought she'd been murdered, Jason would find out and he would suffer, another one of Carla's victims.

Anne's voice interrupted Beth's tumultuous thoughts. "It seems they have evidence that RJ went to see his ex-wife on Friday morning, right around the time of her death. Well now, come to think of it, she wasn't his ex-wife being as they were still married. Gosh, Mom. I thought his wife died years ago. Jason did too. He's really upset that RJ kept her hidden from him all these years."

Remembering her promise to RJ, Beth tried to remain calm. She couldn't tell Anne about the evil that was Carla Scott. And she certainly couldn't tell Anne that she, Anne's mother, had eagerly committed her body and her soul to Jason's father, but she had to know about RJ. "Anne, I, uh… I got to know RJ fairly well while I stayed at his ranch. I doubt that RJ would have kept Jason from his mother if she'd wanted to see him."

Anne laughed softly. "Good old mom, always thinking the best of everyone, even gruff old RJ Scott. RJ keeps his feelings to himself, Mom. It seems to me most people only allow us to see the face they present to the world. Mean inner secrets, they hide deep inside them."

Beth was sick with fear and over-come with anger. The only ugly emotion she didn't feel was doubt. She knew RJ Scott inside and out. She knew his thoughts, his pain, and his dreams, and she knew he had nothing to do with his wife's death. "Anne, please listen to me. I found RJ to be an extremely kind and gentle man. RJ doesn't have a tinge of meanness in him. He could never kill anyone."

"I suppose that's true, Mom. The RJ we know is a decent man and his reputation is what he'll stand on. Besides, he'd been married to his wife for, I guess twenty-six years, so why would he kill her now? He had no motive."

Beth collapsed into the big brown chair. The cushion gave a mighty whoosh. "Mom, are you all right? It sounded like you fell."

Beth felt the sweat running down her face and the chills running up her spine. Even though RJ had gotten her out of Dallas quickly, it was only a matter of time before the whole world knew about them. She knew what the prosecutor would say was RJ's reason to kill his wife. Elizabeth Carlton was his reason. Silent tears formed in Beth's eyes, ran down her cheeks, and buried themselves into wet stains on her pink and white nightgown. Breathless gasps attacked her throat, leaving her speechless and empty.

Anne's voice was heavy with worry. "Mom! Answer me. Did you fall? Should I call 911? If you can't get to the phone, shout if you can. Mom, I'm hanging up and calling 911. Someone will be there quickly."

Beth grabbed the phone and forced herself back to life. "Sorry, Anne. I didn't mean to frighten you. I dropped the phone and was retrieving it from under the chair. I'm all right. I'm fine." She lied.

"Well, thank God you're all right, Mom. We've got enough to worry about with RJ. Okay, well, as long as you're all right, I need to get back to work. Keep your answering machine on in case you're out playing Bridge or at lunch with your lady friends when I call. Uh, well, maybe you'd rather not be bothered with RJ's problems, Mom. After all, you barely know him."

"I know him well enough, Anne." Beth's trembling voice answered. "Please, please call me if anything at all happens to him."

Anne hesitated for a minute. She was becoming worried about her little mother. Her voice sounded so small. It sounded like when her father died. "Mom? Are you crying, Mom?"

Beth couldn't answer. The lump in her throat was choking her and her lips refused to unclench.

Anne's mother's silence said more than words could speak. Anne understood. "I'll call you as soon as I hear anything whatsoever about RJ, Mom. It will be all right. I promise. I love you, Mom."

Beth couldn't speak a decent "goodbye" to her daughter. She couldn't hang up the phone. The empty phone line droned a steady aggravating hum. Soon it was followed by demanding short beeps of a neglected busy signal. Gut wrenching sobs escaped Beth's clenched lips and viciously tore open her heart. Her soul was stripped naked and empty. There were no words.

Beth spent the rest of Sunday in her pink and white night-gown, not bothering to shower or brush her hair, and for the first time in over twenty-five years, she'd neglected church. Her rigid life's routine was completely abandoned in her worry over RJ and she didn't care.

The dreary Sunday turned into a dreary Monday. Beth didn't eat, she couldn't sleep. The phone rang. On the second ring, Beth grabbed the receiver praying it was RJ. It was Anne.

"Mom, something awful has happened." Beth braced herself. "There's a picture on the front page of the Monday Dallas newspaper," Anne hesitated. "The headlines read 'RJ SCOTT'S MYSTERY WOMAN'. Are you still there, Mom?" Anne didn't wait for an answer. "The photo was taken at the airport Saturday, and it's of RJ in a passionate embrace with an unidentified woman. The face of the woman is partially covered by RJ, but Mom, I recognize the person. It's you, isn't it?"

Beth didn't know how to answer. What could she say that wouldn't hurt RJ any further? She didn't answer.

"Mom, please. RJ won't say anything about the woman in the picture. He's protecting her. He's protecting you, Mom. RJ's defense has to know the truth before it gets any worse for him. Please, Mom."

"Anne," Beth began in cautious, deliberate words. She remembered the kiss at the airport and could only imagine what it looked like. She had to minimize the importance of the picture. "RJ and I have a casual interest in one another. It's nothing, really."

"It looked like a really hot kiss, Mom. I hate to ask you this, but just how far has this casual interest between you and RJ gone? Have you been intimate with him?"

Beth thought she'd throw up. "I'm not going to answer that question, Anne. You're my daughter and you have no right to question my morals."

"I'm sorry, Mom. I know you want to help RJ, but RJ won't help himself. We have to know how far your relationship went with him, so we can counter it somehow."

Beth's answer was the sound of soft uncontrolled sobs.

"It's all right, Mom. I understand. I love you, Mom." And Beth was alone again with the angry phone.

Tuesday was worse. Beth broke away from her dedication to the phone. She was sick with worry about RJ, but hunger was making her body weak. Drying her body with a large towel, she wrapped it around herself and took a smaller towel to her hair. Skeptically, she studied herself in the mirror. She looked awful. The worry lines around her eyes did little to offset the deep shadows under eyes. Her warm ivory skin was a cold gray and deep hollows controlled her once rosy cheeks. The sparkle was replaced in her dark eyes with a dead somber glare.

When Beth had left for RJ's Thursday, she'd cleaned out all her food, leaving a lonely jar of dill pickles and a questionable can of chicken noodle soup. The thought of going to the grocer nearly made her nauseous, but it was inevitable. That or starve.

Beth dressed, left her hair hanging in loose damp curls above her shoulders, and walked to the kitchen to open the lonely can of soup. She popped a cup of soup into the microwave and noticed the answering machine blinking. Ignoring her soup, she pushed the recorder button on to hear the message that came in while she was showering. “Beth,” the recording said. “This is Alma Green. Don’t bother to come to my house for Bridge, today. I don’t feel well. No need to return my call.” With all the turmoil, Beth had forgotten Tuesday Bridge at Alma’s. She knew Alma must be really quite ill. For as long as she could remember, Alma Green had the widows Tuesday Bridge on the third Tuesday of the month. Even if Alma was on her death bed, red raspberry iced tea and shortbread cookies would be served. The Tuesday Bridge routine was mandatory.

The phone rang and Beth grabbed it. Mary Edwards’ sweet voice answered. “Elizabeth, how are you feeling, dear?” Mary Edwards was a gentle, kind woman, a Bridge substitute who lived outside the city of Tulsa.

“I’m fine, Mary. How are you?”

“Oh,” the sweet voice answered. “I understood from Alma Green that you were ill. She asked me to take your place for the Bridge group today, so I was just calling to see if you needed anything.”

It hit Beth like a ton of bricks. Alma Green had recognized her picture in the Dallas paper and was distancing the widows’ group from her. Alma Green would smugly confide to the widows at the Bridge group today that Beth was a wanton woman. She’d ask them to pray for Beth; maybe even shed a few tears over Beth’s lack of morals. She’d do her best to destroy Beth as quickly and efficiently as her evil mouth could run.

Sinking into a kitchen chair, Beth thanked her friend and laid the phone back in its cradle. She'd stopped her local newspaper before she left for Dallas, and now she wondered just what was being said about her and RJ in the local newspapers. After sipping a half cup of soup, Beth called both the Tulsa and Dallas newspaper to start up daily delivery as soon as possible. Quickly, she drove to Bern’s Grocery Store for a newspaper and some food.

After selecting simple salad fixings, tuna, a carton of eggs, and a loaf of bread, Beth approached the checkout line where she felt the first, but not the last, and certainly not the worst, of the angry stings of hostility toward her. Alma had been busy.

Recognizing the lady in line ahead of her from church, Beth spoke to the lady. The lady appeared to not hear her. Reaching past her cart, Beth touched the lady’s arm, but the lady turned away from her, ignoring her as though she didn't exist.

When Beth turned to the lady in line behind her, another familiar face from church, the lady pulled away and hurried from the line completely ignoring Beth. As Beth laid her groceries on the roller to be checked out by the checker, the checker slapped a "closed" sign on her counter and exited her booth. Hurt beyond belief, Beth spied Monday's paper that she hadn't received. Quickly, she unfolded the paper and there on the front page was a picture of RJ kissing her at the airport in Dallas, the Poke Police car and Larry waits in the background. The headlines shouted:

THE OTHER WOMAN
"Was RJ Scott's Mystery Woman
The Reason for the Murder?"
Ron Moore, NPI Reporter

Beth couldn't read any further and let the paper fall onto the shelf. Feeling sick to her stomach, her knees ready to buckle, Beth left the cart and food next to the checkout and hurried out of the store.

Livid, Beth slammed the door closed on her little car, remembering the headlines, "THE OTHER WOMAN". Surely, not everyone felt as those ladies did. Everyone knew she wasn't the "other woman type". My lord, she'd never so much as had coffee with a man since Charles' death. She was the epitome of respectability, except for RJ Scott, she reminded herself. Silently, Beth wondered exactly what was "The Other Woman" type.

The anger left Beth and was replaced with a hollow hopelessness. Resting her hands on her steering wheel, Beth regained her composure. Alma had done her job well and Beth was sure Alma had made certain her other friends had seen the picture, too. They all knew she'd been staying at RJ's home during her daughter's wedding, but surely they'd see it as a simple kiss of farewell between two friends. Yes, just a simple kiss. Beth knew she was kidding herself. That was **no** simple kiss. Beth thought about RJ for a moment: his teasing grin, his calloused touch, and his large warm body. She loved him beyond forever and she missed him horribly. She'd give anything on earth just to be with him. He was her love. He was her life.

Beth pushed her precious personal memories of RJ out of her mind. How could her real friends believe that trite composed from the imaginative head of Ron Moore? Most of her friends had met RJ when she brought him to church. Knowing him, how could they possibly believe RJ capable of killing someone? Of course, Alma Green, Mrs. Pious herself, would do what she could to perpetuate the awful story.

Thinking back, Beth remembered Jason talking about Ron Moore when he and RJ first came to her house. Jason had apologized about his grubby appearance, explaining that he'd been working night and day and finally won a court case against Ron Moore, a Dallas news reporter. RJ had warned him of Ron Moore's threats of revenge, but Jason had blown if off and laughed about it. Now, Beth wondered if destroying Jason's father was Ron Moore's revenge against Jason.

Beth entered her home to the ringing of the telephone. It was Anne. "Mom, have you seen Tuesday's Dallas paper?" Anne didn't let her mother answer. "No, you won't receive it until later. Mom, today's headlines are awful. Ron Moore has stooped so low as to put a picture of Dad in the paper."

"Good Lord, Anne. What would your father have to do with all of this?"

"Sit down, Mom, and I'll read the today's headlines to you." Beth found a chair and braced herself. Anne continued:

"RJ SCOTT'S MYSTERY LOVER"
WIDOW OF CHARLES CARLTON
REVERED OKLAHOMA ATTORNEY
By Ron Moore NPI Reporter

The mystery woman, RJ Scott's lover and motive for the murder of Carla Scott, his wife of twenty six years, has been identified as Mrs. Elizabeth Carlton of Tulsa, Oklahoma, widow of the late Charles Carlton, a highly-respected Tulsa attorney.

"I'm not going to read any further, Mom," Anne said. "You'll read it when you get your paper. There are four pictures in the paper, Mom. The first is of RJ at some cattlemen's convention. The second is of Dad when he received the "Citizen of the Year" award. The next picture is of you and RJ embracing at the airport. The forth is a picture of you, opening your front door, evidently when you came home on Saturday. And Mom, way down on the bottom of page two in the Dallas paper is a small article about the suspension of Larry Willis, the sheriff of Poke, Texas. He's being suspended on grounds of negligence with a prisoner, RJ Scott. That picture of you and RJ at the airport shows the sheriff in the background completely ignoring RJ. The paper says that Sheriff Willis was slated to retire next year after twenty-five years of service. Now the poor guy gets nothing. Can you believe this mess, Mom? Now the TV stations have picked up this story, so I'm sure it will just get worse. I've got to go now, but I'll call you later. Bye, Mom."

Beth wandered her house like a lost ghost, as she watched the sunshine filtering through the blinds of her windows turn into the gradual shades of dusk. After miles of pacing, she heard the doorbell ring. Cautiously, Beth opened her door and saw an older model pickup truck pulling away from the curve. When she looked on the bottom step of her porch, she spied a familiar box filled with homemade bread, jams, strawberries, and fresh tomatoes. There was bacon, wrapped in white butcher's wrap, a flat of brown eggs, and a plastic container of pecans. Just when she'd needed them most, Charles' people had come. They didn't judge her. They just wanted to help.

Beth waved gratefully to the truck and leaned down to gather the box of food. As she stood up, she spotted the silver car and the photographer clicking his camera at her. Quickly she ducked back into her house.

After eating enough to quell her growling stomach, Beth placed the food in the refrigerator. She returned to the family room and slumped down in the big brown chair and flipped on the TV with the remote control. The TV stations were having a ball with any sordid details Ron Moore had fed them. One channel was quoting Ron Moore as though he'd been a personal acquaintance of RJ. Beth flipped the channel. The minister on the religion channel was using RJ and her as an example of the aftermath of lust. She flipped the channel; more news about RJ and her. She flipped the channel again, caught herself and flipped back to the previous channel. She heard the young lady reporter mention the name of "Stein's Jewelry". That's where they'd bought the rings, she remembered. Now what? Quickly Beth turned up the volume. The young broadcaster began, whiter than white teeth glowing on her overly tanned face.

"Good Morning, my friends:

Today we learned more about the intriguing romantic saga of RJ Scott, a wealthy rancher and Texas businessman, and Elizabeth Carlton, widow of highly-respected Oklahoma attorney, Charles Carlton, who passed away seven years ago.

RJ Scott's wife of twenty-six years, Carla Desmond Scott, was found dead Friday, leaving a question of the cause of her death. It has been stated by a local news reporter that he had proof that Mr. Scott killed his wife to appease his mistress, Mrs. Elizabeth Carlton.

Upon reading various unsavory articles regarding Mr. Scott and Mrs. Carlton, Mr. LJ Stein of "STEIN'S JEWELRY" of Dallas, called this station and stated he was appalled that the newspapers would print such nonsense without sufficient evidence against Mr. Scott, and he felt it negligent to defame Mrs. Carlton's reputation.

Mr. Stein stated that Mr. Scott wanted only the best diamonds for his future bride, and of course that's why they chose "STEIN'S JEWELRY". When they'd entered his showroom, Mr. Stein was quoted as saying, "RJ Scott said he wanted the fanciest pink diamond ring in the store to give to Mrs. Carlton. Mrs. Carlton stated she was not a fancy woman and didn't want a fancy ring.

"Mr. Scott decided on an engagement ring, a five-caret pink diamond solitaire, mounted on platinum surrounded by miniature diamonds, with a matching

wedding band of five smaller diamonds. Mrs.Carlton decided on a single wedding band inset with pink diamond chips, total carat weight of one quarter. No engagement ring."

Mr. Stein said he'd been at a loss to settle the bantering between the two elders, so he'd gone into his back room in search of some ring catalogues that might suffice both of them. Before he could find what he'd been searching for, he heard a commotion in his showroom. Returning to his showroom, the other patrons were applauding and cheering, some even whistling, as they watched RJ Scott and Elizabeth Carlton embrace with a passion that would have put younger couples to shame. They had settled on the rings.

At first viewing, Mr. Stein said he doubted the unusual ring choices would complement one another, but after seeing the two rings together, he realized it was a perfect fit, just like Mr. Scott and Ms. Carlton.

Mr. Stein said that even though he was remodeling for his grand opening next week at his downtown location of "STEIN'S JEWELRY" with lots of fabulous sales to offer, he felt it was necessary to call the station and make his comments known.

"Myra Sands reporting, Channel 10 WMMQ NEWS, Dallas."

Beth almost laughed. What a way to get some free advertising. Beth threw up her hands and went to bed. After spending countless hours tossing and turning, pulling blankets on, kicking them off, Beth fell into a sleepless expanse of time. A few hours later she gave up.

Early Wednesday morning, the phone rang. It was Anne. "Mom, Jason's with me on the extension." Silence, cold silence.

Beth didn't know what to say to Jason and it was obvious he didn't want to speak to her. "Good morning, Jason," she said. More silence. Beth knew it was coming. Jason wouldn't be able to conceal his anger at her. She'd have to accept it and rise above it. They had to move on for RJ's sake.

"Jason, stop acting like a rotten spoiled little kid. Speak to my mother."

"Hello," was Jason's reply. Silence again.

"Good God, Mom. This whole damn thing just gets crazier and crazier. Have you seen this Mr. Stein, the jeweler on TV? Where'd he come from?" Anne didn't let her answer. "Surely you and RJ hadn't planned to marry. Lord, you just met RJ, Mom."

Beth spoke very slowly, determined to make them understand. "RJ and I have a committed relationship."

Beth heard Jason whisper to Anne, "*I told you she was a husband stealer.*"

She heard Anne whisper to Jason, "*Don't you ever call my mother a husband stealer again, or I'll leave you so fast you'll wonder if I was even here.*"

Gripping the phone so hard her fingers lost all color, Beth cringed.

"Mom, did you know that RJ was still married? Did you know that RJ had kept Jason's mother from him all these years? You didn't know about all of this, did you, Mom? You were just an innocent. Tell Jason that you knew nothing about RJ and his wife, Jason's mother. Tell him, Mom. Please tell him." Beth's chin trembled holding back the tears. Poor Anne, poor Jason.

Jason interrupted Anne. "Elizabeth, did my dad say anything to you about my mother being alive? About them still being married?"

Anne interrupted Jason. "Mom, you wouldn't go along with something like that, would you, Mom? You didn't know, did you?"

Beth didn't respond. What could she say? How did their private love become so sordid, so open for the world's discussion? Beth gave a deep sigh summoning forth a strength deep inside her that she never knew existed. When she finally spoke, her voice was solid and steady. Her thoughts were clear and concise. She was the woman RJ would expect her to be. "Sometimes, marriages just don't work out, Jason, and that's what happened between your dad and Carla. Both of them discovered this shortly after you were born and that's when they separated. Carla moved away, found a new life, and your dad raised you at Scott's End Ranch. From that time on, they had no congenial contact. Believe me, Jason, there was no love between RJ and Carla. They were married in name only."

"Oh, that's a great answer, Elizabeth!" Jason was enraged. "You knew my mother was alive and still married to my dad. Still, you just chose to ignore the fact and indulged in this cheap, dirty affair with him. What did you want out of him, anyway, Elizabeth? His money? You're something else, dragging all of us to church, doing the respectable widow act. What sort of a hypocrite are you anyway?"

Jason was furious, and even though Anne was a new wife, she knew Jason had to dispel his anger before he could move on. Her mother hadn't uttered a sound during Jason's tirade against her, and Anne knew her mother was a lot tougher than anyone thought. Somehow, her little frightened mother had turned into a solid rock. Anne sighed and let Jason continue. "Elizabeth, if my dad didn't love my mother, then why didn't he divorce her?" Jason didn't let her answer. "You said my dad didn't care about my mother and hadn't seen her in years. Then, explain how they have a video of him going into her apartment building on Friday afternoon and coming back out a short time later? Can you explain that, Elizabeth? He did care about her! Ron Moore got one thing right in the paper. You're just the other woman!"

"Jason!" Anne yelled, she'd had enough. "That's not necessary! Your little tantrum won't get RJ out of this mess!"

Anne began to explain what happened after Beth left Dallas. "Mom, RJ had no alibi for the time Carla Scott was killed. They have him on a video going into her building and coming out about ten minutes later. The coroner has the time of death listed pretty close to that time frame. And Mom, yesterday they had no real motive for RJ to kill Carla. Now, this picture of him kissing you at the airport showed up in Sunday's paper. They were simply looking for a motive, Mom. Now, they're saying *YOU* are the motive."

"That's insane." Beth answered waiting for Jason to attack her again. "RJ hadn't seen Carla in fifteen years. He told me that and I believe him. Besides, he didn't have to kill her so he could be with me. I was his, married or not! I love RJ and he loves me."

"Oh, my God!" Jason uttered in disgust under his breath. "Elizabeth, you don't even know my father. The two of you just met a few weeks ago, so how could you be so *in love* with him? That's just a cheap excuse. How could you do this?"

"Shut up, Jason!" Anne yelled at her new husband. "Mom, this whole mess is just awful. Clarisse Martel is an excellent criminal defense lawyer, but she sure doesn't have much to work with. In fact, she has nothing."

"Anne, RJ didn't kill Carla. He couldn't do anything like that. RJ is one of the finest men I've ever known. He wouldn't hurt anyone!"

Anne began again. "We know that, Mom. But, we also know that people have been convicted on much less evidence than they have against him. Unless some miracle happens, I'm afraid he doesn't have a chance. It looks like he'll spend the rest of his life in prison."

Beth put her hand over her mouth to cover her sudden gasp. RJ, who loved the fresh air, the sunshine, nature. Locked up, locked away from everything he loved, he'd die.

"Well, brace yourself, Mom," Anne continued. "There will be reporters and photographers tracking every step you take. RJ is a rich, powerful man, and watching the mighty fall will sell a lot of papers."

"I'm coming to Dallas right away", Beth said. "At least, RJ will know I'm there."

"That's not an option, Elizabeth!" Jason warned aggravation in his voice. "Don't even think about coming to Dallas. Having you here would just cause more trouble. Dad was smart to get you out of here. Yeah, Dad was smart about a lot of things." Jason was quiet for a moment. "All right, Elizabeth," Jason began, reconsidering his outburst at his new mother-in-law. "I'm sorry about my nasty remark about you and my dad, but I'm so damn angry at him for not telling me about my mother being alive! And I just couldn't believe that he told you that he was a married man and you accepted it. Good God, Elizabeth! How could you do something so sleazy? Have you no pride?"

"Jason," Beth ignored the stab at her heart and answered softly, "There's a lot more to this story than I can say, but believe me, your father loves you. If he led you to believe that she was dead, then he had a good reason for it. Just because RJ didn't say anything about her doesn't mean he lied."

"And, sometimes not saying anything can make everything

else a lie." Jason was quiet for a moment. No one said anything. Finally, he continued. "Of course, I'll stick by my Dad, but I wish he'd let me know my mother while she was alive. That wasn't fair to me. It was cruel. Can't you understand that, Elizabeth?"

"Believe me, Jason," Beth's soft mother's voice came alive. "Your father only did what he thought was best for you. He loves you. This time, you've got to trust his judgment. "

Jason ignored her answer completely. "You know what the real candle on this piece of crap cake is, Elizabeth. I have to go to the reading of my mother's will next week. I understand she left me everything she owned." No one said anything for a minute, as they waited for Jason to continue. In an almost childlike voice, he continued, "I would have been a good son to my mother, if my Dad had let me know her. I hope she knows that. God, I don't think I'll ever forgive him for keeping me from her. "

"Jason, my love, what's done, is done. There's no going back." Anne said softly, trying to soothe his pain. "Let's just try and come up with a way to help your dad out of this mess."

"Mom, I know this can't be easy for you." Anne continued, "I know you ***think*** you love RJ, but I'm sure that's because you've been alone so long and he's the first man you've been around. But really Mom, you just barely know RJ. Now, you're being drug into this whole mess, as though you are some *'femme fatale'*. This whole situation is just awful and it's certainly not fair to you."

"Anne, regardless of what you think about RJ and me, please let me come to Dallas," Beth pleaded. "Surely, it can't get any worse than it is now."

"No, Mom, Jason's right. Don't come to Dallas unless the DA's office sends a summons to you. It would be uncomfortable for RJ having you visit him in jail and it would just stir up more trouble. Just stay where you are and stay out of this mess. In time, you'll forget RJ and maybe you'll meet a nice stable man, someone like Dad. I'll call you and let you know what's going on."

"I'll be here, Anne," Beth answered, completely defeated. "I'll be here." Beth remembered the silver car parked across from her house, waiting for her appearance. No, she wouldn't be leaving the house.

Silently, with her hands folded in her lap, Beth sat waiting in her big brown leather chair in the den. She couldn't eat. She didn't read. She didn't sleep. She just sat. Waiting and worrying. *Was this her fault*? She knew RJ was a married man and she'd just wished it away. Now, they'd pay the consequences. He might pay with the rest of his life behind bars. How could this be? Had their love been so wrong that it would destroy them? All they did was love each other. Was that so terrible? He'd tried to get a divorce from Carla, but for some sick reason, she wouldn't let him go. Now, she was dead and instead of them being free of her, she was destroying both of them. This woman who she'd never met was controlling her future. What sort of evil was she? And Silas Stone.... Beth was certain he was the one who called Ron Moore and suggested that RJ had killed Carla.

Beth heard the phone ring. Checking the caller ID, she saw it was Pastor Jim. She couldn't talk to him. She just couldn't be Elizabeth anymore. Waiting for the answering machine to pick up, she heard his voice. "Elizabeth, I've been out of town for a few days, but I'd like to talk to you. I don't know what you're feeling, but I'm a good listener. Please call me." Beth deleted the message and returned to the brown leather chair. She waited.

Thursday, a little after noon, Anne called. The news was worse. Anne told her the DA and RJ's attorneys had met before the arraignment to work out a deal. It didn't go well.

"Mom, Claire Martel tried to dispute the video of RJ coming out of Carla's apartment building. She argued he was barely recognizable under his big gray Stetson. That's when the District Attorney brought in the security guard from the apartment building. Damn it. Hang on a minute, Mom."

Beth heard Anne give copy instructions to her assistant then return to the phone. "The security guard said he was sure it was RJ Scott. He'd seen him parking an old red truck with one green fender in a parking place with a "reserved" sign on it. He said he'd explained to RJ that he couldn't park there because that area was reserved. Instead of moving his truck as he'd been told, RJ demanded to know who it was reserved for. Crap. Hang on, Mom. Let me get this other line. It might be something about RJ."

Beth heard the phone click. Biting her lip until it was nearly raw, she waited until Anne's voice picked up again. "Okay, Mom.

I'm back again. Now, where was I?"

"You were telling me about RJ and the reserved parking." Beth twisted her hair impatiently.

"Yeah, I'm sorry, Mom. The security guard said he told RJ reserved spaces were for "special people" in case they wanted to park there. Hearing that, RJ nearly exploded and said he was pretty damn special too, and RJ brushed right past him and walked into the building. The security guard said he'd written RJ Scott a parking ticket right then and there. That was one reason, he remembered him."

Beth heard Anne say something to someone who'd entered her office. "Damn, this is horrible trying to talk to you and being constantly interrupted. Hang on again, Mom. I'm closing my door, and instructing my assistant to delay all calls unless they're from Jason. The meeting with the DA and our team broke up for a few minutes for lunch, so I ran back to my office to call you real quick and I keep getting interrupted."

Beth heard a shuffle, a door close, and Anne was back. "Are you still there, Mom?"

"Anne, you were telling me about the security guard saying he'd remembered RJ because he'd given him a ticket."

"Yeah, right, Mom. Anyway, when RJ came back down the elevator, the security guard said he could tell RJ was mad as hell. He said 'RJ got in that old red truck and just barreled out of the parking lot.'" Beth heard Anne giggle. "Then the security guard said, 'That damn maniac only stopped long enough to throw the parking ticket in my face.'" Despite the severity of the charge, Beth had to smile.

"Everyone agreed that was definitely RJ Scott," Anne continued. "Even RJ didn't deny it. Clarisse said that anyone that was as blatant in his actions as RJ had been was obviously not trying to cover up some crime. Clarisse said if RJ had killed Carla, surely he would have tried to sneak out the back door of the apartment building. She said maybe he'd even leave his truck there overnight. Anything, so he wouldn't be seen leaving at the time of the murder."

Beth heard Anne take a drink from her water bottle, and then she continued. "It was argued by the DA that he did leave at that time, and he was on videotape. Carla was never seen alive again. The DA said that RJ was so angry with Carla that he picked her up and threw her over the balcony wall. The DA insisted RJ Scott's notorious temper got the best of him this time. Mom, are you still there? I know this is a lot to throw at you."

"I'm here, Anne. Please go on."

Anne took another sip of her water. "Okay, Mom. Anyway, RJ insisted he wasn't guilty. He said he'd never seen Carla. He could hear movement inside the apartment, but she wouldn't answer the door. He said he went there to beg her to give him a divorce. He was prepared to give her anything he owned. All he wanted was his freedom. RJ said when she wouldn't answer the door, he got so angry, he left. He said he hadn't hurt her or touched her, hadn't even seen Carla. RJ said he had no proof of this, except for his word, and he always stood by his word. 'Just, ask anyone', RJ insisted to the DA. 'My word's as good as my handshake or even my name.'

"I felt so sorry for RJ, Mom. He's such a man of honor. His word and his name are so important to him, but this time, RJ's word and his name weren't good enough."

Beth felt familiar tears warming her cheeks for the man she loved, but she wiped them away. It was no time to break down. It was bad and from the sounds of it, it would only get worse.

"I've got to go, Mom. The meeting will start in about five minutes, so I have to fly. I'll call you as soon as I can. Love you. Bye."

Chapter 29

Anne was right. Everything RJ had worked for in his lifetime didn't mean a damn thing to the DA, his lawyers, or even his own son, Jason. The overwhelming evidence against him couldn't be denied, and in the eyes of the law, RJ Scott was guilty. RJ had to accept the guilty plea. All that was left was to determine the degree of his guilt.

After arguing for hours, it was agreed the DA would accept Voluntary Manslaughter. Under the circumstances, and with all the evidence against him, Voluntary Manslaughter was the best Clarisse and the rest of the attorneys could hope for. They had a small victory. They'd been able to save RJ from Murder One or Murder Two. They just had to get RJ to accept these charges. He still insisted he had nothing to do with her death, so after RJ had been escorted back to his cell, it was decided Jason would talk to his dad and urge him to accept the charge. Voluntary Manslaughter was the best he could hope for. Jason was to make his father understand that his fate could have been much worse, had it not been for his attorneys. With good behavior, he could be out of prison in a few years. It was a good deal for RJ.

It had been one long day for RJ Scott. All those damn lawyers agreed he should accept the "guilty" plea to Voluntary Manslaughter. RJ couldn't believe they wanted him to give up and plead "guilty". Hell. He didn't kill Carla. RJ thought those lawyers acted like they'd done something great, getting him charged with Voluntary Manslaughter. That was friggin nuts. They should've proved him innocent, damn it! Didn't his name mean anything? Didn't his reputation stand for anything with that bunch? He'd always been a fair man, never cheated anyone. Now, he was in jail.

RJ insisted he wanted to fight the charges and told Jason to find him some new lawyers. Jason refused because his father *had* the best defense team in Texas. Jason said that if they went to court and RJ lost, RJ might spend the rest of his life in prison, or worse. Jason urged RJ to plead "guilty" to the voluntary manslaughter charge, but RJ knew he couldn't plead guilty to something he didn't do. Jason knew his father had to accept the charges or possibly face death. He couldn't let that happen.

Jason was still angry with his father, but he dearly loved the big, burly man, and regardless of what he'd done in the past, Jason knew he'd eventually forgive his father. He tried to make RJ understand that he had to accept the charges, but RJ still refused. That's when Jason pulled out his trump card, Elizabeth Carlton. Jason knew he'd never be able to get his father to fold on the guilty plea unless he used her, so he did what he had to do to save his father's life.

Solemnly, he watched his father as he paced the dark confines of his jail cell. "The prosecutor will get Elizabeth on the stand, Dad. He'll humiliate her," Jason said. "When they threatened the sheriff over at Poke with permanently losing his job because he allowed you free reign at the airport, Larry finally admitted he'd seen her in your bed, and said he'd seen you coming out of that same bedroom, half dressed in the middle of the afternoon. The papers will label her a slut or worse. Her lady friends at the church will shun her. Do you really want this to happen to this woman you supposedly love?"

RJ stopped his pacing and glared at his son. "I do love her! She knows I love her."

"Then think about her, Dad, if you love her so much. The DA will dig up everything they can think of to humiliate Elizabeth. When they finish with her, she won't have a shred of dignity left. Is that what you want? After this trial is over and you lose, which I'm positive you will, you'll be sitting in the safety of a jail cell. What about Elizabeth Carlton? Where will she be? She won't have you. She'll lose all her friends. Her life won't be worth a piddling damn. Is that what you want for the woman you **love**, Dad? "

RJ knew what the prosecutor could do to Beth, and the visions in his head were ugly. He knew they'd paint her to be a tramp instead of the loving woman she was. They'd humiliate her. She wouldn't be able to walk down the street without people talking bad about her. Hell, no. That wasn't going to happen to his Beth. He wouldn't allow it, not even if he had to stay in prison for the rest of his life. Beth's good name was important to her and he understood that. It would not be taken away from her, not if he could help it.

He'd plead "guilty" to the charge. It'd be all right, RJ decided. He'd make it in prison as long as Beth was waiting for him.

The arraignment was on Monday and Jason said that Judge Henry would probably agree to allow RJ to be released on his own recognizance until the time of his sentencing next Friday. Jason told his father that the Judge knew RJ had always been a decent, law abiding member of the community with no criminal history. So, unless something changed before Monday, RJ would be allowed to go home to Scott's End Ranch, in confinement at the secluded ranch. That was the best Jason or his attorneys could do. RJ had no other choice but to take it. The powerful RJ Scott had been brought down. That was final.

Jason didn't want Elizabeth near his father while he was in confinement at the ranch. In his heart, he resented the love RJ had for Elizabeth and the fact that RJ didn't love the woman who'd given birth to him. He knew his father could be as hard headed as a bull when he'd made up his mind, and he was certain there was a simple misunderstanding between RJ and his biological mother. No one had ever told him any different.

Because of his resentment toward Elizabeth, Jason warned Anne, that they had to keep Elizabeth away from RJ. He said it was because Judge Thaddeus Henry had been assigned to RJ's case. Judge Henry considered himself an authority on the Bible and ruled by his own interpretation. Sentences were handed out, lives altered, according to what chapter of the Bible he was currently interpreting. Word had it that he was currently studying "*2 Samuel 11:1 – 4*", the story of King David's lust for the woman, Bathsheba.

If Elizabeth found out that RJ was out of prison, Jason was certain Elizabeth would come to him at Scott's End Ranch. If Judge Henry discovered the two living together for that week, he'd condemn them as morally iniquitous, possibly sentencing RJ to additional time. Jason said it was imperative that they keep Elizabeth away from RJ.

Anne thought that was ludicrous, but didn't want to see her mother hurt anymore. So, she went along with Jason, and didn't tell her mother that RJ might be free to stay at Scott's End Ranch for a few days before his sentencing.

To keep RJ away from Elizabeth, they'd decided to tell RJ that Elizabeth had ended their relationship and asked that he not call her. RJ was a proud man. Surely he'd see that as a betrayal to him and he'd leave her alone. RJ could afford a small amount of humiliation now to save him years in prison.

It was Sunday. The week from hell was over giving birth to the future of endless misery. Beth wondered if she'd ever sleep again. It was six a.m. She hadn't slept and knew she wouldn't. Over and over in her mind, she replayed the message Pastor Jim had left on her machine, the previous evening.

Pastor Jim said he'd gone to Dallas to see RJ that afternoon. After a lot of sweet talking, the guards agreed to let him see RJ.

Pastor Jim's warm voice was consoling and filled with understanding. "Elizabeth, RJ loves you. He needs you. He's being sent home to Scott's End Ranch on Monday to await the sentencing on Friday. Go to him, Elizabeth. Be there waiting for him. Don't worry what's correct and proper. Don't worry what people will say. If they condemn you without understanding and forgiving, then those people aren't worth your concern. God loves you, Elizabeth. He knows what's in your heart and that's all that matters. Elizabeth, please....decide for yourself what you think is right for you and RJ. Listen to your heart. God wants you to be happy."

Beth rolled over on her side and stared out the window into the early Sunday morning sunshine. Monday, RJ was being released in confinement at his ranch until next Friday. No one told her. Over the last week, she'd argued with Anne and Jason to let her go to RJ. She'd asked, pleaded, begged. They refused. They said that if she was in Dallas, it might stir up more trouble.

"What more was there to stir up?" Beth argued." RJ was going to prison for a crime he didn't commit. His life was ruined. Her life was ruined. What was there possibly left to stir up?"

As she had done so many times in the past week, Beth leaned under her bed and felt for RJ's old cowboy hat that he'd left there weeks before. She could smell him. She could see the dried rings of sweat that had been him. She could feel the weathered strength of the old felt. It was tattered, soiled, beat up, but by God, it still had a lot of life left in it. It had survived and so would they. To hell with what everyone else thought about them. She and RJ didn't have much time left, but she'd make certain they spent it together. Pastor Jim was right. Beth placed the hat back under the bed. RJ would be home tomorrow and she'd be there waiting for him. She'd drive to Scott's End Ranch today, and she'd take her own car. Before she could leave, though, Beth had a few things to clear up, and number one on her list was that awful reporter outside her home.

For the first time in a week, Beth felt energy seep back into her cells. Just knowing she'd be with RJ gave her hope. With renewed enthusiasm, she showered and dried her hair. Quickly, she pulled on her jeans, a white blouse, and wrapped her magenta sweater around her shoulders. As she laced up her tennis shoes, she thought about the clothes she had at RJ's. Everything she needed was still there.

Beth walked to her sun porch and gazed out to the street. The silver car was still waiting, and she wondered if the reporter ever took a break to eat. Didn't he ever have to go to the bathroom? How could these people make their living watching other people suffer? What sort of pleasure did people get from reading about other people's grief? Beth lowered her eyes in shame. How many times had she done the same thing? Read some story in the news, made judgments, had no idea of the real facts.

From inside the porch, she watched the silver car. The young male reporter was watching her. The more she thought about being forced to be a prisoner in her own home, the madder she got. How dare anyone force her to hide as though she'd done something horrible? She loved RJ Scott. He was a good, decent man. Let them judge her if they felt they must, but she was not hiding anymore. To Hell with all of them!

Opening the door of her porch, Beth ran down the steps and across the street to the silver car. As the reporter saw her coming out of the house, she saw him aim his camera toward her. As she approached his car, he lowered the camera in wonder. Beth motioned for him to put his window down. Disbelieving her audacity, he lowered it.

Beth leaned inside his window, hands on her hips in defiance. "If you want pictures of me, then have at it." Quickly, she spun around in front of him. He didn't take any pictures. Beth leaned back inside his car until she was nearly two inches from his nose. "As you must have suspected in your week-long vigilance of me, I'm a very boring person. I can't offer you any excitement whatsoever. Sit there if you want. Take pictures of me, a weary, middle-aged widow, but I promise you, sir, you're just wasting your time."

Beth pulled herself from the window and stood straight and rigid, glaring at him until he lowered his eyes from hers. Satisfied, she crossed the street back to her house and plopped herself on the front steps. Smugly, she watched the reporter as the reporter watched her. After some time, the silver car's engine began to roar and the reporter sped away. He finally realized something about Elizabeth Carlton. She really was very boring.

Pastor Jim Walsh was at a loss of what to do. Over his many years in the clergy, he'd married people, baptized their children, buried some of them, but he'd never been in a situation like the one that now concerned him. Elizabeth Carlton was a devoted member of his church, his friend, and now that she needed him the most, he didn't know how to help her. He'd always been a small town minister with a simple heart. He'd never asked for riches or fame, nor did he want them. He served his congregation and was thankful to do so. His sole purpose on this earth was to be an instrument of God. Now, he wondered if God was testing him. Was God giving him a challenge that he wasn't capable of handling?

Jim had seen the love develop between Elizabeth Carlton and RJ Scott. He'd seen it and was glad it happened. He'd just never expected RJ to still be legally married. Right or wrong, he simply could not condemn them. It wasn't his place to judge. That was God's job. He was just a lowly messenger. A messenger without a clue of what he was supposed to say. Jim had bent God's ear so many times over the past week, he was certain God was sick of listening to him. And, God still refused to answer him.

Saturday, on his own dime, and anxious to help in anyway he could, Pastor Jim Walsh had flown to Dallas to see RJ. He told the officials at the jail that he was RJ's spiritual counselor and wanted to pray with RJ. Of course, RJ didn't know what a "spiritual counselor" was and refused to see him. Laughing softly, Pastor

Walsh sent the guards back to tell RJ it was "Preacher Walsh".

"What do you want, Preacher?" RJ growled, as he entered the interview room. "Is Beth all right?" RJ looked tired and gaunt in his white prison jumpsuit. Without his daily nourishment of sunshine, RJ's ruddy skin had turned a sallow gray. Jim assured RJ that Elizabeth was fine, although he wasn't sure. As Jim stared into the icy blue slits of RJ's eyes, he realized he didn't know why he'd come. There was no way he could help this man.

"Well then, Preacher, what can I do for you, or do you just want to condemn me like everyone else?" The cold blue of RJ's eyes shadowed a flicker of the pain inside the man. "You want to condemn me like my own son does? Well, lay it on me, Preacher, I can take it." Jim didn't answer. He couldn't. RJ continued. "You think I loved a woman when I had no right, and now I have to pay. Well Preacher, I'll tell you right now, I'm not one bit sorry for loving that woman. If I had it to do it all again, I'd love Beth even more. So go ahead Preacher. Take your best shot. Let me have it!"

As Pastor Jim studied the tall defiant man, he could see that RJ's powerful, proud stature, had been replaced with a tired, worn out, angry old man. "RJ, I just came as a friend, and I'm just using my title as Clergy to get to see you; help you pass the time a bit, if you want."

It was obvious that RJ had given up. The loss of respect he'd felt from his son nearly broke his spirit, and seeing his future dreams with Elizabeth destroyed, RJ was a man in the clutch of misery. He'd accepted defeat, something he'd rarely experienced in his life. He had simply lost all hope.

"Well, being a preacher, I just figured you were here to preach." RJ challenged openly.

"Preachers can be friends too. I'm not always on call for preaching. You were kind to me when I came to your children's wedding, and I know you're a good man. If you weren't a good man, Elizabeth Carlton couldn't love you. And RJ, Eliza…Beth does love you."

RJ glared at Pastor Jim. "Beth *used* to love me, Preacher. *Used* to. They told me she gave up on me and doesn't want anything more to do with the likes of me. Said I shouldn't even call her. Hell, I don't blame her."

"Do you really believe that, RJ? To tell you the honest truth, I haven't talked to Beth since all this has happened, but from what you tell me, I guess she's not the woman I thought she was, the woman I respected and called my friend. Just beats me."

"What are you talking about, Preacher. Don't pussy foot with me. I've had enough crap to last me a lifetime."

"I've known Elizabeth Carlton for many years, and she certainly never seemed to be the type of woman who'd turn her back on someone who needed her. I guess I was wrong about her." Pastor Jim lowered his eyes away from the menacing cold glare of RJ Scott.

"Beth's a good woman! Don't you say bad things about her."

"I didn't say that, RJ. You did."

"Bull shit. I'd never say anything bad about Beth. I love that woman."

Pastor Jim looked squarely into RJ's cold blue eyes. "Then explain to me how she **used** to love you, and now she doesn't. When you love someone, you don't stop loving them when things get bad."

"Bcth didn't ask for this mcss, Prcachcr."

"Did you, RJ? Did you ask for this mess?" Jim watched RJ for a moment and knew in his heart that RJ Scott could never have killed his wife. "Beth loves you, and I'll bet she's every bit as miserable as you are. Maybe she's even more miserable. She can't see you or talk to you. She's totally dependent on what she's being told by others. And of course, there's all the garbage she reads in the paper." RJ's eyes dropped to the gray cement floor, his mind deep in thought. "Beth is all alone now, RJ, and from what I know of her, she's hanging on with everything she's got. Don't give up on her. She deserves better."

RJ's eyes raced from the cell floor and searched the preacher's face. "You don't understand, Preacher. They told me Beth doesn't want me anymore."

"Is that the same *they* that's keeping her from coming here to see you? I know Beth would be here if it was at all possible. She'd never turn her back on you."

As RJ lifted his head, Jim could see a tiny gleam in RJ's eyes. It was small, but it was there. "Maybe," RJ answered. "Maybe, but I guess we'll never know."

After a few minutes of silence, much to Jim's amazement, RJ opened up to him. He talked about his childhood, growing up poor. He talked about his unrelenting ambition to regain his family's land and how he'd worked day and night to recover his losses. He said in his careless youth, he'd gotten Carla in a family way. He'd been determined his child would never suffer because of his action, and he married Carla so his child would be legitimate in the eyes of the law. After Jason was born, he gave Carla everything he could think of to get her to stay and be a good mother to Jason. She left them anyway. Maybe it was his fault. He'd never loved the woman. He couldn't love her. That's just the way it was.

"Do you have any regrets in your life, RJ?" Jim asked, trying to help RJ understand himself.

"Oh hell no," RJ replied, quickly. "If I hadn't met Carla, I wouldn't have had Jason. If I hadn't had Jason then he wouldn't have met Anne. And through Anne, I met …." RJ stopped mid-sentence.

"It's all right. I'm not here to condemn you or Beth. It was obvious to me that you both are very devoted to each other; that you love each other deeply. I know I'm going against what I was taught in seminary when I say this, but why is it right to stay married and be with someone you don't love, but it's wrong to be with someone you love but can't marry. Love is not a sin, and sin is not love. Love is God. God is without sin. "

"Yeah, but it seems that God is punishing us, trying to destroy us. And if that's the sort of game God plays, then I don't want any part of God."

"Evil is what's trying to destroy you. God is what will save you. Just give his incredible power a chance."

"Sorry, Preacher, I'm just not one of those goody two-shoes that sits in church, pounding his chest so that everyone can see how fine he is. Nope, I'm just plain old RJ Scott. I do what I can for those that I can, but I don't go to church and have no intention of starting." RJ spoke adamantly, his defenses guarding him.

"God's church is all around you, RJ. It's in the sunshine, the wind, even in the rain. It's in the song of a bird, the howl of a wolf, the birth of an animal. God's church is in all of nature and nature is

God's most perfect church."

Jim could see that he had RJ thinking, but that the "God" talk was making RJ a bit uncomfortable, and that wasn't what he was there to accomplish. "Tell me something," Jim began. "Was the short time that you and Beth had together worth the pain you're going through now? Possibly, you'll spend the rest of your life in prison?"

"It doesn't matter, Preacher. Beth and me…we're supposed to be together." RJ smiled, remembering a far happier time and place. A small twinkle glistened in his eyes turning them into soft turquoise. "Neither heaven nor hell can ever get between Beth and me, and by God it never will. I'll get out of this damn place one of these days and Beth and I can be together. Things will be good for us. I know it."

"I'm glad to hear you thinking like that, RJ. And just remember, when things get tough for you, think about Beth. She's a good woman and she loves you."

"Thanks, Preacher," RJ answered, smiling his big grin. "I needed to hear you say that."

Jim smiled in acknowledgement. RJ Scott had hope again. Pastor Jim Walsh had accomplished his mission. God had indeed heard him, but He certainly worked in mysterious ways.

Pastor Jim Walsh looked over his congregation before the Sunday service began. Still, no Elizabeth. He'd called her several times, but she wouldn't talk to him. He'd even gone to her home, but she wouldn't answer the door. He wondered what it would take to get her back. He wanted to help her; he just didn't know how. Elizabeth Carlton had always been a devoted wife to Charles, and since his death, she'd been the picture of respectability. She'd never dated, dressed in drab clothing, and properly accepted her place on "*Widows Row*". She'd done everything possible to live by the demands of the long suffering Widow's Code. Then she committed the worst violation imaginable. Elizabeth Carlton fell in love with a married man.

Pastor Jim gave a shudder as he recalled mistakes made by other widows and the punishment inflicted on them by Alma and her little group of widows. Every time Alma Green hurt someone in the name of God, it just made him sick, but there was not one thing he could do to stop her. And now he knew it had happened to Elizabeth. He'd heard the evil gossip that was running rampant through his small church, and silently he prayed that God would protect Elizabeth and RJ and give them the strength to survive their bleak futures. There was nothing more he could do.

Elizabeth could hear the music begin in the Church and knew the processional would soon start down the aisle. Trying to be noticed as little as possible, she hurried into the church and walked down the aisle following the processional. The congregation was still standing and singing as she approached Widow's Row. Not knowing what to expect, Beth paused at the end of the Widow's Row waiting for acceptance. She got none. The bony arm of Alma Green stretched up to the next row of seats, forbidding entry to the wanton hussy who was not allowed to sit in the saintly row of good widows. Quickly, Elizabeth moved up several rows to an empty row and sat by herself.

From his view in the front of the church, Pastor Jim Walsh witnessed the cruel gesture that happened to Elizabeth and was filled with disgust. How could these women consider themselves to be good people and be so cruel? Who were these people to pass judgment on Elizabeth?

Pastor Jim could feel the anger welling up about his round Irish face, causing his rosy cheeks to change into a bright crimson red. As he entered his pulpit, he stared out at the clean faces of his parishioners. *Clean faces with dirty hearts. Hearts filled with false pride and small-minded judgment of others.* With a loud clap, he closed his bible and shoved his notes away from him.

The sermon that Pastor Jim gave was not what he'd planned, what he'd worked on all week. That sermon seemed trivial to him. Much to his own surprise, he began a new sermon that he hadn't planned. He could hear his own voice speaking, and as he spoke, he listened. The voice he heard sounded like his, but it was a thundering powerful voice. It was a voice filled with such passion that every member of his congregation sat upright in their seats, certain they were witnessing the very revelation of God Almighty. His voice spoke about little things that people did to cause big hurt to others. He spoke of hurtful actions that made people feel unwelcome. "How can you sit here in God's church, call yourselves followers of God, and turn your back on your neighbor's pain? You don't know what's in your neighbor's heart. You don't hear that person's prayers. That's not your job. That's God's job."

His voice became even louder as he chastised his congregation for casting judgment on others. "Has God taught us to think we are superior to others?" the voice bellowed. "Did God give us the responsibility to condemn our neighbors? No! That is not what God taught us. God taught us to remember the good that people had accomplished, and to stand by their side when their worlds are shaken and dark. Hold out your hand to your neighbor. Give them the strength to withstand the pain. And, there are many kinds of pain. It's not up to us to understand, or condemn their pain. It's up to us to give friendship to those we once called 'friend'. It's such a small offer, but it's the biggest offer, we can ever make. It's God's way. Could we at least **try** to live as God wanted us to live?"

As Pastor Jim left the pulpit, he was certain he heard gasps from his congregation. Never in his life had he shown anger, but there it was, spouted from the holy pulpit of God.

The sermon was over and with the congregation singing the hymn, "*God is an Awesome God*", the preparation of the Eucharist began. As Pastor Jim Walsh looked out over his flock, he noticed Alma Green, her bitter mouth pinched and tight, her body unbending, as she sat all alone on her worthless throne in Widow's Row. Casting his eyes to where Elizabeth sat, he noticed that all the other widows had left their places on Widow's Row and had moved to sit beside Elizabeth.

Pastor Jim knew real joy that day during communion and he smiled toward Heaven. God truly was an awesome God.

As the congregation exited the church, Jim was glad to see Elizabeth had waited to be the last person to shake his hand. "I've missed you, Beth," he said, patting her small hand.

Elizabeth looked at him in wonder. "Beth?"

Pastor Jim smiled. After talking with RJ about her, he could only see her as RJ did. She was Beth. Not knowing if she'd heard his telephone message to her, he continued. "I went to see RJ," he said, and noticed her eyes light up. "He'll get out on bail on

Monday. He misses you."

"I want to be there with him, Jim. I didn't go before, because everyone told me I would just stir up more trouble."

Pastor Jim smiled, "And since when have you and RJ been afraid of trouble?"

Beth smiled warmly at her friend. "After I listened to your phone message, I realized what was right for RJ and me. I had planned to leave for Scott's End Ranch as soon as possible, but I wanted to see you before I left. I wanted to thank you for helping me make the right decision and for telling me about RJ. No one told me RJ was going to be out tomorrow. You're the only one who let me know, the only one who understood.

"I don't know when I'll be coming back here, Jim, but I wanted to let you know that RJ and I will be all right. Whatever happens to us, we'll survive together."

Pastor Jim Walsh smiled his gentle smile. "I know that you will, Beth. You and RJ are both good people. You were fortunate to find each other and I know that you will have a long future together. A blessed future. I just have this feeling."

Beth smiled, knowing that Pastor Jim was the eternal optimist. No matter how bad the weather, he always looked for the sunshine. Then she remembered she had a long drive ahead of her. Quickly she walked away from him.

As she hurried down the steps to her car, he called to her and she stopped and watched as he approached her. "Beth, remember.... I do weddings."

Chapter 30

It was Monday morning and as expected, RJ was given temporary release from jail until his sentencing on Friday. Jason was still livid with anger at his father as he paid the bail for him and waited anxiously for his release. His father had no right to keep his mother from him all those years. If his father didn't love his mother, that was his right, but he had no right to keep Jason from her. Juanita had raised him; and yes, she was a wonderful mother to him, but the woman who'd birthed him was his own flesh and blood. It should have been his decision whether his mother became a part of his life or not. He was over twenty-five years old and his father was still making decisions for him like he was a little child. He'd always trusted his father's judgment without question, but this time his father's judgment was wrong. All wrong.

Jason rose as he spied his tall father walking toward him. He didn't say anything to his father, and RJ all but ignored his son as they walked from the courthouse and climbed into Jason's big SUV. Jason maneuvered the auto through the streets of Dallas and entered onto the highway that would take them to Poke, Texas. Jason stared at the road ahead of him. RJ stared out his window.

Such harsh words had been said between them about Elizabeth Carlton and Jason's mother, that it drove a solid core of anger and doubt between the father and his only son, and it seemed it would be impossible to break this cruel gap.

As they drove the distance to Scott's End Ranch, the silence was awful. Jason pushed the button on his stereo radio to the classical music station. RJ changed it to the country western station. Jason groaned and left the music alone.

The lonely songs of the country singers didn't help RJ's worries or his mood, and as they neared Scott's End Ranch, RJ could stand the suspense no longer. Quickly he leaned over and turned off the radio. He wanted his son to hear his question loud and clear and he didn't want to repeat it. "Jason," he commanded. "Did anybody bother to tell Beth I would be at the ranch?"

Jason rolled his eyes and blew out his breath in disgust. He ignored his father's question.

"Damn it! Don't screw with me. Did you or Anne let Beth know I'm out of jail so that she can come to the ranch for a few days?"

"Good God, Dad!" Jason's shout nearly echoed in the close confines of the car. "I told that woman to stay away from here! You just don't need that sort of trouble! What kind of a sentence do you think Judge Henry would give you, if he knew you were shacked up with your lover for the week?"

RJ's shout over-ruled his son's. "Watch your mouth, Jason. Don't you use that tone in the mention of Beth!"

Jason didn't back down. "Jesus, Dad. Isn't Elizabeth Carlton the reason for all this? You lusted after that woman and she wouldn't have you as a married man, so you got rid of my mother!"

RJ couldn't believe what his son had said. His own son believed he was capable of murder. RJ was furious. "Well, son of a bitch! You really don't believe me, do you? You honestly think I killed Carla so Beth and I could be together! Well, for your information, we didn't let Carla stand between us. Beth was willing to live with me even though I was married."

Jason turned his head away from his father and ignored him. Jason wanted his father to feel the pain of betrayal that he felt, and he knew he could hurt his father more by snubbing him than he could by arguing with him. And more than anything else at that moment in his life, and for the only time in his life, he wanted to hurt his father.

RJ looked at his son, frantic for Jason to believe in him, his anger evaporating and quickly drifting into the awful pain he felt in his heart. RJ leaned across the console separating the two men and placed his hand on his son's shoulder, stroking him with the same love he'd shown Jason when he was a young child. His harsh voice was gone and replaced with a quiet gentle plea. "Son, I had no reason to kill your mother. She didn't stand in the way of Beth and me. Can't you understand that?"

"Well, hell! That doesn't say a whole hell of a lot of good things about the morals of Mrs. Elizabeth Carlton, now does it?" Jason snarled as he turned off the little two lane highway from Poke, Texas, and pulled up to the Scott's End gate.

RJ was infuriated. Jason could think anything he wanted about him, but he would not tolerate Jason's crude remarks about the woman he loved. "Jason, you hypocritical little ass! For all those years, I thought you were the only good thing that ever happened to me. You were the joy of my life. Now, I'm damned well ashamed of you. You're a sorry excuse for a son! Now, just drop me off here at my gate and get the hell out of my sight."

Jason watched as his father entered the code on the security gate. As the gate opened, Jason pulled back onto the small familiar highway leading to Poke, Texas, and back to Dallas. With his long leg, he stomped on the gas, speeding away from the father who'd betrayed him.

"Someone's at the gate!" Juanita exclaimed to Beth, as they watched the movement of the numbers on the gate control. "RJ must be home!"

Beth and Juanita maintained their vigilance beside the Lady in the Fountain and waited to see a car approach the house. There was none. Juanita and Beth looked at each other in wonder and moved outside the garden to have a better look. In the distance, they could see a lone figure walking up the driveway to the ranch. He was a large man. His hair was graying and sun burnt, his face aged from experience.

"It's him, Juanita", Beth shouted back to Juanita as she raced down the winding road. "He's home!" Her heart pounded in her chest as she visualized his strong arms around her: the warmth of his body next to hers, his kiss on her lips, his love.

As RJ walked the long distance from the gate to his home, he could see someone running toward him. It couldn't be Beth. No one told her he was coming home. RJ stopped for a moment and watched the person running toward him. Her dark hair bounced on her magenta sweater, her soft white skin glistening in the midday sunshine. It was his Beth. Quickly, he picked up his step, battling his own body to race faster. He couldn't wait to hold her warm body in his arms, to kiss her sweet lips, to love her.

When the two aging lovers came together, there was no doubts, no regrets, no need for talk or explanations. It was just RJ and his beloved Beth, lost in the blistering desire of their bodies, consumed in the renovation of their tattered souls.

The following morning, RJ lay on his stomach and watched Beth as she slept peacefully next to him. He wanted her to have the pink diamond engagement ring he'd bought her, but he didn't want her to feel she had to marry him by accepting the ring. His name was a name of shame. A name she didn't need to share to know his love. Quietly, he moved from the bed, pulled his jeans up over his naked body and walked to his office. Securing the ring from the safe, he returned to the bedroom and placed the ring case on his empty pillow. RJ watched Beth for a minute, smiled, and went to the bathroom for his shower.

"I think you forgot something, Mr. Scott." RJ leaned out of the large walk-in shower and smiled as Beth dropped her robe and stepped into the shower with him.

"Really, Mrs. Carlton? What did I forget?" RJ pulled Beth to him in the shower, holding her close to his heart, as the soft, warm water joined their frayed souls and caressed their naked bodies. Never had RJ known such joy in his entire life. All the miseries of his past life were forgotten. All the uncertainties of his pitiful future were ignored. This time, this moment in a lifetime, was all that mattered to him. All else was meaningless.

Holding her against him, RJ felt the warm water running down their naked bodies, purifying them, baptizing them in the glory of their unbelievable love. Tenderly, he kissed the woman he loved and wished they never had to leave the peaceful haven of the warm shower. Feeling the warm water run down his rugged face, he smiled as he watched the same stream run down the small scar on Beth's face and run into her eyes. As Beth wiped the water from her eyes, she smiled up at RJ and he noticed the sparkle of the pink diamond. Next to it on her left hand was her simple NOWANDFOREVER wedding band.

Beth pulled away from RJ's arms. "You forgot this, silly. I can't be married without you." Beth slipped RJ's wedding ring on his big finger and smiled up at him through the water running down her face. "Now and forever, I take you for my husband, Randolph James Scott."

RJ knew Beth was playing more of her pretend games. He wanted to play too, but mainly, he wanted to make her happy. "Now and forever, I take you for my wife, Elizabeth Carlton."

Beth smiled through the shower drops, and with both her hands pulled RJ's wet face close to hers. "Beth Carlton Scott, RJ," she corrected. "I marry you in my new name, Beth Carlton Scott."

RJ could barely speak, he was so overcome with emotion. His Beth knew. She understood how devastating the loss of his good name was to him. Yet, she was willing to share his name and wear it with pride. This was what her little, pretend marriage was telling him.

RJ was well aware of the tears welling up in his eyes, but he didn't care. He let the tears run down on top of Beth's head as he pulled his Beth's soft wet body close to him. He held her for a minute and then kissed her softly. Pulling away slightly, he stared deeply into her big brown eyes. "Now and forever, I take you for my wife, Beth Carlton Scott."

RJ accepted the fact that he might be spending the rest of his life in prison for a crime he hadn't committed, but he couldn't get Beth to accept it. Even with the sentencing on Friday, she still held out hope that good things would happen for them. "Maybe some new evidence would appear. Maybe someone would come forward that had seen Carla after RJ had left."Maybe *maybe, maybe*.

Beth had a thousand "*maybes*" that could save them, but RJ knew she was just dreaming. Without denying her, he let her dream for the few days they had left together. These dreams would become memories that would have to sustain RJ for the long days he'd face locked away from all he loved. He'd make the most of them.

Beth was sleeping contentedly next to RJ as she whistled her familiar little bird calls, but RJ couldn't sleep. He had too many things on his mind to waste his precious freedom sleeping. He was well aware that prison life would be hard on him at his age, and just in case he didn't survive it, he wanted to be sure the people and things he loved would be cared for as he wanted. He'd never thought much about dying or about those he'd leave behind. Jason would get most of everything he owned. At least, that's the way he always believed it would be. Now, he wondered if leaving the bulk of his estate to Jason was such a good idea. He knew Jason would always take care of Juanita, Luis and Marco, but the resentment

Jason felt toward Beth was a big worry to RJ.

Yes, Anne would see that her mother was cared for, but at what price for Beth? Would she be forced to live with Anne and Jason and be compelled to suffer Jason's dislike for her? No, RJ would be sure that the woman he loved would be financially secure until her death. If she were living at his big ranch, he knew she'd always be safe and cared for as he wanted. He also knew her silly pride, so he'd been prepared for an argument over her moving to his ranch without him being there. Much to his surprise, Beth was eager to move to Scott's End Ranch. Scott's End Ranch was RJ's home, she'd said earlier that evening, and it would be her home, too. She said she'd feel closer to RJ, even though he wouldn't be there, and she'd be able to visit him in prison. RJ scowled at the thought, but he knew if he wanted to see her, he'd have to let her see him in that awful place. It had to be.

RJ thought about his son and the influence his hard-earned wealth had on his only child. Having great wealth was a big responsibility, and RJ wasn't too sure Jason was ready for so much responsibility at this time of his life. How could he be? RJ had always given to his only child and he'd never asked Jason for anything in return. Now the one thing he asked from his son was to understand his love for Beth, and Jason refused. RJ wondered if his chickens had finally come home to roost.

RJ remembered the boy Jason defended, who'd hit Ron Moore on the highway in his fancy little sports car. He thought about all the useless crap the boy's father's money had bought for his son. Yet, the father had not instilled honor in his son, nor had he ensured his son took the responsibilities for his own actions. What sort of a father was that, RJ wondered, but in his gut, he worried that he was just like that boy's father. Because he'd given Jason anything he'd ever wanted, had he given Jason the idea that material wealth came easy for his own father? Did his son consider him just a money-making machine; a machine that had no feelings? Didn't it ever occur to Jason that what Jason and Anne had together was what RJ had wanted his entire life? Did Jason have so little respect for him that he honestly thought he would kick his mother out of their home and eventually kill her over lust for another woman? Had he taught his son nothing about honor and responsibility?

RJ was well aware that Jason's mother didn't love him and he didn't love her, but if Carla had shown any love for Jason whatsoever, he would have made a life with her for Jason's sake. Yes, he'd have put up with nine kinds of hell, just so Jason would have his real mother, but Carla didn't want it. She said she hated RJ and she hated his snot-nosed kid. She said they'd taken her life away from her and she wanted to be free of both of them.

RJ remembered that cold, dreary night years ago, when he'd driven her to Poke with Jason on his lap. Hell, she wouldn't even hold Jason so he could drive. When they got to an ATM in Poke, RJ withdrew as much money as the machine would allow, gave it to Carla, and left her waiting for the bus to Dallas. He thought he was finally rid of the woman, but he was sure wrong on that one. She'd threatened him all of her life, and now in her death, she'd finally turned his son away from him. There was no way to fight her anymore. RJ had lost his son and he was devastated.

That night Beth had tried to soothe the pain RJ suffered losing the respect of his son. "Every child wants a mother to love them," she whispered as she pulled RJ to her in her large soft bed. "Jason was just ovcrwhclmcd that Carla had bccn so ncar all his lifc and never contacted him. He needed to blame someone, and that someone would have to be his father. Jason will come around in time. When he has his own child, he will understand. You have to be patient, my love." she'd said. "Jason loves you." Beth had repeated these same words over and over to RJ, and he understood, but the lonely ache in his heart for his son remained constant.

RJ rolled over and caressed his one real love, the woman who'd been such a good mother to her own children. He wondered about all the things that could have been for them if they'd met when they were young. But, he recalled, things were different way back then. Beth was different. He was different. It was a lifetime ago.

Juanita and Luis had made excuses to visit friends for the evening, leaving RJ and Beth alone for their final night together. Even though Juanita had made them a romantic candlelight dinner, neither RJ nor Beth had any appetite. Both of them picked at their fine meal with disinterest, eventually giving up and moving to the den settling into the softness of the tan leather sofa. Beth nestled herself into RJ's arms and they sat in silence for some time, both reflecting in the time spent together the past few days.

Over the last few days, they'd spent every minute together, making memories that would keep their hearts alive for the years to come. Every small word was important, every touch was pure pleasure, and every smile was a picture to be locked away inside their memories.

Each sunrise they'd witness together, and as they sipped their coffee in the magic of the early dawn, RJ would describe the beauty he found in the rising of the grand dame'. Every night they made love with the passion of young lovers, eager to face tomorrow. But RJ and Beth were not eager to face tonight's tomorrow. It would be their last one together. Their time together had come to an end.

Burying her head into RJ's warm chest, Beth grounded her tears into RJ's blue chambray shirt. Without uttering a sound, Beth sobbed for the hopeless love they'd found and lost. She was so quiet in her grief that the only way RJ knew she was sobbing was his shirt was stained wet. Hell. RJ didn't mind her tears. He knew how she felt. He wanted to cry, too. For her sake, he didn't.

"It will be all right, Beth. We'll make it," he whispered, pulling her tight against him. "Someday, we'll be together again and nothing in this whole big world will keep us apart. Believe in that, Beth. Please, for me." RJ kissed the tears from her cheeks and smiled, trying to fill her with a hope that even he knew wasn't real.

Jason and Anne hurried through the black wrought iron gates of his father's home and entered the garden. Quickly, they walked past the lady in the fountain and past the glorious plants and topiary. Jason Scott felt sick to his stomach. In fact, he'd never felt this sick in his life. All week long, he'd been miserable with the knowledge that he'd dishonored his beloved father. How could he have accused him of killing his mother? Hell, Anne knew his father better than he did. She'd pointed out to him, in no uncertain words and not sparing one cruel jab, that his father deserved a personal life like everyone else in the world. How long was his father supposed to be punished for his past mistakes? How could Jason possibly suggest that his father could kill anyone, certainly not Jason's mother?

The day he'd accused his father of the horrible crime, Jason knew in his heart that his father hadn't killed his mother, but he'd been so angry he'd lashed out at him. He'd snubbed his father's relationship with Elizabeth and insulted her good name. How could he have done these things to a father who'd spent his entire life, making a good life for his rotten son? Yes, he was a rotten son, certainly not the son that his father could be proud of. He was an arrogant fool, without concern for anyone but himself, a disappointment in his father's eyes. He knew there was no way his father would forgive him, but he had to try. Maybe someday, he could forgive himself.

RJ and Elizabeth's intimate moments were broken by the sound of Jason calling to his father. "Dad", they heard Jason's voice calling as he entered the garden.

"In the den," RJ answered as he watched his son enter into the room followed by Anne. RJ didn't rise to greet his son or Anne, but stayed steadfast on the sofa with his arms tightly around Beth, protecting her from any painful words Jason might say to her.

Thc young man that so much rcscmblcd RJ Scott stood staring at his father for a moment. Tears formed and great falls of watered sorrow flowed openly down his face. He lowered his body and knelt humbly at his father's knee. "Dad, I am so sorry. Will you ever forgive me? I should have trusted you."

RJ didn't respond, but simply glared through icy blue slits at his son.

His apology was not good enough and Jason knew it. He'd hurt his father and insulted the woman his father loved. He'd been so mistaken about both of them. How could he have been so wrong?

Jason moved from in front of his father and knelt in front of Beth. "Elizabeth, can you ever forgive me for the horrible things I said to you. I am so ashamed of myself, how I talked to you. Lord, I don't know if I can ever forgive myself. Please, please, forgive me."

As he knelt in front of her, Beth took his hand in hers and stroked him patiently. "You were hurt, Jason. I'm glad to see you finally understand."

The young man stood and faced his father again, rushes of

tears controlling his sorrow. Quickly, he knelt at his father's knee again, wordlessly begging for his forgiveness. In his hand, he had a crumbled piece of paper.

As angry as RJ had been at Jason, he couldn't stand to see his son so upset. Jason was sorry and RJ understood the pain that had caused his son to lash out at him and the woman he loved, his Beth. Jason had begged Beth's forgiveness and she'd accepted his apology. His son had acknowledged Beth with the respect she was due. Now, RJ would forgive him. RJ held out his arm to his son, his other arm still tightly wrapped around Beth. Like a naughty child, Jason quickly took his place next to this man he adored, grateful for his forgiveness.

Anne plopped her growing body into a plush chair across from the group and observed her mother in the arms of RJ Scott. It seemed so natural for her mother to be with him. Anne thought about her mother and father. Her mother had loved her father, she was certain of that, but she could also see that her mother loved RJ Scott. It really was possible to love two completely different men. Anne came out of her thoughts. "Jason, don't you have something to show your father?"

Jason wiped his eyes and buried his head under his father's large arm. "I can't read it," he whispered, and handed the crumbled yellow letter to his father to read.

"Well, hell son, I don't have on my glasses, so don't expect me to read your letter." RJ smiled, assuming the letter was some sort of a written apology from his son. He couldn't read it because he knew he'd break down crying as hard as his son. He passed the letter to Beth. "Beth, you read it."

Beth picked up RJ's glasses lying on the coffee table. Softly, she began to read the letter.

Friday, May 9

Jason,

My name is Carla Desmond Scott. I am the woman who delivered you into this world, but please don't think of me as your mother. The truth is, I never wanted to be your mother. It was nothing against you personally, Jason.

I just didn't want to be anyone's wife, and certainly no one's mother.

When I was a young girl, my mother died, and I was forced to be a mother to her five children. I resented that very much. My entire young life was spent taking care of someone else's children. I couldn't go to parties, or have dates or do anything that the other girls were doing. I hated my life.

Eventually, my father remarried and I escaped from that miserable existence. I wanted to make up for every dreary day that I had been forced to wipe noses, and change dirty diapers. It was my time and I guess I got a little carried away with the men. I used them for their money, and threw them away whenever someone better came along. No one used me, Jason. I used them.

This was what I did to your father too, Jason. But I got caught. I got pregnant with you. I thought I could force your dad to pay me to have an abortion and have me out of his life, but that backfired. He wanted you, Jason. Before you were even born, he loved you. He was even willing to marry me and give me a big grand house. I tried that, too, but that life was not for me. I left your dad and you and went back to the life I thought would make me happy. It didn't though, because I was broke and couldn't live the lifestyle I wanted.

I certainly didn't want a child, but I told your dad that I wanted you back just to worry him. I knew he'd always put your best interest first, and if that meant he'd have to pay me off, he'd do it. Your dad did as he promised, Jason. He supported me all these years.

The reason I'm writing this letter to you is that I have no one to leave my small estate. I own my apartment, courtesy of your dad, and I have some savings. It's not much, but I refuse to leave it to the stinking government or to some sniveling charity. So, you're the one who'll get it.

Your father was here today, Jason. I didn't bother to answer the door, because I knew he'd ask me for a divorce again. I'd heard he was in love with a lady from Oklahoma and wanted to marry her. This time, though, I would have given him a divorce, because your dad is the best man I've ever known. He deserves to have his life back. However, I decided it was stupid to spend money on a divorce, when I know I would die soon.

I've been told I have to stop drinking, which I will not do. I've been told by the doctors that the sickness, I have is a cruel, painful end to life, which I do not plan to endure. Today, after I finish my last bottle of Scotch, I will simply stand on a stool on my balcony and sail like a free bird out into the wind. This sickness will never take me. I have chosen the way I live and I have chosen the way I will die.

Today I will send this letter to my lawyer's office, with instruction that it is not to be opened until the reading of my will. I don't ask you to forgive me for not loving you, Jason. I just want you to know, it wasn't your fault.

Best Wishes
Carla Desmond Scott

In complete astonishment, Beth took off RJ's glasses and laid them on the table. She grabbed RJ's hand and held it to her face. "RJ, do you know what this means?" She asked, overwhelmed with emotion, tears of happiness filling her eyes.

RJ turned and gazed at the woman he loved, his blue eyes twinkling and full of life again, his face sporting a huge Texas grin. "Well, hell yes, I do, woman. This means we can finally finish our dinner. Damn, I'm starving to death!"

RJ stood and held out his hand to Beth, and the two overjoyed elders started from the room. Realizing they'd left Anne and Jason behind, RJ stopped and turned to Jason and Anne. "Well, come on you two. There's plenty food for all of us."

RJ's attorneys showed the letter from Carla to the DA and all charges were dropped against RJ for the murder of his wife, but somehow, Carla's attorney couldn't accept the letter as proof of RJ's innocence. The handwriting appeared the same, but he was certain something was different.

RJ's attorneys insisted that Carla had been very ill and using a lot of pain killers when she wrote the letter. Of course the handwriting was not exactly the same. How could it be? Carla wanted to make amends with her son before she died as any decent mother would do. Give the poor woman that shred of respect in her death. The case was closed. RJ Scott was an innocent man.

John Morrison, Carla's attorney, had argued these facts over in his head also, but the main thing that bothered him was that he knew his client, Carla. She was a cruel, merciless person. When he'd made out her will, she'd left everything to Jason, but not to leave fond memories for him. She did it to spite RJ Scott. RJ would have to explain her to Jason and she knew Jason would resent his father and blame him. Carla would do anything to have others lives as miserable as her own. Now this woman, who'd been merciless in her life, had supposedly written this kind letter to her son. How could it be? Was it possible that Carla had actually found some empathy for others as she faced death? Was that possible? Or did she fear the hereafter and hoped to gain mercy when she'd given none. As cruel as she'd been in life would this one act of kindness be enough to give her peace for eternity? Maybe, but still John Morrison worried about this.

He had personally gone through Carla's apartment after her death and found nothing to conclude there was any sort of foul play. As her attorney, he'd gone through her personal safe which had been left open before her death. All that was inside the safe was an old bank book and her marriage certificate to RJ Scott. Nothing was out of order. John Morrison closed Carla's files and hurried down to the cold, dark basement vault, where her life's story would be stored. Overhead, he could feel the vibrations of the heavy cars on the busy streets above, evidence of the many lives still active. He didn't like coming down to the gloomy, cold vaults. It was a sad place. Cold and eerie, sort of like he imagined Hell would be.

John shuddered as he carefully locked the vault door with one of many keys on a round steel key ring. Walking up the stairs away from the vault, he hurried his step. Tonight was his son's birthday party. He didn't want to be late. Carla Desmond Scott was forgotten.

Chapter 31

It had been several months since the nightmare ended for RJ and Beth. She'd sold her home in Tulsa and moved to Scott's End Ranch. RJ had bought Beth another car that was long enough for his legs, tall enough so he wouldn't hit his head, but small enough that she wouldn't destroy any hidden mailboxes that got in her way. Knowing her driving, RJ made sure it had a back bumper, warning devise that would alert her to anything in her path.

Beth was driving this car as they returned from seeing Jason and Anne's new home in North Dallas. Having been told that they were expecting twins, the young couple moved to a larger home closer to their parents, great news for all of the family at Scott's End Ranch.

As Beth drove the little car along the highway to Poke, Texas, RJ laid his hand on her leg, and stroked her lovingly. "Beth, would you think I was nuts if I suggested we stop by the cemetery to visit Carla's grave? I don't know why, but I just feel like I have unfinished business with her."

Beth patted his hand on her leg. "I think you need closure to that part of your life, RJ. Seeing her grave might help you to realize that it's finally over."

"I guess I need to tell you about Carla, Cyrus, and me," RJ said, staring off into the country side. "I was always working and didn't pay any attention to the local gossip. I'd seen Carla around with Cyrus, and she was a beautiful, seductive woman. I didn't know why she stayed with Cyrus, but it was obvious that he worshiped the ground she walked on."

RJ cleared his throat and then continued. "Cyrus and I hated each other since we were kids, so when Carla put her moves on me, I jumped in with both feet. I wanted to piss Silas off too, but then I thought she was really interested in me. She wasn't. I was just another one of her conquests. She'd always go back to Cyrus and he'd always take her back. Some months later, she came to me and said she was pregnant by me. I told Carla that if she was sure it was my child, I'd marry her and take care of her and the baby. She agreed and I kept my part of the bargain. Cyrus never forgave me for fathering a child with her and hated me even more if that was possible. After Carla left us, she went back to Cyrus, and he took her back. She stayed with him for a while and then she figured out she could blackmail me and be independent of Cyrus. He hated me for that, too. "

"RJ," Beth said, "you were just a young man, and you tried to do the right thing. You've suffered long enough. Now, it's your turn, our turn. We'll be happy together. Nothing can stop that."

RJ smiled, a contented man.

Exiting the highway, they drove down the narrow gravel road which led to Poke Cemetery. At one time, people had cared for the road, but now the gravel was worn away and the ruts filled with overgrowth. Ancient headstones peaked up from the ground offering a tiny glimpse of lives long past. A few graves had flowers on them, but most were so old that no one visited them anymore. These residents had been forgotten years ago. "I wonder where her grave is." Beth asked, following the narrow road around the cemetery.

"Shouldn't be too hard to find," RJ replied. "We just look for onc that has hard ncw dirt on it and I imaginc that will bc Carla."

They drove further toward the end of the small cemetery. "Stop, Beth," RJ said. "I'm sure I see it now."

Beth stopped the car and turned toward RJ, wondering if he wanted her to go with him.

"Look over there." RJ pointed to a huge headstone that was facing away from them.

In the distance they could see the little man carefully grooming the ground over Carla's grave. With a small broom and a dustpan, Silas Stone removed every stick and every leaf that would take away from the beauty of her grave, his monument he'd created in Carla's honor.

"My God," RJ's voice was whispered. "I never understood how much Silas loved that woman. He couldn't have her in life, so now he cares for her in death." They watched as the little man finished this ritual of adoring worship. He kissed the headstone goodbye, finally assured that Carla would be faithful until his return. Not realizing RJ and Beth had been watching, Silas got into his car and drove away.

RJ got out of the car and walked toward the grave. Beth remained alone in the car, realizing this was something RJ had to experience alone. Silently, she watched as RJ stared at the headstone of the woman who'd controlled his life. After a few moments, he returned to her.

"My Love", RJ said softly, his thoughts deep and far away. "*MY LOVE*" is what Silas had written on her headstone. God, he really loved that woman." RJ and Beth sat in silence for a few minutes. Neither could think kind thoughts about the woman and the way she lived her life, but somehow, they couldn't chide her in death.

"Beth," RJ said, taking her hand in his. "All those many years Silas worshipped Carla, but she never threw him so much as a crumb. How could he stand it?" RJ kissed Beth's hand and pulled her hand to his face, certain she'd stroke him with her love. She did.

"Now, I know why it was so important for Silas to make money. If he had money, he could have Carla. Finally, I understand why he hated me so much." Trying to comprehend Silas' lifetime of pain, RJ paused for a moment and then continued. "Beth, that could have been me. I never knew what love was until I met you. What if you hadn't loved me? God, I would have gone through the same miserable grief, poor old Silas suffered all those years." RJ shook his head in thoughtful wonder. Deep inside his mind, he forgave Silas for all the mean things he'd done and in his heart he knew he'd never hate Silas Stone again.

"But I do love you, Mr. Scott, now and forever," Beth whispered in reverence to the silent surroundings.

RJ leaned across the seat and kissed his wife. "And I love you too, Mrs. Scott, now and forever. So, let's get the hell out of here and go on home."

As Beth backed the car to turn around, RJ sat rigid, carefully listening for any warning beeps, anxious to leave the cemetery just as they'd found it in its silent isolation.

Goldie started to pull her big yellow Cadillac into the single-lane drive to the cemetery, where she'd pay respect to her father and real mother on her Sunday ritual. In the distance, she could see another car exiting the small road. Patiently, she waited her turn, but the car stopped at the end of the road blocking her entry. The car door opened and to her surprise, she saw RJ Scott approaching her car. Quickly, she rolled down her window to speak to him. She hadn't seen him in a long time and had sorely missed his weekly visits. To that day, his key was still hanging on the hook in her bar waiting for him.

"Hey there, Goldie," RJ said, smiling his big grin. "I knew it was you, 'cause no one in the world has a car like you do." RJ placed his big hands on the driver's window sill, and as he leaned toward the homely woman, he realized how much he'd missed her. Goldie was a character like no one he'd ever met, but she was one of the best friends he'd ever had. It was hard giving up a friendship like that, regardless of who she was.

"She's a pretty lady, you got over there in the car, RJ." Goldie motioned to where Beth sat waiting for him. "She's real pretty, a classy-looking gal."

"Would you like to meet her?" RJ asked. He didn't know what Beth would think about Goldie, with her yellow hair and crooked red smile, but he knew Beth would be kind to her.

Quickly Goldie interrupted him, not wanting to feel the disdain she knew his woman would have for her. "No, that's all right. She probably wouldn't understand what it was all about before she came into your life. It's best left alone now." Goldie smiled warmly at the tall man. "You look great, RJ. You look 10 years younger and fit as a fiddle. Been getting a lot of exercise, have you?" she laughed knowingly.

RJ threw back his head and laughed. "Only you, Goldie! You're the only person in this world that would come up with something like that."

Goldie patted RJ's hand as it gripped the side of her door and smiled up at him. "I'm glad to see you doing so good and looking so happy. Now, go on back to your wife. It was good to see you again."

RJ patted her large arm affectionately, "Goodbye, Goldie." RJ waved as he made his way back to Beth. Goldie noticed that RJ must have forgotten to tell her something, because he stopped and walked back toward her.

RJ gazed at her with knowing blue eyes that suddenly grasped many things he'd wondered about in the recent months. He never could understand the letter Carla sent to Jason, the one that saved his own butt from prison. Carla was a mean woman, never cared about anyone but herself. Then, the letter showed up.

Seeing Goldie today, suddenly it all made sense. Leaning inside the driver's side of the big yellow Cadillac, RJ kissed Goldie on her broken face. "Thanks, Nora Jean," he whispered.

As RJ turned from her, he grinned and winked at Goldie, sealing the bond that could never be broken between them. Goldie's broken face turned into a smile that only heaven could have created as she watched RJ walk away from her. Soon RJ and his beautiful wife were gone.

Goldie pulled her long yellow Cadillac onto the small overgrown lane that lead to her parents' graves. Tears of joy filled her eyes smudging the thick makeup that she wore on her chubby face. RJ had known for all those years that she was Carla's sister. Now she understood why he brought her Jason's class pictures and made her aware of everything her nephew had done over the years. Regardless, he'd never told anyone who she was. He'd honored her and respected her wishes.

As Goldie drove her big yellow Cadillac past the site where her sister was buried, she had no regrets about Carla. Her sister's pain here on earth was over. Somehow, though, Goldie knew Carla was in big trouble on the other side.

Goldie pulled her massive body from her plush yellow Cadillac and slowly made her way toward two tall headstones that rested in the shade of a vibrant red Maple tree. As Goldie placed a small bouquet of flowers on her parents' graves, she put the dead flowers that she'd brought last week into a paper bag. Again, her mind brought her back to RJ and the lives they'd known. It was obvious that RJ was happy with his woman, and he'd never need the key to her back room again, but she knew she'd never let another have his key. There were just too many memories attached to that key. She'd just put it with her collection of keys that had belonged to so many of her old boys who'd died in years past. There were a lot more of those old keys than newer ones, hardly worth the effort to keep up the place any more. The gals had gotten older, their kids were grown and they didn't need to work to fill their children's empty stomachs, like years ago. No, it just wasn't worth it anymore.

Maybe she'd move down to her little place in Florida which she purchased some time back as a vacation home. The people were kind to her there, invited her to sit on their porches and drink ice tea with them. They'd even invite her to go out for dinner with them after church. Yes, she'd join the church she'd attended there. Never had anything against churches. They did a lot of good for a lot of folks and they always needed help with the fundraising. Lord, she knew enough about the fundraising needs of charities. She'd given a small fortune to the needs of Poke, Texas.

Yeah, she'd sell her business and move to Florida, where folks treated her with respect. Of course, they didn't know about "Big Goldie's". They only knew what she told them. Her name was "Nora Jean Scott". She'd married a rich rancher who died of a sudden massive heart attack years ago. In her grief she'd raced her horse across the range, lost control of her grip and landed on a steel fence post that disfigured her face.

That's what she told them, and that's all that they needed to know.

Chapter 32

After finishing her morning swim, Beth bathed and dressed for the day. She strolled happily through the garden and stopped to sit by the lady in the fountain. Out of habit, she slipped her hand into the soft rippling water behind her and lovingly surveyed this place of beauty.

It had been five years since she and RJ had been married here in this sanctuary of peace. Juanita had been able to oversee the wedding as she'd always wanted and Luis had outdone himself with the beautiful flowers. Pastor Jim had come from Tulsa to sanctify the happy marriage, which at one time seemed to be a bleak road to nowhere. Beth smiled at the memories of the last five years. Their marriage definitely was not bleak. These last five years had been the happiest time in both their lives. With their two grandchildren often underfoot, the big house had been filled with squeals of childish laughter and the family at Scott's End Ranch enjoyed every minute they were given with their precious grandchildren. Juanita taught them to cook, and Beth taught them to read. Luis taught them to grow flowers and RJ taught them the wonders of Nature.

Soon their grandchildren would begin school and their grandparents knew they'd see them less often. Too soon, they'd grow up and grow away from them, but Beth knew that's the way it should be. Still, they'd miss the children and the sounds of their innocent laughter.

As was his nature, RJ still worked much of the time, but he always had time for Beth and included her in his work, as much as possible, or as much as she wanted. He'd taught her to drive "Big Red", the monster truck. At first, it seemed the old gal was jealous of Beth. She balked and kicked, grinding her gears in rebellion, but in time, she accepted Beth's tender touch and allowed herself to be driven by RJ's "other woman."

On occasion, RJ would discover one of his cows had dropped a calf somewhere and needed to be found quickly. RJ would open the new back gate on the old truck and his boys would jump into the back of the truck ready for the hunt. As though she'd been born to this life, Beth would drive Big Red out onto the range in search of the missing calf. With the two boys on guard on either side of the truck, they would bay in accord when they discovered the missing calf. RJ had learned in the past to keep a tarp handy on the calf hunts in case of accidental poops, so he'd throw the tarp around the calf and settle himself and the calf in the bed of Big Red. Given the signal of his whistle, Beth would bring them back to the ranch's barn properly escorted by RJ's two boys.

Juanita didn't seem to want any help with the upkeep of the large home or with the cooking, which secretly delighted RJ. Juanita said Beth's job was to keep RJ happy and Beth was pleased to do that. She didn't want to invade Juanita's domain, so she let Juanita do as she wanted and Beth helped where she felt she was needed. Shortly after Beth moved into the ranch, she discovered quickly, she'd have more time with her busy husband if she assumed the nuisance payment of the household bills. That worked so well, she assumed control of the ledgers of RJ's cattle business which eased RJ's load considerably. Somehow, though, she knew there was something else she needed to do.

Walking from the garden into the library, Beth gazed at the many books on the shelves of the library, everything from first grade readers to law books. So many young lives had been sculptured from this world of knowledge held safely in place in the arms of the massive wooden book shelves. Passing by the wall of books, Beth sat down at the computer where she often wrote email notes to her children and old friends from Tulsa. Running her fingers through her short dark gray hair, and staring into the light blue screen of the computer, many distant memories began to come to her. At first the words came slowly, hesitantly, as if they were hiding from her. But then, as she forced her thoughts onto the keyboard, the words began to pour out of her fingers as if they'd been hidden far too long. Without effort, she typed faster and faster.

Juanita entered the garden. She hadn't been looking for Beth for any reason, just wondered where she'd been going every morning. It would seem it would be hard to lose track of other members of the home, but it did happen sometime.

Every day after breakfast, Beth would swim. Juanita had tried to tell her that it wasn't good to swim after eating, but Beth would do as she wanted. Lately, though, Juanita noticed Beth's swims kept getting shorter and shorter. It seemed Beth had something she was working on and Juanita wondered if Beth needed her help.

Juanita pushed open the door to RJ's office and stuck her head inside, but Beth wasn't there. With a glance down the garden, Juanita noticed the door to the library was open. Hurrying toward the open door, she saw Beth typing on the keys of the flat board that was connected to the mysterious blue screen. Juanita knew nothing of that machine and, other than dusting it, she never touched it. It scared her.

"What are you doing, Beth?" the older woman asked.

Beth stopped typing and turned in the dark wood swivel chair to speak to Juanita. "I guess it's stupid, Juanita, but I'm trying to write a book." Beth turned back and looked at the screen, silent for a moment, hesitant to share her feelings. As she glanced back to the dark aging face of her friend, she smiled. "I'm trying to write my story, Juanita, but who in this world would want to read the love story of an old woman?"

"Beth," Juanita answered in her aged wisdom, "you've had two great loves in your life. So many women have never had one. Don't you think your story should be shared with others?"

Beth didn't answer. Hearing Juanita's reply, she knew she would continue her book. Deep in thought, she stared at the blue computer screen.

"Is that the beginning of your book," Juanita asked, pointing to a large stack of papers by the printer.

"Yes," Beth answered, "It's pretty rough, just the first draft."

Juanita took off her glasses and cleaned them on the bottom of her skirt, then held out her hand to Beth. "Well, let me see what you've written." Juanita eased herself onto a small couch and carefully flipped through the first few blank pages until she came to the beginning of Beth's book.

THE SEASON OF MAGENTA

Chapter 1

Beth Boudreau
Oleander, Kansas1958

"You are such a stupid little fool, Beth. At least the other girls gave me some resistance, but not you, you little moron."

Juanita smiled. Finally, Beth had found the courage to tell the world her real story. Kicking off her shoes, Juanita slipped her legs under her and settled in. This would be a most unusual love story.

Epilogue

RJ pulled Big Red around the back of the large home, grinning as he noticed the familiar gray van parked behind his garage. Soon, the big house would be filled again with the laughter of children. Sometimes, it took a while to hear the laughter, but RJ knew from experience, eventually the laughter would come. It always did.

In the distance, he could see three small children chasing after a mare and her colt. Eyes alert and wet noses sniffing the crisp, cool air, his two boys jumped from the bed of Big Red and raced to welcome the visiting children in their play.

RJ pulled the block of rock salt from the back of his truck and walked toward the barn. He knew that all of this was due to Beth's book, and he wondered how a book that had never been published could take on such a life of its own, but it had.

It all started after Juanita read Beth's book, he remembered. Juanita had been so impressed with Beth's book that she passed it on to another woman, and that woman passed it on to another woman, and so on until it seemed it had traveled the entire state of Texas.

Beth had written about the violent rape of her childhood, the lingering fears that haunted her daily, and the peace she found after she faced the nightmare. The book was intended as a book of inspiration to rape victims, but it also became a source of hope for others in dire situations. That's how it all really started.

One cold winter night, they got the first phone call from a woman's group in Dallas. They were desperate, they'd said. They had a woman and two small children who were trying to escape the abuse of her common law husband, but there was no safe place for them to go. They'd asked if there was any way Beth and RJ could take the family in, until they could find more permanent shelter for them.

Beth and RJ had agreed, never realizing how Scott's End Ranch would become a haven of hope for so many abused women and their unhappy children. With the safety and security of the ranch, it became a refuge for the mothers to regain their independence and learn to stand on their own two feet. With the many horses, the dogs, and the vast acreage of the land, the big ranch became a place for the children to relax, to play, and to learn to laugh again.

Eventually, the women would get on their feet, pick up their lives and move on, but all of them knew that without Beth and RJ and the security of Scott's End Ranch, they would never have found their new beginnings.

After years of sheltering so many mothers and their children, Beth and RJ realized what a God send "Scott's End Ranch" had been to so many people and decided it was time for a change. The big ranch was not an ending to a long journey as it had been in the times of RJ's ancestors. Instead, the proud ranch had become an end to despair, a symbol of hope for a new beginning. That hope, Beth and RJ decided, would be reflected in the new name of the proud ranch...."Scott's New Beginnings".

About the Author

Brenda Dawson was born in Mississippi, raised in Illinois, and now resides in Oklahoma.

"Season of Magenta" is her first novel to be published, ensuring all dreamers that love has nothing to do with age and that love's zap can happen when least expected...even to the most unlikely people.

Since *A Season of Magenta*, Dawson has written several novels to include:

THE SCOTT SERIES

Petals from the Judas Tree
A Touch of Jasmine
Sammy Blue

Regrets
Indian Blanket

And Children's Books
Monster in the Goldfish Bowl
Prancy

These books are now available wherever books are sold and at

http://2firespublishing.com/.

Please visit Brenda at her website http://brendabdawsonauthor.com/
And as always please give us a review.

Made in the USA
Charleston, SC
07 October 2015